Praise for Angela Thirkell

"Even the most rabid reader of socially significant fiction will be disarmed and seduced into Mrs. Thirkell's camp."

—*New Yorker*

"Mrs. Thirkell's brilliant, easy conversational style carries the reader along in a glow of pleasure."

—*Saturday Review*

"Angela Thirkell has a definite place among American readers. In her own subtle and delicate way, she is completely successful in portraying the riduculous side of the English gentry of the period before the Second World War."

—*Books*

ANGELA THIRKELL

MARLING HALL

A BARSETSHIRE NOVEL

Carroll & Graf Publishers, Inc.
New York

First Carroll & Graf edition 1990

Published by arrangement with Alfred A. Knopf, Inc.

Carroll & Graf Publishers, Inc.
260 Fifth Avenue
New York, NY 10001

ISBN: 0-88184-676-7

Manufactured in the United States of America

CHAPTER ONE

MARLING HALL STANDS ON A LITTLE EMINENCE AMONG what would in more golden days have been called well-wooded parkland. Owing to death duties and other ameliorative influences a number of its fine oaks and elms have been at various times cut down and sold. Those that remain are dying from the head downwards in a disconcerting way for want of woodmen, though even Dean Swift did not have large gaunt leafless branches sticking out of the top of his head like a nightmare of Actaeon. Behind the house meanders the little stream of Rising which after it has flowed through the Risings (High and Low), joins the river near Barchester. Of the fishing, all that can be said is that there is here and there a grayling, but mostly there isn't. The small home farm, which has been for generations a source of great pride, pleasure and financial loss to the Marling squires, is on its last legs, silent victim of a war which has drained it of its labourers and oppressed it with bureaucracy. All this is little pleasure to its present owner, William Marling,

who in late middle age sees his small and much loved
world crumbling beneath his feet during his life and a
fair probability that his family will never be able to
live in Marling Hall after his death. In fact if it were
not for his wife he would have lost heart altogether by
now.

Mrs. Marling, who disliked her name, Amabel, but
had never seen her way to do anything about it, was
an Honourable, as anyone may see who cares to look
her up in Debrett, and connected with most of Barsetshire. She had the tradition of service, the energy, capacity for taking pains and, let us frankly say, the
splendid insensitiveness and the self-confidence that
make the aristocracy of the county what it is. Her father, Lord Nutfield, was a highly undistinguished peer
unknown outside Barsetshire, whose later days were
seriously embittered by the arrival in the House of
Lords of a new creation, indistinguishable from his
own four-hundred-year-old barony except by one letter, and on this subject he was sometimes moved to
speech, though otherwise a silent man.

Very properly the Marlings had two sons and two
daughters. The elder son, Bill, who was a professional
soldier and had a wife and family, had not as yet been
sent abroad. The younger son, Oliver, who was not
married, had been in a business firm in London. At the
outbreak of war he had made frantic efforts to get into
the army but had been turned down as being over age
and having bad eyesight. After some waiting he got
into the Regional Commissioner's office in Barchester,
living at home and going into Barchester by train. His
working hours varied from night duty to day duty, in-
terspersed with a kind of dog watch that made his father say one never knew where Oliver was and, as a
rider, that this war wasn't like the last.

The elder daughter, Lettice, whose husband was
killed at Dunkirk, was living with her two children in
the stables which Mrs. Marling with great foresight
had converted into a self-contained flat in the autumn

of 1939. The younger daughter, Lucy, lived at home and stood no nonsense from anyone.

Mr. and Mrs. Marling would willingly have taken their widowed daughter and her young children into their own home, but Lettice Watson, much as she loved her parents, felt that any personality her husband's death had left her would be battered to death by her mother's efficiency and her younger sister's hearty contempt for anything that did not agree with her own standards, and preferred to make her home in the stables, though her old bedroom was kept for her at the Hall and she often spent a night there.

On the night previous to the opening of this story she had slept at the Hall to see as much as possible of her brother Bill, who was spending a short leave at his old home because he had not time to go to the North of England where his wife was living with her parents and children. Whenever Lettice Watson slept in her old bedroom she woke up in a dream, half believing that she was still a girl at home, yet oppressed with a foreboding that all was not well. As the echoes of her dreams died away she remembered, each time with a fresh pang, all that had happened in the last six years, her very happy marriage, her two little girls, her husband rejoining his ship, the sickening silence and suspense of that week in May, and the news, confirmed by a friend and eye-witness, of her husband's death while taking the retreating soldiers on board. With her inheritance of a practical point of view she admitted that many women were far worse off. Her husband had left her wealthy for her needs, her children were satisfactory, she had her parents and her old home as a background, and to be perfectly frank with herself she also admitted that time was dulling her sense of loss.

"But there one is, alone," she remarked to her reflection in the mirror, eyeing her morning face with some displeasure, "and it seems so silly to be a widow; the sort of thing other people are, not oneself. Oh, dear. Well, there it is," with which philosophy she went down to breakfast.

But if you had known Marling Hall before the war you would have wondered, for instead of going through the gallery and down the large staircase in the wing which was added about 1780, she turned to her left and going through a swinging door threaded a maze of small passages and rather dark back stairs till she emerged near the door into the kitchen yard. Then opening a door on the right she walked into the room where her parents were already breakfasting. This room had been the servants' hall, but when the war began Mrs. Marling, seeing that servants would be increasingly difficult to get, had dismantled all the large rooms on the ground floor, made the panty into a sitting room for the diminished staff and turned the old servants' hall into a dining room with the advantage of being near the kitchen, which had naturally been built as far from the old dining room as possible.

As the servants' hall overlooked part of the garden, the original builder had put the window at a height which prevented anyone looking out. During the nineteenth century the very reasonable idea of treating servants like blackbeetles had led Mr. Marling's grandfather to plant a thick laurel hedge directly in front of the window, to keep the kitchen in its place. This Mrs. Marling, who believed in fresh air, had cut down. To alter the window would have been too expensive, nor in truth did she greatly care if she could see out of it or not, having the very sane idea that a dining room was meant to eat in and one could look out of windows all the rest of the day if one wanted to. Her husband, who never meddled in the house, accepted the change with equanimity and apart from once saying that he felt as if he were in a loose box, ate his meals contentedly. But Lettice, though she blamed herself for it, hated the tempered gloom and once complained to her sister Lucy that she felt as if she were in an aquarium, to which Lucy very truly replied that aquariums were full of water.

"Well, a lions' den," said Lettice, thinking of an engraving in the old nursery where Daniel with an unprepossessing white fringe at the back of his head and a long dressing gown stood eyeing several lions who were cringing till their spines were bent nearly double.

"You couldn't keep lions in the servants' hall," said Lucy kindly. "It's only panelled with matchboarding and they'd rip it out in no time. Who do you think I saw in Barchester yesterday? Old Alec Potter. He says he's got a cow in calf and the vet thinks she'll have a bad time, so he's going to ring me up and I'll go and give a hand. Cows usually have a pretty easy time, but this one hasn't enough stomachs or something, so it's a marvellous chance. And his housekeeper makes the best parsnip wine I've ever tasted and I promised to give her that bit of sugar I saved off not having it in my coffee since the war."

And Lucy went off on her own avocations leaving her sister, who had never before heard of old Alec Potter or his housekeeper, bewildered though full of affectionate if rather exhausted admiration of her omniscient younger sister.

But on this morning Lucy had either had her breakfast or had not yet come down, so Lettice kissed her parents and went to the sideboard to get her breakfast. Sometimes she wished she needn't kiss them; not that she disliked them, but one does not always feel demonstrative at breakfast-time. But on the occasions when she had omitted this ritual, silent anxiety and blame flowed out in such waves that she at once had a guilt complex which lasted her for the rest of the day. So she made a dab at the top of each respected head and poured out her coffee.

"Shall I give you some more, father?" she asked.

Her father said half a cup, and when she put it down by him looked suspiciously at it and then glanced with a resigned look at his wife.

"I know," said Mrs. Marling, returning his look with a sympathetic moral shrug of her shoulders.

"It disgusts me to have a whole cup when I say a half," said Mr. Marling and drank it to the dregs.

"Sorry, father," said Lettice, who had no particular feeling herself about halves or wholes and at once felt that she was seven years old and in disgrace. Her parents exuded patience and resignation while Lettice felt, as she had so often felt, that it was quite useless to be grown up, the mother of two children, "and one that has had losses," she said inside herself with a bitter amusement at the aptness of her quotation, if one was made to feel like a naughty little girl at nine o'clock in the morning. From past experience she knew that to speak or to be silent would meet with equal disapproval after the affair of the coffee, so she thought she might as well speak. But her mother, who to do her justice had thought no more of the affair having shot her bolt, began to speak at the same time, so Lettice stopped suddenly in whatever she was going to say.

"You and Bill were very late going to bed last night," said Mrs. Marling. "I heard the bath water."

This was a favourite complaint of Mrs. Marling's, who had developed a sixth sense for hearing any bath being filled or emptied and suffering the pangs of insomnia in consequence, by which means she scored heavily over her children.

"I had my bath before dinner, mother," said Lettice, involuntarily defending herself. "And I think Bill did too."

"Then I do not know who it could have been," said Mrs. Marling, "but whoever it was I do wish they would be a little more considerate, for the noise of the water running off *always* wakes me. You heard it, didn't you, William?"

"Heard what?" said Mr. Marling. "The bath? Oh, the *bath*. Can't say I did. What was it doing?"

Mrs. Marling transferred her look of resignation and her moral shrug of the shoulders to her daughter, implying rather than actually breathing the words, "Your father!"

"Bill and I were talking about the children," said Lettice apologetically. "We did sit up a bit late because he had to go early this morning. Did you see him off, mother?"

"No sense in seeing people off," said Mr. Marling, bursting into the conversation. "Get up early, don't know how to fill in the time till breakfast. It isn't as if he were on embarcation leave. I did happen to be up a bit before my usual time, but he had gone. He didn't want anyone to see him off. Any coffee left, Lettice?"

His daughter took his cup and filled it carefully to a certain flower on the inside supposed to represent an Imperial Half Coffee-cup. Her heart suddenly felt heavy as she thought of the morning she had seen her husband off for the last time, but she discouraged the feeling and came back to the table.

"That all the coffee?" said her father. "Amabel, you might tell the cook to give us enough coffee. Not rationed yet as far as I know. Well, well, so no one saw Bill off. I remember my mater getting up at 5 o'clock to see me off in 'fourteen, freezing it was too, and—"

But an end was put to what promised to be a very dull story by the arrival of his younger daughter who opened the door in a shattering kind of way and stood there letting a roaring draught blow in from the passage.

"Do you know what I did this morning?" she said to no one in particular. "I saw Job Harrison going across the four acre, so I yelled to him to wait and Turk and I caught him up at the sluices and his wife is *much* better and the other twin's going to live. Goodness, it was cold down at the sluices, not a bit like May."

"'Don't cast a clout till May is out,' my old pater used to say," remarked Mr. Marling. "Sensible, those old sayings. People didn't go about with nothing on in my young days."

"And Turk got a young rabbit," said Lucy. "Turk, Turk!"

At her call a large shaggy dog rushed into the room and began to bark.

"Lucy dear, shut the door," said Mrs. Marling, "and have your breakfast. Down, Turk, down."

Encouraged by these words Turk walked round the table and pushed his large face at everyone, an attention from which Lettice shrank.

"Lie down, Turk, lie down," cried Lucy with the perfunctory voice of the dog lover who neither expects nor desires obedience from her four-footed owner. "The other twin, I mean the one that died, is to be buried to-morrow," she continued, as she poked about among the breakfast dishes. "Thank goodness the hens are laying now. Anyone want this egg? Job doesn't know what to put on its tombstone because it only lived five days, but I said, 'Well, it must have had a name, so Job said it was christened Rezzervah. Sugar please, mother."

"I thought you had given it up," said her mother.

"So I have, mother," said Lucy, whose mouth was very full of scrambled egg and toast, "but I collect it for old Alec Potter's housekeeper, one lump for every cup."

"Rezzervah isn't a name," said Mr. Marling, who had been thinking over the subject. "Where did he get it? In the Bible, eh? Don't remember it there."

"Of course not, father," said Lucy with kindly contempt. "It's because they live in Reservoir Cottages. I saw its coffin yesterday when I was in the village. Fred Panter was making it when I went into the shop to see about having those shelves put up in the Women's Institute. He says it's reckoned lucky to make coffins for twins, so long as it isn't both. I'll tell you what I'll do at the Institute. I'll get Fred to rehang that door into the little room where they boil the kettle. It'll give us twice as much room if it opens the other way round. Bill thought it would be a good plan too. I say, it was rotten of Bill to go off so early. I'd have got up if I'd known, but I had my bath very late last night in the blue bathroom and somehow I overslept. I say, what a noise the water does make going out of that bath. I'll tell you what I'll do, I'll—"

"Lucy dear, one cannot hear oneself speak," said a quiet voice. "Good morning, Mrs. Marling; good morning, Mr. Marling; good morning, Lettice; good morning, Lucy. You might get me my coffee, dear."

Lucy, checked in full career, got up meekly and went to the sideboard while a short, spare, grey-haired elderly woman in a nondescript, dark knitted suit, with a piece of black ribbon tied round her faded neck, sat down next to Lettice, who greeted her as Bunny.

Miss Bunting had spent forty years of her life in instructing the gilded early youth of England before it went to its preparatory school, sometimes residing in the country mansions of its parents, sometimes having classes at their town houses. Mrs. Marling's brothers had all been under her charge, as had in their turn her brothers' various little boys. When London became an undesirable place for classes, Miss Bunting's heart did for the first time in her life blench. Teaching is no inheritance, and an old age as a Distressed Gentlewoman appeared to be the only career open to her when Mrs. Marling, who had the true feudal spirit about old retainers, asked her to come and live at Marling Hall till times were better. Miss Bunting gratefully accepted the offer and had gradually and with great tact become an invaluable cog in the machinery of the house, acting in a ladylike and non-committal way as housekeeper and secretary, and since Dunkirk as occasional governess to Lettice Watson's little girls. She supervised the Red Cross stores that were kept in the dismantled drawing room, she taught Diana and Clare Watson the name of every flower and bird at Marling, she sat up with anyone who was ill and could read aloud for ever, she knitted for all her ex-pupils now on active service, and her sitting room, which used to be the schoolroom, was a land of enchantment to Diana and Clare, where one could make pictures with brightly coloured chalks, sing nursery rhymes with Bunny at the little old upright piano, or, almost better, strum on it without check. Miss Bunting had that sense of her own worth that only the old governess and the old nannie possess, and many peers, including two marquises and a duke, would sooner have faced a revolutionary mob than Miss Bunting's voice when she asked to see if their hands were clean, as was her invariable custom when she met old pupils.

Lucy brought her coffee and was silent for quite two moments while Miss Bunting spoke of the beauty of the May morning which reminded her, she said, of the wonderful weather one spring when she was holiday governess to Lady Emily Leslie's youngest boy.

"Lady Emily Leslie," said Mr. Marling, looking up from his newspaper. "Funny thing you should mention her. I saw something in the *Times* this morning about Martin Leslie. Is he the one you mean?"

"Oh dear, no," said Miss Bunting pityingly, "my pupil was David Leslie, Martin's uncle. Such a clever boy, but he would not brush his hair, and Lady Emily was really no help at all. However, he improved wonderfully under my care. He is flying now. I have a little jug that he gave me when I left, in the shape of an owl. One pours the milk out of its beak. But it is at my married sister's house with my other little treasures. Toast please, Lettice dear."

"I hope Martin's name wasn't in the casualty list, father," said Lettice, who had a private feeling which she tried to discourage that the name of everyone she knew would turn up as killed or missing sooner or later.

"Couldn't say, dear," said her father. "You know the way you see something in the paper and then forget what it was. Might have been on page seven, if there is a page seven to-day. Never know where you are with papers nowadays. No, that's Company Meetings. Wouldn't see young Leslie's name in Company Meetings. Or page three. No, that's Imperial and Foreign. Lord bless me, what we want with foreign news I don't know. Quite enough trouble without that."

"It doesn't matter," said Lettice.

"Martin has been awarded the George Medal for doing something very meritorious with a bomb," said Miss Bunting. "I heard it on the eight o'clock news."

"I say, Bunny, you always get the juicy bits," said Lucy with frank admiration.

"Juicy is hardly the word I would use," said Miss Bunting. "I simply use my ears and my intelligence and remember what is of interest. I acquired the habit when my dear father was so ill. He was nearly blind and very deaf and not altogether in his right mind, so naturally any little scraps of news interested him. And there was no wireless in those days," she added, appearing to take some merit to herself for this fact.

"I wish I could do something with a bomb," said Lucy. "I'll tell you what I'll do. Next time we get an unexploded bomb I'll get Captain Barclay to let me see them explode it. He explodes bombs up the other side of Pook's Piece, where the old quarry is."

"Pook's Piece?" said Mr. Marling, re-emerging from the *Times*. "That's all National Trust now. Bond and Middleton had that meeting about four or five years ago and got it put through. You remember, Amabel. That meeting we couldn't go to. Can't explode bombs on National Trust land. No one will leave land to the National Trust if the military are going to explode bombs on it. Sort of thing Hitler would do."

"I'll tell you what Hitler *would* do, father," said Lucy. "He'd jolly well collect the bomb and chuck it somewhere else where it would blow up a factory or something. If I was Hitler I'll tell you what I'd do. I'd—"

"We have heard enough, Lucy dear, of what you would do," said Miss Bunting, putting the lid back on her private butter ration which she kept in a little earthenware pipkin with a snail on its cover, gift of Lord Henry Palliser aged eight, and kept back owing to its great beauty from the treasures that were at her married sister's house. "The National Trust, as I understand it, holds a trust for the nation, and I fail to see how the exploding, by the military, of German bombs can in any way be said to contravene its aims. The Duke of Omnium was on the Committee and presented Matchings to the Trust. I often took Lord

Henry and Lady Glencora there on Sunday afternoon.
It made a nice walk."

"Matchings?" said Mrs. Marling, who had been
reading her business letters and scribbling answers on
them for Miss Bunting to deal with later. "That is a
very bad bit of land. The Duke tried to sell it to my father, but he wouldn't look at it. What is everyone
doing to-day?"

Lucy fidgeted in her chair, for this daily question of
her mother's, savouring as it did of interference by
parents, annoyed her independent spirit, though she
did not dare to make a vocal protest. Miss Bunting put
on the pince-nez which had quelled many members of
the present House of Lords, and looked at her. Lucy
subsided.

"Bench at Barchester," said Mr. Marling. "I have to
go to an Agricultural Committee at three, so I'll lunch
there. Do you want the car, Amabel?"

Mrs. Marling said she didn't and to be sure to ask if
there was a message from Oliver at the Club.

"Oliver, eh," said Mr. Marling, who appeared to
have forgotten who his younger son was. "What does
he want a message for?"

"A message *from* Oliver," said Mrs. Marling patiently. "You know quite well, William, he was at Pomfret
Towers last night and he might like to come back in
the car with you instead of by train. And don't forget
to call at Pilchard's for the cook's mattress that was
being re-covered. And you might look in at Pinker's to
see if Bill's riding breeches that he left there are ready.
I'll write it all down for you."

"Oh, all right, all right," said Mr. Marling with a
show of ill-temper that did not impress anyone. "Suppose I'm a kind of carrier nowadays. But why no one
could get up and see Bill off, I don't know. I'd have
been down myself, but the boy didn't say when he was
going. Daresay he didn't get any breakfast either.
Don't know what the country's coming to. Here,
Bunny."

He got up, pushed the *Times* across the table at Miss Bunting and went towards the door.

"Dear Bill ate a very good breakfast," said Miss Bunting, rather ostentatiously refolding the *Times* which in Mr. Marling's hands usually looked like an unmade bed. "I slipped on my warm dressing-gown, the one that the Dutchess sent me at Christmas, and my blue boudoir cap, and we had a cosy little tête-à-tête over his egg in my sitting-room and he left his best love for everyone. By the way, Mr. Marling, he took your library book to read in the train. I said I was sure you would not mind."

Mr. Marling did not shut the door in time to prevent his family hearing the loud Damn with which he relieved his feelings. Mrs. Marling went away with her letters.

"Oh, Bunny, you *are* mean!" said Lucy. "Bill promised he'd wake me up and say good-bye."

"He did, Lucy dear, but you went to sleep again," said Miss Bunting. "And you had better go, dear, if you are to get to the Cottage Hospital in time. You know Matron doesn't like you to be late. Lettice and I will do the table."

"I'll tell you what I'll do—" said Lucy.

"No, dear, not now. You will be late," said Miss Bunting, and Lucy left the room, banging the door just so loudly as might be construed by a friendly advocate as pure accident.

As the indoor staff at Marling Hall, which used to be eight, was now reduced to four and a woman from the village who often found herself unable to oblige, it had become a habit that some member of the family should clear away the breakfast things and stack them neatly on a service trolley. Though Lucy was full of good will, her readiness to help had broken more china and bent more forks than her family could bear, so it had been tacitly agreed that Miss Bunting should be in command. Oliver helped as a rule before he went to the Regional Commissioner's Office at Bar-

chester and Lettice if she was spending the night at
the Hall. This morning she and Miss Bunting cleared
the table in silence. Lettice had never talked much as
a child or as a girl and Miss Bunting sometimes wondered why she was so unlike the rest of her family, but
finally attributed it to her grandmother, Mr. Marling's
mother, who had made the lamp-room into a kind of
lay chapel when electric light was installed. Under the
present Mrs. Marling's rule the chapel, which really
only consisted of a blue and white Della Robbia
plaque, some Morris hangings and some rush-bottomed
chairs, had been allowed to relapse. While the children were small their perambulators, outdoor toys,
and later, bicycles were kept in it and there all their
secret societies met. At present it was being used as a
supplementary coal cellar against the winter, but
through all its changes it had been stubbornly called
the lamp-room. Miss Bunting remembered old Mrs.
Marling very well and saw in Lettice the distinction
she had admired in her grandmother and the air of
being as it were withdrawn from what was going on
about her. Not altogether a good thing for a young
woman with children, Miss Bunting thought, but did
not feel called upon to say so.

Both ladies were neat and swift in their movements
and the breakfast things were quickly stacked. The
only difference of opinion was over three clean saucers
and one unused plate which Lettice, with what Miss
Bunting secretly admired as a lordly manner though
her better judgment was against it, was heaping with
the dirty things when the old governess, driven by conscience, interposed.

"Those saucers *separately*, Lettice dear," she said,
"and I think that plate has not been used."

"I didn't notice," said Lettice.

"Well, it is only one or two crumbs," said Miss Bunting. "I will just whisk them off onto the plate that had
the egg on it. I always say one can help the servants in
so many little ways, and keeping the clean and dirty
things separate is one of them."

"Sorry, Bunny," said Lettice, with as little show of feeling as when her father had spoken about his half cup of coffee.

Miss Bunting suddenly wished that Lettice would lose her temper, or argue. It would be more natural, she felt, in a young woman of the present day than accepting the little fads of an old woman. She looked at Lettice, thought of speaking, and held her peace.

"Do you want to come to Rushwater this afternoon, Bunny?" Lettice said. "It's the children's dancing class."

Miss Bunting accepted gratefully.

"It's lucky I've got enough petrol for their dancing and their gym," said Lettice. "Still, one doesn't really want to go anywhere now. I must go through the Red Cross stores this morning, but I'm going down to the stables first. See you at lunch, Bunny."

Miss Bunting looked after her with some displeasure. A young woman of Lettice's age oughtn't to say she didn't want to go anywhere, even if she was a widow. There was Lady Peggy Mason in the last war, who had lost two husbands and married a third before the Armistice, and one would hardly have guessed she was a widow even for the brief periods when she was. But it was no good expecting Lettice to be like Lady Peggy, who was as hard as nails. Besides Lady Peggy wasn't really what you would call *race*, not with that very common grandfather on her mother's side, and Lettice was County right through.

"If only Lord Richard were alive," said Miss Bunting aloud to herself. But Lord Richard was not alive; at least he had last been seen at Calais and by this time no news must be bad news and sure news: and so many of Miss Bunting's pupils were dead now, and so many more would be dead as time went on. Two wars do not keep one's old pupils alive. Miss Bunting sometimes had a dream that she flew—not in an aeroplane but with invisible wings—to Germany and alighting in Hitler's dining room just as he was beginning his lunch, stood in front of him and said, "Kill me, but

don't kill my pupils because I can't bear it." The
dream had always tailed off into incoherence, but it
came again and again, and Miss Bunting had a sneak-
ing feeling, which she condemned firmly as supersti-
tious and even prayed against on Sundays, though
not with real fervour, that if only she could keep
asleep till Hitler answered, the war would somehow
come to an end. But so far she had always woken too
soon.

Lettice went out by the side door, for the front door
with its steps, its elegant pilasters and its fanlight was
not used now that the living rooms were shut up. The
stables were about a furlong from the house, giving
the coachman ample room to get his horses to a spank-
ing trot up the rise and wheel them round smartly at
the front door, where they pawed and champed and
fretted their necks like swans against the bearing rein.
Tradition had it that Mr. Marling's father in his young
days, being an autocrat in the matter of punctuality
and given to the good old tradition of swearing at the
men servants from time to time, had once been at the
front door when the landau and pair, ordered for three
o'clock, had drawn up at the steps before the mellow
stable clock had chimed three. Upon this he had
damned and swore somethink hawful, as the coachman subsequently related, not without pride, to a se-
lect audience at the Marling Arms, and had ordered
him to turn the horses and bring them up again on the
stroke. Lettice's father had equally insisted on punctuality, though without the swearing, but that was before the war when they had the big Daimler and the
two smaller cars and two chauffeurs. Now the chauffeurs had gone to munitions, the Daimler and one of
the smaller cars were laid up for the duration, and
only the smaller family car was being used. Oliver and
Lucy each had a disreputable runabout. Mrs. Marling
had always refused to learn to drive, so if none of her
family were free to drive her she stayed at home or
walked. Lettice was able to help her mother with her

own car which, as we have seen, was otherwise used chiefly for the children's classes, and on other occasions she walked, or bicycled, a mode of progression which frightened her very much.

The stables were built in an L shape, the larger wing of which had been altered to make the flat. The roof over hay lofts and grooms' quarters had been raised, gas and electric light installed, and Lettice was the mistress of a fairly large drawing-room, a small dining-room, a smaller kitchen, a bedroom and bathroom for herself, a tiny spare room, a day and night nursery and a bathroom for nurse and the children. To Diana and Clare's intense delight the entrance was up a real stable staircase, very narrow and almost perpendicular, which to them represented the height of romance, though nurse felt it due to herself to complain at intervals that one couldn't get a pram up. But as the perambulator had a nice dry loose box to live in just under the nursery, no one was really sorry for it.

The Misses Watson, aged five and three, were blissfully engaged at the old horse trough which, with its pump still in working order, stood in one corner of the stable yard. With them was their great friend Ed Pollet, at present almost the only able-bodied man about the place. Ed was for some years porter at Worsted Station, owing to family influence, his uncle, Mr. Patten, being the station-master, but his real genius was with cars, a genius quite undimmed by his being distinctly half-witted in other ways. At a moment of crisis a few years previously he had been lent as temporary chauffeur to Lord Bond and had given such satisfaction that he had been taken on permanently at Staple Park as second chauffeur. When, at the outbreak of war Lord and Lady Bond had let Staple Park to a public school and gone to live in the White House next to their friend and tenant Mr. Middleton at Laverings, Ed had been transferred to Marling Hall as general utility about the garage and with the farm tractor, and now represented the one link with a mechanised world. He cleaned, repaired and drove the

little car and the tractor, worked the engine that made
the electric light, mended anything in the lighting system from a main fuse to the electric iron that the
housemaid left on all night, put washers on taps, repaired the cook's sewing machine and Miss Bunting's typewriter, and understood the electric incuba-
tor as no one else had ever done. In the winter of
1940-41 he had registered, and as the doctor who examined the men found it simpler to do nothing but
test their hearts and pull down their lower lids—a
piece of routine mumbo-jumbo that impressed everyone with his efficiency—it quite escaped his notice
that Ed, who had always been immune to education,
was mentally far below even the standard that the
B.B.C. sets in its broadcasts to the Forces, and passed
him as A.1. Ed would have found himself almost at
once in the Barsetshire Regiment, where he would
probably have become really insane through fright
and homesickness, had not Sir Edmund Pridham, who
took an immense pride in all county idiots, standing
between them and every encroachment of bureaucracy and regarding them on the whole as part of our
National Heritage (as indeed they are), intervened
with the whole force of his position and county authority and forced the doctor to report him quite un-
suitable for any kind of military work and of extreme
value as a reserved worker.

"Bad job that," said Sir Edmund, speaking of the
doctor, "bad job. Men like that ought to be shot. Every
village in England ought to have a village idiot. There
was always an idiot at Worsted and please God there
always will be. Been one there ever since I knew the
place. Doctor's a fool, that's what he is. Sort of man
that would cut you up just for fun. Ed Pollett's all
right in the right place. Aren't you, Ed?"

Ed, who had placidly accepted the medical examination as part of the queerness of the gentry, with no
suspicion of the doom that had been hanging over
him, grinned, and Mr. Marling quickly took him away,
lest the board should reconsider their verdict, while

Sir Edmund went back to see that a communist hair-dresser with no dependents and a fine physique did not slip through the meshes.

This morning Ed had obligingly worked the pump, which was far too high and too heavy for the little girls, and the horse trough was brimming with water which slopped in a delightful way onto their sandalled feet. Three celluloid ducks, a celluloid fish and a small red boat were floating on the water, while Diana and Clare industriously stirred up waves with their hands. Lettice stood watching them, as yet unperceived, thinking, not for the first time, how enchantingly defenceless little girls' arms were in their immature curves, and how adorably frail they looked, though quite misleadingly, as anyone who tries to pick up a child in a temper knows.

"That's Daddy's ship," said Diana, giving the little red boat a push, "and I'm the Germans."

She then threw several handfuls of water over the boat which heeled and sank.

"Now Daddy's drowned," she said cheerfully.

Clare, who found it less trouble not to speak, shrieked with pleasure and Ed grinned sympathetically.

Lettice knew that she ought to go white, put her hand to her heart and gravely lead her little ones into the house. But, mortifying though it might be, she did not think she could give satisfaction in any of these respects. If they could think of Daddy being drowned as a good game, she could only be thankful that it was so. If they had nightmares, or repressions, or complexes about his death it would be far worse. She knew from her own experience exactly what all these feelings were like and did not want anyone else, especially her own little girls with their enchanting boiled macaroni arms, to share her knowledge. So she came up to the trough and smiled at everyone.

"Morning, miss," said Ed, pulling his forelock, an archaism which his various sympathetic employers cherished and which Sir Edmund looked upon as his crowning glory. "Drowning Daddy, the young ladies are."

"That's very nice, Ed," said Lettice. And indeed there was really nothing better to say. "Did you have a nice supper, darlings?"

Both her daughters set their lips tightly and nodded with violence.

"Nurse's brother got free stripes," said Diana and began to explore a crack in the celluloid fish's back with a pink finger.

Lettice considered this remark. It seemed a peculiar kind of thing to get, rather like a Biblical punishment, or possibly a bit of land. A Browning title, "A Bean Stripe; also Apple Eating," floated into her mind. Or were Free Stripes a new kind of ally, like the Free French? But these unprofitable musings were ended by nurse, who, having seen her mistress from the night-nursery window, had come down from a sense of duty to interfere.

"Now Diana, don't get your frock wet," was her very proper greeting to the party. "Clare, don't get your sandals wet or nurse will have to take you in. Good morning, madam."

Lettice said good morning to nurse. Diana, with a serious and intent expression, had now ripped the celluloid fish quite open and was letting the water gurgle in. She looked up with a pleased expression and Lettice felt that if she talked about drowning again she might not be able to bear it.

"Nasty fish," said Diana, suddenly tearing it in two. "All dead."

Clare began to cry.

"Now that's enough, Diana," said nurse, taking the fish's mangled corpse and putting it in her apron pocket. "And stop crying, Clare, and we'll show Mummy the snap of nurse's brother. It's my brother Sid, madam, the one that was the dentist's mechanic. He's just got his stripes and he's a full sergeant. The children were ever so pleased."

She produced a photograph of a young man who looked like an epitome of the whole British Army.

"What lovely moustaches, nurse," said Lettice, unable to think of a more suitable comment.

"Kiss Sid," said Diana, pushing the photograph towards her mother's face.

"That's quite enough, Diana," said nurse, thoroughly shocked. "Now come along, children. We're going down to the shops to get the rations. Really, madam, you'd think Diana was an officer's little girl, not a naval gentleman's. She's been talking about nothing but Sid's stripes ever since the photo come."

"Three stripes, isn't it, nurse?" said Lettice, as her elder daughter's comment became clear. "And you remember it's dancing to-day. I am doing Red Cross stores this morning, and I'll lunch at the Hall, but I'll be back here by half-past two."

The nursery party went off to the village, while Lettice went up to read her letters before going back to the Hall to work.

CHAPTER TWO

AT HALF-PAST TWO LETTICE PUT HER LITTLE GIRLS INTO
her car and drove up to the Hall where Miss Bunting
was waiting. With shrieks of joy the children, who had
been packed into the front seat by their mother, cas-
caded out, flung themselves on the old governess and
dragged her into the back seat, sandwiching her between them and clamouring for the story of David
Leslie who cut all the bristles off his hairbrush because he didn't want to brush his hair. This story Miss
Bunting had told them at least eight times, but its interest never palled and when she came to the climax
where the bristles were found blocking the waste pipe
in the nursery bathroom both little girls screamed
aloud in ecstasy. Lettice, alone in the front of the car,
liked to hear her daughters' squealing voices, and if it
occurred to her that Miss Bunting was a far better en-
tertainer of the young than she was she merely felt
grateful, for much as she adored Diana and Clare, she
also found them highly exhausting.

The road to Rushwater ran through the little village

of Marling Melicent, followed the course of the Rising, went over the hill leaving the Risings in the river valley on the right, and came into Rushwater near the vicarage, which was one mass of evacuees under the able rule of a retired Colonial Bishop who had done locum work at Little Misfit in the beginning of the war and was now doing it with equal enthusiasm at Rushwater, treating his evacuated mothers and children as heathen (which indeed they were) and seeing with his own eyes that the children were properly bathed once a week, regarding it as an only slightly lower form of baptism.

As they passed the vicarage the Bishop emerged with two little girls and Lettice slowed down.

"Ah, Mrs. Watson, we meet again!" said the bishop. "As you see we are just on our way to the dancing class."

Lettice stopped and offered the party a lift if they could fit in. The bishop, who was a man of action and the terror of all backsliders in his sub-equatorial diocese, pushed his two charges into the back, telling them to sit on the floor and himself got in beside Lettice.

"First-rate little tap-dancers those two," he said, jerking a very unepiscopal thumb towards the back of the car. "Father was an acrobat and is in the Middle East now. Name of Valoroso. It's an old name on the halls. The mother had taken to drinking, but I soon settled that."

Lettice asked how.

"Drank with her, knee to knee," said the Bishop. "Only beer of course. I couldn't have done it with whiskey. I find that is the only way with natives. In my diocese they drank 'Mpooka-'Mpooka, filthy stuff, fermented ants' eggs, the female ones, mixed with all sorts of unpleasant things. But I made the chiefs drink all one night with me and next day they were so sick they all took the pledge. I gave them each a Leander cap as a reward—I used to row a bit, you know, and caps were my hobby—and they passed a law forbid-

ding the manufacture of 'Mpooka-'Mpooka. The High
Chief had an interest in a soft drinks factory at Dur-
ban, so we did very well. These children's mother has
taken the pledge and I give her my tea ration to stop
the craving. Now she's a different woman and if any of
the other mothers bring drink in she throws it into the
lily pond. Two of the gold fish died, but the others
seem to like it."

As he finished this interesting story of missionary effort they arrived at Rushwater House which was surrounded in Diana and Clare's eyes with a halo of romance, as having once been the home of the wicked
David Leslie who wouldn't brush his hair. Other cars
with mothers and children were there and the air was
filled with the twitterings of young voices. The dancing class had been started by Mrs. John Leslie for her
own nice dull little girls and a few friends' children
and this was only the second meeting. In the big drawing-room, where most of the furniture was pushed
into corners and dust-sheeted, were a dozen or so
chairs and a tinkling piano at which a middle-aged
woman with a decayed air was sorting music. Another
middle-aged woman with a tired though worthy face
and very neat feet was already exercising one or two
of the early arrivals, holding their hands and making
them count and hop: One, two, three. One, two, three.

Lettice, who was vaguely connected with the Leslies through her mother, kissed Mrs. John Leslie and
introduced Miss Bunting, who enquired after her hostess's father and mother-in-law, Mr. Leslie and Lady
Emily Leslie.

"They are quite well, thank you," said Mrs. John, as
most people called her. "They were staying with my
sister-in-law Agnes Graham when the war began, and
as they are getting on and both a bit invalidish my
husband and Agnes and David talked it over and they
all thought their parents had better stay with Agnes
for the duration, so John and I brought the children
down here. John is Regional Commissioner, you know,
so it is quite convenient, and we try to keep things

straight here. It makes a home for David when he is on leave, except that he much prefers London and practically never comes. And for Martin too, John's nephew who will have the place if he isn't killed. Forgive me, but I must go and talk to Sally."

She went across the room to greet young Lady Pomfret, also a connection of her husband's family, who had brought Lord Mellings, aged three. His lordship did not actively partake in the dancing, but was allowed to skirmish in the back row.

Words cannot describe how Miss Bunting's heart expanded as she found herself in an assemblage where everyone was what she mentally called the right people. And what was more, where practically everyone was connected by blood or by marriage. As the eagle, soaring in lonely majesty, discerns far below the lamb, or in rarer and less probable cases the swaddling child, and drops like a thunderbolt to seize her prey, so did Miss Bunting sustained by her intimate acquaintance with so many of England's gilded youth and fortified by Debrett, pounce upon every relationship and make it her own. In fact she could probably have told many of the young mothers present their exact degree of kin to one another far better than they knew it themselves. Only for a moment did she falter over young Lady Pomfret and in a trice she had it at her fingertips that the present Earl of Pomfret's father, Major Foster, had been second cousin and heir presumptive to the late Lord Pomfret who was Lady Emily Leslie's brother and thus uncle to David Leslie, the reprobate, and uncle by marriage to nice Mrs. John Leslie. Lady Pomfret had been a Miss Wicklow, whose brother Roddy, agent to the late and to the present Earl had married Alice Barton, whose brother Guy had married the Archdeacon's daughter from Plumstead, whose mother had been a Rivers. And so the endless, fascinating chain went on in her mind till via the Honourable George Rivers, cousin to old Lord Pomfret, and his wife who was a niece of old Lord Nutfield, Mrs. Marling's father, she came round again to Lettice Watson, quietly knitting at her side, and rejoiced that she knew her Peerage and her Landed Gentry so well.

Ten or twelve mothers with some nurses in the background were by now established, each with her knitting or other useful work, while their young charges jumped about in a cheerful and inelegant way, laughing a good deal and presenting an agreeable picture. Only the two evacuee children showed any real aptitude for the dance and it was evident that they were rather bored by the amateur nature of the proceedings.

Mrs. John came back and joined Lettice who had been talking to Mrs. John's Nannie.

"It is rather a small class to-day," she said anxiously. "I did hope Clarissa and the little ones would be here. Oh, here they are."

She got up as there came into the room four children; a girl of about nine, two little boys who might have been seven and five and a little girl who could not have been more than three holding her mother's hand.

"Darling Mary," said the mother, giving Mrs. John a soft-enfolding embrace, "here we are, so late, as usual. It was Edith's fault, the wicked one. She ate her pudding so slowly that it made us quite late, didn't it, Edith? So I was quite cross and then Nannie had to put on her blue dress because there was rice pudding on the one she was wearing."

"Rice pudding," said Edith, looking round for approval.

"Agnes darling," said Lettice, receiving in her turn the soft, scented, unemotional embrace. "How are you all? Here is Miss Bunting, who knows David. She is longing to see the children."

Mrs. Graham appeared to find this wish quite natural and sat down by Miss Bunting.

"Of course I remember you so well," she said, turning on Miss Bunting a smile of vague, ravishing sweetness and starry eyes. "David was very naughty the summer you were here and teased everyone dreadfully. I wish you could see James, my eldest boy. He is so like my father, but he is at Eton now. Emmy is exactly like my mother, but she is rather old for this class so I left her with the governess. Darling Clarissa, come and say how do you do to Miss Bunting. She used to give Uncle David lessons when he was a little boy and he was very, very naughty. Clarissa really ought to be with the governess, but she looks so delicious in green that I had to bring her. Darling John, come and say how do you do to Miss Bunting, and Robert too. John is so like my eldest brother who was killed, Martin's father you know, and Robert is very like a photograph of grandfather Pomfret when he was a little boy. Darling Edith, say how do you do."

"Rice pudding," said Edith.

"Wicked one, wicked one," said her mother fondly. "She is called after my aunt who died, Edith Pomfret, and I think she will be very like her when she grows up, though of course there is no relationship. Go and dance now, darlings, and pay attention to Miss Milner, because she is going to show you some lovely dances."

The bevy of children, each with a different kind of ravishing good looks and charm, ran across the room.

Agnes, having exhausted herself in praise of her young, sat benignly quiet, thinking as was her habit of absolutely nothing at all, and occasionally drawing Miss Bunting's attention to Clarissa's way of pointing her toes, or John's bow, or Robert's neat legs, or even more proudly, Edith's habit of leaving the class and performing a private dance in a corner.

"I hoped Cousin Emily would be coming," said Lettice.

"Darling Mamma!" said Agnes. "She did want to come, but it is so much better for her to rest after lunch and she has a thrush that John rescued from the kitchen cat and is trying to make it eat bread and milk, so I persuaded her to lie down. Besides I wanted her to be quite rested for David."

"I thought David was abroad somewhere," said Lettice.

"So did we," said Agnes. "But he rang Robert up at the War Office last night, so he must be back, especially as he said he would come down to-day."

"How is General Graham?" said Lettice.

But her enquiry for Agnes's husband was not answered, for even as she spoke an officer in R.A.F. uniform came into the room and stood looking at the scene. The class suddenly dissolved with shrieks of "Uncle David" from a number of its members. David strode through them and heartily kissed his sister Agnes, whose calm was almost stirred at his greeting.

"How lovely that you have come, David," she said. "You are just in time to see darling Edith do her tap dance."

"No, Agnes," said her brother. "Much as I love you I did not come here with infinite pains and in the teeth of all regulations to see a tap dance. And you don't seem to observe that I am an interesting invalid. I have had jaundice and they have sent me home to recover."

"Emmy had jaundice when she was six," said Agnes proudly. "She was quite ill. I used to read to her every day. We read all the Footly-Tootly books, about the little elves that take care of baby animals and Emmy loved them and got well quite quickly."

"If they are anything like the story of Hobo-Gobo and the fairy Joybell you were reading to the children the summer John got engaged," said David, "I don't wonder Emmy got well quickly. I'd have got well at once."

"We have got Hobo-Gobo in the nursery," said his sister, serenely unconscious of any double meaning, "and you can read it to Edith after tea. But you haven't said How do you do to Lettice, David."

"Where is she?" asked David, looking round.

Lettice held out her hand.

"Good Lord, I didn't know you," said David. "You've done your hair differently and anyway it must be ages since we met. Before the war, wasn't it? And how is Roger?"

Not often in his life had David Leslie been at a loss, but for a moment he wished he were back in Cairo with jaundice. There was a dead silence. Lettice wanted desperately to explain to David that she didn't blame him, that he couldn't have known, that she really didn't mind in the least, that Roger would have been the first to sympathise; but the only outward effect of these varying wishes was that she went first white and then red and said nothing. Even Agnes, into whose mind the idea was slowly creeping that it must be so uncomfortable for darling Lettice if darling David asked such a silly question, could find nothing to say and wished very much that her husband were there as he always knew what to do.

"How often did I tell you in the schoolroom, David, to think before you speak," said a voice at his elbow.

David turned and looked down.

"Bunny!" he cried. "Bless your heart, Bunny my love."

"Sit down," said Miss Bunting.

David sat down and smoothed his hair rather nervously.

"Lettice's husband was killed at Dunkirk," said Miss Bunting in a low, severe voice. "If you read the *Times* properly you would have seen it."

And as she spoke David knew that he was judged, and that it would take all his powers of cajolery and more to reinstate himself in his old governess's good graces. He might have explained that he had been in Canada, the United States and the Argentine most of the previous year on various Government missions, that he had then been sent to the Middle East and been away in Libya where the *Times* was not regularly delivered, that many letters from home had been lost at sea, but nothing, he felt, could make Miss Bunting forgive or condone. For the moment the question of explaining to Lettice was of secondary importance. He nervously wound his wrist watch.

"And don't fidget with things," Miss Bunting added.

Agnes, who had at last grasped the fact that Lettice

might be rather uncomfortable if people asked after her husband a year after he was killed, now joined the attack.

"Darling David, how could you," she said with mild reproach. "It was quite naughty of you and darling Lettice is always so good about it and never cries. Robert admires her very much and says she has behaved splendidly, and her little girls are such darlings. Diana is just older than Robert and Clare is just older than Edith. So now we will forget all about it and you must not be so unkind another time."

At this castigation from his gentle sister David wished more than ever that he were in hospital, or even in the Libyan desert, and would have gone there at once, but that he was rooted to the spot by mortification and embarrassment, sentiments which were as much a stranger to him as he to them.

"I'm awfully sorry, Lettice," he began, but Agnes cast a look of gentle reproach at him, and Miss Bunting, drawing herself up very erect, said distinctly, "Tchk, tchk."

Lettice now recovered herself.

"I am so glad to see you, David," she said, "and you must come over to Marling and see us and I'll show you the last photographs Roger sent me from his ship, and you must meet my little girls."

By a special intervention of Providence the class was now told to get its shoes on for tap dancing and David was again surrounded by a flock of admirers.

"Who do you think that is?" said Lettice to her little girls. "That's David that wouldn't brush his hair. David, these are Diana and Clare."

Diana at once put David through a severe cross-examination on the subject of cutting the bristles off his hair brush, while Clare stood by. David, deeply grateful for this chance of reinstating himself in Lettice's good opinion, so exerted himself to please that Diana refused to put on her tap dancing shoes unless she might sit on his knees to do so. The decayed woman at the piano struck up, Miss Milner clapped her hands and called, "All tap-dancers into the centre" and most of the bevy fluttered away again. From the first it was evident that the two evacuees were swans among very callow ducklings. The amateurs were dismissed after a short lesson with instructions to practise their steps at home, while Miss Milner refreshed herself from her labours by joining in a *pas de trois* with the young professionals. The Colonial Bishop sat beaming at the success of his wards and told Lady Pomfret that they were as good as the witch-dancers at the Festival of the Ripening Maize, though of course quite, *quite* different, he added hastily. But here he was wrong, for Ruby and Marleen Valoroso, when not hampered by the presence of the gentry, could probably have given the witch-dancers points.

"And who is that lovely little girl who dances by herself in a corner?" he asked Lady Pomfret.

"That is Agnes Graham's youngest," said Lady Pomfret. "She is a little older than my little boy. Agnes," she said, leaning across. "I want to introduce Bishop Joram who admires Edith very much. My cousin, Mrs. Graham."

The Colonial Bishop, who was highly susceptible, fell in love with Agnes at once.

"Edith is always like that," said Agnes proudly. "She pays no attention to anyone. I have heard about you from Canon Banister who used to be Vicar here. He says you are being so splendid with evacuees. Are those your children?"

The Bishop said they were, adding hastily that he meant they were not, as he was not married, but was responsible for them. David caught Lettice's eye and found comfort in the flicker of amusement that passed between them. Agnes said, with great sympathy and obvious want of understanding that she *did* so understand and in these times one had to make allowances for all sorts of things. As it was clear that she had settled him in her mind as the father of all the children at the vicarage with a harem of East End wives, he began to explain, but Agnes very sweetly interrupted him.

"I know you will excuse me," she said, "but it is getting on for the children's tea-time and I must hurry. You must come over to lunch one day and meet my mother, who understands everything and adores bishops. Could you come next Sunday?"

The Colonial Bishop looked wretched.

"How stupid I am!" said Agnes, turning her deceptively earnest eyes upon him. "Of course Sunday is a bad day for you. But I shall tell mamma, and I am sure she will write to the Bishop of Barchester about it. And then I could take you to the children's service at half past three, while mamma is resting. Mr. Tompion, our vicar, has a delightful service and we all go and enjoy it so much. Don't we, darling Edith? What does Mr. Tompion tell us on Sundays?"

Edith, a woman of one idea, said rice pudding and was at once removed by her scandalised nurse who had been lurking in the background in case of emergency.

The two evacuees who were quite pleasant looking girls, if a trifle bold-faced, had now put their outdoor shoes on again and approached their guardian.

"These are Ruby and Marleen," said the Bishop to Agnes.

"Mummy," whispered Clarissa loudly and urgently. "Can I go to tea with Ruby and Marleen? They can do the splits."

Whereupon she also was pounced upon by nurse, who deeply disapproved all forms of democracy.

"How nicely you dance," said kind Agnes. "Edith would love to dance like that."

"She's a caution, isn't she," said either Ruby or Marleen, "doing her solo turns."

Even Agnes, who comprehended practically everyone in a general mush of amiability, was assailed by a suspicion that she would not quite like Clarissa to cultivate the Misses Valoroso's acquaintance.

"Come on, mister, we'll be late for tea," said Mar-

leen or Ruby, "and we're going to the pictures at
Southbridge. It's Glamora Tudor. One of my boy
friends got her photo signed. I'm going on the films
when I grow up. Come on."

With a Valoroso hanging on each arm the Bishop
felt he could not do better than go, which he did, accompanied by loud criticisms of nurse as quite a
Madam from his gifted protégées.

"And that," said David, "is the Brave New World."

Mrs. John Leslie said it was so nice to have those
poor bombed children at the class and that it was a
great thing for their own children to mix with all kinds
while they were too young to know the difference.

"No, Mary," said David. "You may have married my
elder brother, but as he is not here I am going to say
that you are talking nonsense. If your children don't
know the difference between those two girls and
Clarissa, it's time you took them to a mental special-
ist."

"But in Russia," said Mrs. John, "all children are
equal."

"And look at them when they've grown up," said
David indignantly. "When did you go all Slavophil,
Mary?"

"I'm not anything-phil, David," said his sister-in-
law, "but Geoffrey Harvey was most interesting about
the Russians the other day at the Middletons. He is
with John at the Regional Commissioner's Office. He
says they are wonderful."

"Well, bless your innocent soul, my love," said
David, "hell hath no fury, though that's a misquota-
tion, like a woman who has heard a long-haired
member of the intelligentsia talking hot air. In less re-
fined circles I should say tripe. I've known Geoffrey
Harvey up and down town off and on for quite long
enough. Give John my love. Bunny, I'm coming over
to see you soon if Lettice will ask me."

Lettice, still anxious to show David that his mistake
had not hurt her, begged him to come whenever he
liked, to which her children added their artless en-

treaties, calling him by the endearing name of Uncle
David, which they had at once picked up from the
young Grahams.

"Robert," said Agnes, who had just caught up with
the preceding conversation, "was on a military mission
to Russia and he didn't like them, so I do not think
they can be very nice."

She looked at David and Mary with the assurance of
a perfect wife.

"Good man, Robert," said David approvingly. "And
now, Agnes, I shall speed ahead of you and catch
mamma unawares, or she will have painted a picture
of the dove returning to the ark on the front door to
welcome me. Do you remember when I came back
from Buenos Aires in 'thirty five how she had painted
Welcome Darling David and a laurel wreath all over
my looking glass for a surprise? I still can't tie my tie
in that glass. If she expects me she is quite capable of
gilding that thrush's claws and beak. I must fly."

Extricating himself from the children who were
hanging onto his legs he blew a kiss to Miss Bunting
and left. The rest of the party quickly followed and
Mrs. John took Miss Milner and the pianist to her sitting room and gave them a good tea before they bicycled back to Barchester, discussing David Leslie with
passionate worship and no rivalry.

During the journey home Diana and Clare, sitting
one on each side of Miss Bunting with their legs sticking straight out in front of them, demanded the story
of how David cut the bristles off his hair brush all over
again. Lettice, alone in front, thought of all the things
she might have said when David asked how Roger
was. Anyone with any sense or any real kindness, she
thought, would have put David at his ease at once by
a few well-chosen words—though what the words
would have been she could not quite imagine. But at
least she could have said *something*, instead of sitting
there like a great booby, going red in the face. It became most important that David should come to Marling Hall as soon as possible, so that she might be quite

sure he did not altogether despise her for her graceless
behaviour, or even worse, fear her for her rudeness,
though after the way she had behaved it was very improbable that she would ever see him again. Six times
she decided to ring him up and repeat her invitation;
six times she decided not to. Perhaps by the exercise of
tactful hinting she could make her mother, a great
stickler for the ties of family, do the ringing up. If only
Roger had been there, she said to herself, he would
have known what to do. And then it surged over her
that if Roger had been there David's blunder could
not have occurred and she laughed at herself for her
folly and then nearly cried when she thought that
Roger could never help her at all now. But to drive
through a mist of unshed tears ("I'm driving with
tears in my eyes," said her mocking self to her) was
stupid when the safety of Diana and Clare and Miss
Bunting depended on her, so she hit her eyes quickly
and violently with her handkerchief and concentrated
on what she was doing. When she got back to the stables nurse appeared at the door.

"Mrs. Marling rang up, madam," she said, "to say
could you go up to the Hall if you wasn't too tired, as
she wants to do something about the Red Cross."

"What was it, nurse?" Lettice asked.

"I couldn't say, madam, I'm sure," said nurse, who
dissociated herself entirely from any war activities,
holding that her brother Sid represented the family
and she, as she often said, was not one to meddle, besides having the children to look after and most of
their washing now and madam's undies as well, not
like when the Commander was at home. "Something
about the Red Cross, Mrs. Marling said. Come along,
Diana and Clare."

The little girls demanded loudly that Miss Bunting
should come up and have tea with them, but Miss
Bunting, whom a long experience had made sensitive
to the finer shades of nursery etiquette, saw in nurse's
eye that the present moment was not propitious. It
might be that the nursery tea was not quite up to visi-

tors' standard, it might be that nurse had some ironing
to do, but whatever it was she knew better than to
thrust herself, or let herself be thrust, on any nursery,
so she said not to-day.

"I'm sure," said nurse, perceptive of Miss Bunting as
someone who knew what was what, "we'd all be very
pleased if Miss Bunting was to come to tea with us another day. Perhaps Miss Bunting would come on Tuesday if she is disengaged and mummy says yes."

Miss Bunting and nurse both knew that mummy
would say yes, but nevertheless the form of asking her
was observed, giving great satisfaction to both parties
who had a very proper feeling for all affairs of proto-
col, and it was arranged that on Tuesday Miss Bunting
should meet the nursery party in the Lime Walk after
lunch, take the children for a walk and come back to
nursery tea. The little girls then went in with nurse,
while Lettice with Miss Bunting drove on to the Hall.

Tea was ready in what used to be the best spare
bedroom but was now turned into the war drawing
room, a fine room on the first floor overlooking the big
lawn and the lime walk which ran down to the Rising
for no reason at all except the pleasant one of making
a lime avenue from the lawn to the river. While they
had their tea Mrs. Marling, a fond but not besotted
grandmother, asked about the dancing class, was
pleased to hear that David Leslie was back, and said
they must ask him to dinner soon. When they had finished tea, the three ladies went to the disused drawing
room downstairs where the afternoon sun pouring
through the open french windows made the room
though uninhabited feel cheerful. Here were stacked
the bundles of dressings, bandages, bedjackets, and
various stores which Mrs. Marling as head of the Barsetshire Red Cross had in her charge. In addition to
what was supplied by all the county working parties a
large consignment of stores from America had recently
been sent to the Hall, and it was these that needed
sorting and labelling. The work was held up from time
to time while the ladies admired the good material

used, material that was not now to be got in England, and each confessed afterwards to severe temptation to keep back a few of the exquisitely sewn or knitted things for private consumption. But honesty prevailed and soon after six everything was in its place. Miss Bunting went to her own quarters while the mother and daughter had a little desultory talk in the upstairs drawing room. Lettice had just got up to go when her brother Oliver came in with a man who she didn't know.

"I've brought Geoffrey Harvey in for a drink, mother," said Oliver, and vouchsafing no further explanation retired into what had been a large dress closet when the drawing room was a bedroom and was now used as a kind of genteel licensed grocer's where some drinks and such odds and ends as biscuits, sweets, cigarettes and other vanishing delicacies were kept. It was a point of honour with the Marling family to put everything of that nature into a common stock, and they were all fairly honest about using the contents except Mr. Marling who had a secret passion for biscuits and was apt to go to the cupboard at odd moments like a boy in a moral story stealing jam. Still, as his son Oliver remarked, the biscuits were paid for with his money, so he deserved first pick. Lettice of course kept her biscuits and sweets for her little girls, but as she hardly ever smoked she put most of the cigarettes she got into the common stock and contributed gin whenever the Marling Arms could supply it.

As long as Oliver was in the cupboard clinking bottles and glasses it was useless to ask him who his friend was, so his mother and sister confined themselves to generalities. Mr. Harvey was a tall, lean man with dark eyes and a great deal of dark hair which was perpetually falling over one eye and as often being thrown back by a toss of his head or put aside by one of his long and very well-shaped hands. To those who admired him this trait was very endearing, having a certain air as of one so innocent and defenceless that he could not even protect himself against his own hair.

To those who disliked him it was but a reason the
more for their (as they considered) well-founded dislike. Lettice was so busy wondering why his name
sounded familiar that she did not consider the question of like or dislike. Mrs. Marling had a general preference for men who were neat and well-groomed, but
as it was her rule never to show her disapproval of her
children's friends till they themselves found they
didn't like them, she asked Mr. Harvey if he knew that
part of the country well in a voice which accurately
conveyed to her son and daughter exactly what she
thought of him. Oliver, collecting glasses and bottles
in the cupboard, smiled to himself and wondered if
Geoffrey Harvey would be quick enough to spot it. He
was still smiling as he emerged with a tray and catching Lettice's eye saw that she had spotted it too, which
made her smile back to him. Mr. Harvey saw her smile
and found it disturbing.

"Sherry, Geoffrey, or gin and whatever we can
offer?" said Oliver. "We are mixing it with some Spanish white wine at the moment, as the village is out of
lime. Mamma, I know you'll have whiskey and soda.
Lettice, a little something to keep the cold out?"

Mr. Harvey asked for sherry, Mrs. Marling took her
whiskey and soda like a man and Lettice shook her
head.

"I will now," said Oliver, "expound your visitor to
you. He was bombed out of London in the last blitz
and came down to some cousins near Barchester, and
owing to his personality is now under John Leslie and
co-equal with me at the Office, only really an inferior
job as he only organises hundreds of typists and what-
nots, while I am allowed to sit in a little room with a
telephone and draw pictures on the blotting paper.
Geoffrey, my mother and my sister Lettice."

Having distributed the drinks he took off his spectacles and held his hand over his eyes for a moment, a
gesture which made his mother and sister each say to
herself, "Oliver's eyes are bad again," and lose all interest in the newcomer.

"Oliver is only pulling my leg," said Mr. Harvey in a deep, melodious voice. "I was really seconded here from the Board of Tape and Sealing Wax because I am rather good at handling masses of dull and mostly useless correspondence and putting people off who want to know things."

"A kind of Tite Barnacle," said Mrs. Marling, testing her man.

"Exactly. How *nice* of you," said Mr. Harvey enthusiastically. "But a very unworthy disciple. And what I want dreadfully is a little house for my sister and myself. If we live any longer with my cousins we shall go mad, and it is certainly not worth paying ten guineas a week which is supposed to include drinks and emphatically doesn't, for the privilege of qualifying for Colney Hatch."

"Who are your cousins?" asked Mrs. Marling.

"I don't suppose you know them," said Mr. Harvey. "They are called Norton and have a quite dreadfully boring garden that people used to come miles to see, all very rare plants that mostly don't come up."

"His mother, Victoria Norton, is a cousin of my husband's," said Mrs. Marling.

"I'm sorry—" Mr. Harvey began, but whether he was sorry for his own unfortunate remarks or for Mr. Marling we shall never know, for Mrs. Marling without paying any attention to him added—"and a dreadful woman with a face like a cabhorse. Her son was at school with Oliver and is quite insufferable and so is his wife."

Mr. Harvey laughed and flung back his hair.

"I remembered old Lady Norton at the Leslies' once, Mamma," said Oliver. "She got the better of a whole lunch party including the Bishop of Barchester and we all had to listen to her account of the way she mulched—it is mulched isn't it, or do I mean squelched—her tenth greenhouse."

Then Lettice remembered that Mrs. John Leslie had spoken of Geoffrey Harvey and felt the relief we all feel when two things click together in our minds. It

made her feel quite friendly towards the newcomer.
True, as David Leslie had said, he was long-haired,
but quite a lot of quite nice men had rather long hair.
Oliver's was fairly long in front, only he kept it very ti-
dily brushed back. And even if David had known Mr.
Harvey up and down town off and on for a long time,
no fair minded person would hold that against anyone.
So she smiled at Mr. Harvey and asked what kind of
house he wanted.

"The dream house, of course," said Mr. Harvey,
mocking himself a trifle obviously. "Just big enough
for Frances and me and our dreadfully faithful cook
who is really Frances' old nurse. But not a little house
with beams that hit your head. Sooner a Council Cottage, however Councilish."

Mrs. Marling said in any case he wouldn't get one.

"I do so understood," said Mr. Harvey. "All for Tol-
puddle Martyrs, and *so* right."

"That is not the way to ingratiate yourself with my
mamma," said Oliver. "Here in Barsetshire we think
but poorly of Dorsetshire. Now if you said the Hog-
glestock martyrs, not that there ever were any, mamma
would smile on your suit."

Mr. Harvey, who liked showing people that he appreciated their remarks, laughed again, and again
flung back his hair. Mrs. Marling, ignoring her son,
embarked upon a catalogue raisonné of houses in the
neighbourhood which had at one time or another been
to let, but as they were all crammed to overflowing
with refugees or people's relations were not worth
practical consideration.

"But mamma," said Lettice, "what about the Red
House? Mrs. Smith is longing to get rid of it and go to
her mother at Torquay. Do you want it furnished or
unfurnished, Mr. Harvey?"

Mr. Harvey said he didn't mind at all, but as most of
his furniture was stored he would prefer unfurnished.
On the other hand, he added, he didn't suppose there
would be the faintest chance of getting it down from

London within the next six months, so perhaps furnished; but anything would be perfect.

"Mrs. Smith wants to let furnished," said Lettice. "She doesn't want to see any of her furniture again, poor thing."

Mr. Harvey said one did so understand that feeling.

"It's because her husband died there," said Oliver. "You wouldn't mind that?"

"My dear, no!" said Mr. Harvey. "It is all so fantastically perfect. Which room did he die in?"

Lettice said in the best bedroom.

"Then I'll have to let Frances sleep in it," said Mr. Harvey regretfully. "I might have seen an elemental, quite too terrifying and marvellous. What is the rent?"

But this was a detail no one knew. Mrs. Marling said if Mr. Harvey really wanted to enquire he had better write to Mrs. Smith. Or perhaps he and his sister would come over one day soon and see it for themselves. Mr. Harvey said his hours of duty were a peculiar kind of jigsaw puzzle, like Oliver's, but he would have a whole day off next week and would tell his sister.

"Ring me up and have tea here then," said Mrs. Marling. "I would like to say lunch, but we are not able to do very much now."

"How one understands that," said Mr. Harvey. "Though nothing to my cousins, I assure you, who simply welcome rationing as an excuse for never asking people to meals and starving their guests. If Frances and I have to sit much longer like the old person of Sheen, who dined off one pea and one bean, with George and Eleanor who is really my cousin, and George, saying in loud voices that they can't think why anyone complains about rations, we shall expire. Thank you so much for your help and now I must be going."

"Do stay and meet my husband," said Mrs. Marling, who wanted that gentleman to cast an eye over the possible tenant of the Red House before she went any further. "Where is your father, Oliver?"

"Isn't he back?" said Oliver.

A great deal of cross-talking then took place from which it emerged that Oliver had come out in Mr. Harvey's car and knew nothing of his father's movements. At the same moment Mr. Marling came in and leaving the door open stood glaring at the company.

"Been waiting in that confounded Club for more than half an hour," he said angrily. "Thought you were coming out with me, Oliver."

"No, papa dear," said Oliver. "I came out with Geoffrey Harvey in his car. Here he is," he added in confirmation of his statement.

"You said I was to wait for Oliver, Amabel," said Mr. Marling. "Waited nearly an hour and then he comes out with a feller I don't know. Afternoon, young man, didn't get your name."

"Geoffrey Harvey, papa dear," said Oliver.

"Oh, all right, all right," said his father. "Thing is your mother said you wanted me to wait for you."

"No, William, I only said would you ask at the Club if there was a message from Oliver in case he could come out with you," said Mrs. Marling, unperturbed. "Did you ask for a message?"

"No, I didn't," said her husband. "What message? No one gives me any messages. I've been sitting over an hour in that Club and that silly feller Norton got hold of me and talked a lot of nonsense about the War Agricultural Committee. Tell you what I said to him though—this'll amuse you, Amabel—he said he was putting a bit of the park under wheat, that bit along the Southbridge Road, so I told him he'd never do any good there. Worst bit of soil for twenty miles round. And you can tell *that* to the Agricultural Committee, I said."

He paused, evidently expecting applause for this brilliant anecdote.

"Eleanor Norton is Mr. Harvey's cousin, William," said his wife.

"Eh?" said Mr. Marling, suddenly afflicted with deafness. "Whose cousin's that?"

"You know you heard quite well, father," said Lettice. "Mr. Harvey has been staying with the Nortons and he wants to look at the Red House. Sit down, darling, and have some sherry."

Mr. Marling allowed himself to be offered a chair and said sherry was poison except with the soup, but he supposed he'd better have some and he couldn't understand what all the fuss was about. If Mr. Carver was staying with the Nortons, why did he want to look at the Red House.

"Not Carver, father, Harvey," said Lettice.

"Oh, all right," said her father. "If you'd been about an hour and a half with that pompous ass Norton talking nonsense about wheat, *you'd* say Carver."

"George is enough to make anyone say Carver, sir," said Mr. Harvey sympathetically. "My sister and I are being starved at Norton Park and we want to find a small house where we can be on our own, not too far from Barchester. Miss Marling said a place called the Red House might be available."

"Lucy? Where is she?" asked Mr. Marling. "I want to talk to her about the young bull."

Mrs. Marling said she hadn't seen Lucy since breakfast, which made her husband ask how the devil it was that Lucy had told Mr. Carver about the Red House. Oliver, realising that the mistake was due to his carelessness, apologised to Mr. Harvey and begged to be allowed to reintroduce his sister as Mrs. Watson. The real Miss Marling, he said, would be back from the Cottage Hospital at any moment. Mr. Harvey in his turn apologised for his unwitting mistake and then said he must really be going.

The door, which Oliver had shut when his father stopped standing in the doorway, was suddenly flung open again by Lucy, in her V.A.D. uniform.

"I say," she said, standing in the open door as her father had done, "I'll tell you what I did to-day. I helped Doctor March to vaccinate two babies. One was Welper's baby, you know father, the man who had the chicken farm, but he's having to give it up because of

grain rationing. It's a fine baby. I held them both
while Dr. March jabbed the stuff in and he says I can
come to his consulting room the day I'm off duty and
help if I like. Whose car is that in the drive? I don't
know the number-plate. I'll tell you what—"

"Lucy, my angel," said Oliver, "it is Geoffrey Harvey's car. He drove me out in it and he wants to take
the Red House. Geoffrey, this is the real Miss Marling."

"Oh, hullo," said Lucy giving Mr. Harvey's arm a
hearty kind of pump-handle shake. "I didn't see you.
You'll like the Red House. It's a bit art, but the beds
are good. I slept there once to keep Mrs. Smith
company when her husband was getting over D.T.
You know he died of it. But I'll tell you what you
ought to do, get the gas oven moved into the scullery
and make the kitchen a sort of dining-room. It'll be
much warmer in the winter."

Mr. Harvey, amused by the strong family likeness
between his host and his host's younger daughter, explained that he must see the Red House before he
took it and was coming over next week with his sister.
He then managed to get away. As he drove back to
Norton Hall he thought how families ran in types. Mr.
Marling, a real character (and he plumed himself on
his collection of characters) and his younger daughter
an absolute replica of him, though the fine, insular
self-confidence which led Mr. Marling to stand in the
doorway bellowing at everyone was not so attractive
in a girl, or a young woman, for Miss Marling must be
at least twenty-five. Anything less like his conception
of Oliver Marling's family there could not be. Yet Oliver's other sister was very like him. Both had a certain
quiet elegance and the reserved though perfectly cor-
dial manners which had attracted him to Oliver in the
Office. He almost wished the elder sister were not
married, for she had all her brother's charm. He would
like to see her smile again in that disturbing way. Very
likely her husband was in the army or away on some
war work and a light flirtation would not come amiss

to ner. The more he thought of her, the more the plan of taking the Red House smiled on him. His London friends, most of whom had managed to get pretty good jobs, would be frightfully envious when they heard he had taken a house where the last occupant had died of D.T. It would knock out completely that conceited young Rivers and his flat where the actress had taken veronal. He felt a sudden spurt of annoyance at the thought of Julian Rivers being an official war artist and paid for it too, all because he was a connection of Lord Pomfret's. But in this he did Julian Rivers less than justice. That odious young man had not asked any help from his cousin, who would not have been much inclined to give it, and by his own arrogance and push as the leading light of the Set of Five, an artistic coterie centring round the Tottenham Court Road, had shoved himself into the job and was now painting munition factories in terms of pre-war surrealism, besides a spot of collage, his portrait of a girl shell-filler done entirely by gluing bits of bus tickets together having had a particular success.

At least, Mr. Harvey reflected, he was not an able-bodied young man who had found a non-combatant job. He was well over military age. He did his work very well at the Board of Tape & Sealing Wax and knew it. Until a few months ago he had been certain of a place in the Honours List, possibly a K.B.E. Whether his work at the Regional Commissioner's Office would sidetrack this he was not sure. He would take care to make a good impression in it and if the impression were not good enough he would manage to get back to Whitehall and his London life, for to live among barbarians in the provinces was no part of his plan. Still, Lettice Watson was not a barbarian and one must make the best of any position in which one found oneself; so he sped on to Norton Park and its amenities in a more hopeful frame of mind.

Meanwhile the unconscious object of his thoughts had gone back to her home over the stables. She found her daughters in bed, very pink and clean, waiting to say their prayers. When they had finished Nurse said,

"I didn't like to trouble you, madam, while the children were saying their prayers, but we couldn't clean our teeth to-night." -

Lettice, rather surprised, asked why.

"I thought Diana was very quiet after tea," said nurse, "but I was ironing and didn't see what she was doing. Just look, madam."

She held up two small toothbrushes, industriously clipped to the bone by the older Miss Watson.

"With the nursery nail scissors, madam, as quiet as you please," she said.

"Oh, Diana, how could you be so naughty," said her mother, trying not to sound loving and making no success of it at all.

"Like Uncle David," said Diana and shut her eyes tightly to show she had gone to sleep.

CHAPTER THREE

On Tuesday, as arranged, Miss Bunting stepped across the lawn to the lime walk. Nurse coming up at almost the same moment with her flock handed them over to Miss Bunting and retired, giving the little girls many injunctions to be good and not worry Miss Bunting and be sure to be back soon after four to get their hands washed for tea. Miss Bunting, who quite understood that the second part of nurse's speech was in *oratio obliqua* for her own benefit, said she had her watch with her and they would be back by a quarter past at the very latest. They then had a delightful walk, chosen by Diana and Clare, to the manure heap, the back of the potting shed, the rubbish heap, the gardener's pig, the barn cat which had six kittens as wild as itself and lay spitting and sparking in a nest of hay, the horrid yet exciting place in the kitchen garden where a rook dangled on a string to keep the birds away, and big rain water tub with scum on the top of it and the little steps that led down to the furnace for the glass houses which could not now be heated. And

all the time Diana asked questions or demanded
stories of naughty children, and Miss Bunting gave the
right answers and recounted the hair-raising deeds of
her naughtiest pupils, and at four-fifteen precisely
they mounted the steep stair to the nursery. Here
nurse, as temporary chatelaine, received the party graciously, made light of a stain on Diana's frock and
Clare's very dirty hands, and took them off to wash.
Miss Bunting, after washing her hands in Lettice's
bathroom, sat down by the nursery window and
thought gratefully of the Marling family who had
saved her from being a distressed gentlewoman. In the
case of Mrs. Marling her very real gratitude was nec-
essarily mixed with the faint contempt that every good
governess must feel for the provider of governess-fod-
der, unable themselves to educate their young, yet
daring to meddle with the educator. For Mrs. Marling's children her feelings were varied. Bill being married and rarely at home was almost a stranger to her,
Lucy was too settled in her rather overbearing ways of
a spoilt younger child to meet with her approval, but
in Oliver and Lettice she saw exactly what she would
wish any pupil of hers to be and felt for them an equal
devotion. Lettice, it is true, scored heavily by having
two little girls, well brought up and amenable to her
influence, but Oliver was a man and she had always
liked boys best, partly because they had an affection
for her that she never quite inspired in their sisters.
Also Oliver had trouble with his eyes and reminded
Miss Bunting of Lord Hugh Skeynes who had to stay
away from Eton for a term and use his eyes as little as
possible while she read book after book to him in the
schoolroom. It seemed a good omen to her that he had
grown up with almost normal eyesight and she
cherished a deep faith that Oliver would emerge in a
few years with an eagle's vision.

Now nurse came back with her charges all neat and
clean and delivered them to Miss Bunting while she
boiled the kettle for tea. The tea being made Diana
scrambled by herself onto a chair with a very fat cush-

ion on it and Clare was lifted into the tall chair,
though it was very obvious that it would not contain
her buxom form much longer. Nurse tied on their
feeders, begged Miss Bunting to sit down and took her
own place opposite.

"Will this be too strong, miss," said nurse as she
poured the tea out of a comfortable brown teapot, "or
shall I add just a little hot water?"

"That will do very nicely, thank you, nurse," said
Miss Bunting. "A little milk please. No sugar, thank
you. I gave up sugar in the last war, though I used to
take two lumps."

"It is quite remarkable the way we all get used to
things," said nurse. "Hand the bread and butter to
Miss Bunting, Diana, and mind you hold it straight.
That's right. Now take a piece for yourself and fold it
nicely in half. I used to be quite a one for sugar myself, but now I never miss it. I always say every lump
you don't take is one up against someone we won't
mention."

While she was speaking nurse doubled a piece of
bread and butter, cut it into fingers and put it on
Clare's plate, and then helped herself.

"It is the same with butter," said Miss Bunting. "I
used to help myself quite recklessly, but now we have
to be careful I find my ration is quite enough for the
week."

"I'm sure I find exactly the same," said nurse. "And
when we think of our brave fighting men, really an
ounce or so of butter seems quite a paltry affair. Don't
drink your milk too fast, Diana."

"I hope you have good news of your brother, nurse,"
said Miss Bunting.

"Sid's got free stripes," said Diana.

"She hears everything," said nurse, looking proudly
at Miss Bunting, who thought this was highly probable. "Yes, Sid has three stripes, hasn't he? I must show
you his photo after tea, miss. Diana, pass the cake to
Miss Bunting. We get very nice cakes from Pulford in

the village, much nicer than the cakes from Barchester."

Diana took a small cake, rammed it into her mouth and handed the plate to Miss Bunting.

"Diana, take that cake out of your mouth at once," said nurse. "What will Miss Bunting say if you choke?"

Diana removed a rather unpleasant mass of cake from her mouth and smiled angelically.

"Some little people," said nurse, "are always over excited when they see company."

"When I was with Lord Lundy," said Miss Bunting, "it was just the same. As soon as anyone came to tea in the schoolroom you would have thought the children were little savages."

"And that's what they'd all be if Some People had their way," said nurse. "I always say, miss, if someone we won't name had been properly brought up we shouldn't be having all this trouble. Clare, don't blow into your milk, you know it's not the way to drink."

"Quite right, nurse," said Miss Bunting approvingly. "There's nothing like the English nursery for making ladies and gentlemen of them."

Nurse, taking this tribute as her right, said she always understood foreigners had no home life to speak of which really made one feel their goings on weren't to be surprised at, but she was sure Miss Bunting was ready for another cup of tea. As she was pouring it out there was a knock on the door and in walked David Leslie.

"Uncle David," said Diana with her mouth full.

Clare, who had her mug to her mouth, said what sounded like "Plum Duff" and choked.

"Now that's enough," said nurse, taking Clare's mug away and wiping her milky moustache off with her feeder. "I don't know what the gentleman will think."

"Bunny, my adored one!" said David. "Good-afternoon, nurse. I suppose you haven't got Mrs. Watson anywhere about? They told me at the Hall she was down here."

"I'm afraid you've just missed her, sir," said nurse, who had not the faintest idea who David was, but recognising him with a nurse's infallible instinct as a proper gentleman, knew it was all right. "She has gone up to tea at the Hall. She went by the walled garden and the flagged walk I think."

"And I came down the drive in my car because I cannot walk, only fly," said David. "Bunny, pray present me."

"This is Mr. David Leslie, nurse," said Miss Bunting. "He's a distant connection of the family's."

"Well, to be sure," said nurse. "You'll excuse my saying so, sir, but I was temporary nurse with Mrs. Graham one summer, before I came to Mrs. Watson, and we used to hear quite a lot about Uncle David in the nursery."

"I'm sure you did," said David, "and not at all to my credit."

"Oh no, sir, I'm sure," said nurse with a superior though respectful smile.

"Well, to make up for it, suppose you invite me to tea," said David. "That is if Miss Bunting doesn't object. Will I do, Bunny?"

He held out his hands, palms upwards.

"And my nails, too," he added, turning them over. "Clean as nurse's apron."

"It's more than they used to be," said Miss Bunting, after looking at them through her pince-nez, while nurse bridled.

Without further ceremony David pulled up a chair between Miss Bunting and Clare. Nurse brought a clean cup, saucer, knife, spoon and plate. The little girls began to get excited. David asked for two lumps of sugar on the grounds that all birds liked sugar and birds flew and he flew, so he must have sugar. Nurse and Miss Bunting, those apostles of self-denial and fighting the blockade, were delighted by his extravagance, both holding secretly that laws were not for well-connected flying officers. Discipline melted. Diana got down from her chair and climbed with

great firmness onto David's knees where she fondled
the lapels of his coat with a loving though buttery
hand and insisted on hanging her own feeder, by this
time in a far from agreeable state, round his neck.
Clare's emotion took the form of drinking copious
draughts of milk while looking at him over or round
the side of her mug, so that most of her milk dribbled
down her chin and nurse had to get a cloth and wipe
up the mess. But though at any other time such of-
fences would have been punished with rigour, or
nipped before they budded, nurse looked on the scene
of debauch with a lenient eye. Partly from a vague
sentiment that we couldn't do too much for our brave
flying heroes, but far more from the feeling, previously
alluded to, that the gentry, and more especially those
with titled relatives, could do no ill.

While nurse cleared away the tea-things and
washed the children's hands and faces, David devoted
himself to Miss Bunting, enquiring earnestly after her
married sister who was a clergyman's widow and her
niece (daughter of the deceased clergyman) who was
a deaconess at Wolverhampton: and though Miss
Bunting knew that he had no interest at all in her relations (as indeed, nor had she, nor had they any in
her) and David knew that she knew, his old governess
could not withstand his cajolery, and melted visibly in
his careless beams.

Now the children returned, ravishingly clean, and it
was Clare's turn to sit on his knees, while Diana plied
him with questions about why he couldn't walk but
only fly, and requested to be taken in his aeroplane. At
this point David suddenly felt, as he so often had in
various scenes of life, that the one thing he wanted
was to be somewhere else. It was never in his scheme
to thwart his own inclinations. Alleging that it would
appear rude if he did not go and see Mrs. Marling he
bade farewell to his hostesses.

"Say good-bye to Uncle David," said nurse, who had
entirely adopted him as one of the family, "and say we
hope he'll come again soon."

Each little girl embraced one of his legs with fervour.

"Good-bye, Bunny," said David to Miss Bunting, his efforts to approach her considerably hampered by his living leg-irons. "Have I been good?"

Miss Bunting looked piercingly at her ex-pupil.

"You cannot fool all the people all the time, David," she said. "You will probably find Lettice and her mother in the village. They are showing some friends the Red House. Anyone will tell you where it is."

Nurse then detached her two limpets from the visitor's legs and David went down the steep stair, his lively nature feeling an unwonted deflation. But nothing had power over him for long, and in two minutes he had shaken off the faint depression caused by his old governess's words and was driving rather too fast down the back drive and so into the village.

Marling Melicent is a pretty village, though not one of Barsetshire's show places, with some good houses of gold-grey stone and some handsome red brick houses anything up to two hundred years old. Here and there an eyesore may be seen in the shape of an Edwardian villa, built indeed of red brick, but of how different a shade and texture from the older buildings. One particularly revolting specimen on the irregular shaped green, two doors off the Marling Arms, caught David's eye and he slowed down, the better to savour its horrors. Built of a hard purple-red brick with patterns of grey brick inlaid on it, the upper story painted with sham timbering, the side nearest the public house consisting chiefly of overlapping tiles of the same uncompromising red as the bricks, with scalloped edges, it had several gables of different sizes, leaded windows flush with the outer wall and a kind of Swiss chalet of a porch. The front door was bright blue. The front garden, to David's reverential joy, had a winding path, a very small pond edged with synthetic rocks, three dwarfs and a toadstool, and a concrete rabbit. A large monkey puzzle blocked what looked like the dining-room window where David could see several coloured

witch balls hanging. The further to enjoy this sight he
stopped altogether, behind a car which was standing
near the front gate. A tall man who had just finished
locking the car looked round and saw David.

"David," he said (and very well he said it David
had to admit) and tossed back a lock of hair.

"Hullo, Geoffrey," said David. "I didn't know you
lived here."

"My dear, I don't yet," said Mr. Harvey, leaning his
arms negligently on the open window of David's car.
"My sister and I want a house. Mrs. Marling and Lettice Watson think this would suit us. Do you know
them?"

David felt unreasonably annoyed at this question.

"The worst of a little car like mine," he said, "is
that if you bend down to talk to anyone inside it you
look so peculiar from behind."

Mr. Harvey straightened himself with a slightly hur-
ried negligence.

"The Marlings are cousins of mine," David continued. "I'm rather ashamed of the sort of house they expect you to live in."

"One does so understand that feeling," said Mr.
Harvey, "but the dwarfs alone are worth the rent the
owner is asking. I don't know what the inside's like.
Come in and see."

He held the front gate open with what David was
quite sure he knew to be feline grace. David locked
his car and walked into the garden.

"So perfectly wrong, don't you think," said Mr. Harvey, indicating the front door. He turned the handle
and stood aside for David to pass. Inside the blue door
was what house agents will call a lobby, about four
feet square, and beyond it a wrought-iron grille, showing a narrow passage and a staircase painted a shiny
green. The two men squeezed with difficulty past a
very thin table with a top painted to imitate marble
and twisted iron legs. Voices were heard on the right.
Mr. Harvey made for a door which had no handle, but
a large rather dirty looking white tassel hanging on a

cord that came through a hole where the handle ought to be.

"Pull the bobbin and the latch will fly up," said David encouragingly.

Mr. Harvey did so and pushed the door open. Before them was the drawing room. Pale green shiny walls, tall gilt lamps, white upholstered chairs and sofa, a large reproduction of a picture of bright red horses, marbled mantelpiece just wide enough for a matchbox to fall off, met their interested eyes. Near the window, below which a negro painted black and gold supported a small semi-circular table of substitute malachite, Mrs. Marling and Lettice were talking to what was obviously Miss Harvey, a woman not quite young, as fair as her brother was dark, with a more determined expression.

"Frances," said Mr. Harvey, "we must have this house. Pure Sloane Square and really, my dear, *too* off-white."

"Oh, David!" said Lettice. "How very nice of you to come. Mother, you remember David. I told you I saw him again the other day at the dancing class. Miss Harvey, this is my cousin, David Leslie. Where did you come from?"

David explained that he had missed her at the Hall, followed her to the stables and had tea with her offspring and Miss Bunting. Mrs. Marling said if they had come to look at the house they had better get it over. Mr. Harvey said the dwarfs had quite made up his mind for him, but Frances had better look at the bedrooms and the kitchens. So the whole party went into the neat, clean tiled kitchen and scullery, looked at the dining-room which had a sham refectory table, a looking-glass with a grille over it all across the end opposite the window, and chairs with imitation vellum seats, and Mr. Harvey kept up a continuous ecstatic murmur of "Off-white; pure, pure Sloane Square." Under Miss Harvey's leadership they then went upstairs and inspected the bath with black glass surround before passing on to the best bedroom.

"I always feel a certain delicacy, or indelicacy, about going into other people's bedrooms," said David, "and there is something about beds that are very flat that says Sin to me."

Mr. Harvey said one so understood that feeling.

"I can't think why," said David warming to his subject, "an almost square divan bed with only a hard bolster and a cover of shiny green and white striped chintz should call to my mind the word Debauchery. One would expect debauchery to mean red plush and electric lights with pink shades. By the way, Geoffrey, where *do* people with beds like that keep their pillows? You ought to know if you are going to live here."

"Perhaps," said Lettice, "people with D.T. aren't allowed pillows. They might suffocate themselves."

Miss Harvey, who had not spoken much but had made notes of things in a very business-like way as she went over the house, said it all depended. With violent cases of dipsomania one had to strap them down, even if one had a male nurse, but she didn't think she or Geoffrey would need it.

"What made you think of D.T., Mrs. Watson?" she asked.

Lettice hesitated and looked at Mr. Harvey. It had not occurred to her that his sister might not know about the late Mr. Smith's death and she wished she had not spoken.

"I never told you, Frances, that the late occupant died of drink," said Mr. Harvey. "So stupid of me."

"It doesn't matter in the least," said his sister.

"I'll sleep in this room if you like," said Mr. Harvey, with just too much carelessness.

"Certainly not," said his sister.

This brief passage gave Lettice a curious impression that the Harvey's were quite independent of outsiders and would not really notice if they all vanished. Miss Harvey except for her fair hair and skin was not unlike her brother, and though her face was stronger she seemed to move with the same impulse. David thought her an uncommonly handsome woman for one who was not quite young, more of a gentleman than her brother and quite worth a little exploring while his leave lasted.

Mrs. Marling, untroubled by such musings, had been considering the matter of the pillows and suddenly saw light.

"Mrs. Smith will know where the pillows are," she said. "She ought to be here now. She knew we were coming."

David, who was near the window, reported that something that no one could mistake for anything but a widow was looking at the dwarfs, on hearing which Mr. Harvey, expressing a fear that she might want to take them away, thus ruining his future happiness, begged everyone to come downstairs. So back to the drawing-room they went, where Mr. Harvey stood at the window eyeing his future landlady malevolently while the rest of the party discussed the decoration and furnishing which happily combined Spanish and Jacobean with functional, or so at least Miss Harvey said, though which the sham vellum lamp shades with semi-transparent pseudo-Canalettos on them and ivory velvet ribbon were, she did not say.

"She is coming in," said Mr. Harvey.

And in came a very thin woman in deep black who had obviously been good-looking once and still had fine eyes. Mrs. Marling and Lettice, who had known her slightly for many years and had no particular interest in her, introduced the possible tenants.

"Of course," said Mrs. Smith, sitting down on the little off-white brocade sofa, its ends lashed to its back by thick oxidised silver ropes, "I would never have dreamt of letting the house while Mr. Smith was alive."

Everyone felt very uncomfortable and at a distinct disadvantage. Everyone, that is, except Mrs. Marling, who having given up some of her valuable time to a deed of kindness for her son Oliver's friend, and knowing that Mrs. Smith wanted to let the house, beat the devil's tattoo impatiently on her bag.

"Miss Harvey and Mr. Harvey, Mrs. Smith," she said.

"I'm sure I'm very pleased to meet you," said Mrs. Smith. "Of course Mr. Smith always did the business and I find it very trying to be left alone like this. I really sleep so badly now that I must get away as soon as possible, and owing to Mr. Smith's affairs being in such a bad way I must let our little nest as well as I can. You don't know what it is to be a widow, Miss Harvey."

Miss Harvey confessed that she didn't, but unwilling to sink too low in her possible landlady's estimation, said she hoped she would some day.

"You never will," said Mrs. Smith. "There aren't two like Mr. Smith in the whole world."

"One does so understand that feeling," said Mr. Harvey.

Mrs. Smith wiped her eyes.

"Pardon me," she said, "but you can't. Mr. Smith had the house beautifully decorated when he bought it a year ago, all to tone. I never thought I would have to let it. You only have to look round the drawing-room to see the sort of man Mr. Smith was."

Lettice and David looked simultaneously at the wastepaper basket which was covered with green brocade and had a shiny coloured reproduction of the Sistine Madonna glued onto it with a dull gold edging.

"Four guineas a week, you said, Mrs. Smith," said Mrs. Marling. "And what about plate and linen?"

Mrs. Smith said she would never have let her house if Mr. Smith were alive. "Mr. Smith always passed the remark," said Mrs. Smith, addressing Mr. Harvey as the weakest opponent, "that the house would be a little gold mine to me if anything were to happen to him, and 'Joyce,' he said—Joyce is my name, you know—'don't take a penny less than four guineas, or five if you leave your silver and your linen.' All the bed linen is in art colouring."

"Very well, that's settled," said Mrs. Marling. "And

my friends can come in almost at once. Who is your lawyer?"

"Mr. Smith was always his own lawyer," said the widow. "You don't know what it is to be alone."

"Keith and Son of Barchester saw about his will, I think," and Mrs. Marling, who had picked up this fact from the senior partner, Mr. Robert Keith, at the time. "So Miss Harvey and her brother will get their lawyer to communicate with them. Is that all right, Miss Harvey?"

Mrs. Smith then took her leave, bidding a farewell to her cottage that made the Harveys appear as oppressors of the poor and unprotected, but much to Mr. Harvey's relief not mentioning the dwarfs. The Harveys thanked Mrs. Marling very much for her help, without which, Mr. Harvey said, they would probably have given the whole thing up in despair, or a least been hypnotised into asking Mrs. Smith to share the house with them till better times. They then went back to Norton Park.

Mrs. Marling and Lettice had walked down from the Hall and were quite ready to walk back, but David insisted on running them up in his little car, and as a matter of course came in for a drink. What he wanted, in so far as he ever really wanted anything, was to see something of his cousin Lettice and make an impression on her that would wipe out his stupid question about her husband. But Mrs. Marling, who had strong family feelings, instituted an exhaustive inquiry into the whole of the Leslie family, numbering at present some sixteen or eighteen, besides Martin Leslie's mother and her second husband, an American, and her American children. So time slipped away till David said he must go.

Lettice, whose heart still smote her because she had not yet explained to David that he had not hurt her, had also hoped to have a few words with her cousin, but with her mother present it was impossible. She recognised, without rancour, that it always had been and always would be impossible to talk to her own

friends when her masterful mother was present. For
this reason, as we know, she had preferred to live in
the flat over the stables where at least she had solitude
when she needed it and could ask a friend to tea. Ever
since she was a child she remembered her mother taking possession of all her own friends, not from any jeal-
ousy of them or any wish to attach them to herself,
but because having been brought up as one of a large
family with a great many county and public interests,
she could hardly envisage any but a communal life.
Anyone who came near Marling had to be drawn into
her orbit. She felt no need for privacy herself. Her bedroom, her sitting-room, her interests, her time, were all
public. Devoted to the service of others, full of
abounding energy, it never occurred to her that other
people might like to retire from the glare of family life
from time to time. Lettice could think of more than
one girl or young man, in the days when she lived at
home, whom she would have liked as a friend, and
would have cultivated in her own diffident way had
not her mother, with the best intentions in the world,
forcibly drawn the newcomers into the family vortex,
absorbed them, and left Lettice a little in the shadow.
One of the things that had made Lettice like her husband so very much, even before she loved him, was his
total absence of fear where her mother was concerned.
Having seen the girl he wanted to marry, he had gone
straight to his goal, which was to see as much of her as
he could and get her for his own. Mrs. Marling, always
willing to please her children though she usually managed to spoil the pleasure, had asked him to stay and
for the first time in her life had met someone who
politely brushed all her plan-making aside and merely
said, in answer to all suggestions of family picnics or
other outings, that he would like to take Lettice for a
walk, or a drive in his car, or in the canoe on the Rising. To none of these pleasures had Mrs. Marling any
adequate objection, and being a sensible woman used
to suffering fools on committees, she left the young
people to their own devices. When they said they were

engaged she was honestly delighted and expected to
see them, having, as it were, got that trouble off their
chests, rejoin the family circle. That they still preferred their own society was to her inexplicable.

To Lettice the inexplicable thing was that anyone
could resist her mother, and, as we have said, part of
her devotion to her husband may be attributed to her
admiration of his courage. Her elder brother Bill and
his wife were as family-minded as her mother, and her
sister Lucy bade fair to be even more masterful. Her
ally was her brother Oliver, only a little older than
herself and equally diffident, though he had early developed a technique for melting away from his mother's possessive influence which Lettice could not emu-
late. He had lived in London, she had married and left
home. Now circumstances—the end, for the time
being, of the firm in which he was a partner, her husband's death—had brought them both back to their
old home. Though Lettice had the independence that
her income and her separate establishment over the
stables gave her, her silent nature had fallen again
under her mother's sway. She knew it and had not the
heart or the strength to resist. Sometimes she wished
she had taken a house farther away and had vaguely
set about looking for one. Then the impossibility of
ever explaining to her mother why she should do so,
her gratitude for all the love and kindness that accepted her as a child of the house again and did not probe
her feelings, made her feel that she would be a devil
to leave Marling. And she knew that her father would
miss her. As for Lucy, she was extremely fond of that
roistering young woman whom she humbly recognised to be thirty-six times as energetic and capable as
she could ever be; and if Lucy's fine egoism sometimes
made her stop her ears mentally and shrink into herself, she showed no sign. Lucy had taken her place as
Miss Marling and on this position she did not want to
infringe, so she was more quiet than ever.

Oliver saw a good deal of this and it worried him.
That Lettice should be near her old home at present

was right and proper, but he realised that she was one of those natures that can only make a few real decisions in their lives. One such effort she had made when she married, an effort which had been amply justified in her great happiness and her two little girls. Whether she would ever exert herself again, Oliver not very hopefully wondered. If she did not, no one could do it for her, and as long as her parents lived she would remain a charming shadow about their house and estate. This Oliver would not be. He gave in to his parents with pleasant grace, but like a blob of quicksilver he was apt to split under their hands only to reunite as himself somewhere else. To remain at home was no part of his plan. After the war he intended to go back to London, where one could see one's own oculist. For Oliver's oculist had disappeared into the Army at the beginning of the war and he had chanced upon a very unlovable gentleman whose attitude towards his patients was that if his glasses did not suit them, something must be wrong with their eyes and it was entirely their own fault. Oliver, smarting under a large consultation fee and a very expensive pair of spectacles which made him feel rather sick and a good deal blinder than he was, had put the spectacles away and resigned himself to using his old ones and supporting his headaches till his own dear Mr. Pilman came back from wherever he was. Meanwhile he proposed to look after his sister Lettice whenever her gentle obstinacy would allow itself to be looked after.

On this day he happened to get back from Barchester at the moment when David, baulked for once by his cousin Amabel's determination to follow the Leslies into their last ramifications, gave up the game and was preparing to go. The sight of a fellow man encouraged him not to go, and he and Oliver had a short but agreeable conversation about their prep school and Mr. Panton who had hairs growing out of his ears, over a gin and lime; for the lime, our readers will be glad to hear, had now come in at the grocer's.

"Do you mind," said David to Oliver, as he held his

glass to be refilled, "if I talk to you out of the side of my mouth?"

Oliver said he would like it of all things.

"Then," said David, proceeding to do so, "could you possibly call your mother off? I have been trying to say something to Lettice for seventy-five minutes quite in vain."

He then put his face in order again.

"If your intentions are honourable I might do something," said Oliver. "Mamma, dear!"

"Yes, Oliver," said his mother.

"God bless you, kind gentleman," said David, out of the other side of his mouth.

"How many bedrooms has Joyce got?" said Oliver.

His mother said the best bedroom where Mr. Smith had died, the dressing-room and the other little room. Why? she added. Because, said Oliver, the Harveys thought they might be having an old governess to stay with them, and if so, where would they put her? Mrs. Marling said of course she had forgotten there was that extra room that Mr. Smith added when he built the garage. It was true it only had a staircase from the kitchen, but if they put their maid there it would be all right, as there was a gas fire and running water. Then the governess could have the little room. It would be nice if she came, Mrs. Marling added, as she and Bunny could meet.

"Good God, mamma dear," said Oliver. "You cannot throw old governesses together like that. There is measure in everything. They may be deadly enemies at sight. I'm sure the Harveys' old lady hasn't had as many highly-connected pupils as Bunny—nobody has —and there would be Feelings."

Mrs. Marling, who appeared to have a disposition to put two of a suit together as if governesses were a poker hand, argued the question, led on by her undutiful son, which gave David his opening. He moved to Lettice and having got his opening didn't know what to do with it, a state of things not at all normal to him which displeased him greatly. So he temporized and asked after the little girls.

Lettice said they were very well and looked distractedly at her empty glass.

"Let me get you another drink," said David, taking the glass. "I know one ought to know people seven years to poke their fires, but I believe it's less for cocktails. I don't mean to poke them, of course."

"No, thanks," said Lettice, "though I do suppose being cousins and having known each other practically all our lives, though hardly ever meeting, you could poke a cocktail if you liked, though how one would do it I don't know."

"Then I'll poke one at myself," said David, picking up the shaker and filling his glass. "Lettice—"

But at the same moment his cousin said, "David."

"Shakespeare—Browning," said David briefly. "And now you carry on. Sorry."

"It was only," said Lettice, going rather pink, "that I wanted to say that it may sound horrid, but I don't mind if people talk about Roger a bit. I don't really mind even if mother does. In fact I like them to if they feel like it—but not if they don't, of course. And I'm sure Roger would agree."

David quite understood the courage behind his cousin's jumbled remarks and admitted to himself, a person with whom he was upon very frank terms, that she was braver than he was.

"I wanted to mention that myself," he said, "but I am a coward by nature. I hadn't heard that Roger was killed until Bunny told me at the dancing class. There didn't seem to be any way of apologising. I never met him except at your wedding, but I'm sure he was a frightfully good sort."

"Thank you," said Lettice. "That's absolutely all right. Only I was afraid I'd been churlish and frightened you. So I am very glad I haven't."

The cousins looked at each other and felt much more comfortable. Mrs. Marling having demonstrated to Oliver that one touch of governessing made all ex-governesses kin and failed in the very least to convince him, turned to David, or rather turned on him, such was her vigour, and invited him to dinner the week after next if he was still on leave.

David accepted and finally said good-bye. As he was starting his car, another car drove up and a young woman and an officer got out.

"Hullo," said the young woman. "Are you about the pig swill?"

"I wish I were," said David regretfully. "Who ought I to be?"

"I thought you were from the aerodrome," said the young woman. "Flight Commander Jackson said he'd send someone over to arrange about letting me have some. We could do with buckets. I'll tell you what, if you are going to the aerodrome will you tell him that he simply must send that pig stuff over at once, because I can't spare anyone to go. Lucy Marling."

"O coz, coz, coz, my pretty little coz," said David, adding, "The Bard."

"What do you mean Kuz?" said Miss Marling. The light of intelligence then dawned in her and she seized David's hand.

"Of course you're David!" she cried. "Tom, this is David Leslie, he's a kind of cousin of mine. This is Tom Barclay, I mean he's a captain, and he's going to let me see them explode the next bomb."

Captain Barclay, a pleasant-faced man of about David's age, shook hands and said he would certainly not let Miss Marling see any bombs exploded and would probably lose his stripes if he did.

"Oh rot," said Lucy, "you promised me. I ought to know how to explode bombs, because you never know and if there was one here Daddy would fuss like anything. I suppose Ed could do it, he's our sort of chauffeur, a bit mental but he's a marvel with his hands. I'll tell you what, next time you have a bomb I'll bring Ed and then he can see what to do."

"No promise ever passed these pure lips," said Captain Barclay, quite unperturbed by Lucy's insistence. "And no one, mental or otherwise, is coming."

"And don't say you will tell Captain Barclay what, Lucy, once more, for I cannot bear it," said David. "Barclay, your speaking countenance is familiar to me. Was it New York?"

"I thought so," said Captain Barclay. "It was."

"And was it the party someone threw the night we all got back from a West Indian cruise?"

"It was," said Captain Barclay. "And who the host was I never knew, but I remembered your face at once."

"I think," said David, "you and I were the last to pass out, such is the Bulldog Breed. We must meet again. I'm with my sister at Little Misfit. Good-bye, Lucy, I'm coming to dinner here the week after next and I'll beat you at six-pack bézique afterwards. See you again, Barclay."

He drove off down the drive.

"I'll tell you what," said Lucy to her escort, "come in and have a drink."

Captain Barclay, seeing no reason against this, followed his companion up to the drawing-room and was introduced to Mrs. Marling, Lettice and Oliver. In Mrs. Marling he saw an authoritative woman in good, unostentatious county clothes, so like his county mother's county friends that he felt at home at once, the more so as she discovered within three minutes that his mother was a distant cousin of Lord Stoke and thus vaguely connected, though by no means related, to her husband's mother.

"If you had your way, mamma dear," said Oliver, "everyone would be so related that the whole of Barsetshire would be within the forbidden degrees of affinity. Talking of which, Barclay, do you happen to be married?"

Captain Barclay said Good Lord, no.

"That's all right," said Oliver. "Not but what I am all in favour of matrimony, but it is well to know. We had several officers billeted here early in the war who practically got engaged to the doctors' daughters and what not, till their wives came to visit them. It distinctly lowered one's opinion of military men."

"I'll tell you what," said Lucy, who was tired of county relationships, "there ought to be a law to make men who are married wear rings."

"Like Frenchmen," said Captain Barclay.

Lettice said Or bulls, Oliver countered with pigs, and Lettice added that bright was the ring of words when the something or other sang them. Oliver cried out against bad puns, and Captain Barclay, who was used to that kind of silliness at home, smiled and said nothing and thought his sisters would like Mrs. Watson and her brother.

"Hullo, daddy," said Lucy as her father came in. "This is Tom Barclay."

"How de do, how de do," said Mr. Marling, putting on to his older offsprings' intense pleasure what they called his olde Englishe Squire manner. "Berkeley, eh? Used to be a feller called Berkeley who rode to hounds over Nutfield way. Never much liked the man. He was riding a nice little mare one day, I remember, in nineteen three or four, and all his false teeth came out when she jumped the big fence near Starveacres. Bad business, bad business."

He shook his head mournfully and asked Oliver for a whisky and soda.

"What happened, sir?" said Captain Barclay.

"Shockin' thing," said Mr. Marling, throwing himself into his part with renewed vigour. "Mare put her off forefoot on them and galloped a field with 'em before she pulled up. Went dead lame. And old Berkeley tried to swear without a tooth in his head."

"You're all wrong, daddy," said his daughter Lucy in the loud voice that she considered suitable for idiots and parents. "It's Barclay, not Berkeley, and Tom's people live in Yorkshire."

"All right, all right, I *said* Berkeley," said her father. "And you needn't shout. I'm not deaf yet."

"Lucy meant Bark, not Berk," said Oliver.

"Like spelling it Derby and pronouncing it Darby," said Lettice, to help him.

At the sudden introduction of Derby Mr. Marling lost his bearings completely and said if young people would do nothing but mumble they couldn't expect anyone to understand and though he'd like to see Hitler in a concentration camp, it wouldn't do people who mumbled any harm to have a taste of Hitler's methods. *He'd* teach them to mumble, he added.

Captain Barclay, whose father lately dead had been much such another kind but ferocious gentleman, with a strong conviction that this war wasn't like the last, felt sorry for his host and explained in just the right voice, as far from mumbling as it was from shouting, that he spelt his name Barclay and his mother had been Dora Stoke before her marriage. Having assimilated these facts Mr. Marling forgot his rage and said he remembered his mother quite well at the Hunt Ball at Rising Castle in 'ninety-seven. Mrs. Marling, grateful to the new guest, asked him if he would dine with them soon. Lucy stood ungracefully with her legs too wide apart and watched with complacence her captive's progress in her parents' good opinions; for though she considered most of their views entirely worthless, she still secretly attached a certain value to their reception of her friends.

Then Captain Barclay, looking at his watch, said he must go at once, so Lucy escorted him downstairs.

"Please say good-bye to your sister and your brother for me," said Captain Barclay as he got into his car. "They disappeared while I was talking to your father. And thanks for the drink."

"Well, don't forget about the bombs," said Lucy, who believed in the power of repetition. "And I'll tell you what. If we get a bomb here, I'll telephone to you at once, and then you can get it before the people at Southbridge get here, and then you can let me see you explode it."

Captain Barclay refused to commit himself, saluted and drove away. In the drive he overtook Lettice who was on her way to her stables escorted by Oliver, and stopped to say good-bye.

"You were so good with father," said Lettice. "He is a little deaf, but it is mostly wilful inattention."

"He is secretly rather proud of not listening to what people say," said Oliver. "A peculiar passion, but parents are peculiar."

Captain Barclay said they were indeed, and his governor had been as peculiar as the best of them.

"But one is very proud of them for being peculiar," said Lettice. "Anyone who is a character ought to have sixpence to encourage them. And as I'm a parent I hope to get peculiar myself in time."

Then Captain Barclay drove on, much pleased by his afternoon. Lucy, who had annexed him a fortnight earlier at a sherry party, was not his ideal woman, but he found her an excellent sort of fellow. Of Mr. and Mrs. Marling we already know his opinion. Oliver Marling and that charming Mrs. Watson stirred his interest. Their similarity in good looks, their private world of small jokes, the reticence that went with their friendliness, interested and attracted him. He hoped to see a good deal of the family during his stay in those parts.

CHAPTER FOUR

WORDS CANNOT EXPRESS HOW TRYING MRS. SMITH WAS during the next three weeks. Her lawyers and the Harveys' lawyers soon got to grips over the lease which was very simple, and as far as signing and sealing went all was well. But the more the lease was signed the more her passion for her own house grew, and that in a very disconcerting way. While the inventory was being made she haunted the house, removing small pieces of portable property with sentiments rooted in her past, or, even more annoying, of use for the immediate future, thus driving the elderly clerk who was doing the work nearly mad. At first the Harveys laughed at the affair, saying that she would soon be going to Torquay and it must be very hard to be parted from one's possessions, but as the days passed, Torquay became a kind of El Dorado, the unattainable goal of nebulous desires. It gradually became known that the mother with whom she was going to stay, far from being as people had supposed a dear old lady in a lace cap, was a very vigorous woman of seventy who lived with twelve cats and a slave friend of sixty-five. The enthusiasm which had brought mother and daughter together in the early days of Mrs. Smith's bereavement had as rapidly waned. The mother had reflected that Joyce and the slave friend never got on well, which upset the pussies. The daughter had reflected upon the horrors of being shut up with her mother and her companion and the cats, and having let her house at a good rent, decided to go as a lodger to Mrs. Cox who had been a cook in good families and had a bedroom and sitting-room for gentlewomen.

"And you see, Mr. Harvey," said Mrs. Smith, meeting that gentleman, much to his surprise, in what he was now legally entitled to call his dining-room, although he had not yet slept in the house, "I shall kill two birds with one stone. I shall save the fare to Torquay and I shall be able to keep an eye on my wee home. I have got my own latch key, so I shall just slip in and out if I want anything, like a fairy, and be no trouble to anyone. I just ran over to find the coal-tongs. Mrs. Cox has mislaid hers."

As she spoke she brandished a pair of modern machine-hand-wrought antique tongs or pincers which had been hanging by the fireplace.

"I suppose there is another pair here," said Mr. Harvey, very much wishing that his sister were with him. But she had gone to London the day before, leaving him with instructions to go over to Marling Melicent and see if the groceries and coal she had ordered had come in and was coming down in the afternoon with their maid.

"You won't need a fire in this room," said Mrs. Smith. "It has the morning sun. Mr. Smith never liked to have a fire because of the art fireplace. We always used the electric heater. We just switched it on, or rather the girl did, a few minutes before breakfast and quite enjoyed the heat it gave, and the moment breakfast was finished Mr. Smith would switch it off with his own hands. I never thought then that I would be living in rooms."

Mr. Harvey at once felt so guilty that he nearly asked her to give up her rooms and live at the Red House, but, reflecting how much he would dislike it, he didn't. He looked with great disfavour at his landlady who was wandering about and fingering some books that he had brought with him. His dislike for her increased, for his books were to him like parent, child and wife. What particularly annoyed him was that she had such fine eyes in her thin ravaged face. If all her features had been like her pursed-up discontented mouth he could have hated her wholeheartedly, but her eyes demanded his grudging admiration. Then he looked at the art fireplace where art was exemplified in rough variegated bricks with a few Swedish tiles inset, and vowed vindictively to himself that he would let coal fires roar up it as long as there was any coal in England.

"I see you are quite a reader," said Mrs. Smith, picking up a volume and looking at the title. "Mr. Smith never had much time for it. He said human nature was like a book to him and an ever-open book. Strarkie. Is it a nice book?"

Mr. Harvey, in despair, almost snatched Lytton Strachey's *Elizabeth and Essex* from her hand.

"No, it's not very nice," he said. "I don't think you'd like it."

"Well, I'll just take it back with me and see," said Mrs. Smith. "You'll find I'll often be in and out to borrow a book. I gave up my library subscription when Mr. Smith died, and I quite miss not having a book."

"I'm afraid that is my sister's," said Mr. Harvey, still clinging to his child. He then thought Mrs. Smith would take offence, but she glided—for he could think of no other word to express the decency of her widow's walk—from the room, and saying that now they were neighbours they would be seeing each other quite often, continued to glide down the serpentine walk, through the garden gate and away across the green.

If, Mr. Harvey thought, this was what things were

going to be like, he and his sister would have done better to stay at Norton Park, where at least there was the park between them and the world. He wondered if he could have the lock of the front door changed, but reflecting that one could also get into the house by the kitchen door, the verandah door at the back, and by the garage, he gave it up in despair, resolving that his sister should deal with it all when she came. With almost trembling fingers he put his books in the sideboard and locked it, though convinced that Mrs. Smith would have a duplicate key of that as well as of the kitchen, verandah and garage doors, and was just going when a stalwart form walked across the grass, disdaining the serpentine walk, and disclosed itself as Lucy Marling carrying a large basket.

"Hullo," said Lucy. "Mother thought you and your sister would like some peas and things as you're moving in to-day. How's Joyce?"

"You don't mean my sister, do you?" said Mr. Harvey. "She's Frances."

"No, Joyce," said Lucy rather impatiently. "You know, the one this house belongs to."

"Oh, Mrs. Smith," said Mr. Harvey. "Is she a friend of yours? I wish you would ask her not to come and take things out of the house now we have taken it. She has got two saucepans and a reading lamp and she has just taken the dining-room tongs."

"Good old Joyce," said Lucy unsympathetically. "Oh, and mother said would you and your sister come to dinner next Tuesday at eight. David Leslie's coming and Tom Barclay. And she wants the basket back. I'll tell you what, you'd better put the veg and things in the wire basket in the scullery if Joyce hasn't taken it. Come on."

She strode into the scullery, tipped the contents of her basket into a kind of wire vegetable rack in three tiers, shelled a couple of pea pods and ate the contents, eyeing her host as she did so in a way that alarmed him very much.

"You write things, don't you?" she said severely.

Mr. Harvey said he had written a few poems.

"I mean books," said Lucy patiently.

Mr. Harvey said his novel about Pico della Mirandola had pleased some critics, and like a mettled
though nervous steed flung back his lock of hair.

"What I mean is you're literary, aren't you?" said
Lucy, breaking a young carrot in half and putting the
thin end in her mouth. "I mean you know lots of people in London like Mrs. Rivers and George Knox. I
like their books awfully."

Mr. Harvey, who despised both these successful authors and disliked the first, said rather huffily that he
found it more difficult to get a suitable subject than
Mrs. Rivers or Mr. Knox, as his public was not content
with meretricious work.

"Well, I'll tell you what," said Lucy. "If you can't
think of a good subject, you ought to do a book about
Joyce. You'd hardly have to do anything but just write
down what she says. I've often thought of writing a
book about her myself, but I don't know the right way
to begin. You could make it awfully funny and I'd tell
you lots of things about her."

Mr. Harvey smiled as agreeably as he could.

"You ought to meet Mrs. Morland," Lucy continued,
almost pushing Mr. Harvey before her along the narrow passage to the front door. "She's the nicest literary
person I know, not a bit like an author. I mean she is
just like an ordinary person, not affected. I've written
down some of the funny things Joyce said and I'll let
you have them if you like to make a book with. Don't
forget Tuesday at eight. Good Lord, it's twelve and
I've got an Allotments Committee. Good-bye."

Mr. Harvey, at last free of women, gave his hair a
misogynistic toss, lit a cigarette and went back to the
task of checking the groceries in which Mrs. Smith
had interrupted him. Women were insufferable! That
wretched Mrs. Smith filching fire-tongs and trying to
filch books. That boorish Miss Marling who thought
she could write a book and wanted him to meet Mrs.
Morland. At the thought of Mrs. Morland he felt the

scorn that only a writer who sells his work by the
hundred can feel for a writer who sells hers by the
thousand. If life at the Red House were to be like that,
he and Frances would be as dull as they were with the
Nortons, though certainly more free. Then he thought
of Tuesday and his spirits rose. A dinner party, even in
war time, was a pleasant distraction. He would probably meet that attractive Mrs. Watson again. Then he
reflected that he might with equal probability sit next
to that quite insupportable Miss Marling, at which
thought he put a tick against the washing soda so violently that he broke his pencil. So he left the rest of
the job for his sister and drove back to Norton Park to
eat his last lunch, collect his luggage and meet his sister at Barchester.

On Tuesday evening David Leslie, the Harveys and
Captain Barclay arrived punctually at eight. When we
say evening, it was in the eyes of God, as David remarked to Miss Bunting, six o'clock on a fine summer's
afternoon.

"You need not try to shock me, David," said Miss
Bunting. "If Mr. Churchill wishes us to have Double
Summer Time, He knows best."

This remarkable religious creed so enchanted David
that he kissed his old governess's hand with great
courtesy.

"God bless you, Miss Bunting," he said. "It is deeds
like this that win the Empire. How are Lettice's
charming children?"

"Diana and Clare, as I suppose you have forgotten
their names," said Miss Bunting, "are very well. You
had better ask Lettice what Diana's last exploit was.
Very flattering to you."

"You pique my curiosity," said David, who was now
tired of this game. "I shall fly like Ariel and ask her."

"No need; you are sitting next to her at dinner," said
Miss Bunting. "Tell me about your mother."

David did so, not without an occasional glance towards his cousin Lettice who was talking to Mr. Har-

vey, and not without an occasional absentmindedness
in his speech.

"I always said, David, that your manners were from
the head, not from the heart," said Miss Bunting. "You
can go now."

"Like a faithful though half-witted hound, the more
you beat me the more I adore you, even to cringing,"
said David, "especially as I need your advice. What do
you think of Geoffrey Harvey?"

But Mrs. Marling swept her party downstairs to the
dining-room and neither by word nor by look did
David get an answer to his question.

Mr. Marling, who rather disliked dinner parties unless he knew everyone present, was naturally suspi-
cious of Captain Barclay and the Harveys. On Captain
Barclay he was prepared to suspend judgment as a feller who was a pukka soldier, but his disapproval of
Mr. Harvey, though based on nothing stronger than a
dislike for fellers who didn't cut their hair properly,
was only held in check by his sense of duty as a host.
As for Miss Harvey, she was a lady, which was enough
to command his tolerance, and good-looking into the
bargain, so he was not displeased to have her next to
him at dinner.

"And what are you doing, lady?" he enquired. This
mode of address, a part of the Olde Englishe Squire
make-up, gave great pleasure to Oliver who was on
the other side of Miss Harvey and caused him to wink
at Lettice, opposite, who had also overheard it.

Miss Harvey said she was working in the Regional
Commissioner's office, in the same department as Oliver.

"Well, well, that's all new since my time," said Mr.
Marling. "What's it all about, eh?"

Miss Harvey, in her pleasantly modulated voice,
said she was sure Oliver must have explained it to his
father much better than she could.

"No one tells me anything," said Mr. Marling,
changing to what Oliver and Lettice called Mr. Gum-
midge. "I'm an old man and out of date I suppose and

the children go their own way. I don't understand this war at all."

Miss Harvey, showing great sympathy, led her host on to talk of the last war and his own Territorial exploits, so that he cheered up a good deal and told her several very interesting stories without much point. Oliver, on her other side, was grateful for her attention to his father, to whom he was fondly and exasperatedly attached, and telegraphed approval to Lettice, who was getting on very well with David. David, an expert on other people's feelings so long as they did not involve his own, had spotted almost at once in Lettice her habit of taking a second place. He saw that her mother entirely domineered her, though in all kindness; he saw that her father was very fond of her and took her for granted; he saw that her sister Lucy, though doubtless very fond of her too, would always shout her down and not so much push her out of the way as stride over her as if she were not there. Behind this triple barrier he guessed a new-found cousin who would laugh at his own kind of joke. It would be amusing to help this lovely moth—for butterfly was not a suitable name for Lettice—out of the family cocoon. Also it would be a pleasantly safe game. In David's experience charming women, and even some who were not so charming, were apt to take him a little too seriously, but this Lettice would not do. They were cousins, which was not romantic, Roger had only been dead a year, and more than this, David, who had had a good deal of experience, was quite sure that Lettice could set to a partner very prettily if encouraged, without the faintest dint in her affections. Had he thought such a misfortune possible he would not have contemplated a cousinly flirtation. Ever since the summer some six or seven years ago when two ladies, one being his present sister-in-law Mrs. John Leslie, had refused him in one morning, when he had not the faintest intention of proposing, he had had occasional fits of wariness. But here he instinctively felt he was safe. So he applied himself to amusing Lettice and to his great pleasure found that not only did he make her laugh, but she was making him laugh. And what was more, she showed no particular disposition to talk about her children.

"I cannot tell you," he said, "how restful it is to be at a party where no one mentions the nursery. And when I say that, I mean how very nice it is that you don't, for no one else is in a position to do so. At least if the Harveys or Barclay have nurseries they conceal it. My darling sister Agnes has not one idea in her head outside her offspring, and by the time her youngest daughter—if Edith is to be the youngest, which you never knew with Agnes, has left the nursery, Emmy will be married and Agnes will begin all over again with grandchildren. A black outlook for an uncle."

"Why—" Lettice began.

"Stop," said David. "I know exactly what you are going to say. The reason I haven't got a nursery of my own is, surprising as it may seem, that I have not got a wife. Sometimes my kind friends try to find one for me and I feel sentimental and sad. But then I reflect that I might become a wife-beater and remain contented with my humble lot as a roving blade. I expect you adore those nice little girls of yours, even though you restrain yourself from being a bore about them."

"Diana and Clare you mean," said Lettice, though whether as a statement or as a small reproof for his forgetfulness David was not sure. "I think they are very nice little girls, but if I hadn't got nurse I mightn't like them so much. Nurses really make mother-love possible. So do the Bunnies, later on. I think Roger was more devoted to the children than I am, but he saw so little of them that it was fairly easy."

"You take the words out of one's mouth," said David admiringly. "The words that one couldn't quite say oneself but strongly feels within one. I like mother-love myself. My divine mamma is a living example of how adorable and maddening it can be. Never for one moment is one safe from her putting her head into the room to see what one is doing and try to make one do it differently. Well, here's to all the Nannies and Bunnies that keep it alive."

He raised his glass, caught Miss Bunting's eye across the table and drank to her. That lady, who was talking to Mr. Harvey, smiled grimly. Mr. Harvey looked faintly surprised.

"Once you have known them in the schoolroom they never change," said Miss Bunting. "Now tell me more about yourself."

From some women this would come as a flattering invitation, implying a deep and almost more than sisterly interest; and even if one knew that it was only surface charm, the charm was there none the less. From Miss Bunting the remark paid no tribute to the fascination of Mr. Harvey's life and doings at all. Rather did he feel like a heretic who has had an unexpected respite from the Grand Inquisitor and is now about to be subjected again to the question, for Miss Bunting, with a detached interest in men as children of a larger growth, had so put him through his paces, ferreted out his past and enquired into his present, that he very much wished she wouldn't, the more so as she obviously found his whole career not up to her standard. Under her unemotional catechism he had confessed to the wrong school, the wrong university, including the wrong college in it, the wrong branch of the Civil Service. He was not married (and if he had been he felt by now morally certain that Miss Bunting would have coolly disapproved his choice of a wife), he cultivated the society of writers and painters who in her estimation did not exist at all, he wrote poems that Miss Bunting had not read and showed no sign of wishing to read. As for his novel about Pico della Mirandola, Miss Bunting, in a perfectly ladylike way displayed such a knowledge of names and dates as left him feeling very small; for it must be confessed that though he had worked up his subject with considerable industry he had allowed himself to drag in characters who, historically speaking, were hardly contemporaries till, as a very young reviewer who had just

discovered the Poetry of the Anti-Jacobin and wished
to display his knowledge searingly remarked, the
novel was not unlike the procession at the end of *The
Double Arrangement*. The allusion passed over the
heads of most of his readers who were distressingly
young in mind if not in years and read for the most
part sixpenny books of a decidedly pink tendency, but
it had rankled in Mr. Harvey, who was silly enough to
subscribe to a press-cutting bureau and read all his
notices.

"You should read some of Mrs. Barton's historical
novels about 15th and 16th century Italy," said Miss
Bunting. "I have found them very useful when telling
some of my older pupils facts about the Renaissance
period."

Mr. Harvey would have liked to say that he thought
Mrs. Barton's books very dull and pedantic, also that
neither he nor his public were pupils, older or
younger, of Miss Bunting's; but though he would have
been quite rude to anyone of his own set who had so
presumed, something told him that rudeness to Miss
Bunting would not be wise, and as that lady went on
eating as if he were not there he was not sorry to be
addressed by Mrs. Marling, who, after having a quiet
conversation with Captain Barclay about families, did
her duty by asking Mr. Harvey how he was getting on
at the Red House.

"Very well," said Mr. Harvey. "Our maid likes it,
which my sister appears to think the principal thing at
present, and the beds are extremely comfortable. We
can't thank you enough for having found it for us. In
fact if Mrs. Smith would go to Torquay all would be
perfect."

"Is she giving trouble?" Mrs. Marling asked with interest.

"I wouldn't like to seem ungrateful," said Mr. Harvey, "but she has very original ideas about the relations of landlord and tenant. As fas as I can make out
she looks on us as a kind of dépôt or universal store."

"Troublesome woman Joyce is," said Mrs. Marling

with what Mr. Harvey considered very insufficient sympathy.

"It's not so much the saucepans and the reading lamp," said Mr. Harvey, "but the day we moved in she took the fire-tongs from the dining-room, last week she borrowed the electric kettle, and this afternoon, so our maid tells us, she took four pillow cases. It is a little awkward, because we are on duty at the Regional Commissioner's office and can't very well defend ourselves."

"Annoying woman," said Mrs. Marling, again with provoking complacency. "One doesn't wonder that her husband drank, though to do him justice he drank pretty heavily before he married her. You had better let Lucy know. Are you very busy?"

Mr. Harvey, a little placated by the question, said he was working on a book of poems in his leisure time, but the Muse, he said, tossing his hair back vaguely in that tutelary genius's direction, was not propitious amid the clash of war.

"Clash?" said Mrs. Marling. "I haven't heard of anything in these parts for some months. The last bomb in this district was in February. I meant busy at the office."

Mr. Harvey, well trained in his Government Department, made a non-committal answer that would have satisfied his chiefs, but did not satisfy Mrs. Marling. To her the Regional Commissioner's office was but a branch of the county activities among which her whole life had been passed. John Leslie, the head of it, was a cousin; various other cousins and old county friends were scattered up and down it and undoubtedly a good many so-called secrets were told to Mrs. Marling as a matter of course. And as John Leslie said, if all the girls who sat at the telephones or the tele-printers knew what was happening, he saw no reason why Amabel Marling, who could probably have run the office just as well as he could and was as safe as they made them, shouldn't know too. But he knew, and Mrs. Marling knew, that if a secret was important

enough to be kept from the clerks and typists she was
not the woman to enquire into it on her own account.
All of which made Mrs. Marling a little impatient of
Mr. Harvey and she said she hoped the affair of the
yellow at Skeynes had blown over. This tactless allusion to the mistake of a woman official in Mr. Harvey's
department who had mixed up the purple and yellow
raider signals naturally annoyed him and made him
say that it were, perhaps, better not to discuss these
things in public.

"Public?" said Mrs. Marling, looking round the
table. "You know and your sister knows and Oliver
knows, and if it comes to that I know. I daresay Lettice and Lucy know too; but it isn't worth talking
about. Are you going to keep hens?"

Mr. Harvey, annoyed by her undepartmental attitude, said that he found hens peculiarly revolting.
There was, he said, something about their glassy eyes
and their passion for suicide in front of his car that
made him feel he would rather go without eggs for
ever than keep them.

"That is, of course, the alternative," said Mrs. Marling. "I'll speak to your sister about it after dinner. I
think Lucy knows a farmer with some pullets for sale
and they'll be up to thirty shillings before we know
where we are, so you'd better get them now. And you
might have a few ducks too. There is a little pond in
your garden."

"Oh, I don't think Mrs. Smith would care for ducks
in her water-garden," said Mr. Harvey, seeing in his
mind's eye a vision of ducks among the dwarfs and
toadstools.

"Don't worry. I'll get Lucy to speak to her," said
Mrs. Marling. "I'm sure she can get you some layers
and you can always eat them later on if they are not
satisfactory."

She then gave him a great deal of valuable advice
about pullets, layers, chicken-food, and nesting boxes,
offered to send down some grain from the farm and
advocated the occasional introduction of a cock to

liven the hens up; or as an alternative livener-up
Epsom salts in their drinking water. Mr. Harvey hated
his hostess more and more. He had not written a book
of poems and a novel about Pico della Mirandola, besides being a recognised intellectual in his own set,
merely to be ordered to keep hens. And what was
worse, Mrs. Marling, rising from the table, said she
would speak to his sister at once about keeping fowls
and Mr. Harvey saw no way of getting at his sister and
warning her without making himself conspicuous.

By this time David and Lucy were making such a
noise that everyone was glad to get up except Mr.
Marling whose slight though wilful deafness enabled
him to bear his younger daughter's voice better than
most people.

"Lucy!" said Mrs. Marling, across the clamour.

"Oh, mother—" Lucy began, but Miss Bunting in
her turn said "Lucy," without raising her voice.

"Oh, all right," said Lucy. "I'll tell you what, mother, let's sit in the Stone Parlour. It's so hot indoors."

Mrs. Marling was quite willing. Mr. Marling said,
What was all that about the Stone Parlour. As no one
took much notice, he stopped being deaf and said if
people liked to catch their death of damp that was all
right; but everyone knew that it had not rained for
three weeks, so no sympathy was offered and the
company drifted out of the side door and along the
gravel walk which lay along the west front of the
house. At the end of the walk, at the south-west corner
of the house, Mr. Marling's great-grandfather had
built out a little two-storied pavilion. The lower story
was open to the west and north with stone pillars that
supported an upper room much coveted by Marling
schoolboy sons. From its window many a home-made
rope ladder had been let down before dawn for romantic filibustering expeditions. True, the adventurers
could just as well have gone down by the back stairs,
but such is youth.

Owing to its aspect the Stone Parlour was not much
use in an English spring, but as the summer waxed

and the sun at setting passed round northwards, the
last light shone upon it and streaked the grass below
the lime avenue with gold. Here coffee was brought,
and chairs were placed in the parlour or just outside it
on the grass.

When Mrs. Marling had suggested an adjournment,
Mr. Harvey had a flash of hope that he might snatch a
word with his sister and warn her against hens, but
Lucy, with the frank selfishness of those who are determined to do kind deeds for their fellow creatures,
pounced on him as he came out of the back door and
clung to his side, the better to develop to him her plan
for writing a book about Mrs. Smith, the anecdotes to
be supplied by herself, the hack work of putting them
on to paper by him. She had read lots of books, she
said, that weren't half as funny as Joyce was, and she
was sure everyone would simply roar with laughter.

"I'll tell you what," she added, "you ought to meet
Adrian Coates who publishes Mrs. Morland's books.
He's awfully nice and publishes lots of books. I'm sure
he'd publish a book about Joyce. Does he publish your
books or are they too highbrow?"

Mr. Harvey said rather huffily that his publishers
were Johns and Fairfield.

"Oh, I know," said Lucy. "They're frightfully highbrow. They published old Lord Pomfret's book."

Mr. Harvey nearly groaned aloud. If ever a peer
had written a bad autobiography, Lord Pomfret's *A
Landowner in Five Reigns* was the worst. It had sold,
Mr. Harvey and his friends had been obliged grudgingly to concede, but by an ill-deserved piece of luck.
That it was in any way to be compared with Lionel
Harvest's *Cast Me Abroad* (a scathing exposure of
Broadcasting House written after he had inherited his
great-uncle General Harvest's fortune and retired from
public life) was not to be thought of, and if Lord
Pomfret's book had sold ten thousand copies and Harvest's seven hundred and fifty in spite of his friends
rallying in the weeklies, it simply proved that the public were fools. In Russia, as Lionel Harvest too often

told his friends, a book like his would have been published by the State and sold at least a quarter of a million copies.

Instead of groaning he said to Lucy that he wanted just one word with his sister. Two steps brought him to her side, but unfortunately an equal number of steps had brought David Leslie to her other side.

"Frances," said Mr. Harvey urgently.

"No, Geoffrey," said David, who had been sufficiently bored by Mr. Harvey at one or two intellectual sherry parties to enjoy cutting him out even with his sister, who was certainly a very handsome girl, if girl you could call it, "you did not bring your sister out to dinner to persecute her with your unwelcome attentions. Miss Harvey, I shall not sleep sound o' nights—pardon the expression, not mine but the Bard's—unless you tell me what colour the art sheets are that your landlady mentioned the day I helped you to look at the house."

"Frances," said Mr. Harvey, "I just wanted to tell you—"

"Wait a moment, Geoffrey," said his sister, who loved him but could not forget that she was the elder by eighteen months. "The sheets are in two sets; the best ones are peach, or apricot, I'm not sure which, the second best are apricot, or possibly peach. There are also some rather inferior ones for guests which must have been boiled by the laundry as they simply look dirty by any kind of light."

"Perfect!" said David.

"And there are bath towels with bath mats to match in mermaid green," said Miss Harvey, "and pale purple face towels."

"And are there guest towels?" said David passionately.

"I will not deceive you, there *are* guest towels," said Miss Harvey proudly. "You know them because they are too small to use and have GUEST embroidered on them. From the look of them I should say Mr. Smith was in the habit of wiping his razor on them."

David laughed so much that Mr. Harvey was able to say once more to his sister, "Frances, Mrs. Marling wants to talk to you about hens—" but before he could say any more Mrs. Marling came up behind him.

"Yes," said Mrs. Marling, "I was just telling your brother that you must keep hens. Of course the way the government has behaved about the whole egg question is perfectly scandalous, but that's neither here nor there. Our duty is to keep backyard fowls and increase the country's egg production. Lucy knows of some good pullets you could get at a reasonable price and there is an old shed in the doctor's garden next door that I know he would let you have for ten shillings. I'll send Ed our chauffeur-handyman down, he can alter it for you."

"Ed is half-witted," said Oliver, who having enjoyed Miss Harvey's society at dinner had gravitated back to her, "because his mother had an affair with one of Lord Pomfret's keepers before he was born. I mean before Ed was born, not the keeper."

Miss Harvey expressed astonishment with her fine eyes.

"Don't put me out of my stride, Oliver," said his mother. "I want Miss Harvey to keep hens, and I thought Doctor March might let her have that rickety little shed where he used to keep that dreadful goat. By the way, Oliver, I wonder if we ought to keep a goat."

"But why, mamma dear," said Oliver, "when we have three cows? Or only as a mascot?"

"Well, you never know," said Mrs. Marling. "Much as I dislike goats' milk, we might be very glad of it if things get bad."

"No, mamma dear, we mightn't" said Oliver. "And even if the invasion comes here and drives our cows away I would rather pine and die than drink that filthy stuff. Besides, you don't see the Germans overlooking a goat in the scrimmage. They'd have it, or I suppose I ought to say her if it's a question of milk, at Corps Headquarters before you could say knife."

"I expect they'd cut her head off long before they got her as far as Headquarters," said Miss Harvey sympathetically. "I once lived with a goat for a few months and I'd have cut her head off myself if I'd had a sword. Devils!"

Oliver laughed and settled himself more comfortably in his deck chair, if the word comfortable can be applied to those draped skeletons. If Frances Harvey could appreciate the devilishness of goats she was a woman after his own heart. He had liked her in the office where their work threw them together a good deal, but to have her in his own home was an experiment. He had felt some faint qualms, for Geoffrey, though they got on well enough, was not quite his style and Geoffrey's sister might not fit into the atmosphere of Marling. Now, to see her listening to his mother, asking intelligent questions about wire netting and grain ration, handsome and self-possessed, made his heart feel an unaccustomed glow. Not falling in love, for he knew those symptoms quite well. Simply great pleasure in the society of a clever, practical, good-looking woman.

Mr. Harvey, despairing about hens, for he knew that if his sister approved the idea, hens they would certainly have, picked his way among deck chairs, wicker chairs, wood and canvas upright chairs, cane chairs, to where Lettice was standing with her father and Captain Barclay.

"Come and help us," said Lettice. "We can't remember who Lord Stoke's mother was."

"Yes, who was she?" said Mr. Marling to Mr. Harvey. "You ought to know, Carver."

"It is Mr. Harvey, father, not Mr. Carver," said Lettice gently, smiling at Mr. Harvey to show that she at least was under no delusion.

"I'm afraid I don't know, sir," said Mr. Harvey, conscious as he spoke of something like a gimlet in his back.

"Hum! Carver'd have known," said Mr. Marling, letting himself down into a cane armchair with a flat green cushion. "*His* mother was a sister of Victoria Norton's."

Mr. Harvey hated the unknown Carver as much as he had hated his hostess and wished he had blue, or least county blood, and all the while the sensation of something boring into his back made him vaguely uncomfortable.

"Let's see," said Captain Barclay. "Old Lord Stoke's second wife was from Yorkshire, wasn't she? Lucasta Bond was her only child."

Mr. Harvey hated Captain Barclay who knew who people's second wives and second wives' only children were even more than he hated the unknown Carver or his hostess, but still saw no place in the conversation for himself. Lettice smiled again to encourage him.

"Old Lord Stoke's first wife was a Miss Hooper, an heiress from Somerset," said Miss Bunting appearing from behind Mr. Harvey, who then realised to his horror that it was her eye of scorn that had been looking right through his back.

"*That's* it," said Captain Barclay, much relieved. "She was a daughter of Squire Hooper of Rumpton who drove the last coach right across the churchyard before it was taken off the road. Won't you sit down, Miss Bunting?"

He brought forward a comfortable cushioned chair.

"No, thank you," said Miss Bunting, quite kindly. "The upright one."

Captain Barclay hastened to place it near Mr. Marling.

"There, if you please," said Miss Bunting, indicating a position just outside the little circle.

Captain Barclay put the chair where she wanted it and Miss Bunting sat down. Lettice, Captain Barclay and Mr. Harvey sat down too.

While Mr. Marling and Captain Barclay finally threshed out the ramifications of Lord Stoke's family, Mr. Harvey, who felt more and more nervous of Miss Bunting, asked Lettice in a low voice if Miss Bunting was offended.

"Oh dear, no," said Lettice. "She always sits on a very stiff chair a little away from us. I am not quite sure if it is to show that she knows her place or to keep us in our places. The result is much the same and rather petrifying."

"What a nuisance she must be," said Mr. Harvey in a low but sympathetic voice.

"Oh no," said Lettice, surprised, "we adore her."

She then asked very kindly about the Red House, and Mr. Harvey felt that he had been elusively snubbed. But he put the feeling away to annoy himself with at night and joined in the talk which had now left Lord Stoke and become general. They were all getting on very nicely when Lucy, who had taken David to look at two young bullocks, came back and pouncing on Captain Barclay, whom she regarded as her personal property, said she had to go over to the Cottage Hospital for half an hour and he had better come too.

"Come, come, Lucy," said David. "My car is just as good as Barclay's and he doesn't want to go with you, while I do. In all the wide borders my car is the best. Reconsider it."

"Oh rot," said Lucy good humouredly. "Come on, Tom."

"Ruin seize thee, ruthless Lucy," said David, who did not really care in the least whether he went with Lucy or not. "If you be not driven by me, What care I by whom driven you be. I shall go and cut someone out."

Captain Barclay excused himself and got up. David stood looking a very handsome figure against the sunset while he swiftly meditated. To cut out Harvey with Lettice would be fun. Equally it would be fun to cut out Oliver with Miss Harvey. After wavering for a second he decided on Mr. Harvey as the nearer prey and took Captain Barclay's chair, from which he had an excellent view of his cousin Lettice. With the devilish motive of annoying Mr. Harvey he asked Mr. Marling how the entries for the Skeynes Agricultural were going that year and if Lady Norton was sending anything.

Mr. Marling, overjoyed at an opportunity for exhibiting pessimism, said there was foot and mouth disease at Chaldicotes and he didn't suppose there would be a show at all. That, he added, was the sort of thing the confounded Ministry of Arigculture did. Just the sort of thing they would do when he had two of the best heifers he had ever bred. As for the Norton Park herd, he knew nothing about them.

"Geoffrey will know," said David, looking at Mr. Harvey who was quietly though firmly telling Lettice about his new book of poems. "He has been staying at the Nortons, hasn't he? Geoffrey, excuse my interrupting, but Cousin William wants to know what the Nortons are sending to Skeynes."

Mr. Harvey, pulled away from the pleasant occupation of talking about himself, stared uncomprehendingly at Mr. Marling.

"Is it the shorthorn or the polled Angus, Carver?" said Mr. Marling.

"Do you mean a cow?" said Mr. Harvey.

"Of course father does," said Lettice, coming to his rescue. "Father you *must* remember that it is Mr. Harvey, not Carver. Mr. Harvey works in John Leslie's office with Oliver and writes poetry."

"Well, Carver'd have known," said Mr. Marling, who appeared to bear a permanent grudge against Mr. Harvey for not being someone else. "Poetry, eh? Not what it was in my young days. My father used to have them all to dinner. Tennyson and Browning and that lot. You wouldn't have heard of them."

Mr. Harvey, whose poetic circle had, for reasons best known to no one, elected to patronise Tennyson, tried to protest, but Mr. Marling, vaguely feeling that he had somehow wronged that fellow Carver and anxious as a host to make amends to his guest, however little he liked him, came heavily over him like a tank.

"All this modern stuff is what you young men like," he announced grudgingly, but determined to make a handsome job of it. "Kipling and A. P. Herbert and that lot. I don't know much about it, the old stuff was good enough for me, but there's some pretty poetry in *Punch* sometimes. Ever write for *Punch?*"

Mr. Harvey, who looked upon T. S. Eliot as a back number, could not at once find words to explain how little he would demean himself by writing for *Punch*, which had rejected several of his poems, and while he struggled for self-expression his host continued,

"Stephen Phillips. You'd never have heard of him, but he wrote a lot of good stuff, plays and that. I remember as well as if it were yesterday seein' old—now what the devil was his name, you know who I mean, the actor everyone was talkin' about, actin' in that play of Phillips's about, dash it all I don't remember things as I used to, it's all this war. Lettice, what was the play when two young people fall in love while they are readin' somethin'?"

Lettice, sorry for Mr. Harvey, but amused at her father's rapid progress in his Olde Squire character, wished that Oliver were there, but seeing David's expression she realised that he understood, and it was with a voice perilously near a giggle that she suggested Paolo and Francesca.

Mr. Marling then lost interest and went into his study to answer letters and fill up forms. Lettice applied herself to soothing Mr. Harvey, who was quite ready to talk about his poems again. David, satisfied with his effort, got up and found himself face to face with Miss Bunting whose presence, just out of his range of vision, he had quite forgotten.

"Up to mischief as usual, David," said his old governess.

David said he hated being misjudged.

"I am not misjudging you," said Miss Bunting. "But I don't mind your getting into mischief in that quarter. It is not what WE want here."

David was not quite sure whether her royal pronoun referred to herself or to the whole Marling family, so he said nothing.

"I am going upstairs to my room now," said Miss Bunting. "I always boil a kettle on the gas ring which

Mrs. Marling kindly had installed for me and make
myself some tisane. I acquired the habit when I went
to the Riviera as companion to the Dowager Marchioness of Hartletop one year. It is very soothing. If
ever you care for a cup I shall be glad to see you. I
never lose interest in my old pupils. Good night."

"Let me see you home," said David and with great
gravity accompanied Miss Bunting as far as the side
door where he bade her good night and returned,
much refreshed, to help in the hen discussion. Miss
Harvey had already mastered most of the theory of
hen-keeping as laid down by Mrs. Marling and was
making notes of various official pamphlets and rules
connected with those inhuman birds. Oliver, who was
often tired in the evening, was amused by her eager-
ness and sat comfortably quiet, throwing in an unhelp-
ful word from time to time. The strange late light of
the long summer evening, curiously artificial as if all
nature knew that its course was being run in a channel
not its own, lay very clear on the lime avenue and the
meadows beyond the Rising to where the distant line
of the downs was darkening against the fading glory
in the north-west.

"On such a night as this," David remarked, pulling a
chair up near Miss Harvey, "it seems almost sacrile-
gious to talk of fowls. Miss Harvey, have you no soul?
If you have, Cousin Amabel will grind its bones to
make chicken food. Why not take a turn in the lime
avenue with me instead?"

With unflattering want of confusion Miss Harvey
said she would be delighted.

"Why don't you go, too, Oliver?" said his mother,
but Oliver said he felt too lazy. Mrs. Marling looked
anxiously at him.

"Eyes?" she said.

Oliver nodded. They sat in silence while the dusk
crept over the lime trees and the meadows. Mrs. Marling longed to comfort her son, but respected his wish
that his frequent fatigue should be ignored. Oliver valued deeply in his mother her power of standing aside

and laying no burden of affection on him. They understood each other pretty well and cared for each other without words, without obligation. Presently Oliver got up, kissed his mother and went away. Mrs. Marling followed him with her eyes to the corner of the house, with her thoughts to his room. She was not one of those mothers who have to come into their grown-up sons' rooms and wake them up to see if they are comfortably asleep, nor did she ever ask questions. In return Oliver told her just as much as he thought fit, which is so much kinder to one's mother than telling her everything. Her one wish for him was that he should marry happily. So far he had felt no enduring flame. Now Frances Harvey had brought her good looks and her clever mind into their intimate circle and Mrs. Marling wondered if his daily work with her was to have the usual effect of propinquity. She was ready to lose him to whatever woman he chose to love, but whether Miss Harvey would be that woman she could not guess.

The voices of Lettice and Mr. Harvey sounded in quiet talk from where they were sitting. The voices of David and Miss Harvey who were returning from the lime avenue came across the lawn in laughter. All else was still. The trees grew black against a sky now clear emerald. The air chilled. Mrs. Marling was just going in when a door in the Stone Parlour wall was opened and a loud noise burst out, which was Lucy, followed with less noise by Captain Barclay. Lucy at once made enquiries for everyone, and hearing that David was walking with Miss Harvey, called aloud "Six-pack bézique, David!" at the top of her powerful voice.

David, who to tell the truth had exhausted the possibilities of Miss Harvey for the moment, shouted back to her, and the whole company went into the house. The Harveys with polite cries against the lateness of their visit said good-bye. Captain Barclay lingered for a few moments. Much as he enjoyed Lucy's company he had hoped for a talk with her sister, but this had not been. Lettice said good-bye with one of her encouraging smiles and he went back to camp thinking that the evening had on the whole been well spent.

"Lucy, you really must go to bed," said Mrs. Marling. "Good-bye, David. Come again soon."

"I say," said Lucy, "we never played bézique."

"I can't if you go gallivanting with the military," said David. "I'll come another day. What a nice fellow Barclay is."

"I'll tell you what—" Lucy began.

"No, you won't," said David. "Good-night and go to bed."

He kissed his cousin Lucy in an unemotional way and went off, thinking with some pleasure of his persecution of Geoffrey Harvey.

Mr. Harvey, who was a little afraid of his sister, drove her home and put the car away. When he came into the house he found her in the drawing-room.

"We aren't going to have hens, are we?" he said anxiously.

"Of course we are," said his sister.

"Well then, is there anything to drink?" said Mr. Harvey.

"Only gin and lime," said his sister. "I told Hilda to leave it out. It's all we've got left. There's the tray."

On the tray was a piece of paper addressed to "Miss Harvy" in an unknown and laborious writing.

"Who wants to write you letters?" said Mr. Harvey.

"'Mrs. Smith as borrowed the lime because it ran out'," his sister read aloud.

"Oh God!" said Mr. Harvey. "Cows, and poetry, and now that woman has taken the lime juice. I wish we had stayed at Norton Park."

"No, you don't," said Miss Harvey. "Lettice Watson wasn't at Norton Park."

CHAPTER FIVE

IF MR. HARVEY HOPED THAT HIS SISTER AND MRS. MAR-
ling would forget about hens, he was the more deceived. Miss Harvey rang up the Hall. Mrs. Marling
rang up Dr. March. Miss Harvey rang up her brother
who was on duty at the Regional Commissioner's Office
that day, and asked him if he could get Wednesday off
as it was also her day off. Mr. Harvey said he supposed
he could, rang off abruptly, and was so rude to his
senior typist that she was able to finish the sleeve of a
jumper while he got over it.

Lucy, getting wind of all this, arranged with Octavia Crawley who was doing a month at the Cottage
Hospital to take her duty on Wednesday, promising
her what in hospital language was called a Caesar, a
form of operation to which Octavia was at the moment
much attached. She then told everyone what till her
father said, For God's sake then *take* Ed and don't let's
hear any more about it. Ed, delighted to be of use,
came down to the Red House with a wheelbarrow
containing a piece of corrugated iron about four foot

99

by six, and some dilapidated wire netting, both taken
by him off the village scrap-metal heap where they
were slowly rusting to death because it seemed to be
no one's business to collect them.

The delightful hot weather had broken, but
Wednesday was not an unpleasant day, with quite
warm intervals. Mr. Harvey, though very much annoyed with his sister for being hen-minded, was not
above putting on a pair of green corduroy trousers and
a paler green Aertex shirt with short sleeves, in which
he felt rather dashing. His sister, despising fancy
dress, was wearing a tailored boiler suit, and we must
grudgingly admit that she was one of the few women
who could do it. The proceedings as arranged by
Lucy, who kindly allowed Miss Harvey to act as vice-
president, were to begin with the removal of Dr.
March's old shed by Ed and the estate carpenter, who
could then re-erect it in a slightly different form in the
back garden of the Red House. After this a kind of
hen-house bee was to take place, everyone helping to
make perches, put up wire netting and in general arrange for the comfort of the new tenants. The Harveys
had offered a fork lunch, David Leslie who had heard
about it was coming with some drinks, and later in the
afternoon Lucy, with the aid of Captain Barclay who
tended to spend most of his free time at Marling,
would fetch the hens from the farm where they had
been residing and instal them.

About eleven o'clock Ed, balancing his corrugated
iron and wire netting in the wheelbarrow like Blon-
din, arrived at the Red House and went to the back
door, where Hilda, once the Harveys' undernurse and
now their maid, was preparing not to approve of the
hen scheme. Not that she disliked fowls. On the contrary she had delighted her employers' childhood by
tales of her sister in the country who had married a
farmer, and drew glowing pictures of her own future
bringing up hundreds and thousands of pullets by
hand. But she still had towards her ex-children the

very proper nursery-maid attitude of seeing what they were doing and telling them not to, and ever since the great hen question had been mooted she had shown a tendency to exaggerate the less favourable aspects of hen-keeping. According to her Sibylline utterances while dusting the drawing-room, making the beds, or standing in the kitchen with a blank face while Miss Harvey suggested dishes for lunch or dinner, all day-old chickens were cockerels, if one bought pullets they did not lay for seven years, if one bought laying hens they ceased to lay or laid double-yolked eggs and died. All hens died if possible just before one could kill them for eating and must be burnt. Having hens was more trouble than a whole nursery of children. There was no proper food to get in war time. Anyone who tried to keep hens must have over twelve or under fifty or the Government would do something about it. Hens meant grain and meal. Everyone knew the Government had sent all the grain to Canada to be safe, and as for the meal it was what anyone would call less than no good at all; besides, where there was meal there were rats and where rats were she could not possibly stay.

Ed knocked at the back door which was opened by a tall, middle-aged woman with short, unwaved, greying hair, a tight-lipped mouth which when opened showed quantities of very unconvincing false teeth, and an unwelcoming expression. She wore a gaily coloured cotton frock of no particular cut and a flowered overall that crossed behind. Most people who came to the back door were stricken with terror by her appearance, but Ed had no such feelings, for by a piece of great good luck she was extremely like his mother to whom, for no reason except that she took all his wages and paid him a very small weekly allowance, he was quite devoted. So remembering his manners he took off his cap and smiled.

Hilda, seeing a strange man before her, was convinced that he was a gypsy, a tramp, a German, or a burglar's confederate come to spy out the best way of getting into the house at night, and was preparing to turn him off by force if necessary and certainly by the rough side of her tongue, when he smiled his slow, Barsetshire and, we must add, half-witted smile.

Hilda was no sentimentalist, for a lifetime in the nursery does not encourage that attitude, but she had one soft spot in her heart for her elder nephew Albert who had been killed near Ypres. True Albert had been a sergeant-major with a hideous moustache and a medal-covered chest which he stuck out like anything, while Ed was clean-shaven and had a slow, shambling walk, but there was something in the stranger before her that brought Albert very vividly to her mind.

"Well, young man," she said, "what's the matter?"

Ed smiled again and said Miss Lucy had told him to come about the shed.

"What shed?" said Hilda, just as sharply as his own mother might have said it.

Ed rolled his cap up in his hands.

"I dunno," he said, looking admiringly at Hilda. "Mr. Govern, he'll know."

"And who's Mr. Govern?" said Hilda, with just his mother's impatience, but without the addition of You Great Fool.

"He's to be here at eleven," said Ed.

"Well, a cup of tea won't do you any harm," said Hilda and opened the back door wide.

She pushed Ed into the kitchen, shoved him on to a chair, banged a large cup of tea and a plate of bread and some vague cheese substitute called Spread down in front of him, banged another cup down for herself and put her elbows on the table.

To Ed's gentle and permanently mystified soul this was no stranger than anything else in his life, so he chumped his bread and Spread and drank his tea, into which Hilda had put a generous spoonful of sugar.

"And what's your name?" said Hilda.

Her guest said it was Ed, and Mr. Govern had said to be at the Red House at eleven with the wheelbarrow.

"About those hens, I'll be bound," said Hilda. "Mucky creatures they are, near as mucky as ducks. And I know who'll have to feed them."

"You will, miss," said Ed. "Mother feeds our hens. She won't let me."

Another knock at the door interrupted their conversation. Hilda opened it. A weather-beaten man with a long nose was standing outside. He wore a carpenter's apron under his jacket and carried his carpenter's bag.

"It never rains but it pours," said Hilda grimly.

"Mr. Govern said he would be here at eleven," said Ed, who by tilting his chair onto its hind legs could see what was happening at the back door.

"Mr. Marling's estate carpenter, madam," said Mr. Govern. "Is Pollet in there?"

"If that's Pollett he's there all right," said Hilda, "having a cup of tea."

"He's a bit wanting, you know," said Mr. Govern, "and if you'll excuse me I'll come in and have a look."

"Have a cup of tea you mean," said Hilda, not averse to additional male society.

She stood aside while Mr. Govern wiped his feet violently, and ushered him into the kitchen. Under the beneficent atmosphere of strong tea and a quite unrationed amount of sugar Mr. Govern explained that Miss Lucy wanted him to take down that there shed of Dr. March's and turn it into a hen house. It was, he said, no kind of a job, not what he called a job, with the gate into the ten acre crying out to be rehung and Mrs. Marling wanting the kitchen door mended and Miss Lettice's bathroom door needing a bit planing away where it stuck on the linoleum, but Miss Lucy was a one-er for having things done, so done it must be.

"Well, if it's got to be done, you and Mr. Pollett had better do it," said Hilda. "And what may *your* name be?"

"Govern, miss," said the carpenter. "Christened James, but my old woman she always called me Govern. She died two years ago come Christmas and I

made her coffin. A good job it was too. I'd had that bit
of elm lying by for five year."

"Well my name's Plane and the sooner you know it
the better," said Hilda, suddenly becoming the under-
nurse. "Now get along to your work."

"Plane by name, miss, but not by appearance," said
the gallant Mr. Govern. "Quite the name for a carpenter's mate as one might say. Come on, Ed, and thank
Miss Plane for the tea."

Ed rolled his cap, smiled his ravishing smile and
murmured, "That's oke, miss."

"You'd better call me auntie," said Hilda to Ed.
"And if you want a cup of tea any time, let me know,
and Mr. Govern too. There's plenty here. Have you
got your dinners with you?"

Ed shyly produced from a pocket a small packet
wrapped in a dirty rag and laid it on the table.

"Mother said that's all I could have," he said.

"It'll do nicely for the chickens when they come,"
said Hilda, contemptuously poking the contents with
one finger. "You come up here at dinner time, Ed, and
I'll find something for you."

"I wish I wasn't going home for my own dinner,
miss," said Mr. Govern, "but I dessay my niece won't
remember to put it on the fire. She's quite flighty since
she got the job as postman. If my old woman had seen
her in leggings she'd have died of laughing. It seems a
pity she wasn't spared."

At this broad hint Hilda invited Mr. Govern to share
pot luck, and the church clock having by now struck
half past eleven her guests went off to Dr. March's
garden and began to take down the shed.

At half past twelve Mrs. Marling arrived at the Red
House and found the Harveys looking disconsolately
at the mess Govern and Ed were making. The
goatshed had been removed in sections and was being
re-erected near the end of the garden. Sawdust lay
thick on the ground and wire netting and corrugated
iron blocked the path.

"Look here, Govern," said Mrs. Marling, hardly

waiting to greet the Harveys, " that won't do. There's too much shade down here. The chickens won't get any sun."

Govern said he supposed the lady and gentleman wanted vegetables and unless he put the hen house right on the vegetables this was the only place.

"By the way," said Miss Harvey, "are we to let the hens loose in the garden? I suppose they'll eat all the vegetables if we do. Couldn't we have a wired-in run for them, Geoffrey, on the lawn?"

"You won't get any wire," said Mrs. Marling with authority. "Not a foot to be had anywhere. Lucky if you can wire a little run for them round the house. Where did you get that wire, Ed?"

"She's O.K.," said Ed. "Ed found her."

"That will do nicely," said Mrs. Marling, measuring it with a professional eye. "You'll be wanting to get your dinner now, Govern."

Govern touched his cap and put by his tools. Then followed by Ed he took his way towards the Harveys' kitchen, much to the owners' surprise.

Mrs. Marling laughed.

"Govern always finds a friend," she said. "How long has he known your maid?"

"I didn't know he knew her at all," said Miss Harvey.

"I daresay he didn't," said Mrs. Marling cryptically. "How do you manage with only one maid. She's a good age, isn't she?"

"Not so very old," said Mr. Harvey. "She was our under-nurse and quite a young one at that. And Frances has found a girl to come in and help in the morning."

"You are lucky," said Mrs. Marling. "I didn't know there was a girl in the village. Who is it?"

"Her name is Millie," said Miss Harvey. "A red-haired girl."

"Not Millie Poulter?" said Mrs. Marling. "I suppose you know she lives with her aunt."

Miss Harvey said Millie had said something about an aunt, but she hadn't paid much attention.

"Well, you'd better," said Mrs. Marling, moving towards the house. "Dear, dear, how late Lettice and David are. Her aunt is Mrs. Cox, where Mrs. Smith is lodging. You'll find it a bit inconvenient, but Millie ought to be called up soon."

Mrs. Marling did mean, though she knew she would repent it afterwards, to put Miss Harvey in her place. People who came to live in a village should, according to her code, take an intelligent interest in their neighbours. If Miss Harvey had not discovered since she had been at the Red House that her daily girl was to all intents and purposes a spy from her landlady's camp, she had only herself to blame.

"That accounts for the lime juice," said Miss Harvey thoughtfully, but concealing her annoyance very well. "Do come in. I am sure David won't be long."

"And why that proprietary air about David?" said Mrs. Marling uncharitably to herself. Not that she cared who David's friends were, but David as such was a relation and one must keep an eye on family ties.

Even as they got to the house David's little car drove up. He was driving Lettice, and the back of the car seemed to consist chiefly of bottles.

"Hi! Geoffrey, come and help," said David. "You take the drink while I put my head in the boot."

So speaking he opened the hole at the back where dirt and string live and with some difficulty pulled out a roll of chicken wire, which he carried into the garden and dumped in the porch.

"My dear David!" said Mrs. Marling. "Where on earth did you get that? I thought there wasn't a foot left in the country."

"No more there was," said David. "But let me defer my narrative till we get inside, because I want to make a good impression on Frances, though why in a boiler suit I cannot tell. For you alone I did it, Frances. I heard that Barton had got a lot of pre-war wire net-

ting for the alterations he was making for the Trustees
at Brandon Abbey, and I knew his wife wanted onions
and a setting, or clutch, if I make myself clear, of hens
if you will excuse my dragging them in when we shall
hear quite enough about them before the end of the
day. Agnes has unlimited onions. Mary appears to
have unlimited clutches, so we did business. And how
delightful the drawing-room looks. A little more off-
white even than before."

Miss Harvey thanked David warmly for the wire
and rather wished she were not wearing a boiler suit.
The party then adjourned to the dining-room. The
fork lunch was a figure of speech, for the food that
Miss Harvey and Hilda had provided required spoons
and knives as well, and was very good. David un-
corked his bottles and demanded ice. Hilda, summoned from entertaining Mr. Govern and Ed, brought
in a tray of cubes and retired. Lettice congratulated
Mr. Harvey on his green corduroys.

"I'm so glad you like them," said Mr. Harvey, tossing back his hair in a gratified way. "They do give one
colour in this drab world."

Lettice said she always found green made her look
rather sallow.

Mr. Harvey said one did so understand that, but he
meant a dash of colour in the landscape, at least he
didn't quite mean landscape, but the surroundings, the
ambiance as it were. The sad thing was, he said, that it
would take at least thirteen coupons to replace his
shirt and trousers, even if they could be got again,
which he doubted.

"I suppose," said David to Miss Harvey, "you wear
those dungarees or oshkoshes—pardon the ignorance
of a mere male—to save coupons. How wise. Everyone
ought to be in uniform and then we wouldn't spend
any coupons and do the government in the eye."

Miss Harvey said she doubted whether the government would notice, but certainly uniform was an excellent idea as no coupons were needed.

"I wish they weren't," said Mrs. Marling. "I was

talking to Cousin William this morning, David, about
new clothes for Ed Pollett when he drives the car. The
tractor had gone right through the seats of his
breeches and his jacket is shockingly shabby. Cousin
William always gave the chauffeurs their uniforms of
course, but he can't spare his own coupons. Ed's mother says she doesn't see why she should give up Ed's
coupons for clothes that he doesn't wear at home, and
I see her point."

"It will be the same with the maids, of course," said
Lettice, "and with nurse. I always supplied her uniforms and now neither of us can really afford the coupons. It is very awkward. I could put her into boiler
suits, but she wouldn't look as nice as you do, Frances.
Nor would mother's maids."

"I hadn't thought of that," said Miss Harvey. "Luckily Hilda has always worn her own clothes, so I'm
safe."

"Was that Hilda who brought the ice?" David
asked. "I like her clothes. But seriously, Cousin Amabel, what are you going to do about Ed? Would Moss
Bros. help; or a marine store, whatever that is?"

"I should think there isn't a secondhand pair of
chauffeur's breeches left in England," said Mrs. Marling. "You don't know one do you, Mr. Harvey?" she
added, suddenly realising that the host and hostess
were rather being left out of the conversation.

"I wish I did," said Mr. Harvey. "I could ask at the
Regional Commissioner's Office if anyone has a pair."

"What I call really *Bolshevik*," said Lettice, becoming quite animated as she thought of her wrongs, "was
having to give one coupon for a black velvet glove to
put coal on the fire with that I promised to Lucasta
Bond. She had never heard of them and wanted one
dreadfully. I was furious. Does the government think
one would use a black glove, which is really only a
bag with a thumb, to go to church with, or shopping?"

"Not Bolshevik," said Mr. Harvey deprecatingly.

"Oh, isn't that the word?" said Lettice. "I mean all
horrid and Soviet anyway."

Mr. Harvey was about to protest against this depreciatory use of the word, but luckily a torrent of complaint burst forth from the company, each member of which had a personal grudge against the whole coupon system. Mrs. Marling's Burberry, wearing out from sheer spite, had run into fourteen coupons. Miss Harvey had been forced to give two coupons for a piece of blue ring velvet to make a turban and having spent it in the making was so much to the bad. Mr. Harvey had to get a new evening suit owing to the enemy action of moths and was twenty-six out of pocket. Lettice had felt obliged by misplaced generosity to give six to a friend who was getting married and couldn't get a trousseau on her own coupons, and now deeply regretted it.

"Join the Air Force and see the world," said David. "Look at the lovely uniform all coupon free. But my heart is broken in another way. I can't give six pairs of stockings to all the girls I know, and the handbags are beneath my contempt. It's enough to make one wish there wasn't a war."

The hubbub of complaint rose higher than ever. Lettice suddenly saw Mr. Harvey's eyes assume a Gorgon-struck expression. Following their direction she saw that the door was open and Mrs. Smith was standing there. The tumult died down.

"Oh, can I do anything for you?" said Miss Harvey, the first to pull herself together.

"I am sure I didn't mean to intrude," said Mrs. Smith, "especially in my own house, for I know exactly how Mr. Smith used to feel when people came in unexpectedly, but I thought I'd just bring the lime juice bottle back. You'll excuse my having borrowed it last night, won't you, but I had none and Millie, my landlady's niece you know, happened to say there was a bottle open at Red House and your maid being out I said to Millie, 'Just run across, I'm sure Miss Harvey won't mind.' So she just ran over and such a bright girl she wrote a little note to explain, which I hope you found."

"It was quite all right," said Miss Harvey manfully.

"So I thought you'd like the bottle back," said Mrs. Smith suddenly producing it from a basket. "We are told to waste nothing and I thought you would like to put it with the other bottles for the salvage. It just needs rinsing."

She thrust into Miss Harvey's unwilling hand the empty, sticky lime juice bottle. Everyone hoped she would go. But as she didn't, it became incumbent on the rest of the party to do something.

"Well, Joyce, I hope you are comfortable at Mrs. Cox's," said Mrs. Marling, while Lettice said much the same.

"Do sit down," said Mr. Harvey, bringing a chair forward.

"If it isn't Miss Perry that used to teach in the infant school at Rushwater!" said David. "And I thought it was Mrs. Smith. And how are you?"

The ci-devant Miss Perry looked down at her mourning as though to hint that she was but half a Smith since her husband's death.

"What you want is a drink," said David, pouring several things into the cocktail shaker. "One good bottle deserves another. Come on, Mrs. Smith, put it down."

"I hardly like to," said the widow. "You know Mr. Smith had a slight weakness that way and it quite put me against it. Not but what he was always the gentleman."

"Once a gentleman always a gentleman," said David. "Here you are."

Mrs. Smith bridled and sipped the drink.

"Now tell me all your troubles," said David, while his audience sat fascinated and admiring.

"Mr. Smith was in business, Mr. Leslie," said the widow. "I never thought he'd be taken. We had just furnished the nest and got everything cosy when he went. I never thought I would be living in lodgings before a year was out. My health isn't what it was and I feel the loss of my own things about me."

"Never mind," said David. "Have another short one? That's the spirit. Now, Mrs. Smith, you must look on the bright side. Mr. and Miss Harvey are keeping the nest beautifully clean and soon there'll be some chicks, I mean in the garden. Have you seen the lovely hen house they are making?"

Mrs. Smith said Mr. Smith could never abide poultry.

"Nor can Miss Harvey," said David. "No one can, but we must all be brave in war time. Think of our gallant flying men."

Mrs. Marling, who was afraid that someone might giggle, suggested that they should all go into the garden and see how the work was getting on, or Lucy would arrive with the hens and have nowhere to put them. Mrs. Smith said she would just like a peep at her lovely drawing-room and went across the passage.

"For God's sake, David, remove her," said the agonised Mr. Harvey. "You seem to have some power over her. She'll take the arm-chairs and sofa if we're not quick."

They all followed Mrs. Smith into the drawing-room where she stood in an ecstasy of nostalgic admiration.

"Every single thing was paid for before Mr. Smith died," she said. "Cash and comfort was his motto. Now he's dead I haven't much of either, but it is a pleasure to roam about the old haunts. Are you using the art blotter, Miss Harvey? If you aren't I would like to spirit it away to my lodgings. It was at that very blotter that I sent out the funeral notices. It was in the *Daily Telegraph* and the *Infant Scholastic Weekly* and the *Barsetshire Chronicle*. Mr. Smith's business friends sent a lovely wreath with an inscription. I would like you to come to tea in my little room one day and see the mementoes."

As she spoke she lifted the olive velvet blotter, inlaid with oxidised gold braid and dripping with tassels, and clutched it convulsively.

Miss Harvey looked helplessly at her brother and said Of course Mrs. Smith must take it.

David, who as usual was getting bored by the scene, said he thought he saw Govern digging a hole in the turf, which caused Mrs. Smith to hurry out, blotter in hand.

"Well; enough, no more," said David reflectively, "'tis not so off-white now as it was before. We'd better go after her, or she'll take all the peas and my wire."

By the time they got into the garden Govern and Ed were hard at work again. Both the Harveys had a turn for carpentering and acquitted themselves quite credit-ably, even by Govern's standards, in putting the wire up round the run. Mrs. Marling, having satisfied her-self that all was going well, went back to the Hall to do some Red Cross work, so Lettice and David were left to watch the workers. There was, under a birch tree, a curved garden seat constructed and painted to resemble stone, evidently a part of the off-white deco-rative scheme. On each of its arms a concrete basin with a concrete pigeon on its edge prevented anyone from sitting or leaning. Here Lettice and David estab-lished themselves. A few yards away they had the pleasant sight of other people working. The sun came out, the breeze only stirred the smallest branches, Mrs. Smith was absent-mindedly among the peas with her basket as David had foretold.

David and his cousin looked at one another and laughed.

"Lord!" said David. "Fancy meeting the ex-Miss Perry here. My darling mamma, who will show her heavenly charity to everyone, used to have her to tea once or twice a year and if I was at home I always escaped by the window. She is the sort that thinks mamma is so nice, but a little *queer*, don't you think: as indeed she is, bless her. By the way, the thrush died, they always do, and she kept the corpse for two days while she painted its portrait in water colours and then Agnes took it away and the children buried it. Clarissa wrote a poem about it which I can't re-member. It ended,

> See our thrush doth now arise
> And to heaven he quickly flies.

Not really good. Oh Lord! how dull children can be."

Lettice did not answer. Since she had re-made David's acquaintance she had thought much of him. Sometimes she thought with pleasure of his charming ways, his gift of laughter, his ridiculous mock-seriousness. Then she would think of his other moods; his way of suddenly being bored and dropping whatever he was doing and saying, of melting away whenever he was not being amused or interested; his perhaps rather heartless baiting of people like Mrs. Smith who, it was true, did not feel it—at least she hoped they didn't—but who might at any moment awake to the fact that they were being made a motley to the view and be bitterly perplexed or wounded. He had baited Geoffrey Harvey that night in the Stone Parlour, making him show his ignorance about cows; and she was not sure but that he had set her father and Geoffrey at cross-purposes about poetry for his own amusement. And what was worse, she too had become part of his private entertainment and had only just stopped herself laughing at her father. Was David a bad influence, she vaguely wondered. Even if he was, she, a woman with two children, was too old to be corrupted by him. Surely she could share his amusement and yet not feel any contempt for his victims. Perhaps she could even influence him to be more tolerant; a thought which shows that she was not very experienced after all.

David, watching his cousin's musing face, wondered how he had happened to miss seeing her for so many years and blamed himself. Her faint seriousness, her readiness to laugh when the ice was broken, the fascinating way in which the ice froze again between visit and visit and had to be thawed till laughter came; all this attracted him more than he had been attracted for some time. It was a small, fresh experience for David Leslie to find a delightful woman whom he was at liberty to love as a cousin without prejudice to loving her if he wished as a friend, or as his long-sought-for love. Nothing would have induced him to think of a wife in terms of pleasing his family, but if he did consider making Lettice his wife he knew his parents and Agnes and John would approve wholeheartedly. Lettice had a quiet distinction of manner, good enough looks for any man, the right kind of birth and background. She had loved Roger evidently and though she loved him did not give David the impression that her heart was sunk in the sea before Dunkirk. True there were children, but they were agreeable and well behaved and their half brothers and sisters would not be so very much younger. Money David did not need, but that his wife should have money of her own would not be unpleasing. There was no hurry. He was on leave and had heard that he would be employed in England for some time to come. The field was clear. If Mr. Harvey had any thoughts about her, David did not consider it a serious matter. He had already established a supremacy over Mr. Harvey in the matter of the polled Angus—rather unfairly, he admitted to himself, for the time he had spent a few years ago in the Argentine buying and examining cattle for his father had made him an authority in a small way—and so had an easy lead.

It was therefore all the more disconcerting when his cousin, coming back from her musing trance, suddenly said,

"David, you were really not very kind to Geoffrey the other night. He might easily have seen you were egging him on, and so might father."

"Bless your heart, my love," said David, with a stirring of guilty feelings to which he was not at all accustomed, "he needs no egging. No more than old Perry— I beg her pardon, La Smith—does."

"But I think you were rather unkind to Mrs. Smith," said Lettice, womanishly seizing this weak point. "I really thought she would see that you were mocking her."

"What lovely words you use," said David admiringly. "Anyone else would have said making fun of her."

"Well, they would have meant the same thing," said Lettice spiritedly. "David, I know I laugh when you are like that because I can't help it, but do you really need to mock so much? Don't you ever like people enough not to laugh at them?"

"That question, my love, requires some notice and a power of consideration," said David. "So far I may truthfully say no. And when you know how much I adore my mamma and how often I laugh at her, you will realise the full extent of—I can't remember how I was going to end that sentence, but anyway you will realise how difficult it is. If I ever met anyone, a woman particularly, that I didn't laugh at, it would either be because she was so dull that she had nothing in her to laugh about, or because she made me feel that I couldn't and needn't mock; and then how dull I'd be."

"You don't mock me," said Lettice with great simplicity, "but I don't find you at all dull."

"Bless your heart," said David, "how little do you understand the implications of your brilliant cousin. What I am trying to say, in halting words, is that if I were head over ears in love, which somehow I've never quite been yet, it would make me so stupid that I would be as dull as ditchwater."

"I do get confused, David, with all your brilliance," said Lettice, "but I still think it isn't very kind to laugh at Joyce in front of her face, though I admit she fully deserves it."

"Listen, love," said David, the thought flashing through his mind that if anyone but Lettice had been so gently obstinate over such a trifle he would have found an excellent excuse for getting away ten minutes ago, "I will now tell you something. You believe it is your duty to tell me that."

"I never said anything about duty at all," Lettice exclaimed indignantly. "I just thought you were not very kind to Geoffrey and Joyce."

"I'll tell you what, as your sister Lucy would say," said David. "You may not have said duty, but you thought duty. And let me tell you, love, that in my peculiar and useless life I have learnt one thing. It is never one's duty to tell people unpleasant things, because they only make them miserable and usually aren't true. If you meet the word duty, it always means telling your friends something that hurts them. Have you ever known anyone who felt it his or her duty to tell you something nice?"

"But people often say nice things to me," said Lettice.

"Yes, my owl, they do, I am sure," said David. "But not from a sense of duty; because they want to. Has anyone ever said to you, 'I am sorry, Mrs. Watson, but I feel it my duty to tell you that you are being a very good mother and looking after your children who do you great credit'?"

Lettice opened her eyes wide and said of course not.

"There you are," said David. "And if they want to say that you are behaving shockingly and bringing up your children like guttersnipes, it is not duty, it is really because they want to."

"I do my best to bring them up well," said Lettice, looking anxious.

"Half-wit; nincompoop; in fact Woman," said David, very affectionately. "It is hopeless to talk to you, and I feel it is my painful duty to tell you that you are the very nicest cousin I have and that your daughters are perfection, though I wish they wouldn't hug my legs so hard when we meet, for it spoils the creases in my trousers. Now we will stop talking sense. Besides, I hear a noise which is unmistakably telling people what, and I associate it with your sister Lucy."

Even as he spoke Lucy came round the side of the house carrying a pair of hens in a professional way by the legs, upside down.

"Hi, Govern!" she shouted. "Is the house ready?"

Govern, who was putting up perches inside the hen

house, withdrew his head from it and shouted, "Yes, Miss Lucy."

"Tell Ed to come here then," Lucy shouted back.

Ed came up with his unhastening walk, took delivery of the hens from Lucy and put them into the run. The hens shook out all their feathers to express their surprise at finding themselves on their feet again and began to peck about.

"All right, Tom," Lucy shouted towards the front of the house, "you can bring the others. I've got the rest in a crate," she explained to David and Lettice, "but there wasn't room for these two. Oh, there you are, Tom. Come on."

She strode off towards the hen run, followed by Captain Barclay and David, who obligingly helped to carry the crate. Govern had just put the fastening on the door of the run, the hens were decanted, the door shut and the new tenants left to sort themselves.

"I wonder, ought we to feed them at once," said Miss Harvey, getting up from her knees and banging some of the earth off her boiler suit.

"I believe," said David, "one butters their paws. Oughtn't we to have a Harvest Home? Or perhaps Peace-Egging. Or would that be tempting Providence?"

Mr. Harvey laughed and said one did so understand that feeling, but he was sure Providence would find Peace-Egging a restful change from what it was doing at present.

"But really, I mean," said Miss Harvey anxiously, "ought I to give them something to eat? I've put water in the run, but perhaps they'd feel happier with some bread or some scraps."

"They'll be all right," said Lucy robustly. "They were eating up till the last moment at Farmer Hobbing's and this earth is only just dug up. Who's going to feed them?"

Ed, who was helping Govern to collect his tools, looked up. A remark made earlier in the day echoed in his brain.

"Auntie," he said, smiling at Miss Harvey.

Miss Harvey, who knew that Ed was wanting, looked alarmed.

"Beg pardon, miss," said Govern, "it's your maid he means. She told Ed to call her auntie. She understands hens all right. Thank you, sir," he added, as Mr. Harvey tipped him, "a pleasure I'm sure. Come on, Ed; auntie's got some tea for you. Good evening, miss. Good evening, Miss Lucy."

He walked away towards the kitchen followed by Ed.

"I don't pretend to understand country life," said Mr. Harvey, "but our Hilda is a farmer's daughter and her sister married a farmer, so I expect she knows all about it."

"I'll tell you what, I'll go and talk to her," said Lucy, and went hot foot after Govern and Ed.

David and Captain Barclay lit cigarettes and fell into talk about men they knew. Miss Harvey went indoors to tidy herself and Mr. Harvey took himself and his green corduroys to where Lettice was still sitting.

"A green thought in a green shade," he said admiringly to Lettice as he sat down.

"Really pale blue," said Lettice kindly. "Green makes me so yellow. Oh, but I said that at lunch time. Unless you meant you were the green thought."

Mr. Harvey felt a slight exasperation, and the word merry-thought floated unbidden and unwanted into his mind.

"And talking of green thoughts," said Lettice, "have you noticed that Mrs. Smith spent quite half an hour among the pea-sticks?"

Mr. Harvey said he really thought that was Frances's business, and he expected every morning to wake up and find Mrs. Smith had taken the pillow from under his head.

"Joyce is a very trying woman," said Lettice placidly.

"You all say that," said Mr. Harvey with a touch of impatience, "but it doesn't make her any better."

Lettice looked at him with interest. To those with real roots in the country the intolerance of the city-dweller who comes among them for the neighbours who are part of their surroundings is always a little surprising. The Marlings had accepted Joyce Perry, ever since she came among them as the wife of Mr. Smith, as a natural phenomenon, and did not enquire. Mr. Smith, apart from his weakness about spirituous drink, was a respectable corn and seed merchant trading in Barchester, whose father had been a respectable corn and seed merchant before him. Both also supplied coal, and though Mr. Marling got most of his by the truckload, he had dealt with father and son for smaller quantities. The Smiths, with all their qualities and defects, were therefore part of the Marling world, and that Mrs. Smith was a troublesome woman was accepted like the weather or the rates. If Mr. Harvey could not get on with her, it was simply that he did not belong to the Marling world. We doubt whether Mr. Harvey would quite have understood this.

"Oliver says you are very busy this week," said Lettice, knowing that men like to talk about their work. "He would have liked to get the afternoon off and see the hen-house too, but John Leslie had to be away and couldn't spare him."

It is below one's dignity to be jealous of someone's brother, but Mr. Harvey felt a slight annoyance that his work should be less indispensable than Oliver's. He then tried to check this feeling. The result was a silence which Lettice, well-trained in good manners, did not allow to becoming embarrassing.

"I expect you are able to write your poetry while you are at the office," she said. "Oliver says there is a lot of spare time."

Mr. Harvey was again mildly annoyed that his muse should be considered as a stop-gap, but answered that he found it very difficult to work in fits and starts and really needed leisure to produce his best work. But he had, he said, been working on some translations lately.

"Do tell me about it," said Lettice, wondering if

nurse and the children who were coming down in the old pony cart to fetch her would be much longer.

"I don't know if you came across a little book called *A Diabolist of the Restoration* by a man called Hilary Grant," he said. "A slight study, but quite well done, of a minor French poet of the Romantic Period."

"Oh, Hilary Grant who married Lavinia Brandon's daughter over at Pomfret Madrigal," said Lettice. "We all thought the old aunt, Miss Brandon, at Brandon Abbey, would leave him a fortune, but she left all her money to a charity. I think Hilary is in the Intelligence Corps now. His mother used to make him go to Italy and he spoke Italian quite well. Do you know Mrs. Brandon? She wasn't anyone very particular, but she is very charming and a great friend of Sir Edmund Pridham whom you must know; everyone does."

If Lettice had not looked so charming and had such a pleasant voice, Mr. Harvey would have put on the famous manner with which he was used to crush people who would do the talking. When one has carefully led up to a delightful conversation about oneself, it is mortifying to find one's elegant audience much more interested in county ramifications; and not even county, he said rather bitterly to himself, thinking of Lettice's description of Mrs. Brandon's family. Nor did he wish his title to fame to be judged by his knowing or not knowing Sir Edmund Pridham. He had more than once had occasion to come up against Sir Edmund on county business at the Regional Commissioner's Office, and had on every occasion been worsted by that gentleman, who knew his county and its organisations inside out and had a baffling habit of standing no nonsense from anybody, or even worse, ignoring the decrees and precedence and going straight to John Leslie, who valued his help and advice highly.

"I never knew Hilary had written a book," Lettice added.

Mr. Harvey, deciding that it would be below him to lose his temper, explained that Hilary Grant had printed as an appendix the little collection of verse entitled

Belphégor which was the only extant work of the poet
Jehan le Capet, whose real name was Eugène Duval.
These poems he was translating.

"And will they sell well?" asked Lettice, who knew
from Mrs. Morland that authors wrote because they
had to earn their living.

If Mr. Harvey had not been sitting down he would
have stamped with rage at Lettice's want of tact. Then
he looked again at her and felt it didn't really matter if
she had tact or not, so long as she made so harmonious
a picture upon the curved seat, under the birch tree,
so he ignored the question.

"There is one sonnet," he said, "which I confess I
find difficult. It is, as it were, a glorification of his mistress, in the type of the many-breasted goddess. The
last two lines run:

'Maîtresse féconde qui portes dan tes reins
Bavants les trop ignobles jumeaux de tes seins.'"

"How well you speak French," said Lettice.

"The enjambement of these lines," continued Mr.
Harvey, gratified that his accent had not passed unnoticed, but quite determined not to be side-tracked, "is
unusual in le Capet and seems to point forward to
Mallarmé. I hammered out a couplet yesterday that
seemed to me to me not without merit. But you shall
judge.

"'Wide-wombèd whore—'"

"I simply cannot bear," said Lettice firmly, passing
over this embarrassing sample, "poetry that has the
word 'breast' in it. I don't know why. Modern poetry
at least. And there is nurse and the children. Well,
darlings; say how do you do to Mr. Harvey."

Diana and Clare behaved very well. Miss Harvey,
now clothed in a silk frock, came to say tea was ready
and begged Lettice to let the children stay. Nurse graciously gave permission, Captain Barclay and David
were collected and they all went indoors. Miss Harvey
apologised for tea being a little late, but said she had

not dared to ask for it till Govern and Ed had gone.
Hilda brought in the teapot and hot water.

"Would your little girls like tea with us," said Miss
Harvey to Lettice, "or in the kitchen? Hilda used to be
my and Geoffrey's nurserymaid and she loves children."

"I'm sure the children would love to have tea in the
kitchen if nurse has no objection," said nurse, speaking
as one royalty to another through an ambassador.

"Will that be all right, Hilda?" said Miss Harvey.

"I'm sure I don't mind if nurse and the young ladies
have their tea in the kitchen," said Hilda, secretly flat-
tered at being raised to the honorary status of full
nurse. "And Miss Lucy said to say she was just coming,
Miss Frances. She's been helping me wash up the tea-
things after those men. Will you come this way,
nurse."

Having thus implied that the entertainment of Govern and Ed was a painful duty foisted upon her by her
mistress, Hilda withdrew, followed by nurse and the
children. Lucy then burst into the room.

"I never knew Joyce had such a good scullery," she
said. "I say, Frances, I saw Joyce going across to Mrs.
Cox's with about a peck of peas. What a nuisance
she'll be. I'll tell you what, your maid does awfully
good teas. Govern and Ed had just finished and she
had given them a marvellous meal; sardines and cold
rice pudding and cold mashed potatoes and beetroot
and cake. I talked to her about the hens and she understands everything. She knows how to kill hens too,
so if any of yours don't lay and you want to eat them
she can do it. It's a thing I've always wanted to learn
and she's going to show me as soon as you want one
killed. One ought to know how to kill hens."

Her eyes sparkled with enthusiasm and she dropped
a piece of scone face downwards on the carpet which
was of asymmetrical geometrical designs in tones of
beige.

"Tut, tut," said David reprovingly, as he picked it
up. "It is well known that the only difference between

butter and margarine is that you can get out butter
stains but not margarine stains. I am willing to lay you
sixpence, Frances, that your landlady will smell out
the stain before this tea-party is over and commit
hara-kiri, or whatever its silly name is, on the carpet to
make you lose face."

"Don't," said Miss Harvey piteously.

"I won't," said David. "Couresty to women has always been my motto. I did know an English family in
the Argentine that used to shoot their hens, because
they were afraid to wring their necks. But they had
the whole wide pampas to do it in, so it didn't matter
if their shots flew wide."

Lucy laughed so good-humouredly that David re-
nounced teasing her as a poor job and turned his attention to Miss Harvey. They had plenty of common acquaintance in the Harveys' London world and were
able to be quite unkind and funny about them. Lucy
meanwhile attached herself to Mr. Harvey, desiring to
know all he would tell her about his work at the Regional Commissioner's Office, rather, he gathered, so
that she might be ready to do it all herself in any
emergency. This left Captain Barclay free to talk to
Lettice, which he was so seldom able to do. Not that
he had anything special to say to her, but they had a
pleasant background of the same kind of friends and
ways of living. Lettice was never less than courteous
to people she was talking to, and this afternoon her
manners had the added courtesy which often comes
from one's mind being elsewhere and being conscious
of the fact. Under her conversation her mind was running on David. That he should have called her a half-
wit and a nincompoop gave her a secret pleasure, to
which his addition of Woman as a final epithet of op-
probrium somehow added zest. She wondered a good
deal whether David was right about duty. Looking at
the question impartially, or what passed in her mind
for impartially, she saw that there was much to be said
for David's point of view. Certainly when people like
Lucasta Bond had taken upon themselves to tell her

things for what they mistakenly considered her good, she had hated them with a mortal hatred that only death could quench, and only the passage of a week or so had dropped into the gulf of oblivion. She went hot and cold. Had her words to David made him as angry as Lucasta Bond's had made her? Would he lie awake planning bitter repartees, as she had planned them against Lucasta? If so, life was too hard to bear. A gentle pricking rose behind her eyes. Then the thought of crying before company made her ashamed. She laughed at herself inside, the pricking subsided, and as David, in the middle of being quite chivalrously impertinent to Miss Harvey, smiled at her with what she knew was a secret smile for her alone, her spirits rose, and she was able to show her liveliest appreciation of what she had not heard Captain Barclay saying about Lord Stoke. Captain Barclay thought she had never looked more charming and that he would like his mother and sisters to see her.

Time had been passing. Lettice got up and said they must go. The Harveys expressed their gratitude for the way in which everyone had rallied.

"By the way," said Miss Harvey, "our old governess that we mentioned to you is coming next week. I wonder if I might bring her up to the Hall one day. It would be such a pleasure to her and she will be rather alone as I am in the office most days."

Lettice said she was sure her mother would be delighted.

"I don't want to hurry or disturb anyone," said David, "but as Heaven is my witness I see my Miss Perry, your Mrs. Smith going down the garden again with her basket. Geoffrey, you had better go and look. She may have come to get the rest of the peas."

Mr. Harvey looked so harassed that Lettice was sorry for him.

Lucy volunteered to fetch the children and bring them round to the front door, so the rest of the party went down the little winding path to the front gate, accompanied by their host and hostess. In the road was the pony cart, Ed at the pony's head talking to it in a confidential way that the pony perfectly understood. Nurse and the children joined them, with Lucy and Hilda in attendance. Lettice was just going to get into the pony cart when Captain Barclay came forward.

"I'd like to drive you back if I may," he said. "I've got my car here and plenty of petrol."

"Oh—thank you," said Lettice, irresolute, for she was not sure if nurse would approve.

"That'll be nice for mummy to go in the gentleman's car, won't it," said nurse to her young charges, "and Ed can drive us up. Get in, Ed."

Ed, his face all rapture, got in and took the reins. Diana and Clare were lifted in, nurse mounted behind them. Suddenly Ed's face blanched.

"Look out, auntie," he said to Hilda. "She's coming."

Everyone looked round and saw Mrs. Smith emerging from the front gate holding her basket triumphantly.

"What a piece of luck that I was here," she said almost brightly. "I just happened to be passing with my basket and I thought to myself, 'Well now, suppose those fowls have commenced to lay?' So I just slipped down to the run and looked in the box and found—what do you think?"

David suggested *sotto voce* a time bomb.

"A dear, wee egg!" said Mrs. Smith. "So now, isn't that nice. Quite the end of a perfect day."

An uncomfortable silence fell. It was plain that Mrs. Smith having found the egg meant to keep it. Noblesse obliged the Harveys not to expostulate and they exchanged agonised and hating looks behind their landlady's back. Even David was at a loss.

"Thank you, m'm," said Hilda, dexterously taking the basket before Mrs. Smith knew she was there. "I'll put it away and I'll tell Millie to take the basket back when she comes to-morrow."

She whisked round the side of the house and vanished.

Everyone feverishly said good-bye to Mrs. Smith, who however appeared to take the incident as part of the day's work. Mr. Harvey, in an ecstasy of terror lest she should have taken offence, said she must meet their old governess, Mademoiselle Duchaux, when she came next week.

"Oh, I did not know she was French," said Mrs. Smith. "I used to like the poetry of Victor Yugo very much when I was a girl. I daresay she knows some. Well, I must be wending my way."

The company breathed again. Diana and Clare said "Gee-up," and Ed flapped the reins on the pony's back, who trotted obediently away. Lettice got into Captain Barclay's car and Lucy demanded to be taken to the Cottage Hospital.

"I'll tell *you* what, my girl," said David. "You'll come in my car with me. It's on my way back."

In a few moments they were at the Cottage Hospital. As the car drove up, an uninteresting girl, who was Octavia Crawley, came to the door in V.A.D. uniform.

"Hullo," she said to Lucy, "it was a rotten Caesar, absolutely straightforward. They had one at the Barchester General with the most ghastly complications last week. Oh, and mother says she hopes you'll all come to tea next time you're in Barchester. Is he your brother? Oh, and Matron wants you at once."

"Cousin," said Lucy. "Good-bye, David."

She banged into the hospital. Octavia gave David a bored look, as to one who was not likely to supply any wounds, burns, scalds, fractures, or haemorrhages and went into the Hospital.

"If that's the Dean's daughter, no wonder people write to the *Times* about the state of the Church of England," said David to his car, and went back to Little Misfit.

CHAPTER SIX

Miss Lucy Marling was a strong believer in what she called wearing people down. Having a great deal of energy, an insatiable desire for practical information and no false modesty, her way of getting anything she wanted was to batter people till from sheer fatigue or exasperation they gave in. A happy few, among whom may be counted her brother Oliver, were proof against her assaults. Lucy had long cherished a wish to know every detail of what was done at the Regional Commissioner's Office, how it was done and who did it, but Oliver, though he had no very vital secrets to give away and did not at all mistrust his younger sister's discretion, thought the less said the better and evaded all her more searching enquiries. When Lucy had thoroughly mastered this fact she with great simplicity turned her powerful mind on to Mr. Harvey who, while properly discreet, gave her a certain amount of interesting detail. Mr. Harvey, who was quite used to the admiration of young women both in his capacity as poet and as Civil

Servant, found in Lucy's gentlemanly attitude a certain zest and rather enjoyed her company, looking
upon her as a Roman of the empire might have looked
upon a gigantic Gaul who had become domesticated
in his house.

"I'll tell you what," said Mr. Harvey, who much to
his own annoyance had been infected by Lucy's
phraseology, "why not come to the Office one day
when you are in Barchester? When I'm on day duty
I'm never very busy between six and seven and I'll
show you some of the working."

This invitation was given at Melicent Halt, the
nearest station for Marling. Before the war there had
been talk of shutting the station, but with petrol short-
age everyone now used it for shopping in Barchester,
or to go in the other direction to Southbridge. Lucy
had come down in the pony cart on a Friday after tea
to collect some fertiliser from the Parcels Office and
Mr. Harvey was waiting for the down train from Barchester. It was a single line, and the up and down
trains passed one another at Melicent Halt and even in
war time were apt to linger while their guards and
engine-drivers exchanged news, collected the washing,
or did some bartering of cigarettes and onions.

A very old gentleman with a Newgate frill, his
wicked old face seamed with the dirt and wrinkles of a
long disgraceful life, was talking to the ticket clerk
who was also the porter.

"Russians?" said the old gentleman. "If a Russian
was to say, 'Take a fill of tobacco, mate,' I'd take the
fill of tobacco."

"Our Russian comrades would give you a fill of tobacco all right, Mr. Nandy," said the ticket clerk, who
was an unfortunate example of a little too much reading of sixpenny pink books. "And you'd give them a
fill."

"I wouldn't give no Russian a fill no nor no one
else," said the old gentleman, chuckling malevolently.
"Anyone as gives away a fill of baccy is a fool. You
can't get a good fill of baccy nowadays, no nor a good

glass of beer neither. Them Russians gets everything. I heard Mr. Churchill say that on the wireless, but they won't get my baccy, nor my beer. What's the time, Bill?"

The ticket clerk said five minutes to six.

"I'm off to the Hop Pole then," said the wicked old gentleman. "I'll show them Russians who'll get a pint of beer first, them or me."

And spitting quite horribly the wicked old gentleman hobbled off to the Hop Pole.

"That's old Henry Nandy," said Lucy proudly to Mr. Harvey. "He drinks and smokes all day long and lives in one room and it simply *stinks*. He's supposed to be rolling in money."

"Funny the way Mr. Nandy carries on, miss," said the ticket clerk, who always meant to assert the solidarity of the intelligent workers by refusing the antiquated titles of miss, sir, or madam to travellers, and was always—for the worst of us are not perfect—a little shy of putting his theory into practice. "He doesn't seem to get the idear of Russia."

"Mr. Harvey knows all about Russia and things," said Lucy tolerantly. "I'll tell you what, Geoffrey, you ought to talk to Bill Morple about Russia. He's frightfully keen about it and he's read quite a lot. I must say I think it's all rather rot myself."

Mr. Harvey, though deeply conscious of the superiority of everything Russian over everything English, did not at all want to have a public debate with the ticket clerk. Lucy, to his horror, appeared to be considering herself in the light of a boxing match referee and to be ready to order all seconds out of the ring, so it was with much relief that he heard the jarring bell which announced the approach of the down train. Bill Morple vanished into the booking office and the distant engine hooted as it came through the cutting. Lucy, who believed among her other articles of faith in doing things herself, her opinion of other people's powers of mind or action being low, took advantage of Bill Morple's absence to storm the Parcels Office and get her bag of fertiliser. As she dragged it along the platform she banged into Mr. Harvey.

"Oh, sorry Geoffrey," she said.

"And who is that?" said a voice behind her in an extremely correct English accent.

"Oh, Lucy, I want you to know Mademoiselle Duchaux," said Mr. Harvey, laying a detaining hand on her arm.

Lucy kindly shook it off, for she hated anything in the nature of what she called "pawing" (though to do Mr. Harvey justice he had no such intentions and would have shuddered at the thought), and looked round. An elderly woman, neatly dressed in exactly the right clothes, her grey hair perfectly done under a suitable hat, was looking at her with obvious curiosity.

"This is Lucy Marling," said Mr. Harvey in a placating way. "Mademoiselle Duchaux."

"She is Miss Marling, I presume," said Mlle Duchaux, withholding her approval or disapproval of Lucy till she had a thorough explanation of her.

"Oh, how do you do," said Lucy. "You're the one Geoffrey said about that was his governess. He talks awfully good French."

Mlle Duchaux was rent by emotions. Part of her was pleased that her ex-pupil should have done her credit; the other part resented the apparent patronage of a si disgracieuse jeune personne unspeakably. And indeed Lucy, in a very old shapeless coat and skirt, a shabby felt hat, dirty string gloves, dragging a large bag of some evil-smelling stuff, was not an object of aesthetic pleasure. Then Mlle Duchaux's hard eye observed her well-groomed hair and her well-cut, well-cleaned shoes and her well-fitting stockings and recognised her for what she was.

"Frances has spoken to me of you in her letters," said Mlle Duchaux more graciously. "It seems that you are doing great national work, looking after gardens and fowls and nursing. Une vraie patriote enfin."

"Good Lord, no!" said Lucy, properly shocked by the use of the word patriot. "I just muck about the

place a bit. But the Cottage Hospital's quite decent.
I'll tell you what, Geoffrey, would Mlle Duchaux like
to see over it? Matron would love to show her the
wards and we've got a Caesar and two lots of twins
just now. Ring me up."

Sketching a kind of salute to Mlle Duchaux she
strode off, stowed away her fertiliser in the pony cart,
picked up the postmaster's wife who had been down
to see her aunt in Railway Cottages, a nasty little row
of 1870 functional dwellings, and drove away. Mr.
Harvey, who was very helpless with luggage, at last
got Bill Morple to attend to him and packed his ex-
governess and her suitcases into his car.

"Lucy Marling is a delightful young woman," he
said with false ease as they drove towards Marling.
"She really runs the whole place and I don't know anyone I'd sooner go to in a crisis."

"Heureusement que les crises ne sont pas trop
fréquentes," said Mlle Duchaux aloud to herself.

"I know she looked a bit peculiar this morning," said
Mr. Harvey, basely apologising for Lucy. "She is rather a rough diamond."

"On ne s'en aperçoit que trop," said Mlle Duchaux
with icy detachment.

Mr. Harvey regretted unspeakably that he and
Frances had ever asked their guest to pay them a visit
and wondered how long a fortnight would last. Thank
heaven he would be at the office a great deal of the
time and so would Frances. Mlle Duchaux was visiting
them for a holiday before taking up some job which
she had not particularised. So long as the job remained
fixed for that day fortnight he could bear it. In fact he
would have to bear it, for one cannot turn an ex-govern-
ess away from one's door. So, summoning all the traditions of the Civil Service to his rescue, he exerted
himself to appease Mlle Duchaux and got back to the
Red House with no further unpleasantness.

When Lucy got back to the Hall she dumped her
fertiliser in the gardener's shed, put the pony and cart
away, helped Ed to grease the car, a long overdue job

which afforded the participants intense pleasure, and
gave herself a kind of rub down before dinner. At
least we can think of no other description of her
sketchy and dégagé toilette. During the meal she took
the opportunity of telling her parents what on several
points, and as Oliver was on duty and Lettice dining
in her stablehouse, there was no one to save them.
Mrs. Marling, more than usually busy with her Red
Cross work while some of her committee were having
apologetic holidays which they much needed, let her
daughter talk on. Mr. Marling, also deep in county
business, merely wondered why the feller who had
taken the Red House, Carver or something, wanted a
governess, and talked aloud to himself about the ini-
quities of Government departments and his hatred of
interference. So Lucy was able unchecked to persuade
her mother that the proper thing for them to do was to
go and call on Mlle Duchaux on the following afternoon. In normal circumstances Mrs. Marling would
have pleaded press of work, but a desire to see for herself how the Harveys' hens were getting on made her
agree to Lucy's plan.

Accordingly, next day Lucy and her mother walked
down to the village, enquired at the post office after
the postmaster's wife's aunt, saw Dr. March about the
under housemaid who had sprained her thumb, and
walked up the little winding path to the Red House.
As it was a normal English day in late summer, the
Harveys and their guest were sitting in the drawing-
room with a wood fire. Hilda threw Mrs. Marling and
Lucy into the room and went back to her kitchen to
get tea. Introductions took place. Mlle Duchaux, recognising the County in Mrs. Marling, was very pleasant
and it was soon discovered that she had taught French
to a nephew of Mrs. Marling's who had gone into the
Consular service and died of fever. Hilda brought in
tea.

"What an amusing tea-service," said Mrs. Marling,
looking at the china.

"I'm never quite sure if it is amusing or exasperating," said Mr. Harvey.

"Exasperating," said his sister, taking up the square black teapot with a sunk spout and pouring tea into square mustard-coloured cups with a few black circles on them. She then passed to Mrs. Marling a black milk jug whose handle was flush with its outer wall, if we make ourselves clear, while the fingers of the holder went into a recess which bulged inside the jug into the milk.

"It's Swedish," said Lucy. "Joyce told me so when Mr. Smith bought it."

"Les Suédois!" said Mlle Duchaux with venom.

There did not seem to be any answer to this.

"Did you know," said Mrs. Marling, turning to Mlle Duchaux and changing the conversation, "that my poor nephew left a widow? He had married a charming Austrian girl before the war, and we can't get any news of her."

"Les Autrichiens!" said Mlle Duchaux, to any powers of vengeance that happened to be about.

"But luckily there aren't any children," said Mrs. Marling, hoping to pacify the situation.

"Ça je le crois bien!" said Mlle Duchaux, with such awful wealth of meaning that even Mrs. Marling felt conversational helplessness descend on her.

"I don't know whose fault it was," said Lucy in an open-minded way. "Sometimes of course people just can't have children. There was a woman that came into the Barchester General Octavia said—"

"I do hope, Miss Harvey," said Mrs. Marling desperately interrupting her younger daughter, "that you will bring Mlle Duchaux to tea before she goes. Would one day next week suit you?"

After a great deal of consultation about dates, for both ladies were busy women, a day was decided. Mlle Duchaux expressed great pleasure at the prospect of visiting the château and peace reigned again. Mrs. Marling enquired after the fowls.

"The brown pullets have given us a few eggs," said

Miss Harvey, "and the white Leghorns are laying splendidly. Hilda is actually laying some down. I can't tell you how grateful we are to you for making us keep them."

"I have often wondered why Leghorn," said Mr. Harvey. "It seems curious to go to Italy to get white hens. Now if—"

"Les Italiens!" said Mlle Duchaux, almost spitting with hatred.

"—if it were straw hats it would seem more reasonable," Mr. Harvey bravely continued.

Mrs. Marling, hurrying to fill the breach, was just about to say that she remembered seeing the *Chapeau de Paille d'Italie* in Paris as a young woman, but terrified of the possible effect of the word Italie on Mlle Duchaux, hastily amended her words and said how very amusing Labiche's farces were. Mlle Duchaux, recovering herself, gave a short, capable and quite unwanted lecture on Labiche and the Palais-Royal, and harmony was restored till Hilda opened the door and stood looking at the company.

"We haven't quite finished, Hilda," said Miss Harvey.

"It isn't that, Miss Frances," said Hilda. "Did you remember it's National Savings to-day? I just seen Mrs. Smith go into Dr. March and she'll be here next. I thought you'd like to know."

She approached the tea-table, announced that they would need more hot water and took the jug away.

"Such a nuisance," said Miss Harvey plaintively. "I would far rather put bits of money straight into War Loan or something by cheque, but we felt we ought to join the Marling Savings Group as we are living here."

"We didn't know how much to subscribe," said Mr. Harvey. "Half-a-crown a week seems very mean, but we thought it would look proud to give more. We do put all we can into Government Bonds. But to have half-crowns ready on Saturday afternoons is really worse than the Germans."

He looked nervously at Mlle Duchaux, thinking that

she might say "Les Allemands!" but she remained unmoved.

"And having Mrs. Smith to collect it is so awful,"
said Miss Harvey in her turn. "It gives her such a
chance to see what we are doing and take things away.
Hilda won't give her a chance in the kitchen, but I
don't know how to stop her in the house."

The front door bell rang and Hilda was heard scur-
rying along the passage.

"She's here," said Hilda, hastily putting a jug of hot
water on the table before opening the front door.

"I am quite a stranger," said Mrs. Smith as she came
in. "But the war, you know. I have been out collecting
since half-past three and am nearly at the end of my
tether."

There was nothing for Miss Harvey to do but to ask
her to have some tea and introduce her to Mlle Duchaux, who had been looking at Mrs. Smith as if she
were a grammatical mistake in a French essay.

"Pleased to make your acquaintance I'm sure," said
Mrs. Smith. "I used to read a lot of Victor Yugo's
poems when I was young."

"Ah oui, les vers de Victor Hugo," said Mlle Duchaux, with a cold clarity and precision worthy of the
house of Molière.

"You speak French," said Mrs. Smith with interest.
"Vous êtes free French? J'admeer beaucoup General
de Gole, le leader des Free French."

Mlle Duchaux said nothing, but it was evident that
she resented Mrs. Smith's attachment to the General.

"Je viens collecter les National Savings tous les
week-ends," Mrs. Smith explained to Mlle Duchaux.
"Nous avons un National Savings Group à Marling et
je collecte pour lui. Presque tout le monde a été not at
home aujourd'hui. Thank you so much, Miss Harvey, a
cup of tea was just what I wanted. Les coupes de thé
sont si anglais," she added to Mlle Duchaux.

That lady was for once entirely taken aback and
could only ejaculate, "Oh, yes," in a way that quite

confirmed Mrs. Smith's opinion of French people. Having finished her tea she opened her bag.

"Well, as I am here, I had better do my little bit of war-work," she said going to the writing table. "Oh dear, where is the blotting book? There was one here, in art velours."

She looked suspiciously about for thieves. Miss Harvey said with some diffidence that she thought Mrs. Smith had taken it away with her not long ago.

"So I did," said Mrs. Smith, becoming tearful. "I find my poor memory is not what it was since Mr. Smith died. Vous savvay," she said to Mlle Duchaux, "que je suis soule since Mr. Smith passed on. Il est très triste."

"It is indeed very sad to be alone," said Mrs. Marling hastily, fearing the effect of Mrs. Smith's statement on Mlle Duchaux.

"Now the half-crowns," said Mrs. Smith, who had got her books and papers in order. "Half-a-crown for you, Miss Harvey, and half-a-crown for your brother and a shilling for Hilda. That's right, isn't it."

Miss Harvey said how stupid, she had forgotten to get change at the Post Office that morning and appealed to her brother. Mr. Harvey produced a ten shilling note and looked at it in a stupefied way. Mrs. Smith said she would see if she had change.

"Now let us see," she said. "That is five shillings for Mr. and Miss Harvey and one shilling for Hilda. Six shillings altogether. And I have just two florins here, so that is four shillings change, how lucky."

Mr. Harvey handed her the ten shilling note, received the two florins, and looked perplexed.

"That's all right, Geoffrey," said his sister. "I give you half-a-crown and Hilda gives you a shilling; then you'll have seven and six."

"But I gave Mrs. Smith half a sovereign," said Mr. Harvey.

"Yes, but you owed her half-a-crown for your National Savings," said Miss Harvey. "So now that's right."

"I've only four shillings here," said Mr. Harvey.

"Well, then, I'll pay you back now," said his sister, "and then we'll be square. No I can't, I've only got a half-crown and a florin. Look, I'll pay you the half-crown and see if Hilda has change for the florin and then I can give you her shilling."

"Don't trouble," said Mrs. Marling, "I think I've got two shillings. No, I haven't, but I've got a shilling and a sixpence. I'll give your brother the shilling and you the sixpence, and then if you give me the half-crown that will be right."

"No, it won't, mother," said Lucy. "You're trying to do Frances out of a shilling."

"But it's a shilling she *wants*," said Mrs. Marling.

"I'll tell you what," said Lucy. "Everyone put their money back and we'll start fresh."

After a good deal of disorder during which a six-pence fell down the back of the sofa and was fished up by Miss Harvey together with a dirty duster obviously stuffed there by Hilda when called away from her work, everyone had his or her own money again. Everyone spoke at once and in two minutes the muddle was worse than before.

"Nous ne sommes pas pratical comme vous," said Mrs. Smith to Mlle Duchaux.

This might have gone on till black out, but most luckily Hilda came in to clear away the tea things. She was carrying a plate with six shillings on it.

"Here's the National Savings," she announced. "I knew you'd need them, so I took them out of the house-keeping."

"Oh thank you, Hilda," said Miss Harvey taking the money. "Then I owe you a shilling, don't I."

"That's all right, Miss Frances," said Hilda magnanimously, and whisking the tea things on to a tray she left the room.

"And to think this is going on all over England every day of the week," said Mr. Harvey with a gesture of despair. "I don't suppose there is more than one person in every ten who can understand change,"

Mrs. Smith said it was quite dreadful and often made her wish she hadn't taken up National Savings, but we must all do our bit.

"I expect you would manage it much better in France, Mlle Duchaux," said Mrs. Marling, while Mr. Harvey murmured, "order, not manage" under his breath.

"Ah par exemple, on ne payerait pas," said Mlle Duchaux with patriotic fervor.

"Vous payriez en franks," said Mrs. Smith, "qui sont beaucoup plus faciles. Les shillings sont plus difficiles que les franks et beaucoup plus valuables."

This unwitting attack on the value of the franc made Mlle Duchaux so angry that as Lucy said afterwards to her mother she expected her to guillotine them all, but she controlled her rage and merely looked daggers at Mrs. Smith, who then said she must wend her way. That she should be leaving without carrying away some article of portable property was so remarkable that the Harveys held their breath. But they might just as well have let it go, for at the door of the drawing-room Mrs. Smith turned and said she had quite run out of matches and might she just borrow a few to light her gas ring and boil her milk at night. Without much enthusiasm Mr. Harvey took a box out of his pocket.

"Just four or five," said Mrs. Smith humbly, "and I am sure I can find an old box of Mrs. Cox's to strike them on."

Lucy was almost sure that she heard Mr. Harvey say Damn, but with great politeness he begged Mrs. Smith to take the box. Mrs. Smith said she couldn't dream of such a thing and put it in her bag. Mr. Harvey escorted her to the door.

As he came back to the drawing-room a great silent sigh of relief rose from the company.

"Joyce is so troublesome," said Mrs. Marling. "Well, we must get along now. I do hope, Mademoiselle Duchaux, that you will be able to come to tea. Lucy would come and fetch you in the pony cart and per-

haps we could arrange a day, Frances, when you and
Oliver get off duty at four and he could bring you out
with him."

A date was provisionally fixed, when Lucy uttered a
loud exclamation.

"I'll tell you what," said Lucy. "Joyce has gone off
without her National Savings."

Several eye-witnesses contradicted her.

"Miss Marling is quite right," said Mlle Duchaux in
her excellent English. "When you all returned the
money and began the calculations afresh, Geoffrey
had back his ten shillings. The poor lady has not got
her six shillings at all."

"But what about the six shillings Hilda brought in?"
said Mrs. Marling.

"Good Lord, I have still got them," said Miss Harvey. "I must let Mrs. Smith have them on Monday.
How stupid! Still, it was very nice of Hilda to say she
wouldn't let me pay her shilling. She is really keen on
National Savings."

"Now, I *will* tell you what," said Lucy, frowning
with the effort of her thoughts. "Hilda took all the National Savings money out of your housekeeping
money, didn't she? Well then, you have paid her shilling once. And if you give her another shilling you'll
have paid it twice."

"You are perfectly right," said Mr. Harvey. "It all
goes to show that the so-called educated classes are
not fit to be trusted with money. Now in Russia there
is far too much real educated intelligence for that.
Mere infants there would have managed this affair
better than we have."

"Ces Russes! ne m'en parlez pas!" said Mlle Duchaux with a serpent's hiss.

Mrs. Marling and Lucy said good-bye and went
home. At dinner Mr. Marling asked what they had
been doing and on hearing about Mlle Duchaux and
the National Savings said things weren't like that in
his young days. Lucy looked at Oliver for sympathy,
but his eyes were painful and though he smiled it was

from affection, not from understanding. Lucy felt rather alone.

By Monday Oliver was much better and quite ready to
arrange a plan for driving Miss Harvey out from Barchester. The arrangement of a provisional day was rat-
ified and when it arrived Lucy according to plan took
the pony cart down to the Red House, collected Mlle
Duchaux and drove her up to the Hall. At least not
quite to the Hall, for there was the question of the
pony, so Lucy stopped at the stables and asked her
guest if she would mind walking the rest of the way.
Mlle Duchaux got out and stood despising the pump
while Lucy hurled the pony into his loose box till next
wanted. Just then voices were heard on the steep staircase; Lettice and her daughters saying good-bye to
Miss Bunting who had been giving the children a little
light instruction. Miss Bunting came downstairs, and
Diana and Clare appeared at the nursery window
from which they hung, shrieking loving farewells.
Catching sight of their Aunt Lucy they screamed more
loudly than ever.

"Hullo!" shouted Lucy.

"Hullo!" shouted Diana and Clare.

Nurse then appeared behind them, smiled graciously at Lucy and told her young charges not to. Diana
and Clare disappeared with a final wave to Miss Bunting.

"Hullo, Bunny," said Lucy, hitting herself all over to
remove the pony's hairs. "We'll come up to the Hall
with you."

"I have the pleasure of meeting—?" said Mlle Duchaux.

"Oh, I'd forgotten you didn't know Bunny," said
Lucy. "This is Mlle Duchaux, the one she's staying
with the Harveys."

Mlle Duchaux assumed an expression which made it
quite clear that she did not like waiting by a pump,
that the children whoever they might happen to be
who shouted so loudly were very badly brought up,

that Lucy was not conversant with the rules of good society, and that it was impossible for her to speak to the person called "Bunny" without a formal introduction. All these shades passed unperceived by Lucy. Every one of these shades were appreciated by Miss Bunting, who remarked courteously, with an excellent English-French accent,

"Miss Bunting, ancienne institutrice dans la famille Marling."

Mlle Duchaux, the conventions now being satisfied, burst into a torrent of French, but though Miss Bunting was no mean French scholar she had no intention of hazarding herself before a rival governess and placidly answered in English, conversing affably with Lucy and the stranger all the way up to the Hall.

If we have given the impression that the two ex-governesses did not cotton to each other, that is exactly the impression we wished to create. Mlle Duchaux felt the natural contempt of a French governess, who had spent most of her life in England where the mere fact of her being a foreigner gave her a certain status, for an English governess who spoke rather good French. Miss Bunting felt the even more natural, though less plainly shown contempt of a first-rate English governess who had always taught in good families for a foreigner who would never know what really good families were. In Mlle Duchaux's silent criticism of Diana and Clare, and of Lucy, her truly British heart saw the ignorance and self-satisfaction of a nation which would always say Sir Smith and broadly speaking had neither the word home nor the word gentleman in its vernacular. Mlle Duchaux was in her turn more than aware of Miss Bunting's feeling of superiority, and the only person wholly at her ease was Lucy, who never noticed likes and dislikes unless people actually hit each other or said something outrageously rude.

"I'll tell you what, Bunny," said Lucy. "I haven't put the pony away properly in case I drive Frances and

Mlle Duchaux back, so why don't you come too, just for the drive."

"How do you call your pony?" said Mlle Duchaux.

"Oh, anyhow," said Lucy. "Oh, I see, you mean *what* do I call him. Well, I usually call him Pony, because his real name is Poniatowski. He was a Russian or something and it sounded a good sort of name for a pony.

"Polish," said Mlle Duchaux, unable to resist imparting information. "Quant à ces Polonais—mais passons outre. Stanislas Poniatowski was the last king of Poland."

"Stanislas Augustus," said Miss Bunting. "But of course it was he that you meant. It was his brother who joined with Napoleon in that unfortunate invasion of Russia."

These apparently innocent words had exactly the effect that Miss Bunting intended. Mlle Duchaux had for the moment confused the two Poniatowskis and could have exclaimed with the ballad-maker, "Earl Percy sees my fall," substituting of course Miss Bunting for Earl Percy. As for Miss Bunting's simple statement about Napoleon, Mlle Duchaux considered it a reflection upon the Emperor and a partisan attitude (as exemplified in the word unfortunate) towards the Russians, for whom, unless White Russians, she had no use at all.

"Unfortunate for Napoleon, I mean," Miss Bunting added, as they reached the back door of the Hall. "I think you will find your mother in the drawing-room, Lucy, where I will join you."

She went to her bedroom to set her little front of false hair to rights while Lucy took Mlle Duchaux upstairs. Mrs. Marling asked Mlle Duchaux how the Harveys were liking their house. Mlle Duchaux said they found it very comfortable though of course they regretted Norton Park. Before this interesting topic was quite exhausted Oliver and Miss Harvey came in as did Miss Bunting, who as usual sat on an upright chair at a slight distance from the party and surveyed them all impartially. Mlle Duchaux sat on a sofa with her very neat ankles and her rather short fat legs much in evidence, hoping that the nonchalance of her attitude would strike Miss Bunting, who however thought but poorly of it.

Oliver was in good spirits. The pain in his eyes which went and came regardless of times, seasons, weathers, food, spectacles or anything else, had elected to retire since Sunday and as usual he forgot that he had ever had it. The work at the office had been little but routine of late and in his many spare moments he had seen a great deal of Miss Harvey. He admitted to himself that since her coming the office had been far more amusing. Nice, hard-working and conscientious as the secretaries and typists were, he could not talk to them easily. Cinemas, the rationing of cosmetics, the disappearance of silk stockings, and new stitches for jumpers knitted with non-coupon wool appeared to be the limit of their conversational powers. They were quick, intelligent, obedient, ready to stay overtime whenever wanted, and Oliver marvelled, as many others have marvelled, at the gulf which was set between himself and his friends and what were at the present moment the actual pillars, if not the saviours of society. In Miss Harvey he found an assistant as quick, intelligent and obedient as the best and one with whom he could talk his own talk. If Miss Harvey pretended an interest in the seventeenth-century poets who were Oliver's private passion, she was only doing her duty as a pleasant woman. Whether Oliver was entirely deceived by her interest we cannot say. To discuss *The Worme of the Flesh and the Worme of the Spirit*, that rare metaphysical poem of Thos. Bohun, Canon of Barchester from 1657 to 1665, when he rashly made a journey to London to observe the effect of the Plague upon human bodies and never returned, was a very pleasant way of filling in spare time at the office. On that very morning Oliver, looking up something in the Barchester Public Library, had been met by the excited librarian with a volume of

Bohun's collected works which had been found
while sorting old books for salvage. How it had
got into the salvage, he could not say, unless it had
been by the zeal of his late woman assistant who had
instituted a private drive to replace 17th and 18th century sermons by contemporary communist literature.

"But I'm glad to say the A.T.S. have got her," said
the librarian, an enthusiast with a game leg left over
from the last war. "She came to see us yesterday looking like a sodden ginger pudding. You can take the
book, Marling, and keep it over the weekend. Then I'll
recatalogue it."

Oliver rapidly examined the volume and saw with a
leaping heart that at least two poems in it were unfa-
miliar to him. He put it in his pocket, finished his research, went to the office where he worked hard till
four o'clock and then drove Miss Harvey out to Marling.

The conversation at tea was almost embarrassingly
bilingual. The Marlings all spoke what may be called
County Family French and considered it a proper act
of courtesy to use the language of their guest when
addressing her. Miss Harvey, though she spoke quite
well, had a natural disinclination to make any mistakes
in front of her old governess who had a paralysing effect on her accent and syntax, so she kept to English,
throwing in a few words of French from time to time.
These she used when speaking to any of the Marlings.
They on the other hand had a fine English self-con-
sciousness about speaking in French to a compatriot
and preferred to answer Miss Harvey in their native
tongue. Mlle Duchaux, very much at her ease and very
much determined that her audience should realise it,
graciously spoke now the French of Touraine, which
as all of her pupils were sick of hearing was her native
province, now a highly colloquial and idiomatic form
of English which had the effect of making Oliver and
Lucy nearly have the giggles. Miss Bunting alone kept
her head. Knowing that she was perfect she simply
continued to sit bold upright at an awkward distance

from the tea-table and uphold the character and language of an English gentlewoman.

"Vous prenez du sucre, mademoiselle?" said Mrs. Marling pouring out tea.

"Je ne dis pas non," said Mlle Duchaux. "Ah! le bon sucre de France, combien je le regrette!"

She took two lumps.

"I am very sweet-tooth," she announced.

"One can always make up in quantity what one cannot get in quality," said Miss Bunting. "Lucy dear, pass the sandwiches to Mlle Duchaux."

"Je dois dire," said Mlle Duchaux taking two, "que votre margarine est infecte. Quand je pense au bon beurre qu'on avait en France, le beurre si frais, si délicieux—et dire qu'on se trouve forcé de manger cette espèce de graisse! Je veux bien prendre encore un sandwich, Miss Marling."

"It is so lucky," said Miss Harvey, "that we are having fairly good weather for Mlle Duchaux's visit. We have had tea out of doors twice."

"And frankly," said Mlle Duchaux, suddenly becoming English, "it was two times too much. Enough is as good as a feast of this climate. Je vais vous dire une chose, madame," she continued, interrupting Mrs. Marling who was talking to Oliver, "vous devriez installer des calorifères. Si vous aviez vu l'appartement de ma belle-soeur à Orléans, un si joli appartement, bien meublé, bien chauffé, the very last word in comfort, a snug little nest as you say. Votre château doit être froid comme tout, l'hiver. Take my advice, get your people to install central heating. It will not be expensive. I see you have quantities of trees in your property. Vous les ferez abattre, vous les brûlerez, un point c'est tout. Je veux bien prendre un de ces petits gâteaux, seulement pour l'essayer. Ce n'est pas comme nos gâteaux chez nous. Ah, les pâtisseries d'Orléans, they would make you lick your lips. The water comes into my mouth only to think of them. Enfin, il faut se résigner. Si vous m'offriez encore un gâteau—merci, mademoiselle Lucie. Il faut manager pour vivre."

"I hear," said Oliver politely, "that you are taking some kind of Government job, Mlle Duchaux. I hope it will be an interesting one."

"I have engaged myself as directress of an institution in which French ladies will work for their country," said Mlle Duchaux. "We shall organise, des thés, des dancings, enfin everything to give the French Tommy a rousing good time when he comes back on leave."

"Where does he come on leave from?" asked Lucy.

Everyone flung themselves into the breach and discussed some one thing, some another, chiefly hens, a subject on which Mlle Duchaux, not being strong on fowls, felt it better not to express an opinion, beyond remarking that there was nothing in England comparable with a bonne poularde de Bresse, and that no English cook could accommodate fowls as a French cook did.

Miss Bunting said aloud to herself that words which looked the same in both languages and had different meanings were a most interesting study. She herself, she said, learnt something nearly every day from the delightful dictionary of the late M. Chevalley whose death was such a loss to scholarship.

"Well, well, well," said Mr. Marling, coming heavily in and leaving the door open. "Havin' a hen-party, Amabel? I suppose you haven't kept some tea for me?"

"Papa dear," said Oliver getting up, "Frances has brought a friend, Mlle Duchaux, to tea. My father, Mlle Duchaux."

He shut the door and sat down again.

"And how are *you* mademoiselle," said Mr. Marling, letting himself down into his chair. "Enjoyin' our part of the world, eh? No Germans here, thank the Lord and hope there never will be. Nasty business about France, very nasty. I'm an old man now and I daresay my children will tell you I don't keep up to date, but the French are exactly like what they were in 'fourteen to 'eighteen. My regiment got badly let down by 'em in our sector. Well, my wife will show you the place. Not much to see now."

"I was just saying to Mrs. Marling," said Mlle Duchaux who was so startled by her host's Olde English manner that she did not, luckily, altogether follow his drift, "that you should install central heating here. I see your grounds are well wooded. You should have some trees felled to burn them and it would not cost you a half-penny."

Mr. Marling went purple in the face, but being of a courteous nature and trained to the sacredness of guests, he merely swallowed his tea at a gulp, heaved himself up again and saying he must go and look at a horse's legs, left the room without shutting the door.

"Mais il est tout à fait charmant, monsieur Marling," said Mlle Duchaux. "Ecoutez, monsieur Oliver, si vous vouliez bien fermer la porte—je ne peux pas m'habituer à vos courants d'air anglais. Oui, charmant. Il a tout à fait l'air d'un country gentleman."

This seemed so probable that Mrs. Marling could only murmur something apologetic about his being very busy.

Miss Harvey who was by now in a state of gibbering nerves at her old governess's behaviour got up and said they must go, as she believed Lucy was going to drive them back. Lucy said Bunny was coming too and she'd go and get the pony cart up from the stables.

"You can't all get into the pony cart," said Oliver. "Look here, Lucy, you drive Mlle Duchaux and Bunny, and I'll walk down with Frances—unless you are tired," he added.

Frances, who was not relishing the prospect of being a fourth at very close quarters in the pony cart, said the walk would do her good after her day in the office.

"I'll tell you what then," said Lucy, "we'll walk down to the stables and pick up the pony cart and Frances can come when she likes. Come on, Mlle Duchaux."

Mlle Duchaux embarked upon a fine arabesque of farewell, which from suggestions for a complete reconstruction of Marling Hall and the park, rose to a vigorous denunciation of English cooking.

"Mais je dois dire une chose," she said as she shook hands with Mrs. Marling, "vous mangez beaucoup trop en Angleterre, une nourriture excessive qui ne convient pas à ce temps de guerre. C'est un défaut de la race, je le sais, mais il me semble qu'à l'heure actuelle les Anglais pourraient et devraient se rendre compte de leurs défauts et tâcher de les corriger. C'est un crime contre l'humanité que les Anglais et les Américains se bourrent à leur aise pendant que mes compatriotes, si braves, si courageux, périssent de faim. Vous ne m'en voudrez pas de vous avoir parlé avec cette franchise toute française: nous sommes comme ça, nous autres."

Lucy said in a loud mutinous aside that the Free French at the Convalescent Home at Southbridge ate nothing but butter.

"Alors, c'est au revoir, n'est ce pas," said Mlle Duchaux ignoring or not hearing this protest, "et merci mille fois, màdame, de votre charmant accueil. Vos petits gâteaux ne sont pas mauvais: vous pourriez même dire à votre cuisinière de m'en envoyer, n'est ce pas. J'aime beaucoup les friandises."

Miss Bunting saying with great composure that they must not keep the pony waiting, led Mlle Duchaux from the room.

"I can't tip the pony cart over, or I might hurt Bunny," said Lucy darkly as she followed them.

Mrs. Marling and Oliver hardly dared to exchange looks for fear of hurting Miss Harvey's feelings, but she was only too ready to apologise for the behaviour of her old governess.

"Mlle Duchaux never used to be like that," she said. "I suppose it's very awful for French people now, and being Free seems to be so difficult. I'm sure she didn't *mean* to say anything, Mrs. Marling."

Mrs. Marling begged her not to feel responsible so kindly that she cheered up. Mrs. Marling then went to write letters for the District Nursing Committee and left her son and her guest alone. Miss Harvey said she ought to be getting back, so she and Oliver walked across the lawn towards the lime avenue which was a short cut to the village. The Double Summer Time light, which was so harsh at tea-time, was just beginning to soften as they strolled down the avenue towards the Rising. The late afternoon was calm, their steps matched, they felt no particular need to speak. When they reached the further end where a white gate leads to the footbridge across the little river, Oliver stopped and looked back at his home. Its dignified garden front was an eternal joy to him and he felt that his companion was sharing it.

"What a perfect home," said Miss Harvey in a low voice.

"I love it quite unreasonably," said Oliver. "I can't say that I was ever really unhappy at school or college, but I always had Marling in my mind, and however much I looked forward to coming home, it was never so good as the thing itself."

"When your father dies—forgive me—" said Miss Harvey, "I do hope you will be able to go on living here."

Oliver said he hoped that would not be for many years. He sank into a reverie, thinking of the place without his father and mother, trying to imagine Bill and his wife as master and mistress. Bill's wife, though not exactly his sort, was a thoroughly nice woman, well trained to a sense of family duty, and he felt quite certain that she would always have a bed for him. Probably that rather uncomfortable little room near the top of the back stair by the baize door into which hunting bachelors were occasionally thrust would be known as "Oliver's room" and the children would come and jump on him in bed or watch him shave if they were not too old by then. Too old by then: what a

way to put it, as if he were hoping his parents would
die next year, though at moments he wondered if his
father, confused and depressed in a rapidly changing
world where all he stood for was being battered and
undermined by friend and foe alike, would not be
rather glad to slip out of it; though he would do his
duty as long as he could stand or see or hear. He
sighed.

"Sad thoughts?" said Miss Harvey, with so exactly
the right tone of sympathetic yet discreet interest that
she was quite delighted with herself.

"Graves and worms and epitaphs," said Oliver lightly. "And talking of which, Frances, look what I have
got."

He took Bohun's book from his pocket and opened
it at the title page.

"The librarian at the Public Library rescued this
from the salvage," he said. "Do you see the date?"

"Sixteen sixty-five," said Miss Harvey, gazing at a
woodcut of the Rev. Thos. Bohun, M.A., with a skull
cap, gown and bands, and his nose rather out of drawing.

"That is to say," said Oliver, "two years later than
the recognised edition. And there are two poems in it
that have never been noticed in any criticism of Bohun's work."

"How marvellous!" breathed Miss Harvey.

"It is rather fascinating," said Oliver, "to think that
by some trick of fortune this is the only copy known to
be extant. He went up to London in the year of the
Plague and died there, and it is quite possible that in
the general fear and confusion his new book was lost or
burnt and this one copy, sent to some friend in Barchester, has survived. This poem, *To his Mistrefs, on
feeing fundrie Worme-caftes,* has probably never been
read until today."

He held the open book so that she could see it. Miss
Harvey, leaning towards him, looked at the yellowed
page with its elegant italics and long esses and read,

" 'As *Wormes* their *Bodies'* earthern *Images*
   Vpon the *grounde* (groundlings themfelves in-
     deede)
   Do voide, themfelves a *Father,* yet a *fonne:*
   So I, my *Body's* race through thine b'ing runne,
   Do void (nor can avoid) th'immortal *Feed—*'

I mean Seed," said Miss Harvey correcting herself,

" 'Making (with thine) our true *Effigies.*' "

She stopped.

"A very Bohun-like conceit," said Oliver. "One can take it as a type of the immortality of the soul, or of the body."

"Yes, yes," said Miss Harvey thoughtfully. "He means that worm-casts—"

She paused.

"Of course the body and the soul were eternally mingled in Bohun's metaphysics," said Oliver.

"Yes," said Miss Harvey, adding with an air of can-dour, "but I don't think I *quite* follow his argument."

"It seems to me clear enough," said Oliver. "The worm makes the worm-cast which though made of earth is the complete copy of itself. The lover, desiring to perpetuate himself, does so—"

He paused.

"Yes, I see the analogy," said Miss Harvey.

They both paused. It was the very dickens, Oliver reflected, that one could not examine a simple meta-physical poem by a respectable Canon of Barchester without feeling uncomfortable. He and Frances were rational beings, experienced in the world, used to liter-ature, but there was no doubt about it they were both shying away from the simple metaphysical poem. Re-gretfully he came to the conclusion that they were just too old to discuss this mingling of the sacred and pro-fane with real freedom. He could think of dozens of young people, round about his sister Lucy's age of twenty-five or so, who would thrash out the whole question of worm casts with academic interest and no feeling of constraint. Lucy herself would probably call it rot, which was of course an attitude. His parents would simply have read it, accepted it as a seventeenth-century poem and thought no more about it. But he and Frances stood between two generations and much as he had wished to discuss the poem in all its bearings he was forced to realise that it could not be done. With a spurt of rancour against the Canon who had brought this confusion on his mind, he shut the book and put it into his pocket.

As for Miss Harvey, she felt, not for the first time, how silly men were. Any child could understand the implications of the poem. She could think of dozens of intelligent women friends who would have analysed it word by word, laying full stress on its biological and psychological significance. But men were so apt to be squeamish. Still, she liked Oliver and if he were going to live at Marling, she did not shrink from considering that she might live at Marling too, for that would have been quite as squeamish. By a common impulse they walked on, across the footbridge and the water meadow, up by the allotments and so came into the village near the forge. Here they parted with a slightly clinging handclasp and a comfortable feeling that they would meet again at the office next day, and Oliver walked slowly back to the Hall.

At dinner there was a considerable amount of discussion about the tea-party. Lucy said Mlle Duchaux seemed to have enjoyed driving back in the pony cart and how funny it was that she had been driving two governesses in what used to be called the governess cart.

"Did you and Frances have a nice walk?" she asked Oliver.

Oliver said very nice.

"Oh, I forgot," said Lucy. "Mlle Duchaux says she has a nephew in the Free French and if he comes anywhere near here can he come and see us? So I said of course, only to telephone first. Was that all right, mother?"

"Yes, I suppose so," said her mother. "And will you ask Octavia to tell her mother that I would be very glad to have tea with her on Friday if it suits. I have a committee in Barchester that afternoon."

"I've got to go in too about the chickens' rations," said Lucy. "I'll tell you what, I'll ring Geoffrey up, he promised he'd let me see him at work in the office and you could come too. And I'll tell you what—"

"Je dois vous dire une chose," Miss Bunting quoted softly.

Lucy stared; then her face and neck crimsoned.

"Oh Bunny, you don't mean I'm like Mlle Duchaux," she said anxiously.

"Not a bit, Lucy dear," said the old governess, "but you do work your catchwords to death."

"I say, I *am* sorry," said Lucy with genuine and unforced contrition. "Why didn't you say before, like the time I always said 'definitely'? I've quite stopped that. I'll tell you what, I'll definitely try to remember—"

She stopped as her mother, her brother and Miss Bunting began to laugh and in a moment had wholeheartedly joined them. Mr. Marling said what on earth were they all laughing at and if no one would take the trouble to speak plainly no one could understand what they said.

CHAPTER SEVEN

OCTAVIA CRAWLEY, WHO THOUGH VERY DULL WAS RELI-
able, told her mother that Mrs. Marling and Lucy
would like to come to tea and Mrs. Crawley said that
would fit in very well as the Choristers' Parents' Club
meeting was not till half-past five, and she hoped Lettice would come too. On hearing this Lucy telephoned
to Mr. Harvey and instructed him to show her over the
Regional Commissioner's office after tea. Mr. Harvey
not having the presence of mind to say no said yes,
adding that it would be very nice if Lettice cared to
come too. Both these invitations were used by Lucy as
a battering ram to make her sister come, who in any
case liked Mrs. Crawley and was pleased at the idea
of seeing where Oliver worked; also Barchester was a
good central point where one might see people one
wanted to see. So on the Friday Lucy drove her mother
and sister into Barchester and delivered them at the
Deanery.

In the drawing-room, that fine room on the first
floor overlooking the Close, they found Mrs. Crawley

and Octavia who was having twenty-four hours off duty and looked as plain in her private clothes as she did in uniform, though not quite so shapeless. Mrs. Marling, who had not seen her for some time, asked after the Dean's ex-chaplain, Mr. Needham, to whom Octavia had been engaged since the beginning of the war.

"Oh, Tommy's very well," said Octavia with a faint air of animation. "He likes Iceland awfully. He saw a film in Reykjavik with Glamora Tudor in it. He wants to go to Russia."

"I hope he won't," said Mrs. Marling. "It will be so anxious for you."

"I wish *I* was going," said Octavia. "I've never had any proper frost-bite cases and I expect I'd get millions there, but that beast Matron says she couldn't spare me even if I was allowed to go."

"I didn't know nurses were being sent out," said Mrs. Marling.

A general conversation characterised by partial knowledge hovering on the verge of ignorance then took place, during which it was decided that no one knew if nurses were being sent or not, that if they were it was a shame, and it was a shame if they weren't. This conversation might have gone on for ever had not the Dean come in with Mrs. Morland, the novelist, who was a friend of everyone present.

"Laura, how nice!" said Mrs. Crawley.

"I was trying to get some tapioca, though quite in vain," said Mrs. Morland, "and I saw the Dean on the other side of the road so I went across. How are you, Mrs. Marling? Lettice dear; and Lucy; and Octavia. How is Tommy?"

"He's awfully well," said Octavia. "He saw an awfully good film at Reykjavik of Glamora Tudor. He wants to go to Russia. I think it's awfully mean, because he'll see all the frost-bite cases and I want frightfully to see some and no one knows if I could get there. People's hands and feet and faces are *ghastly*

when they've been frost-bitten and they often get gan-
grened."

Exhausted by this outburst she sank into a pleasant
reverie of a wardful of hideously mutilated patients.

Lettice enquired after Mrs. Morland's new book.

"Adrian Coates wants it by the New Year," said Mrs.
Morland in her tragedy voice, "so I am working practically night and day. Of course there may not be a New
Year at all, but one just goes on as if there would be. If
it weren't for the Russians I could manage."

And what, said the Dean, had the Russians done.

"Nothing," said Mrs. Morland. "At least I mean they
are wonderful of course, though it seems a little unreasonable to call them allies, because allies are people
that help one."

The Dean said laughingly that they all knew his devotion to the Finns, as indeed they did, for he had
talked of little else for the first year of the war owing
to having been on a cruise to the Capitals of Northern
Europe before the outbreak of hostilities; but in spite
of his deep, he might say his profound admiration for
that gallant little nation he could not, in his conscience, withhold an equal meed of admiration for their
quondam oppressors, now so magnificently holding
their own against the German hordes. And how, he
said, could any nation render greater help to a sister
nation than by holding in check the common foe.

"Yes, of course," said Mrs. Morland, always only too
ready to agree with anyone at the moment because she
so hated arguments which often made her hairpins
come out. "Of course it is really *heroic* of them to fight
for their liberty and burn everything and I am sure if
we had to burn Barchester we would think twice, but
what I mean is two people being attacked by the same
person doesn't make them allies. At least not if allies is
what I always think of it as, which is people who fly to
one another's help against anything, but they never
flew to our help about anything at all—when I say flying I don't mean aeroplanes of course."

The Dean said with a patient voice that our dear

Laura did not quite understand the principles which governed our alliance with the Soviet government. He who was not against us, if he might turn the phrase, was for us and—

"But Turkey isn't against us, and no one could say she was for us," said Lucy, who had no hairpins and rather liked arguments.

And, the Dean continued, there was no doubt that Russia, by her magnificent resistance, was doing more for us than any declared ally.

"I cannot forget," said Mrs. Morland, "who killed the Tsar and his wife and the poor little Tsarevitch and all those extremely good-looking girls."

The Dean so far forgot himself as to say rather crossly that we had beheaded Charles I.

"That," said Mrs. Morland majestically, "is exactly what I mean. Look how pleased everyone was when Cromwell died and Charles II came back. Cromwell must have been very like Hitler."

This snipe-flight from Russia to Germany disconcerted the Dean, who said huffily that the comparison was most unfortunate, as Cromwell was one of the most enlightened rulers England had known and look what had happened to the Stuarts only twenty-eight years after the Restoration.

"Seventy, eighty, eighty-eight," said Mrs. Morland counting on her fingers. "The flight of James II. But no one cut his head off. Besides I cannot bear Cromwell on account of that wart on his face which he could easily have done something about, though I'm not sure if wearing a chauffeur's cap like Stalin isn't just as bad. But then the Russians are eleven days behind us, aren't they."

The Dean kept an offended silence. Mrs. Crawley said she thought it was thirteen days by now and Mrs. Marling said hadn't they altered that, like our having Double Summer Time.

"I'll tell you what," said Lucy. "Let's look in the Encyclopaedia, Dr. Crawley."

"It's no good looking in father's Encylopaedia," said

Octavia, "because it has only got to where Dr. Livingstone hasn't been found yet."

"But Dr. Livingstone wasn't in Russia," said Mrs. Morland, perplexed but tenacious.

"No, in Africa," said Mrs. Crawley, who felt that as a Dean's wife she ought to intervene when missionaries were concerned.

The Dean said that Dr. Livingstone was beside the point.

Lettice, who had not yet felt called upon to speak, thought she had better say something calming and mentioned the Russian ballet.

"I wish," said Octavia, "that I could see a Russian ballet dancer's feet. They get in a ghastly state going about on tip-toe like that. If I went to Russia I might see some."

The Dean cast an unloving look on his unmarried daughter, and might even have spoken to her sharply, though it would have made no impression on her at all, but that the parlourmaid announced Mr. Leslie, and David came in.

"David, how nice!" said Mrs. Crawley, whose family when younger had been apt to chorus "how nice" when visitors arrived, so that their mother should not get it in first.

"I apologise for bursting in on you unannounced," said David, "or rather underannounced because your parlourmaid, though heaven knows I gave her my correct rank as His Majesty's Regulations command, is so anxious to show that she was once underparlourmaid at Rushwater that I wonder she didn't announce me as Mr. David, but hearing from a sure hand that two or three were to be gathered here—sorry Dr. Crawley—I thought I'd make it three or four. And hundreds of Marlings, fair fa' their sonsie faces."

His cousins greeted him and if Lettice looked a little confused no one noticed.

"But I am showing gross discourtesy," said David, looking at Mrs. Morland who, her colour heightened by her dialectical exercises, her hair escaping as usual from its pins, her hat at a decidedly unfashionable angle, sat looking like a second-class Sibyl.

"Oh, I am so sorry," said Mrs. Crawley. "One always takes it for granted that people know each other, though why they should I can't think. Laura, this is David Leslie. You ought to know Mrs. Morland's name, David, even if you haven't met her. You must have read her books."

"I don't see why at all. How do you do," said Mrs. Morland, who hated this form of introduction almost more than she hated the people who told her proudly how many friends they had lent her books to.

"Not Mrs. Morland who writes the books about Madame Koska's workshop!" said David. "I confess to my shame that I used not to be a reader of your books, but when I got into the Air Force I found the whole mess reading you and saw light."

Mrs. Morland was so pleased that two large brown hairpins fell out of her. David picked them up and restored them.

"Do they *really?*" said Mrs. Morland, who was never so surprised as when anyone liked her hardworking books.

"Word of one of our gallant airmen," said David. "And what is more I have one of your books, only a six-penny I admit, but the rank is but the guinea stamp, in my pocket. If you would write my name in it, the whole mess will be green with envy."

"Of course I will," said Mrs. Morland, her eyes beginning to brim with emotion and grabbling in her bag.

"If it is a pen, have mine," said David. "True I shall never be able to use it again owing to its hallowed association, but what of it? Sign please."

"What shall I say?" Mrs. Morland enquired earnestly. "I can't say 'David Leslie with love from Laura Morland', because I didn't give it to you. I know what."

She wrote something and handed the book to David with a pleased yet guilty look.

" 'I wish I had given this book to David Leslie,' " he

read. "A perfect inscription, Mrs. Morland. Do you always write that?"

Mrs. Morland had the grace to look slightly confused and said she sometimes did.

"Now I know you as well as if we had played together," said David, "and if I might have my pen back—. Thank you," he added as Mrs. Morland stopped putting it into her bag in her confusion. "And I can assure you that the daredevils of the air will toast you with a rousing cheer when I show them the book."

"We were having a very interesting talk about Russia just before you came in, David," said Mrs. Crawley.

"You can't have been," said David. "Not interesting. Ignorant possibly."

"It was jolly ignorant," said Lucy cheerfully. "The Dean and Mrs. Morland were having an argument about Russia and no one knew if they had stopped having Easter at the wrong time or not, but Dr. Crawley won't have a word against them."

The Dean said that Lucy exaggerated. None, he said, could admire the magnificent resistance of the Soviet more than he, but at the same time he could not but bear in mind, and the more especially since he had been privileged to tour the northern capitals of Europe just before the war, the undoubted oppressions exercised by the Russians in past years on a very gallant though unfortunately at the present moment misled little nation. He would, he said, deem himself a time-server were he to hold his peace on this subject. If one nation commanded our respect, that nation, whatever its subsequent deplorable and misguided policy, was the Finnish nation. All men of good will, he said, must needs think with him. Since the heroic ages no nation had compared with the Finns. Strong in purpose, lovers of truth and freedom, the Finns—

Mrs. Morland, who had kept her eyes shut in a very alarming way, suddenly opened them and said, "No," so loudly that the Dean, to everyone's relief, stopped.

"Why 'No'?" said David, voicing everyone's curiosity.

"I know," said Mrs. Morland, pushing her hair back with both hands in a very unbecoming way, "that I am not good at explaining, but one thing I can never forget, and that is my fur coat."

"None of us can," said David sympathetically. "But tell us some more."

"The winter before last," said Mrs. Morland, looking round dramatically, "when Finland was being gallant, and the Russians were making so much progress in spite of everyone fighting in white nightgowns in the snow, I let the Finns have my fur coat. To be quite truthful it was only my second best one, but I had paid three pounds to have it done up and there were years of wear in it and I *hated* parting with it. But I can't bear to think of people being cold, though I daresay Dr. Crawley would tell us that the Russians were cold too, only not gallant just then, so I did it up in a very large uncomfortable parcel, because you know how things like fur coats simply bulge out of everything, and sent it to the Finnish Relief Fund."

She paused for breath and David, who was enjoying himself hugely, said he hoped they had acknowledged it.

"They did," said Mrs. Morland impressively. "But no sooner had the Finns got my fur coat than they made peace with Russia. That is neither here nor there. If they wished to make peace that is entirely their own affair. But they had no business to take my fur coat under false pretences. If one gives people wedding presents and the marriage is broken off, they send the presents back."

"And your funeral baked fur coat Did coldly furnish forth the armistice table," said David.

"So I am very sorry," said Mrs. Morland, taking no notice of David's Hamlet-words, "but that is a thing I never can forgive. Being gallant is one thing, but taking my fur coat under false pretences is another and

though I may forget, for it is perfectly extraordinary
how one forgets things, forgive I never shall."

David was so enchanted by Mrs. Morland that he
would willingly have lingered at her side, but though
she thought he was a very pleasant young man, as indeed he was, her real wish was to talk to Mrs. Crawley
about grown-up things like servants and rationing.
The Dean had by now got into talk with Mrs. Marling
about a large Red Cross meeting at Barchester at
which he was to speak, so David was able to take his
cup of tea over to where his cousin Lettice was sitting
on a small sofa. The peculiarity of this sofa was that a
determined woman could fill it entirely or make room
for a companion. Mrs. Brandon had made good use of
both these possibilities at the big Deanery dinner
party in the first winter of the war and though she had
been assisted by the chiffon dress of floating scarves
that she was wearing, Lettice Watson, in a plain silk
dress and a light woollen coat, performed the same
miracle with apparent ease. As David approached she
appeared to fill the seat. By the time he reached her
she had shrunk into herself and left a space inviting
him to sit down.

When Lettice had heard of the invitation to tea with
Mrs. Crawley and the subsequent treat of going over
the Regional Commissioner's Office, she had as we
know accepted both. During the next few days not
very much happened. The children were rather trying,
she wasted five coupons on buying a pair of shoes that
she didn't really like, the Harveys were both on day
duty, Captain Barclay had been away for ten days on
a short course. More and more did her thoughts turn
to her Cousin David as an amuser or livener-up. What
she would have liked to do was to ring David up and
ask him to dine with her in her stable, but if she did
this she feared three things. David might be away in
which case she might have to leave a message with
Agnes Graham's butler and he might not bother to
ring her up when he came back; if he did come she

was not quite sure whether nurse would approve; and again if he did come she was perfectly sure that her mother, without any idea that she was intruding, would probably ask all about David's visit, and even suggest that he and Lettice should both come and dine at the Hall.

Lettice was angry with herself. David was her cousin and if she chose to ask him to dinner no one could say anything, certainly not Agnes's butler, certainly not nurse, though she could do a good deal by a terrifying reticence. Everyone knew that her mother always asked probing questions and expected circumstantial answers without the faintest wish to pry. But the fact remained that Lettice, a respectable widow nearer thirty than twenty, with an establishment and an income of her own, felt a diffidence for which she couldn't account at the thought of ringing up her cousin.

"It's idiotic," she said indignantly to herself. "You aren't in love with David and he isn't in love with you. And why on earth you don't ask him to dinner and have done with it, I can't think."

And so she had gone on wavering, sometimes going so far as to take the telephone receiver off, once actually asking for Agnes's number. She had then quietly hung up again but the Exchange, who knew her very well, kindly rang her up a few minutes later to say she was through to General Graham's. David was not in and she had to have a quite idiotic conversation with Agnes about the children, in the course of which Agnes mentioned that she was going to town on Thursday for the night. When she had rung off Lettice began to think and a little to dream. All through Wednesday she made up her mind and unmade it. On Thursday she was busy in the morning over Red Cross work with her mother and fully occupied in the afternoon with her daughters, for it was nurse's afternoon out and Miss Bunting who so often came to the rescue was helping at a Bring and Buy Sale in Southbridge. By the time she had bathed her little girls and put

them to bed she was very tired and depressed. Her
evening meal was tasteless and when her maid, who
was really quite a good cook, had cleared it away and
gone home, she sat alone without even the twilight to
soothe her, for Double Summer Time was still raging
far into the night. Life loomed before her as an eterni-
ty of looking after children and being alone in the evening. Roger was gone and nothing would bring him
back. She felt tears very close to the surface and got
up and walked angrily about, hitting her eyes with her
handkerchief.

Suddenly she could bear herself no longer. She took
off the receiver and asked for Agnes's number. While
the Southbridge exchange on which she was bandied
words with the Nutfield exchange to which Little Misfit belonged, she was able to change her mind a dozen
times and was just about to replace the receiver very
quietly, hoping, for such are the self-deceptive powers
of human nature, that the exchange would not notice,
when the voice of Agnes Graham's butler said this was
Nutfield 703.

"Oh, is that you, Parfitt?" said Lettice, in great confusion. "It's Mrs. Watson. I wonder if Mr. David is
in?"

Parfitt's voice asked her to wait a moment. She held
the receiver, listening eagerly, breathing rather fast
and wishing she had the courage to ring off.

"Hullo, love," said David's voice.

Her courage returned and she suddenly felt as light-
hearted as she had been miserable a few moments earlier.

"Hullo, David," she said. "I was frightfully bored to-
night, so I thought I'd talk to you. How are Agnes and
Cousin Emily?"

"Agnes has gone to London," said David. "My
adored mamma is writing her memoirs which I must
say consist chiefly of a great many odd bits of paper
with things written on them that she can't read. She
has got that nice Miss Merriman staying here that
used to be Aunt Edith Pomfret's secretary."

"How lovely," said Lettice. "And when does Agnes come back?"

"To-morrow afternoon," said David, "as too well I know, because I am under oath to fetch her from Barchester at 7.5."

"And mother and Lucy and I are having tea at the Deanery," said Lettice. "What a pity Agnes will be so late or we could all have met."

"Would you like us to have met?" said David.

Lettice was silent for an instant. Would David think her unmaidenly—ridiculous and inappropriate word—if she said yes? Could she bear to break her own heart, though preserving her dignity, by saying no?

"Because in that case," said David, apparently going on with his side of the conversation though Lettice felt that several hours had elapsed, "I shall, by a curious coincidence, also go to tea at the Deanery. After all, he christened me."

Lettice heard herself say that they were going on to see the Regional Commissioner's Office, so David mustn't be too late.

"That suits me down to the ground," said David. "I want to see John, and I can pin him down at the office. Give those delightful children of yours Uncle David's love and tell Bunny I never forget her. I must fly now. Good-bye, love. Matthew, Mark, Luke and John, Bless the bed that you lay on, Four corners to your bed, but this is really an unnecessary wish, for no bed I have ever seen had either less or more than four. Bless you, love, good-night."

"Tea-time then, at the Deanery," said Lettice, but the telephone was irresponsive.

She hung up the receiver and smiled. But even as she settled herself with a book doubts began to assail her. Evidently she had bored David or he would not have rung off. David must be so used to people ringing him up that one only made oneself cheap by doing it. David would now think that she was one of those women that were always ringing him up. Perhaps he would be so revolted that he would not come to the

Deanery. She longed to ring him up again and make
sure that he really understood it was tomorrow. Nothing on earth would induce her to ring him up again.
Oh, if only Roger would come and make it all right.
The mounting passion of tears brimmed over. No use
now to hit her eyes with her handkerchief, nothing for
it but a half blind search for more handkerchiefs, a
loud and undignified sniffing. She could not even
enjoy the luxury of crying in peace, for nurse might be
back at any moment and would see her bunged-up
eyes and swollen nose. In despair she decided to go to
bed and say she had a headache. Without more than
an occasional choke she undressed, went through all
the ritual of creaming and cleaning and was safely in
bed when the telephone rang and at the same moment
she heard nurse come in.

"Oh, please will you see what it is, nurse," she called
to nurse. "I forgot to switch the telephone through to
my room."

Maddeningly, nurse shut the drawing-room door.
Lettice strained her ears and could just hear nurse's
voice saying, "Hold on a minute, sir." Her heart leapt.
David had rung her up. She lifted the receiver of the
telephone by her bed.

"Is it you?" she said, her whole being concentrated
upon the voice that was to answer. "I hoped you
would ring up somehow."

"How very nice of you," said a man's voice, a very
kind, pleasant voice, not David's, though his was
pleasant enough (but was it kind?). Her heart rose,
turned and fell. David had not thought of her again.

"I hope I am not disturbing you so late," the voice
continued. "I only got back from the course to-night,
rather unexpectedly, and I wanted to know how you
were and your mother and Lucy."

"All very well, thank you," said Lettice. "Do come
and see us soon. Any time this week-end."

"Thank you very much," said the voice. "I have so
often thought of you and Diana and Clare. I mustn't

keep you up now. I'll certainly come over on Saturday
or Sunday. Take care of yourself. Good night."

Lettice lay back on her pillows. To expect David
and to find Captain Barclay was a blow. But her own
candour with herself compelled her to admit that if
David had rung up she would have been as disturbed
and distracted—whatever he had said—as she had
been when he rang off earlier. Her heart had sunk
when she heard Captain Barclay's voice indeed, but
undeniably her heart was much comforted now,
calmer, not making her cry.

Nurse looked in and said good night.

"I'll tell you what, my girl," said Lettice vindictively
to herself as soon as nurse had gone, "David isn't good
for you, so just get that into your head."

Grateful to Captain Barclay for having broken David's spell she went to sleep quite happily.

Next morning she woke with the rather holy feeling
that a good fit of crying often brings, a feeling as of
one who had shed the trammels of the flesh and now
floated, a beautiful disembodied spirit, above all
earthly emotions, which did not prevent her feeling
more and more nervous as the hour for tea at the
Deanery approached. Of two things she was quite certain: either David would not come, or if he did come
he would eschew her company. In consequence of this
she made but a poor figure in the interesting political
discussion which had been going on. Then David had
come in, the sun had shone, the birds (which were
two very tiresome seed-spitting budgerigars in the
Deanery back drawing-room) had sung, quite deafen-
ingly, and now David had come to sit beside her with
his cup of tea. She realised that she was like Finished
Coquettes in books who keep a seat next to them for
their admirers and break all hearts. Not that she
thought the Dean's heart was broken, for everyone
knew that his only human passion was hatred of his
bishop, and there were no other gentlemen present.

But David was there and to her own great relief she
suddenly felt quite normal again.

"I adored your ringing me up last night," said
David.

Lettice could not at the moment remember what the
Finished Coquette would say, so she smiled, which
David seemed to find quite satisfactory.

"I adore being rung up more than anything," he
said. "It is so exciting not to know who it is."

"Is it never exciting when you do know?" said Lettice, manfully striving to play her rôle, but before
David could answer, Mrs. Marling, swivelling herself
round, chair and all, made a third in the conversation,
asking after Lady Emily's health. Finished Coquettes,
Lettice thought rather bitterly, had boudoirs where
they could see people alone, and far from having
mothers who interrupted them in and out of season
they had confidantes who rose and silently left the
room murmuring an excuse, or soubrettes to whom
they said, "You may go, child; and if the Marquis
should call, I have the vapours."

"I ought to have gone to see Cousin Emily long
ago," said Mrs. Marling, "but one is so busy; and the
petrol. Will you give her my love, David, and ask if
she would like some of us to come over. It will depend
on my petrol, but I can manage somehow."

David said he knew his mother would love a visit,
and promised to ask Agnes to ring up about it. He
then began to lose interest in the tea-party. Lettice
saw that his thoughts were straying and mistakenly
blamed her mother in her mind. Luckily Lucy, who
had been holding her breath while the Dean said what
he had to say about the Future of Europe, seized an
instant's pause to say in a loud voice that it was time
to go to the Regional Commissioner's Office. Her
mother, with more tact, said to Mrs. Crawley that she
knew her Choristers' Parents' Meeting would be waiting for her and took her flock away, saying good-bye
to David.

"Oh, David," said Lettice, "didn't you want to see John?"

But David did not hear.

Lettice's heart was not in the least broken, but she got into the car with her mother and Lucy feeling that all occasions did conspire against her. She was far too apt to imagine the scenes of her life as she would like them to be and to feel disproportionate disappointment when they turned out to be as they were. Her lively fancy had pictured David taking her to the office in his car and a great deal of laughter and a spice of tenderness. It was now obvious that he had never seriously considered visiting the office and everything felt very flat. But she valiantly pulled herself together and by the time they arrived was ready to show interest in anything and everything.

The Regional Commissioner's Office, a very hideous building on the outskirts of Barchester, had been a Commercial College (if the expression means anything) which failed at the beginning of the war. It had then been taken over by the Government and now housed the organisation that was to run that part of England in case of a serious crisis. John Leslie had been appointed Regional Commissioner almost as soon as the scheme came into being. Under him a number of officials picked from various walks in life worked in shifts so that the office was fully staffed for the whole twenty-four hours. The shifts were arranged with dog watches as it were, so that no one had the same hours for more than a few days together, which was very practical as far as work was concerned but was apt to drive their various wives, housekeepers, parents and landladies almost demented. So far Mr. Harvey and his sister had mostly managed to get the same times on and off duty, which economised petrol. Oliver more often walked to Melicent Halt and went by train to Barchester while the weather was good.

The entrance was presided over by a policeman who knew the Marlings quite well, his parents being the estate cowman and his wife, so the party went in without any difficulty and sat on a very hard bench in a corridor while the policeman sent a boy scout to tell Oliver. After a short wait during which Lucy showed the scout with the aid of his scarf how to wring a hen's neck, for faithful to her practice of seeing how things were done, she had studied the technique of this useful art with Hilda, Oliver appeared and said Geoffrey would be busy for a few moments and would then join them. Meanwhile he suggested that they should come and see his room.

It is a curious fact that the mental impression one has formed of an unknown place is so immediately and completely overlaid by the sight of the actual place that it is practically impossible to remember what one had imagined. Mrs. Marling, Lettice and Lucy had each her own conception of what Oliver's room would be like, but as the door was opened each of these visions was wiped out, never to be recovered. What they did see was a very uninteresting-looking room, rather too tall for its size, with two ugly plate glass sash windows, a table, a desk and some chairs. Miss Harvey was seated at the table doing something that looked very professional with some papers.

"Don't let us disturb you, Frances," said Mrs. Marling. "What a nice room you have to work in."

"No, mamma dear," said Oliver. "Only a mother could call it that, and even a mother's partial eye must admit that it is quite hideous, besides looking out on to the gasworks and the soap factory and getting the benefit of the doubtless very healthy smells from them both. Geoffrey has a much more amusing room. Do sit down and he will be here in a moment."

"What exactly *is* a Regional Commissioner?" said Lucy. "I mean I know John is our one, but what exactly do you do?"

"I'm afraid I mustn't say exactly," said Oliver, "but broadly speaking if we were cut off from London by the railway being blown up and all the telephones being down and the wireless jammed, John would at

once become king of Barsetshire and the surrounding
counties and give us all our orders."

Mrs. Marling said it was very nice to feel that John
was at the head of things because his father had always done so much for the county.

"And that reminds me, Oliver," she said, "that David
says Cousin Emily would like us to go over. If I go
next week would you be free any day?"

Miss Harvey opened a drawer, took out a paper and
handed it to Oliver.

"I'm sorry, mamma dear," he said after looking at it,
"but my times are hopeless next week. You and Lettice
or Lucy will have to go; I simply can't. Where did you
see David?"

His sister Lucy said at the Deanery and she would
tell them what, the Dean talked an awful lot of rot and
Mrs. Morland was there and what exactly did Oliver
and Frances *do*.

"Well, most of it is fairly secret," said Oliver, "and
fairly important. Here," he said, opening a door and
showing them a small room, empty except for some
telephones, "are my special telephones that would be
very important if anything happened. I'm afraid I
can't tell you any more. This room used to be the
speed test room for the shorthand pupils when it was
a Commercial College."

"I thought you would be much busier," said Lucy
reproachfully. "More like a real office. I say, they're
going to have some Free French at the Barchester
General. Octavia told me at tea-time. I wonder what
colour they'll be."

It was so obvious to Oliver that his family's visit to
his room was an anti-climax and that the smallest
event of Marling life was of more interest than his files
and telephones that he had not the heart to ask his sister Lucy what she meant. To his great relief Mr. Harvey then came in and invited the whole party to come
and see his room.

Mr. Harvey's room gave far more satisfaction than
Oliver's. Not only was it much larger and not so high,

but it was in a semi-basement, its windows were
boarded up and it was entirely lit by electric light.
Several girls were knitting, some maps hung on the
wall, a kind of tape machine was ticking away by itself
in a corner. Mrs. Marling, recognising in one of the
knitters the girl who used to be at the pigeon-hole
marked G. to M. in the cashier's office at Pilchard's
Stores, entered into a most interesting conversation
with her about the probability of soap being rationed.

"How quiet you are here, Geoffrey," said Lettice. "It
doesn't feel like a war at all.

Mr. Harvey said this was usually a slack time.

"You might show them how the teleprinter works,"
said Oliver.

"If you think it would amuse them," said Mr. Harvey doubtingly. "You see, Lettice, there is a kind of
central organisation, and we are only an arm or a leg
of it, as it were, but if a crisis happens we bud off on
our own and become a centre ourselves. By the way,
Oliver, what a marvellous find that was of yours. Too
perfectly Bun, my dear. Frances told me."

"Bun?" said Oliver, who admitted to himself that he
was not up to Mr. Harvey's Bloomsburyisms.

"Your Canon of Barchester," said Mr. Harvey, turning his back on the teleprinter.

"Oh, Bohun," said Oliver.

"I think you'll find that his contemporaries called
him Bun," said Mr. Harvey.

"To rhyme with Donne," said Miss Harvey.

"But I don't admit Dun," said Oliver.

Lucy, who took an interest in intellectual conversation, said Mr. Miller at Pomfret Madrigal said Don,
because she had heard him because he had written a
book about him and, what did Geoffrey *do* in his
room?

"I mean, I don't want to ask questions about secrets," she said, "but I mean do you really *do* anything
or just sit here in case?"

Lettice looked anxiously at Lucy who was, she
thought, showing an embarrassing amount of interest.

For her own part she thought it was very interesting to see the office and the maps and telephones and machines, but she had a strong feeling that it was better for her not to know what they were about in case she suddenly met a German and told him all about it. And if one was to be perfectly truthful with oneself the machines and telephones and maps were really not very interesting. If something dreadful was happening like Buckingham Palace being blown up and all the secret telephones were being used and the machines pouring out yards of bad news on reels of paper and tidings of dismay being fixed with coloured flags all over the map, she felt her interest would rise. But to see Miss Cowshay from the cashier's office at Pilchard's and, as she suddenly realised, the exquisite creature called Amanda who used to be the receptionist, dreadful word, at Maidenhair, the best Barchester hairdresser's, sitting at a desk with things clamped over her ears, made her feel that it was all a kind of self-important game that Oliver and Geoffrey and Frances were playing.

There was rather a noise as Oliver was still arguing with Miss Harvey and her brother about Bun, and Lucy was asking questions, so that John and David Leslie came in without being noticed, except by Lettice, whose heart battered her so violently that she had to tell it quite contemptuously how confident she had been all along that David would come. John, who was as kind as could be, took charge of Lucy and explained everything to her while David approached Lettice.

"I hoped you would wait till I came," he said.

Lettice knew that any woman of spirit would say that she had not noticed whether he was there or not, but she also knew her own incapacity for putting a good face on her lies, so she smiled at him. Her smile was meant to convey that she cared not a whit about his movements, but it is rarely that our smiles look from the outside as they feel from the inside.

"What a pleasing anxious being you are," said David.

Lettice looked startled.

"You do worry, love," said David. "I may be a laggard in love, but I am not a dastard in war, and nothing would have induced me not to come here when you were coming. Look at old John teaching Lucy's young ideas how to shoot. You wouldn't believe it, Lettice, but it was I who got John married. He and Mary were so full of delicacy that they were quite paralytic and I more or less knocked their heads together. Lord! Lord! I can make happy endings for other people, but I can't make one for myself. And now I must go back to Little Misfit or Agnes will ask me how I could be so cross and naughty as to be late for dinner. Farewell, thou art just about the right dearness for my possessing. Give my love and good-bye to Cousin Amabel."

He picked up the end of Lettice's scarf, kissed it, waved his hand to the company in general and was gone.

"Mr. David Leslie *is* a nice gentleman," said Miss Cowshay with a simpering sigh. "I always say, Mrs. Marling, that Mr. David Leslie is quite my beau ideel of a gentleman."

Amanda said one could always tell a gentleman by the way he acted and Mr. David Leslie always acted like a gentleman, while another young female, the slave of the teleprinter, said he'd look lovely on the films. Lettice felt how true it was about people being sisters under their skin, but was glad on the whole that it didn't show outwardly.

As David had gone there seemed to be nothing to stay for and Lettice was quite glad when her mother finished talking to Miss Cowshay and summoned Lucy to drive them home. Oliver and the Harveys escorted them to the front door and then went back to their work.

"You didn't mind my telling Geoffrey about Bohun's poem, did you?" said Miss Harvey to Oliver.

"I thought you said Bun," said Oliver, in whom the episode still rankled.

"Only in front of Geoffrey," said Miss Harvey, with a downcast eye and sidelong glance which Oliver found very alluring.

"I don't mind in the least," he said, opening the door of his room for her.

"But I do, a little," said Miss Harvey, laying her fingers very lightly on his arm and withdrawing them swiftly. "It was amusing when Bohun was our secret. But I know I am silly."

It did occur to Oliver that if she wanted it to be a secret, telling it to her brother was not the best way of keeping it hidden, but he made every allowance, and did not begin his work again for an appreciable space of time.

At dinner Mr. Marling asked as usual what they had all been doing, and before anyone could answer gave them a very dull and detailed account of his own day, including a good deal of abuse of various fellers who had not seen eye to eye with him on various subjects. When he had grumbled himself out, his wife with her usual even humour said they had had a very nice tea at the Deanery and then a very interesting visit to the Regional Commissioner's Office.

"And whom do you think we saw there, William?" she said. "That nice girl, Miss Cowshay, who used to be in the cashier's office at Pilchard's. I always paid my bills to her and she used to cash cheques for me."

Mr. Marling said why couldn't they always have the beans cooked like that and what the deuce was a girl from Pilchard's doing in the Commissioner's Office.

"I told you, William, she is working there," said Mrs. Marling.

"Never said any such thing, my dear," said Mr. Marling. "Never mentioned a word about the girl workin' there, did she now, Miss Bunting?"

"Mrs. Marling did not mention it in so many words," said Miss Bunting, "there you are perfectly right. But I confess I understood her to mean that the girl worked there, or she would not have been there at all. Lucy dear, the water please."

"It was splendid, father," said Lucy. "John Leslie showed me everything. You know, everything that's happening everywhere in all sorts of secret ways, and the Barchester Fire Engines have to go as far as Badmouth if there's a raid. I'll tell you what, I'll see if Captain Grant at the Fire Station will let me do A.F.S. for a bit this autumn. I'd simply love to go down to Budmouth in a raid and help with the hose. And David was there but he was talking to Lettice. Oh mother, I'm sorry, I forgot to telephone to Octavia. I won't be a moment. It's about the Free French."

"Finish your coffee first, Lucy dear," said Miss Bunting, and Lucy, to her own great surprise, finished it.

"Amabel," said Mr. Marling when his younger daughter had bolted her coffee and gone to telephone, "Lettice is seeing quite a lot of young Leslie. No business of mine, but you're her mother. Don't want the child to be disappointed, you know. David's a good boy, but he and Lettice—wouldn't do."

To avoid any comment on his remarks he lighted a cigar and went away to his study.

"Why did William say that?" said Mrs. Marling, half to herself, half to Miss Bunting.

"Men often understand men better than women do," said Miss Bunting. "When Lady Griselda Palliser was running after Lord Humberton, before he married Miss Rivers of course, it was her father, the Duke of Omnium, who drew the Duchess's attention to it and events proved his Grace to be perfectly right. Lord Humberton was a good enough young man, but he could not be considered for Lady Griselda. The Duchess said to me afterwards, 'Bunny, I thought the Duke was making un unnecessary fuss, but I now see that he was perfectly right'."

"Well," said Mrs. Marling with her usual candour, "I must say I think William is making a quite unnecessary amount of fuss. And as for running after men, that is a thing Lettice has never done."

"Lettice has an excellent character," said Miss Bunting. "I know few of my pupils who are more what I would wish. But she is so retired as a rule that a small advance from her means more than all Lady Griselda's rather hoydenish way of pursuing Lord Humberton. She is too much alone."

"I daresay you are right," said Mrs. Marling. "It's all rather worrying. But I think you exaggerate, Bunny. After all, they are cousins. We might go through, that list of dressings for the Nutfield Hospital now."

Miss Bunting signified her acquiescence. But the thought of Lettice exposed to unhappiness remained with her and that night she dreamt her Dream about Hitler more clearly than usual.

CHAPTER EIGHT

It was a phenomenon well known to David Leslie's friends that from time to time, usually just when he appeared most settled, he would submerge as it were, and for a week or a fortnight or even a month or two, no one would know where he was. Then he would reappear, as charming as ever but quite silent about where he had been or what he had been doing. The truth, as he well knew himself, was that he feared boredom as he feared nothing else, and among the boring things of life he counted close human relationships. His mother, his sister Agnes, he adored and with them he felt safe. With all other human beings, however delightful they might be, however flattering their affection for him might be, he too quickly felt that he had had enough. Very often he left a wound behind by his rapid flight, but when he came back the scar was healed and no rancour was felt, because, as his sister-in-law had once remarked, he was so very Davidish. Had he possessed inner contentment, no one would have been happier.

Now, after cultivating the society of the Marlings and of his cousin Lettice in particular, he suddenly resented his own affection for them and felt he must be gone. A special job of work came his way and he vanished, with only an Air Ministry address for letters. This news reached the Marlings through Agnes Graham, who rang up about their proposed visit to her mother.

"Darling mamma so particularly wants you, cousin Amabel," she said, "because she is in great difficulties about writing her reminiscences and she says you are the only person who can tell her what year your father went in the Big Wheel at Earl's Court Exhibition."

Mrs. Marling asked why.

"I am sure," said Agnes's unruffled voice, "that I have not the faintest idea, but mamma has Lord Nutfield's name written on a piece of notepaper with Windsor Castle on it, so she thought you might know."

Mrs. Marling felt the faint bewilderment that so often overcame Lady Emily Leslie's friends when her ladyship began to explain anything, and to avoid fuller explanation told Agnes they would be delighted to come to tea and rang off, as she knew Agnes's powers of going on talking and wanted to write some letters before she went down to tea with Lettice.

The occasion was Clare Watson's fourth birthday which was being celebrated by a small party and a cake with four candles. The guests were originally Mrs. Marling and Miss Bunting. To them had been added Mlle Duchaux and Captain Barclay; the former from pure kindness as it was her last day with the Harveys and both of them were on duty and, we may say, had made but a half-hearted effort to change their hours, the latter also from pure kindness, because he appeared to like coming to Marling and to be rather unemployed at the moment.

Since the visit to the Regional Commissioner's Office and David's disappearance some time had passed. September was well into its last week and even Double Summer Time did not make the evenings last after

dinner. Lettice had missed David a good deal, but to
her own surprise and even relief she had not pined.
On the contrary, she had quite enjoyed herself. Captain Barclay had been to Marling for lunch, for tea, for
dinner, for the night, for tennis and for no particular
reason, and though Lettice did not feel with him the
pleasurable excitement, uncertainty and general unsat-
isfactoriness that she felt with David, she had found
him very agreeable company and had promised to go
and stay with his people in Yorkshire for a few days,
later in the autumn. Intricate though the ramifications
were, it had been established that, via the late Lord
Stoke, Captain Barclay was if not a relation at any rate
a distant connection by marriage, so everyone felt very
comfortable and called him Tom.

Lucy looked on his progress with an indulgent eye.
It was clearly understood in her mind at any rate that
he was her property, and this being so she was quite
happy to let him amuse himself with Lettice, or in any
other way he chose. As for staying with his people, she
would have refused the invitation at once, on the
grounds of having far too much to do at home and in
the neighbourhood and in general not wanting to:
which was perhaps why the invitation was not given.
For Captain Barclay's mother in Yorkshire, while delighted to ask Lettice Watson when her son suggested
it, saw no reason to ask Lucy Marling when he had not
suggested it. As for his sisters, if they had thought
about it at all they would have said the same, but as
they were busy being very efficient in war work and
all wore uniform, they naturally had a kindly contempt for a brother who was merely a professional soldier, and for any of his friends.

The auspicious day was marred by two contre-
temps. The first was that Clare was sick after breakfast
owing to emotion and the sight of her birthday cake
which nurse had rashly left in the kitchen where she
could see it; but she was none the worse and was considered to have acted on the whole in a way creditable
to human nature. The second and really bad misfor-

tune was that Mrs. Smith who had come up to the
Hall to ask if Mr. Marling would sign a legal paper for
her, met Mrs. Marling at the door just as she was leaving and walked down the drive with her. On hearing
where Mrs. Marling was going, or rather on ferreting
it out of her, she became so lachrymose on the subject
of her own loneliness and childlessness, that Mrs.
Marling, though she knew that Mrs. Smith had married at an age which made any chance of a family of
quite Sarah-like improbability, was weak enough to
say that she knew Lettice would be pleased if she
would come in for a moment. Lettice was not particularly pleased, but she realised her mother's position
and did not wish to make it more uncomfortable.
Moreover, the feeling, to which we have before alluded, of Mrs. Smith as a kind of vassal or dependant
having a claim on her courtesy was strong in her, so
she welcomed the unwelcome guest very kindly.

The tea-table was very well spread considering that
the war had been going on for more than two years. In
preparation for Clare's birthday nurse and the maid
had hoarded sugar, the Marling fowls had supplied
eggs, butter had been sent by various American
friends, and the result was a very unwarlike cake with
an iced top and CLARE written on it in pink. There
was also bread and real butter, honey sent by Captain
Barclay's mother from her own bees, various very
good little biscuits of oatmeal, Hovis flour and whole-
meal, confected by nurse who was a very good hand at
such delicacies in a trifling, lady-like amateur manner
that did not compromise her dignity, and as a special
treat some sandwiches filled with grated chocolate, the
gift of Lucy, who could not come till after tea because
she was driving convalescent soldiers from the Barchester General Hospital and had very nobly sacri-
ficed a slab of chocolate given to her by a grateful
Canadian sergeant.

When everything was in place nurse, bearing herself
high and disposedly, marshalled the company to their
seats. Captain Barclay was placed between Diana and

Clare, who had temporarily transferred their affections to him. Nurse who knew quite well that Mrs. Smith was a gate-crasher kept her next to herself, for she had gathered from Hilda that Mrs. Smith had a weakness for portable property and wished to keep an eye on her. The little girls were told to say their grace. Diana, who was rapidly approaching the age when to say one's grace in public becomes a shameful ordeal, looked rather sulky. Nurse said, Now then, we mustn't have any silliness with Miss Bunting here, which remark relegated Mlle Duchaux and Mrs. Smith to their proper place in a most satisfactory manner. Diana shut her eyes, put her hands together and said her grace in a very fat, complaining voice.

Clare, just because Diana had sulked, was seized by the spirit of showing that she was very good. Clasping her hands and screwing her eyes up till nothing but her long lashes could be seen, she hurriedly said some words in gibberish and opening her eyes looked round with an expression of sanctity. Lettice of course adored them both, each for her peculiar wickedness. Nurse while thoroughly disapproving chose to say nothing, silently daring Mrs. Smith and Mlle Duchaux to find any fault with her charges. The tension being now relaxed nurse began to pour out tea and Diana passed the bread and butter to Mrs. Smith.

"Just a morsel," said Mrs. Smith, "for I am never one for tea. Mr. Smith was just the same. What a sweet sight some little people are, Mrs. Watson. They remind me of those lovely lines of Victor Yugo's. I cannot exactly call them to mind but maddemersell would remember."

Mlle Duchaux, who hated being called mademoiselle like that more than anything in her life as a governess, said she regretted that she did not know to which lines Mrs. Smith was referring.

"One of those beautiful poems where Yugo is a grandfather, I think," said Mrs. Smith. "Something about Linnercence, the innocent child you know, having a palm in its hand, a palm-branch I should say."

" 'L'innocence au ciel tient la palme'," said Mlle Duchaux, unable to resist the opportunity of showing off.

"The very words!" exclaimed Mrs. Smith. "So *feeling*. And how does it go on? Ah, it comes back to me, 'Et sur la terre le hoquet'."

It did great credit to Mlle Duchaux that she did not betray the faintest emotion. Miss Bunting had an instant's indecision. Should she show by a slight twitch of the mouth that she fully appreciated Mrs. Smith's peculiar reading of the line, or should she sacrifice her own fair name and uphold the name of Britain by keeping Mlle Duchaux guessing. Her indecision lasted but a moment. Nor by look nor by sign did that admirable woman betray Mrs. Smith. She asked Captain Barclay if he would pass her a chocolate sandwich and spoke of the difficulty of getting plain chocolate in Barchester or in London.

Mrs. Smith said, Of course, we must keep every bit for the kiddies.

Clare, who had to nurse's scandal been feeding herself with both hands, suddenly remarked "Joggolate," and opened her mouth very wide to show that it was full of chocolate sandwich.

"Shut your mouth, Clare," said Miss Bunting. And we may remark here that no other woman in the world would nurse have allowed to give such an order to one of her own charges. Not that she minded the order itself so much, but that the order should be cheerfully and obediently obeyed was a great test of her self-control. There was an imperceptible pause while steel grated on steel. The opponents saluted and retired, each with greater respect for the other. "I cannot at all agree with you, Mrs. Smith," Miss Bunting resumed. "'There is far too much fuss about children now. Oranges and chocolate for children only! Rubbish! *My* pupils did not have such pampering. Lord Henry had a piece of chocolate after lunch on Sundays. And as for oranges, when I was young there *were* no oranges. They came in at Christmas, so sour that one could not possibly eat them without sugar and we had one occusionally for a treat and a tangerine of course in the toe of our Christmas stocking. I do not see that I am any the less robust. All this fuss about orange juice for babies is very undignified. If English children were intended to have oranges, doubtless Providence would have arranged for them to grow here."

"I must say I rather agree with you, Bunny," said Mrs. Marling. "We never got more than an after lunch piece of chocolate. And as for spinach, no natural child can stand it."

"But, Mrs. Marling, the kiddies need the vitamins," said Mrs. Smith.

"Show me a vitamin, Joyce, and I'll believe you," said Mrs. Marling. "People don't want vitamins, they want what they want."

"And to take oranges away from grown-ups who do want them and force children to have oranges when they want fish and chips!" said Miss Bunting.

Captain Barclay said he would rather have fish and chips any day and what about a Society for the Prevention of Cruelty to Adults?

Lettice, looking lovingly at her daughters, said she often thought herself of founding a Herod Society.

"What children need," said Mlle Duchaux, who had always found the frivolity of the English deeply shocking, "is good soup, though of course you others do not understand the art of making real soup. Give a French woman a bone and a crust and an onion and she will produce a nourishing and fortifying soup, fit for a king."

"I should think a bone and a crust is about all they have now, poor creatures," said Mrs. Smith. "And if they have an onion it is more than we have. Really one would think Someone we won't mention here had a spite against onions, such a bad year it's been."

The subject of onions was discussed in all its aspects while Mlle Duchaux ate with a steady purpose which, as Lettice said afterwards, made her think of Madame Defarge. Clare cut her cake by proxy, the proxy being her mother, and everyone had a little to wish her good luck. The children then said their after-tea grace and were removed to have their hands and faces sponged.

"I am so sorry," said Lettice. "Not smoking makes one forget, but I've got some here. Mlle Duchaux, will you have one? I'm afraid they're only Virginian."

"Merci, je ne fume point," said Mlle Duchaux with a clarity that would have won a round of applause at the Théâtre Français.

Miss Bunting, who occasionally indulged, immediately took one of Lettice's cigarettes and inhaled in a most dashing and devil-may-care way, pushing back her chair and crossing her elegant elderly legs, while she eyed Mlle Duchaux in a controlled but provocative way. Mrs. Smith murmured that Mr. Smith didn't like to see ladies smoking, but was quite a chimney himself.

Now the little girls, pink and clean, came back and threw themselves upon Captain Barclay.

"Bando," said Clare.

"She means piano," said Lettice with quite unjustifiable pride. "She wants her nursery rhymes. Would it bore you frightfully, Tom, if we had a few?"

Captain Barclay removed Diana and Clare from his legs and went over to the little piano. Nursery Rhymes, he said, were on the whole the governing principle of his life, and which ones did Lettice use? On seeing old copies of the *Baby's Opera* and the *Baby's Bouquet*, he exclaimed delightedly that he liked them better than anything in the world, and in all seriousness sat down and began to play some of the tunes, adding pleasing harmonies to the accompaniments which even their most nostalgic admirers cannot deny to be barren and unimaginative in the extreme. Clare wormed herself on to his knees. Lettice pulled up a chair and took Diana on her lap. Gradually the children were entirely ignored as the two grown-ups passed eagerly from page to page, Captain Barclay even providing like Mr. Frank Churchill a slight but correct second. Mrs. Marling and Miss Bunting let themselves go back in thought to so many childhoods in the old sheltered days. Mrs. Marling saw herself in the years before the new century, sitting on her mother's lap, hearing those same songs: she saw her elder children hearing them from her—Lucy had never cared for them. Miss Bunting had visions of one schoolroom after another, always with its well-used upright piano at which she used to play those songs for her younger charges till they escaped her and went to their prep. schools. Neither lady was over-given to sentiment, but each found herself in that uncomfortable predicament when one wants to wipe one's eyes and blow one's nose yet does not wish to be seen doing it.

"Did you ever know one called *The Silly Little Baa?*" said Captain Barclay to Lettice.

She turned over a heap of music and drew out a thin, long-shaped book of songs, worn with much use, which she opened and placed on the music stand.

"Diana and Clare both know it," said Lettice, taking the opportunity of coughing and we regret to say sniffing slightly.

"Come on then," said Captain Barclay.

" 'What do you think a silly little Baa
    Said one day to his mamma,
    I want to go away to those hills afar,"

sang Lettice and Diana and Clare. The story unrolled itself as the Baa, against all his mamma's advice, ran away by the bright moonlight, When the pretty little stars gave a pretty little light, And thought Oh how pleasant to be out at night, until he came to the dark, dark wood; And then oh, *how* he wished he had been good, For the cruel wolf nearly made him its food. Lettice's voice began to quaver perilously. Diana looked up at her mother and stopped singing. Captain Barclay went on; the shepherd kind and good Hastened away to the dark, dark wood And (with far too many words jammed together in one line after the best traditions of English poetry) saved the little lamb from being the cruel wolf's food.

"Now, it's all right," said Captain Barclay *sotto voce* with a side glance at Lettice, "Come on."

" 'Then the kind shepherd took up the little Baa,
Away from the wood where he'd wandered so far,
Back to the side of his own mamma
In the safe, safe fold where the little lambs are,' "

he sang, with hearty but inexpert help from Clare. Diana, overcome as she always was by the beauty and pathos of the song, burst into a fit of crying and hurled herself into her mother's arms. Lettice, equally overcome, tried hard not to show it, failed, and putting Diana down went precipitately into her bedroom. Mrs. Marling and Miss Bunting applied themselves to comforting Diana, which usefully hid their own emotion.

"Mais, qu'est ce qu'elle a, Mrs. Watson?" said Mlle Duchaux.

"Je pense qu'elle pense de son mari," said Mrs. Smith reproachfully. "Il était un marin, vous savez."

"Mais cette histoire d'une brebis égarée—ça n'a rien a faire avec la marine," said Mlle Duchaux with the inexorable logic of the French.

"Vous ne comprenez pas," said Mrs. Smith, enfolding herself in an aura of pitying Britishness against all foreigners.

By this time Diana was comforted, Lettice had come back quite restored, and Clare on Captain Barclay's knees was playing single notes with a fat finger, to her own deep satisfaction. Captain Barclay did not feel comfortable. Somehow he had made Lettice cry. That Diana should cry was natural, his sisters had cried when they were small and most of the little girls he had known were apt to cry for a moment if anything went wrong. But for Lettice to cry, Lettice whom he had always found so gently gay, so pleasant a companion, whom he always left with a warm feeling at his heart, was shattering. In fact, he thought, while he held Clare's finger to play the tune of *Three Blind Mice* and supplied a bass with his left hand, he was a

brute. There was probably something connected with
that song that struck a deep sacred chord in her. Perhaps her husband used to sing it to her when they
were engaged. But at this flight of fancy his sensible
mind pulled itself up short and he laughed, so that
Clare laughed too.

"Come here, Diana, and I'll tell you a story on the
piano about some giants and some dwarfs," he said, "if
Clare will sit still."

The story consisted of loud bangings in the bass
(giants), small twitterings in the treble (dwarfs), the
approach of the two parties, an awful scrimmage in
the middle of the piano in which Diana and Clare
joined with all their might, the withdrawal of the com-
batants *glissando*, and finally sleepy twitterings in the
treble and peaceful grumblings in the bass. The little
girls shrieked with joy and begged for it again, but
Captain Barclay, scattering them right and left, suddenly turned into a grown-up again. Lucy came in
from driving her convalescents and after eating a large
slice of birthday cake said she would drive Mlle Duchaux and Mrs. Smith back as she wanted to ask Hilda
about killing ducks and if you killed them the same
way as hens. Tom, she added, could come too. Captain
Barclay did not want to come too. He wanted if possible to have a word with Lettice and make some kind
of apology. But Lucy was not a person one could dis-
obey and he could think of no plausible, nor indeed
any courteous excuse. So he said good-bye to all his
hostesses, dropped his gloves behind the radiator in
the hall and followed Lucy downstairs. That strong-
minded young woman opened both the doors of the
back seat and saying to Mlle Duchaux and Mrs. Smith,
"Get in one each side," ordered Captain Barclay to sit
by her in front. The journey was soon over. Mlle Duchaux was dropped at the Red House, and Mrs. Smith,
with embarrassing humility, said she would get out
there as she knew Miss Marling had so many calls on
her petrol. In vain did Lucy point out that by going
round the village green, which she meant to do in any

case to avoid turning the car in the narrow bit of road outside the Harveys, she would pass Mrs. Cox's door. Mrs. Smith again protested. Lucy was not one to waste words, so she said All right, started her car violently and asked Captain Barclay where he had left his car because she hadn't seen it in the stable yard. Captain Barclay said quite right, he had left it up at the Hall, but he couldn't find his gloves and had a kind of inner conviction that he must have left them at Lettice's, so she would drop him there.

"I expect they're in your car all the time," said Lucy.

Captain Barclay said he remembered having them as he walked down the drive.

"Well then, you go up and see if they're there," said Lucy, "and I'll wait for you and run you up to the Hall."

"No," said Captain Barclay firmly. "I'm sure they're at Lettice's. I'll tell you what, you drop me there and then you can go on and look in my car. If you don't come back I'll know they aren't there."

He noticed with a faint irritation that it was he who had told Lucy what and not she who had told him and wondered if his disingenuous suggestion would convince Lucy. Apparently it did, for she nodded and, whisking the car in a masterly way round the green, turned in at the gate at the bottom of the hill.

"Good-bye," said Mlle Duchaux, extending her well-gloved hand to Mrs. Smith outside the gate of the Red House.

"Au revaw but not good-bye, we hope," said Mrs. Smith, making no effort to take the offered hand, "but I am just going to pop in for a moment to see how the dear garden is. You can't think how I miss my little garden, and having to buy vegetables is dreadful. Ever since I married Mr. Smith I have had a little bit of garden and now with things the price they are—but I always say we have much to be thankful for, so I'll just pop along and have a look."

With which words she edged past Mlle Duchaux,

skirted the pond and made for the little kitchen garden. Here Mr. Harvey, in grey flannel trousers, a yellow pull-over, and bare feet in sandals, was picking
some late beans in a very dilettante way with his back
to her. A basket was on the path nearby.

"Quite a stranger, Mr. Harvey," said Mrs. Smith.

Mr. Harvey turned round and nearly dropped a
handful of beans.

"Quite a start it gave me to see you there," said Mrs.
Smith. "Many's the time I used to come down the garden from the house when I'd been helping the girl to
get the supper, to tell Mr. Smith we were just dishing
up. He had quite a fancy for beans and liked to pick
those runners himself. Gentlemen have their ways."

"I'm not really so very keen on picking beans," said
Mr. Harvey, anxiously disclaiming any point of affinity with the late Mr. Smith. "Hilda wanted some and
my sister wanted to write some letters, so I thought I
might as well go."

"Ah, you may put it on them, but it's really your
own kind heart," said Mrs. Smith. "Mr. Smith was just
such another one. Kindness was his motto as you
might say."

Mr. Harvey said he was sure it was and threw his
beans at the basket. Some went in and some again did
not.

Mrs. Smith, remarking that Mr. Smith though fond
of gardening was quite awkward with his hands,
picked up the beans, put them in his basket, and to
Mr. Harvey's great terror stepped on to the bean
patch, where she walked along the other side of the
row that Mr. Harvey was picking, sometimes culling a
few herself, sometimes pushing the basket at him so
that he might drop his beans in it. In vain did he suggest that she must be tired. Mrs. Smith said with very
beautiful resignation that she was always fatigued but
tried not to think of Self. By this time they had got to
the far end of the bean row and Mr. Harvey, emerging
from his tendrilled prison, thanked Mrs. Smith for her
help and said Hilda would be waiting for the beans.

Accordingly they set out homewards, Mrs. Smith carefully holding the basket on the side away from her companion and ignoring his offer to carry it. Where the little path to the back door branched off behind the laurel hedge Mr. Harvey tried to stop, but as Mrs. Smith walked on he unwillingly followed her. At the lily pond she paused.

"Do you know, Mr. Harvey," she said, raising her large, sad eyes to her tenant in a way that made him feel like mud, "those dear dwarfs were Mr. Smith's last purchase before he passed over. We had been to the afternoon session at the Barchester Odeon and he was so taken by Snow-white that he went straight to Pilchard's next day and bought these statues as a kind of souvenir. True it is that he was not quite himself when he bought them, owing to something at supper with some gentlemen friends after the pictures that didn't agree with him, but once having bought them he was quite taken with them as you might say. When I thought of going to Torquay my one real regret was the dwarfs."

Mr. Harvey heard himself saying that the dwarfs would not run away and blanched at the effect his landlady's conversation was having upon his conversational style.

"But someone might run away with them," said Mrs. Smith in what Mr. Harvey to his horror realised to be an arch manner. "I sometimes feel I could just pop one of them under my arm and carry him off. Just for auld lang syne."

Mr. Harvey by this time would gladly have put all the dwarfs into the wheelbarrow and taken them over to Mrs. Cox's if by so doing he could have got rid of his landlady. They had now reached the garden gate and he was just about to open it, his hand was indeed on the latch, when Mrs. Smith laid her rather predatory and dry-skinned hand with its wide wedding ring on his.

"Pardon *me*," she said tragically. "I know I am very foolish, but I like to feel that I can open and shut this dear little gate myself. You must excuse me if I say, Mr. Harvey, that being able to pop over and see my little home whenever I like has been quite a comfort."

Mr. Harvey, alarmedly conscious of his hand imprisoned under hers, said, Oh, not at all.

"You do not know, Mr. Harvey," said Mrs. Smith, releasing him as she opened the gate, "what it is to be a widow. It quite does me good to see my little home with a man about it, so if I pop in and out you must just take no notice at all. I shall just creep in like a mouse, and if you and Miss Harvey are doing anything literary I shall take what I want quite quietly and run away again."

With a smile that froze Mr. Harvey to the marrow and a look of her fine ravaged eyes, she made off across the green. Mr. Harvey went into the house and was just going upstairs when Hilda came out of the kitchen.

"Where's my beans, Mr. Geoffrey?" she said. "Beans don't string themselves and they aren't as young as they was."

Mr. Harvey looked round helplessly.

"I think Mrs. Smith must have taken them by mistake," he said.

Hilda looked at him, went back into her kitchen and slammed the door with such violence that Miss Harvey looked out of her bedroom.

"I suppose Hilda is upset because you let Mrs. Smith have the beans," she said coldly. "I saw you from my window. Really, Geoffrey, you are too feeble for words."

"I couldn't help it," said her brother, too wretched to push back his lock which hung damply over one eye.

"Help it!" said Miss Harvey with the impatient contempt of an elder sister for a younger brother. "If she asked you to marry her you'd be too feeble to say no. If there aren't any beans we can't have them. Don't be too long with the bath."

Mr. Harvey vengefully turned on a very deep, hot

bath. If Frances chose to treat him as a child he could
at least keep her out of the bathroom; a puerile revenge it was true, but a satisfactory one. As he lay in
the steaming water, the hot tap running and so depriv-
ing factories, railway engines, warships and canteens
of the fuel necessary to their existence, he was suddenly transfixed by a thought of horror. When his sister
talked of Mrs. Smith wanting to marry him had she
meant anything? He knew that she hadn't; it was
merely an outburst of temper such as life with Frances
had accustomed him to. Yet it made him uncomfortable, so uncomfortable that he tried to turn off the hot
water with his toes, swore with agony and got out of
the bath. Dinner was accompanied by silent hatred
from Hilda, a certain amount of nagging from his sister and the clearly expressed and unfavourable opinions of Mlle Duchaux on Miss Bunting, so that Mr.
Harvey heartily wished the war were over and he
were back in Whitehall.

Lucy decanted Captain Barclay in the stable yard and
agreeable to her promise went on to the Hall to see if
his gloves were in his car. In normal times, her kind
heart would have prompted her to drive his car down
to the stables for him, but he had very properly left it
locked, so she looked through the windows but could
not see any gloves. Her father came up at that moment
and talked with her about some ploughing, then she
had to go to the kitchen to fetch two eggs for Ed's
mother who had been unwell and by this time it was
so late that she decided to drive down to the stables,
leave the eggs with Ed who always lingered there as
long as possible, and kindly drive Captain Barclay up
to the Hall.

Captain Barclay went up the steep stair with a faint
but unmistakable pounding of his heart and rang the
bell. The maid had run down to see her mother before
supper and nurse was putting the children to bed, so
the door was opened by Lettice, who said, "Oh."

This word may be interpreted in various ways. It certainly did not sound hostile, and as Lettice stood aside for him to enter the little hall he took it as kindly meant.

"No one ever rings, they just come straight in," said Lettice, "so I couldn't imagine who it was."

"I thought I might have left my gloves here," said Captain Barclay.

Lettice said that she didn't think any gloves had been seen, but if he would come in she would ask nurse. She came back in a moment with the news that nurse knew nothing of them.

"But you must have left them *somewhere*," said Lettice earnestly. "Do you think you had them when you came?"

Captain Barclay said with great truth that he was perfectly sure he had them when he came and how extraordinary it was that things got mislaid just when one wanted them. Lettice said when one particularly wanted things they had a way of vanishing, and turned over several sofa cushions. Captain Barclay, with a sense of guilt tempered with elation, looked behind the piano.

"I am terribly sorry," said Lettice anxiously.

"Too stupid of me," said Captain Barclay. "By the way, I hope Diana wasn't really upset by the *Silly Little Baa*. It's certainly an awfully sad song and I felt rather a brute when she began to cry."

"Oh, she always cries at that," said Lettice. "So do I."

At these simple words a great weight was lifted from Captain Barclay's soul.

"And we both rather enjoy crying," Lettice added.

This confession seemed to Captain Barclay so rare and beautiful that he had nothing to say.

"It is funny," Lettice continued, half to herself, "how agreeable crying can be when there is really nothing to cry about; and it doesn't make one so hideous. But if you are really miserable and try not to cry you get all choked, and then when it comes unchoked

it is quite dreadful and one can't stop and one looks all
swollen and disgusting."

Captain Barclay looked at her most sympathetically,
but still found nothing to say.

"I am so very sorry about your gloves," Lettice said,
suddenly becoming the hostess again.

"I'm sure I'll find them somewhere," said Captain
Barclay, more or less truthfully.

Lettice began to move cushions again, to feel down
the back of the sofa, to look in such improbable places
as the inside of the upright piano. Captain Barclay
could bear her misguided efforts no longer. She was
tiring herself by her fruitless searching and the fault
was his.

"I'm awfully sorry, Lettice," he said, "but I left my
gloves in the hall."

"Are you sure?" said Lettice. "They weren't there
when you came in just now. At least I didn't see them."

She went towards the door. To see her thus abasing
herself to menial tasks (for so Captain Barclay more
or less put it to himself, though not exactly in those
words) for his sake, for the sake of a deliberate and
black-souled liar, was too much for him. He strode
across the room and got hold of the door handle before she could touch it.

"They are behind the radiator in the hall," he said,
with simple nobility.

"Have you just remembered?" said his hostess with
interest. "Let me look."

"Well, as a matter of fact," said Captain Barclay, de-
scending from his noble altitudes and opening the
door, "I put them there on purpose. Here they are, if
you don't believe me." And so saying he reached down
behind the radiator and fished up his gloves, with
small bits of fluff and flue sticking to them.

"Oh dear!" said Lettice distressed. "I am *always* telling May she must dust behind the radiator."

She stood with her head a little on one side thinking. Captain Barclay's last words seemed to her singularly devoid of sense. Why the fact of their being be-

hind the radiator should prove that he had put them
there she didn't see. And even if he had, why he
should put his gloves in such a silly and, most regrettably, such a dusty place she could not think, when
suddenly a thought came into her mind that made her
feel as if she were blushing.

"Do you mean you dropped them there on purpose,
Tom?" she said, as a quite new light on the affair.

"Absolutely on purpose," said Captain Barclay, observing with slight nervousness her rising colour and
wondering how angry she was.

This interesting conversation then stopped dead
while its owners stood tongue-tied.

"The fact is," said Captain Barclay in a rather rough
voice which he did not recognise as his own, so that he
had to stop, clear his throat and start again. "The fact
is I frightfully wanted to tell you how frightfully sorry
I was about making Diana cry, but there were too
many people about and Lucy wanted me to go down
to the village with her. So I chucked my gloves behind
the radiator to make an excuse for coming back."

"How very nice of you," said Lettice earnestly. "But
Diana wasn't really unhappy. She was only enjoying
being unhappy."

Captain Barclay would have liked to shake Lettice.
After quite a quarter of an hour's argle-bargling they
were just where they had started.

"It doesn't really matter about Diana," he said with
the calm of desperation. "It's you that it matters about.
I can't bear having seen you cry. If I was thoughtless,
if I hit on a song that hurt you, something your husband liked perhaps, or—"

"Oh, Tom! how dear of you!" said Lettice, at last
grasping his drift, "I think it is the nicest thought anyone has ever had of me. No, no, nothing to do with
Roger. I have always cried all my life at the *Silly Little Baa*. Roger used to laugh at me for it, and really I
laugh at myself."

"Are you sure?" said Captain Barclay, still suspi-
cious.

"Quite sure," said Lettice. "Dear Tom, don't think me very horrid, but there is practically nothing that makes me unhappy now about Roger. It used to be quite dreadful, but you now one does get used to things."

Her voice sounded infinitely touching to her guest. He said nothing, for a true instinct made him aware that she was lightening her soul of some burden and his part was to stand by.

"You know," she continued, looking very hard at a point on the wall a little to the right of Captain Barclay, "it isn't Roger himself that I miss so much now, and I know it sounds heartless, but it just happens to be the truth, as having a man about the house. Not anyone special, but just to smell a pipe in a room, or Harris tweed in the hall, or to feel that someone else ought to have the *Times* first; just idiotic things. I'm sorry. I didn't meant to talk about myself. Don't hate me. It's difficult enough to know if one is being truthful or only enjoying letting go. I really am being truthful, but I have enjoyed letting go too."

Captain Barclay could find nothing better to say than that it was absolutely all right, so he said it with conviction, adding that he must go at once or he would be late.

"Your gloves," said Lettice, picking them up from the radiator where he had laid them. "Or do you want to put them down behind the radiator again?"

"Yes," said Captain Barclay.

And with such emphasis did he say it that the image of David Leslie might have been driven from Lettice's mind for good, if at that moment Lucy had not come banging up the stairs and banged into the flat.

"Come on, Tom," she said. "I'll drive you back to your car. It's frightfully late."

Captain Barclay could not push Lucy downstairs, so he laughed and thanked her. Lettice fully realised that Tom was Lucy's property, so she did not attempt to keep him. For a mad instant she thought of dropping his gloves behind the radiator again. Then her upbringing told her that though it would be amusing, though Captain Barclay would at once understand the signal, though it would mean another visit and possibly the fun of talking about oneself again, that it could not be done, because a lady would not do it. So she said good-bye. Lucy clattered down the stairs and Captain Barclay followed her. Lettice shut the door and went to say good night to her daughters.

CHAPTER NINE

WE WILL NOW TRANSPORT OURSELVES TO HOLDINGS, THE gentlemanly residence of Major-General Robert Graham, C.B., at Little Misfit. Commodious and comfortable, built by his great-grandfather in the Regency Stucco era, it was under Agnes Graham's rule a warm and scented abode of peace, with children prettily seen and pleasantly heard at the right times, and incredibly an almost pre-war staff, although of peculiar middle age or extreme youth. Here Agnes, whose husband was at present in the War Office, was housing her father Mr. Leslie and her mother Lady Emily Leslie. Mr. Leslie, who had been very ill just before the beginning of the war and to his great fury forbidden to ride or to walk much, had driven his wife and family nearly mad by insisting on doing both and collapsing. So Agnes, as we already know, had taken advantage of a visit that her parents were paying her to keep them both under her soft wing. Mr. Leslie grumbled a good deal, but Agnes only said, "Poor darling papa," looking at him with doves' eyes. Rushwater, under the care of John Leslie, Mary Leslie and the agent Macpherson, was well looked after and every few weeks Mr. Leslie was driven over to pay a state call, inspect the place, find fault, say it was high time he was dead, and come back to tell his wife how well John was doing.

Sweet and even as Agnes's temper was, we must admit that without the providential coming of Miss Merriman she might have found her beloved mamma mildly speaking a handful. Miss Merriman, as all that part of the county knew, had been the perfect companion for some years to the late Countess of Pomfret. At Pomfret Towers, at the Casa Strelsa in Florence, in the London house, she had exercised unswerving and equable rule over servants English and foreign, kept the accounts, answered the letters, seen that incoming and outgoing guests were provided with the right trains and cars, arranged the allotment of bedrooms and places at dinner, talked with the same calm to prime ministers, fox-hunting neighbours, or pert nieces, been perfectly friendly to everyone, yet kept an invisible barrier between herself and the world. She was Merry to all the Pomfrets' friends, yet no one used and few knew her Christian name. To any advances she opposed a courteous steeliness that had never been broken. When old Lord Pomfret's heir, his distant cousin young Mr. Foster had come to live at the Towers, she had come to care for him very deeply but had schooled herself to remember that there were fifteen years between them and he was the heir to an earldom, and when he married Sally Wicklow, the agent's sister, none was more unfeignedly sincere in her congratulations than Miss Merriman.

Her countess's death was a blow that she felt none the less because it was not unexpected. She mourned her with the same silent fidelity that had gone to her feeling for Gillie Foster. A legacy from the countess together with her own means made her sufficiently independent, and for a time she lived with a sister. But Lady Pomfret's friends all remembered her and wanted her and by degrees she became a kind of visiting

secretary to a large circle of titled or county families.
It was while she was in Shropshire with Lady Harber-
ton, formerly Phoebe Rivers and a niece of Lord Pomfret, helping her with a large christening party, that
Mr. Leslie had fallen ill. Agnes Graham had invoked
her aid to keep Lady Emily company at Rushwater
and when she transported her parents to Holdings
Miss Merriman had come too and appeared likely to
remain for the present. The late Lord Pomfret had
been Lady Emily's brother, so there was much common ground. Miss Merriman after a week of quiet observation, had taken the measure of her entrancing,
wilful and maddening new employer and was now
able, much to Agnes's relief, to circumvent her in most
of her meddlesome and impracticable schemes: for her
ladyship, though much lamer of late and often in pain,
had not abated a whit of her brilliant and many-facet-
ed outbursts whether into society, painting, literature,
the church, the village, or war activities.

When war broke out, shortly after the Leslies had
gone to Holdings and it had been decided that they
should not for the present go back to Rushwater, Lady
Emily had conceived a scheme for brightening the
blackout by stencilling bright designs of her own creation on all the black curtains and frames that were
hurriedly being put up. Agnes had made over to her
mother two large rooms on the ground floor as bedroom and sitting-room. Here Miss Merriman under
Lady Emily's directions, had cut holes in pieces of card-
board to make stencils and had driven her ladyship into
Barchester to lay in a store of bright paints and large
stiff brushes, also to buy the very largest kitchen table
at Messrs. Pilchard's to serve as a work table.

Her ladyship then added to the distractions of war
by insisting on a personal expedition to all the servants' bedrooms, the better to decide what kind of colour design would suit each member of the staff. Even
Agnes blenched at the thought of intruding upon the
awful vastness of the cook's bedroom and the kitchen
maid's Regency garret, but Miss Merriman unpertur-

bedly accompanied her employer up the steep stairs
that led to the servants' quarters, low rooms on the top
floor behind elegant little pilasters which considerably
obstructed the view, and stood by while Lady Emily
indulged in detailed examination of such fascinating
objects as the cook's blue sateen nightgown case and
the kitchen maid's collection of threepenny novelettes.
Only one room remained a mystery to her ladyship,
the room belonging to her French maid, Conque,
whom she had brought with her from Rushwater.
Conque, who mistrusted all her fellow servants, had
during forty years' service in England always carried
the key of her bedroom about with her and as she was
never known to have been ill, no one had ever obtained access to her room. Her ladyship was therefore
not able to decide what design would be most suitable, and when Conque under great pressure brought
her the black curtains that she had sewn and put up
herself, Lady Emily emblazoned them with her ver-
sion of a Gallic cock and the Cross of Lorraine—to the
great annoyance of Conque, who was a devout though
completely unpractising Catholic and complained that
the double cross n'avait pas de sens commun. "Et
quant au Saint-Esprit," she added scornfully, in refer-
ence to the cock, "ce n'est pas ressemblant du tout.
Mais enfin puisque miladi le désire—" and with a
shrug of her shoulders she took her curtains back to
her room where she put them up the wrong way round
and so avoided any further annoyance.

For the first eighteen months of war Lady Emily
had been fully occupied by her grandchildren at
Holdings and at Rushwater, the care of her husband,
and occasional visits to relations first in her car, then
as petrol became scarce, by train, always accompanied
and guarded by the indefatigable Miss Merriman who
found that she had a double duty as Conque, after a
lifetime spent in England, was quite incapable of
taking a ticket for her mistress or speaking to a porter,
and had on three separate occasions left valuable pieces
of luggage or clothing in the train. Now however

the discomfort of travel and her increasing lameness
kept Lady Emily at home, so she had conceived the
idea of writing an autobiography. It seemed to her
loving family very improbable that the book would
ever take shape, but it afforded intense pleasure to the
author. Day after day she and Miss Merriman would
sit down at the kitchen table (which her ladyship had
painted pale blue and decorated with arabesques of
gold) to attack their task. Day after day Lady Emily
would be attracted in every direction by the most delightful red herrings, running into blind alleys among
her great-grandparents, divagating into her grandmother's exchange of letters with the Duke of Wel-
lington, rambling into the Italian branch of the Pomfret family, re-reading old diaries, going through collec-
tions of daguerreotypes and old photograph albums,
driving over to Pomfret Towers to ask young Lady
Pomfret who knew nothing about it the year in
which the late earl had opened the new wing of the
Barchester General Hospital, re-reading aloud all the
letters her three sons had written her from school, college, the navy, or the army, making elaborate genealog-
ical tables for which no sheet of paper was ever big
enough, turning out the contents of various silk bags
containing pieces of old dresses, each with a story attached which she could not remember, filling a
number of threepenny exercise books with her elegant
flowing writing and refusing to number the pages so
that not even Miss Merriman could find her way about
in them, making additional notes on half sheets, or as
paper became a subject for economy on old envelopes
slit open, which she left about in books and among her
gloves or read aloud, apropos of nothing, at dinner.

In all these activities Miss Merriman was a zealous
and untiring helper, beside reading aloud Surtees and
Barsetshire Place Names to Mr. Leslie, helping Agnes
with her sewing parties and other war work, and keeping on good terms with the nursery, and to her it was
that Lady Emily first expressed her desire to see the
Marlings again.

Although Lady Emily was a great cultivator of family ties and had always made Rushwater a kind of clearing house for all family news, this was not her sole reason for wishing to renew relations with Marling Hall. She loved all her children with an embracing and almost indiscriminating love, but if she had a favourite it was David. Selfish and unreliable as he was in many ways he had a devotion for his mother which made him in a fit of dixhuitièmerie compare himself with the Chevalier de Boufflers, while by no means attributing to his domesticated mamma the characteristics of Madame de Boufflers, and the tie between them was very close. How much Lady Emily knew of his frequent attachments to charming women, or even of the more frequent attachments to him, David could not be quite sure, but he really did his best to spare his mother uneasiness by telling her nothing and heaping her with affection and small gifts whenever he came to see her. It was naturally Lady Emily's deep wish to see David happily married and her heart would have opened widely to any bride that he brought home. That it would have opened more widely to a wife from her own set is just possible, but so far no bride, county or otherwise, had been produced. During the summer David's sudden spate of visits to Marling had roused her ladyship's interest and wish to interfere to a very high pitch. Agnes and Miss Merriman had managed to restrain her, and David's visits had stopped for some time. But her curiosity was by now so roused that nothing would serve her but to see Lettice Marling for herself and decide whether there was "anything in it," though how she proposed to find out no one knew.

Accordingly Agnes had telephoned, the day for a visit had been arranged, and on a fine late September afternoon Agnes and Lady Emily with Miss Merriman were seated in the drawing-room with their work waiting for their guests. Agnes's work was sea-boot stockings which she knitted with speedy skill on the grounds that the grease in the wool kept her lovely

hands soft. Lady Emily was making a khaki scarf, had
been making it for nearly a year, and was likely, as far
as anyone could see, to finish it a few days after the
end of the war, if then. Not only was she nearly always
occupied with other things, with her vast correspondence, with her grandchildren, her painting, her
decorating, her autobiography, the mending of the
prayer and hymn books in Little Misfit church, a work
which entailed yards of transparent adhesive mending
papor with which she patched the torn pages rather
crookedly or replaced them in the wrong part of the
book and became festooned in a kind of spider's wob
of paper in the process, but knitting had never been
one of her accomplishments. Agnes had suggested that
her mother should make many-tailed bandages, for
her sewing was exquisite, but Lady Emily said that
would not be like real war work and she must do
something difficult. So Miss Merriman went by train to
Barchester and bought khaki wool and knitting needles and cast on the stiches for a scarf. Her ladyship explained that to do any work really well one must begin
from the very beginning and unravelled Miss Merriman's work with a mischievous face. Miss Merriman
composedly wound the ravellings into a ball and
began teaching her employer how to cast on, a task
which after the loss of two and a half pairs of needles,
some of which were afterwards found as far afield as
in the dolls' house in the nursery and others never
found at all, was at the end of six weeks more or less
successfully accomplished. As Lady Emily had vague
recollections of having been taught to knit in her
youth by a German governess with the wool wound
round her left hand fingers and Miss Merriman,
though a skilled knitter, could only knit in the English
way, the period of instruction was complicated and
lengthy. At last Lady Emily was fairly launched and
proceeded to perform bravura variations on the theme
of plain knitting in every row. What she achieved in
the way of adding stitches, of losing stitches, of in-
venting stitches that no one had ever met before, of

finding a long ladder where none had been five minutes earlier, of discovering a peculiar knotted lump twenty rows back and insisting on unravelling to that point because nothing was too good or good enough for the soldiers and picking up her row with double its number of stitches, only those who have tried to guide a mother's early steps in knitting can understand. At the present time her scarf, which varied from nine inches to nineteen in width and had a curiously serpentine appearance when it did not look triangular, was about five feet long. Agnes thought Miss Merriman might now cast off, but Lady Emily, with floating memories of a Rugger scarf of John's at his public school, insisted that it must be at least double the length and continued her Penelope web.

"I really think, mamma," said Agnes for the third or fourth time since Lady Emily had emerged at four o'clock from her afternoon rest, "that you are quite wrong about David. If he were really fond of Lettice he would come back and see her; besides one must remember she is a widow."

"Of course she is a widow," said Lady Emily, "because she has those two little girls."

"They are nearly the same ages as Robert and Edith," said Agnes, her lovely face assuming a look of maternal pride, "only Diana is a little older than Robert. Besides," she added earnestly, "I do not think that her being a widow has anything to do with it. Widows can quite well marry again and after all John was a widower when he married Mary. Of course they would not marry just yet as poor Roger has only been dead a year. No, it is getting on for eighteen months which makes *such* a difference. Mamma, you are knitting in the wrong direction."

Lady Emily having, as she often did, picked up her knitting in the middle of a row and started backwards, had now discovered a curious loophole in her work and was looking at it with intelligent interest. Miss Merriman put down her Air-Force-blue sock and came to the rescue.

"You know, mamma," said Agnes, "Mrs. Stoner who is Mr. Middleton's sister, the architect that we met at Lucasta Bond's, married a man whose name I have forgotten who is Mr. Middleton's partner, and she was certainly a widow, but then she only had step-children."

Lady Emily considered this aspect of the affair and said step-children were of course quite different from one's own children because they could marry each other.

"Mamma!" said Agnes.

"You know quite well what I mean, Agnes," said her ladyship. "Children that have *quite* different parents and then one of each sort dies and the ones who are left get married, can get married to each other without the faintest difficulty, though it is so perplexing to outsiders. But as David hasn't any children of his own they can't marry Lettice's girls. If he marries Lettice they must have some boys and they can all come to Rushwater when the war is over and use the nurseries again. Thank you, Merry, that is perfect, and now," said her ladyship, taking the knitting from her secretary's hands and pulling one needle right out of its stitches, "I can go on beautifully."

Miss Merriman without a word took the knitting from her employer, and Parfitt introduced Mrs. Marling, Lettice, Lucy and Miss Bunting. This lady had been brought partly for the pleasure of the drive, partly to meet Lady Emily again and partly, though nothing would have induced her to admit it, because she wanted to see Miss Merriman whose fame as the perfect secretary-companion had long ago reached her ears. Agnes coming forward enfolded the Marling ladies in her dispassionate, scented embrace, shook hands with Miss Bunting and led the party to her mother.

Mrs. Marling who had not seen Lady Emily since Mr. Leslie's illness was at first shocked by the change in her. Her cousin Emily's handsome ravaged face was whiter than ever, or rather of an exquisite colourless parchment look. Her bright dark eyes looked more cav-

ernous, the delicate bones of nose, cheeks and chin
were more visible than of old, and she made no effort
to rise. But when she spoke her face lighted up with
all the glow of affection that Mrs. Marling remembered from her earliest days, her thin sensitive mouth
retained its entrancing curves, and the lace and scarves
with which she had mobled her head gave her the
noble look of an ageless and distinctly mischievous
sibyl. Mrs. Marling saw that the flame in Lady Emily
was not quenched by her years and wondered, as she
often had, at Agnes's gentle imperturbability with her
adorable and disconcerting mother.

"And Cousin Amabel," said Agnes, "you remember
Miss Merriman at Pomfret Towers. Merry, you know
Lettice and Lucy, don't you. And I want you to know
Miss Bunting."

The two éminences grises, if we may apply so
equivocal a name to two so very respectable ladies,
shook hands, looked at each other and acknowledged
in that one glance each an equal. It became clear to
both ladies that they were the cradle, the guardian
power that brought such beings as Agnes, Lettice,
David, Lady Emily in safety through the trials of
childhood and of the world. Not for a day, Miss Merriman knew, could she have taught and controlled the
schoolroom as Miss Bunting had done; nor for her was
it to tell the sons of dukes on their twenty-first birthday that their hair needed brushing or that their appearance at the christening of their eldest sons left
much, by Miss Bunting's standards, to be desired. Not
for a day, Miss Bunting realised, could she have kept
her patience with the quicksilver spirit, that windblown
fountain, that irresponsible fiend angelical, Lady Emily
Leslie; nor could she have dealt with her letters, her
servants, her writings, her myriad avocations. In the
look that passed between Miss Bunting and Miss Merriman a Throne spoke to a Throne and a silent language
sped between them which none else in the room could
understand, which none else might share.

"And now we must have a long comfortable talk all

about our young people," said Lady Emily to Mrs.
Marling. "Come and sit quite near me."

This invitation Mrs. Marling found some difficulty
in accepting, for Lady Emily who was seated in a very
large comfortable armchair with her feet on a hassock
and a shawl over both, constituting a stumbling block
for the unwary, had a lacquer table strewn with painting materials on one side of her and on the other a
charming papier-mâché-topped table with mother of
pearl inlay supported not very securely by one leg and
three claws, on which were a number of books top-
pling on the verge of a fall. When we add that her ladyship had a kind of large writing board with a green
baize cover laid across her chair from arm to arm covered with exercise books and loose sheets of paper, it
will be seen that no very intimate conversation with
her was possible.

Mrs. Marling strode over the hassock and pulled up
a small chair with a low seat which she wedged up
against the papier-mâché table and sat down. Two
books fell off and lay sprawling face downwards on
the floor. Miss Merriman picked them up and was
about to bestow them elsewhere in safety when her
employer protested.

"Back on the little table, please Merry, just where
they were," said Lady Emily, "because I do find," she
continued to Mrs. Marling, "that if one knows where
things are one is so much more comfortable. What
books were they, Merry?"

Miss Merriman, replacing the books on the table
though in a slightly safer position, said one was Lady
Norton's garden anthology, *Herbs of Grace,* and the
other Mrs. Morland's last novel.

"Victoria Norton's book is quite dreadful," said her
ladyship taking the whole room into her confidence.
"Snippets about gardens, what David calls 'God-wots,'
and *so* many misprints. And a stupid title because it
isn't about herbs at all and makes one think of St. John
of Jerusalem, not that she does belong to it, which

somehow makes it worse. Shall I like Mrs. Morland's book Merry?"

Miss Merriman said she had been reading it aloud to her on the previous evening and thought she had enjoyed it.

"Of course; I enjoyed it immensely," said Lady Emily, her loving hawk's eyes sparkling, "I know I did, because I was thinking all the time that if someone could get a little petrol from somewhere Merry could drive me over to see Victoria Norton and I would give her a list of all the misprints. I made one in bed this morning and I have it somewhere."

Her ladyship stretched out her hand to the other table and upset a glass of painting water. Miss Merriman produced a duster from a drawer and mopped up the mess.

"Here it is," said Lady Emily triumphantly, "only I painted some doves and some fishes on the same piece of paper so it is rather mixed."

With some pride she produced a piece of paper where one of her untaught delicious arabesques of flying fish and floating birds strayed among a good deal of writing half of which was upside down.

"There," she said triumphantly, handing it to Mrs. Marling, and then returning, as she always did, however long the divagation, to her earlier theme, she asked if Mrs. Morland's boys were all well.

Mrs. Marling, who had luckily informed herself from Mrs. Crawley the day she went to tea at the Deanery, said that so far all Mrs. Morland's boys were safe. The three elder had been serving in various ways since the early days of the war and Tony, the youngest after considerable muddle and delay from the War Office had at last got into a Field Artillery OCTU and was going to Powderham in Middleshire. This news drove Lady Emily into a welter of kind plans for writing to various friends who lived at distances varying from sixty to a hundred and sixty miles from Powderham and telling them they must ask Mrs. Morland's boy to lunch, when Parfit came in with the tea things.

"Now we will have a real sit-down tea at the table," said her ladyship, "and I shall get up and join you and have a talk to Miss Bunting, who was always so wonderful at schoolroom tea and used to make darling David cut his nails, though it was years before he could cut his right hand with his left, which sounds as if one were flying in the face of the Bible, but I daresay there weren't any nail scissors then. Now I shall get up."

In one more second both tables would have been knocked over, the writing board and its contents all over the floor and her ladyship probably tripped up with her own shawl and hassock, but the admirable and all-foreseeing Miss Merriman, swift as lightning but more practical, whisked away the writing board, replaced it by a plain oak board on which Lady Emily could have her tea, tidied the shawl, pushed the hassock more comfortably under her employer's feet, put another cushion behind her, and all with such decision, neatness and speed that the visitors stood amazed and Miss Bunting's expert's admiration went up several degrees.

Tea was not peaceful, for Lady Emily, demanding private talks with each one of her guests, succeeded in getting Mrs. Marling, Lettice and Lucy grouped round her, thus paralysing all intimate conversation, while she read aloud and discussed with herself various fragments of her autobiography, which acquired a good deal of butter and crumbs in the process.

"I want you all to help me," she said. "Amabel, I am sure you will remember the year my brother opened the new wing of the Barchester General Hospital, because I know you were abroad with your father then which made it stick in my memory."

Mrs. Marling, who hadn't the faintest idea and didn't know that the late Lord Pomfret had opened the wing, had to confess complete ignorance.

"I will look up the files of the *Barchester Chronicle*, Lady Emily, next time I go into Barchester," said Miss Merriman from the tea table.

"And another thing I *cannot* remember," said Lady
Emily, distractedly rearranging the scarf round her
face, "is how many men we had at Rushwater when it
was an Officers' Hospital in the war—I mean THE
war, not this one which is not in the least one's idea of
what a war is like. Lucy dear, you are at a hospital
aren't you, I am sure you would know. We gave up
most of the house, including having a ward in the drawing-room, so that would give you some idea."

Lucy was for once completely at a loss and tongue-
tied. Miss Merriman, without apparently interrupting
her conversation with Agnes and Miss Bunting, said
she would ring up the agent at Rushwater and get the
exact figures from him.

"Then that is all our business for to-day," said her ladyship with a great air of being the very competent
chairman of a committee. "And now I want to talk to
Lettice. David says your children are adorable. You
must bring them over here one day. Dear child, I was
so grieved about your husband, but we won't speak of
it now. David says you are quite wonderful. Of course
everyone adores David, but you and I know how adorable he *really* is. If he is spared to us in this war," said
Lady Emily, thinking, as she often did, of her first-
born, killed before Arras, so long ago now, "he must
marry and settle down. He has been enjoying himself
quite long enough."

Mrs. Marling and Lucy in a frenzy of embarrassment had been talking loudly and at random to each
other during her ladyship's speech. Lettice, also acute-
ly uncomfortable, for she could not make out whether
her cousin Emily's words were directed at her, or were
merely, as seemed more probably, her ladyship conversing aloud with herself, heartily wished that her
mother and sister would not be so ostentatiously tactful, for it made everything much worse. It was no
pleasure to her to hear that everyone adored David
and she was not sure whether she shared Cousin Emily's feelings about knowing how adorable he really
was. He had not been very adorable to her. He had

come over to Marling a great deal and amused and excited her and made her wonder what she really felt and then he had vanished without a word, without telephoning. On the whole she hated him, but did not see her way to telling the state of her mind to Cousin Emily, so as usual she took refuge in a smile.

Before Lady Emily could do any more damage the contents of the schoolroom and nursery were disgorged into the room. Emmy, Clarissa, John, Robert and Edith said How do you do with exquisite courtesy and want of interest to the visitors and flung themselves into an angelic group round their grandmother, all talking at once. It appeared that at nursery tea Robert had put a piece of crust under the rim of his plate to avoid eating it, which Nannie's eagle eye had at once spotted. He had been made to finish it but Edith, inflamed by his heroic action, had taken out of her mouth her piece of crust and put it into John's saucer. No one could quite bear to make her eat it; the nurserymaid had borne it way, Nannie had preached a sermon on waste in war time which had made John and Robert offer to give up all their crusts for the poor soldiers for the duration of the war, while Edith had cried so loudly for her crust that the nurserymaid had been told to fetch it back and put it in the canary's cage. When the story reached this point Lady Emily drew a picture of the canary eating the crust for John and Robert, while Edith danced a private dance with a transfigured face, singing in a very tuneless voice "Crust, canary; canary, crust" over and over again.

Emmy, old enough to feel a little out of it, attached herself to Lucy who showed her with a scarf exactly how one wrung a chicken's neck, so earning Emmy's undying admiration. Clarissa, standing where the schoolroom and nursery meet and never quite sure to which camp she belonged, got behind her grandmother's chair and with very elegant fingers looked through Lady Emily's painting materials till she found a soft black lead pencil and a piece of clean paper and drew knights and princesses. Robert and John having ad-

mired the canary, asked for it to be in a cage, so Lady
Emily drew a cage over it and Robert drew some bird-
seed very large and John drew a very crooked pot of
water for the canary to drink from.

Agnes, seated between Mrs. Marling and Lettice,
explained with gentle persistency the cleverness of
James (at Eton), the mental gifts of Emmy (at that
moment strangling her eighth turkey-cock under
Lucy's instructions), the exceptional sweetness of
Clarissa, the kindness and courage of John and Robert
and the brilliant gifts of Edith, who tired of dancing
had got her grandmother's embroidery bag and was
neatly disentangling her silks.

"If only Robert did not have to be at the War Office
so much, it would be quite perfect," said Agnes, "but
really the war has been quite a good thing in some
ways, because Robert was always going away on Military Missions and as there is nowhere left to go now,
we do get him at the weekend quite often. You know,
Cousin Amabel, he went on a mission to Russia about
five years ago, and I am so glad he went then, because
if he had gone there now it would really be most uncomfortable never knowing where he was, because
there is a different bit of the map in the *Times* every
day and often they put in pieces of country that one
does not know at all."

Mrs. Marling, whose head, strong though it was,
was beginning to reel, said they ought to be going, but
Agnes begged them to wait a few minutes as her father, who remained in his room from lunch till after
tea, so very much wanted to see them, and despatched
Miss Merriman to see if he was ready.

In a few moments Miss Merriman came back with
Mr. Leslie. Mrs. Marling was again shocked by the
change in him, but again as soon as the unreasonable
surprise that we all feel when years have aged our
friends had spent itself, she saw the Mr. Leslie that
she knew emerging from and as it were overlaying the
half stranger who had for a moment appeared to her
eyes. Mr. Leslie was genuinely pleased to see the

Marling family and enquired minutely after Mr. Marling and Oliver and after Bill and his family, who were apt to be forgotten by outsiders because they were so seldom in the South.

"And who's that young lady?" he asked, indicating Lucy.

"That's Lucy, Cousin Henry," said Mrs. Marling.

"Lord bless me, so it is," said Mr. Leslie. "I thought she was still in the schoolroom."

Her mother called to her to come and talk to Cousin Henry. Lucy, with Emmy glued to her side, came across the room and shook hands, tempering her vigour as she saw how frail Mr. Leslie had become.

"Pleased to see you again, my dear," said Mr. Leslie. "Come and sit down. And are you the young lady David has been telling us about? He was over at Marling nearly every day till he went on his course."

Most unluckily, his wife overhearing his question, her genius for meddling suddenly took possession of her.

"Henry," she called, "it is Lucy you are talking to, not Lettice. It is Lettice that David visited every day. Lettice and I had a lovely talk about darling David. She understands him perfectly and is longing to talk to you about him. Yes, Robert, the canary must have a garden of course and we will give him a watering can and a rake."

Having done her deed of mischief she again became absorbed in her drawing.

"So it is Lettice that David goes to see, is it?" said Mr. Leslie, kindly. "Well, he's a good boy. I don't pretend to understand these young men and he never sticks to anything nor to anybody: never has yet. But he'll have to think of settling some day. We thought he'd marry Mary, you know; but it turned out to be John all the time. He must bring you over here to see us when he comes back."

Acute discomfort reigned. Mrs. Marling, who was very courageous and realised better than either of her daughters how little Mr. Leslie's mistake really mattered, explained with kind firmness that Lettice's husband had been killed before Dunkirk and that she was living with her two little girls at Marling.

"Poor girl, poor girl," said Mr. Leslie, laying his hand on Lettice's very kindly. "We lost our eldest boy you know, at Arras. His mother was wonderful about it. I don't know how I'd have got on without her. And you have to get on by yourself. You must come over and see Emily more often. And don't let David be a trouble to you. He's bone selfish, always was. Expects girls to hang about waiting for him, and the girls will do it and it makes the boy worse than he is; but he's a good boy."

Lettice was touched by Mr. Leslie's kindness and a little frightened by his words about David. They chimed too well with her own unacknowledged thoughts. She was no girl, though to Mr. Leslie she might seem one, but had she not waited for David, hung on to him at the other end of a telephone; was she not one of the foolish women who helped to spoil him, who believed his charming, easy flattery?

"I'd love to come over and see you and Cousin Emily again," she said. "And David is no trouble at all. He is so nice to my little girls."

"We are all very fond of David—" Mrs. Marling began, anxious to ease the situation and pass on to other subjects.

"I'll tell you what," said Lucy, recovering her poise, "David is—"

And then, always timing his entries perfectly with his usual perfect luck, who stood in the doorway but David.

"Bless you all," he said, shutting the door behind him. "Home is the airman, home from the air, as far as one can be who has done nothing but mind his books and go to lectures. Mamma darling!"

He went over to his mother, wormed his way among his nephews and nieces and kissed her happy uplifted face.

"And papa," he said, kissing his father with complete unselfconsciousness, "and Agnes, and millions of Marlings, too divine. Cousin Amabel, I am longing to come over and see you all. Lettice, my precious, how are your daughters whose names I do not pretend to remember though I adore their faces? And Lucy, my love, we must have our six-pack bézique."

"Darling David, it is so nice to see you," said Agnes from the tea-table. "Darling Edith has nearly learnt a poem to say to you. And here are Miss Bunting and Merry."

"Blest pair of sirens," said David, kissing a hand of each lady

Miss Merriman, who knew David's place better than he knew it himself, said "How do you do, David," and quietly went over to where Mr. Leslie was sitting.

"Well, David, showing off as usual," said Miss Bunting.

"Quite right, Bunny," said David outwardly unabashed. "Is there any tea left, Agnes?"

"Ring, darling, and we'll have some," said Agnes, with less than her usual attention, her eyes following Miss Merriman. A look passed between them which Miss Merriman evidently understood, for she left the room with purpose in her step. The children crowded round Uncle David, the fresh tea was brought, social turmoil reigned. Then by a side door Miss Merriman came back and with her a nurse in uniform and crackling cap and apron.

"Anything wrong?" said David to his sister.

"Not wrong, darling," said Agnes, "but we have Nurse Chiffinch here to look after papa just now. She nursed Hermione Rivers when she had influenza at Pomfret Towers and is quite invaluable. Darling Edith calls her Iffy."

"Now, Mr. Leslie," said excellent Nurse Chiffinch, "here comes the spoil-sport. We mustn't have you tired with the flying son at home. Quite a tea-party too."

"Hullo, nurse," said Lucy. "Barchester General, Ward D, winter before last."

"If it isn't V.A.D. Marling!" said Nurse Chiffinch.

"Do you remember the floating kidney case?" said Lucy.

"I never laughed so much in my life," said Nurse Chiffinch. "Now I must take Mr. Leslie away to have a little shut-eye before dinner as we have the Flight-Lieutenant, isn't it, at home. We shall be seeing you again I hope, Miss Marling. Now, Mr. Leslie, we will have a nice little rest before dinner and be as fresh as a daisy."

With kind skill she helped Mr. Leslie to get up, waited placidly while he said good-bye to his guests and escorted him from the room. His wife looked after him, her bright eyes veiled with anxiety, but as soon as the door was shut she gave her whole attention to the children again.

"Poor papa gets so tired," said Agnes, reducing the whole episode to every-day level by her unemotional statement. "Now Edith must say her poem to David and then she must go to bed."

"And we must really go," said Mrs. Marling.

"I wonder, Miss Bunting," said Miss Merriman as Edith was produced to recite her poem, "whether you would care to see the room where Lady Emily works. She has been doing a great deal of her charming painting lately. I expect you saw it at Rushwater."

"I would like it very much," said Miss Bunting. "When I was at Rushwater," she continued as the two ladies quietly left the drawing-room and went across the hall to Lady Emily's sitting-room, "Lady Emily decorated the Peony Dressing-room most beautifully. She painted the washing stand and all the chairs and the window seats with a Peony design and the paint would not dry for weeks. How is Lady Emily, Miss Merriman?"

"Wonderfully well," said Miss Merriman. "Do sit here by the fire. She is anxious about Mr. Leslie, but very happy with Mrs. Graham and the children, and very busy with her book."

"And Mr. Leslie?" said Miss Bunting.

"Not well," said Miss Merriman. "His heart is not good and his mind is easily tired. Mrs. Graham is wonderful with him. I think if David were to marry suitably and settle down he would be glad."

"I do not think," said Miss Bunting, speaking with the authority of her age and her long knowledge of little boys who had grown to big boys and to men, "that David will settle. Or not till very late, if ever."

"That is my impression too," said Miss Merriman, wise with her long habit of observation and discretion. "I have felt that since I first saw him as a schoolboy at Lord Pomfret's and I am glad to find that you feel the same, as you have known him so much longer and more intimately. And in any case I do not think he has met the right woman for his wife as yet."

"Nor do I," said Miss Bunting. "Not in this part of Barsetshire at any rate. Are these Lady Emily's paintings?" she added, looking through her pince-nez at some vivid water-colour drawings of deer and doves prancing and soaring among bright foliage.

"Yes, she did these on a large piece of coarse paper that was wrapped round the books from the London Library," said Miss Merriman. "I wish she had done them on something more durable, but she uses whatever comes to her hand. How lovely Mrs. Watson looks."

"She does," said Miss Bunting, gratified. "But she is too much alone. Commander Watson's death was a great blow. She has behaved excellently, but she broods too much. I wish I could see her happily married again. She needs a great deal of patience and a strong character to lean on. So difficult to find."

"Yes, indeed," said Miss Merriman. "I cannot think of anyone. Not in this part of Barsetshire at any rate. I think from the noise that Edith has finished her poem, Miss Bunting. Perhaps we had better go back to the drawing-room. Lady Emily may want me."

Without exchanging another word or even another glance the éminences grises left the room, having settled everything by the light of their knowledge and experience. The fates might mock at their decisions and

reverse them all, but they knew that they were right in
principle and that anyone who strayed from the path
they saw would be the unhappier for it. That Lettice
should not stray was Miss Bunting's silent prayer. As
for David, though quite fond of him she felt that no
anxiety or pity need be wasted on one who was so well
equipped to look after himself.

In the drawing-room Edith, flushed with success,
was finishing for the third time that short but excellent
moral poem immortalised in *The Daisy*, accompany-
ing it by a kind of rhythmic dance of her own inven-
tion.

> Come, Pretty, Cat!
>   Come here to me,
> I want to pat
>   You on my knee.
>
> Go, naughty Tray;
>   By barking thus,
> You'll drive away
>   My pretty Puss.

Her fat yet elegant form, her dancing feet, her im-
perfect diction enchanted all her hearers, but it was
too evident that the spirit of poetry had intoxicated
her and that in a minute she would be quite out of
hand, when Nannie appeared with the nurserymaid in
tow.

"That's quite enough now, Edith," said Nannie, graciously acknowledging the Marling family's presence.
"Say good-night to Grannie and Mother and Uncle
David and all the ladies and come along to bed. And
send your love to Diana and Clare. Now John and Robert, you come along with Ivy. I will leave Emmy and
Clarissa here, madam, just while Edith has her bath
and then I'll send Ivy for them and they had better not
get excited or Emmy will have the nightmare again."

With the ability of a Field Marshal Nannie de-
ployed her troops, turned the enemy's flank and took
the hostile forces into protective custody.

"John and Robert and Edith are so little that they have to go to bed," said Clarissa loftily.

"Clarissa has to go to bed at seven," said Emmy informatively, "but I go to bed at half past seven."

"Now we will have some lovely reading aloud," said Agnes, apparently oblivious of her guests. "Mamma darling, where *is* Undine? You were reading it to the children last night."

"I simply. Cannot. Think," said Lady Emily, dividing her words by full stops the better to express her detachment from the whole subject.

"Yes, Lady Emily, you had it in your sitting-room this morning and painted Undine with blue-green hair inside the cover," said Miss Merriman. "I'll get it."

Mrs. Marling felt that the family atmosphere of Holdings was closing round her like treacle and she and her party would gradually be absorbed and live there unnoticed till they died. It was now or never. She stepped over the hassock and said good-bye to Lady Emily.

"Come again," said Lady Emily, flashing one of her brilliant smiles at the guests. "I had a great deal more to say to you, but I can't think what it was. It is so good for Henry to see his friends. He is older, and I can't do very much for him now. Lettice darling, come and see us again soon. David must fetch you over and we will have a long talk about him. Miss Bunting, it was so good of you to come and see me. It made me remember our schoolroom days and how dreadfully dirty David's hands used to be."

"I always said," said Miss Bunting, "that David was never clean from the day Nannie Allen left till his last year at school. In the schoolroom he had to be clean, but elsewhere he was extremely dirty."

"God bless you, Bunny," said David, putting his arm round her shoulders and patting the upper part of her arm. "Among the crowd of servile sycophants you alone recall me to my better self, and I must say remind me rather unnecessarily of my worse self. Lord!

how dirty I used to be behind the ears and under the collar. But always the gentleman."

Miss Bunting disengaged herself from David with as little interest as if his arm had been a strand of a climbing plant and said good-bye to Agnes and Miss Merriman. The Marling party left the room and even as they left it Mrs. Marling, turning her head, saw Agnes settling herself with her knitting on the sofa near her mother, Emmy and Clarissa curling up one on each side of her, Lady Emily looking madly for her spectacles and Miss Merriman pointing out that she was wearing them. Mrs. Marling would not have changed her family for Lady Emily's, but seeing their complete self-sufficiency and their absorption in one another she felt a faint envy. Then she reflected how much nicer her own children were and the envy passed, though not the recollection of the family scene.

David saw them into the car. Lucy was driving and Lettice sitting beside her. David kept his hand upon the lowered glass.

"When shall I come and see you, Lettice?" he said. "This year, next year? They have given me another holiday because there isn't anything for me to do. And I want to see Frances Harvey again and annoy her. I feel she has uncharted depths."

To Lettice's fury the heart that did not find David in the least adorable rose, panted and sank again.

"I'm not frightfully busy," she said. "Ring me up."

Lucy, impatient, for it was growing dark, drove off. Lettice was able to spend the journey home in wishing she had answered David as the Finished Coquette would have answered. Now she would listen for the telephone bell and her voice would not be her own voice; her thoughts would revolve exhaustingly round one subject. And always she would be wondering if nurse or her mother thought David meant more to her than any other friend. A ridiculous thought for anyone to have, she told herself loftily, and knew she was not telling the truth.

CHAPTER TEN

THE ONE GOOD THING, AS LUCY REMARKED, THAT COULD
be said for the war was that time went so fast. Meals,
work, sleep, day, night, blackout, followed each other
on an ever more swiftly turning wheel. Oliver said that
it was the one aim of his life to discover whether bed-
time or getting-up-time came the more often. Opinion
on this subject was divided, Lettice holding that one
did nothing but go to bed, Lucy that one did nothing
but get up. Mrs. Marling thought it was on the whole
breakfast which occurred more frequently than any
other milestone in the twenty-four hours. Mr. Marling,
enquiring what they were all talkin' about, said Nonsense, you couldn't alter time any more than the Government could with that damned Double Summer
Time which to his certain knowledge had so upset his
best Jersey that she had slipped her calf, a statement
which led Lucy into such lugubrious details of the too
often sensitive Jersey's trials that Oliver begged her
rather to tell them about the thyroid operation at the

Cottage Hospital, a request with which she obligingly
complied and at quite wearisome length.

As the autumn ran its course every household in
Barsetshire, and indeed all over England, became
more and more like a small beleagured garrison or an
ark resting on Ararat. Servants were called up, or
rushed into reserved occupations to avoid being con-
scripted, a word to which they attached some sinister
meaning including an attack on their liberty to entertain members of H.M. Forces at bed and board at
their employer's expense. Gardeners and chauffeurs
had mostly gone except the aged, or boys just leaving
school who had been carefully and successfully
trained to despise the land and defy authority, though
Ed, we are glad to say, continued in his mentally de-
fective kindness and mild wisdom to reign over the
stableyard at Marling Hall. The early blackout, besides taking anything from ten minutes to half an hour
to do according to the size of the house, cut off evening visiting altogether. The rationing of petrol, more
stringent and rightly so, cut people off from most of
their friends, while the 600 highly-paid men and girls
employed at the aeroplane reconditioning works near
where Captain Barclay was stationed, were driven in
motor coaches to and from their work over distances
varying from five hundred yards to a mile and a half
every day, besides being driven over to Barchester to
the cinema every week at their employers' expense. A
great many people who wrote to thank friends or relations in Canada and the United States for small presents of food had their letters returned to them by the
Censor with a typewritten slip saying that they were
soliciting food, a word which roused the recipients to
frenzy and made them wonder how they could ever
explain to their kind friends abroad how much they
had enjoyed the half pound of cheese, the half pound
of chocolates and the fifty cigarettes. Gin vanished
and re-appeared, more frequently the former. Clothing coupons which looked such an imposing array
when issued melted to nothing before the onslaught of

a coat and skirt, or a winter overcoat. A new kind of gold-digging was evolved by women of all ages, who took up the attitude that their husbands, sons, brothers and men friends would never need any new clothes and so might as well let them have their coupons. About two million gas masks and three million identity cards were left in buses or trains or lost at home. Soap flakes caused much annoyance by being so scarce. Small articles of haberdashery were unprocurable, or soared to fantastic prices. Milk rationing drove everyone from the dairyman to the consumer demented. Powdered milk was nominally issued though many dairy farmers were unable to supply it, and a little later the Food Controller made his stirring announcement that a certain amount of powdered milk that had gone bad would be released for the use of cats engaged on work of national importance such as mousing. Women fed their odious little dogs on pounds of meat obtained illicitly from their butcher or by standing for an hour or two in a queue for meat which was variously said to be horseflesh or bombed cows. An increasing number of people dug up bits of their lawn and planted vegetables or kept hens, while a great many others said it was a shame to destroy the turf and the young people must have their tennis. A day's shopping in London which used to be one of Barchester's relaxations now became almost impossible, partly because one spent the whole day going from shop to shop and not getting anything, partly because the cheap day ticket could not be used for the return journey between four and six, and to pay 2s 1d. more for a period ticket was more than flesh and blood could bear. First-class carriages were done away with on all the shorter runs, which enabled all the people who had been travelling first-class with a third-class ticket to go on doing so and to occupy their leisure by scratching and scraping the blackout off the windows. Also the restaurants in London were rushing downhill with joyous abandon, many of them serving at war prices food that no Barsetshire house-wife would have

allowed to appear at her own table, while the over-
worked and overtipped waiters were alternately
lachrymose and insolent. Millions of people, old and
young, attained the Greater Freedom by not cleaning
their shoes.

A great many people became violently and in
most cases very ignorantly Jugo-Slavo-, Czecho-, Po-
lo-, Sino-, Russo-, Uruguay- and many other phils,
while another and equally large section announced
that it hated all foreigners including certain portions
of the Empire and the British Isles, and always had:
but they both meant pretty much the same thing and
experienced much relief by airing their opinions in
railway carriages or at dinner. The newspapers became a great deal smaller and were just as silly. The
vast mass of slightly subnormal electors who had acquired the habit of turning on the wireless as soon as
they got up and leaving it on till they went to bed, including all those who had taken advantage of a joyful
state of national upheaval not to pay for their licences,
were informed that a Mr. Pickles had been sent by
heaven in answer to their request and continued to
leave the wireless on. Not long afterwards they were
informed that Mr. Pickles had at their request been
despatched to wherever it was he came from, and left
the wireless on even more than before. But apart from
these disasters of war most people were very good, not
least among them the elderly whose world had been
broken and who knew they could not live to see civilisation remade, even if the young wanted to remake it
in their own sense of the word.

With this brief and prejudiced survey we will leave
world issues and return to Marling Melicent.

Here hens bulked very large through the autumn.
Everyone had said How easy to keep hens, of course
every cottager has a few and they cost you absolutely
nothing. But the stern voice of disillusionment as experienced at the Red House informed the Harveys
that those insane animals cost a great deal, laid with
reluctance and died with enthusiasm. Even Hilda

could not altogether quell them, in spite of her previous experience. If they were left in the run they sulked, refused to jump for cabbages dangling from strings, went broody and had to be put in padded cells to recover. If they were allowed to walk about the garden they ate every green vegetable they could see, or pushed their way like serpents through small gaps in the hedge or loose places in the fence into Dr. March's garden on one side or Colonel Propert's on the other. Chicken wire was now practically unprocurable, so apart from trying to block the holes with some old bits of tennis net, in which the best layer nearly hung herself one Sunday while everyone was at church, nothing could be done. The Harveys, having the intellectual's humanitarian feelings towards animals on whom kindness is entirely wasted, refused to shut them up and it became one of Mr. Harvey's most disliked tasks to have to go round to one or other of his neighbours in answer to an angry telephone call and catch one of his flock. At first he chased them kindly and brought them back in his arms, trying to placate them with kind words, but as winter drew on and everything got colder and muddier he learnt to carry them by the legs, using language that made the works of his favourite modern authors sound tame. Miss Harvey, who was very good at business on the theoretical side, worked out that their eggs had cost them about nine and sixpence each first and last, but then, as she so truly pointed out, they did have the eggs.

It was one of the annoyances of this time that Mrs. Smith showed unexpected gifts and a really magic touch with fowls. Little as the Harveys wished to have her about the place, they had to admit that the mere sight of her in the garden would cause the most moulting and dejected hen to brisk up, the broody to begin to take notice, the layer to redouble her efforts. The catering at the Red House with master and mistress out for a good many meals did not give much in the way of scraps, so Mrs. Smith took the largest gardening basket, one of which Mr. Harvey was particularly

fond, and after the manner of an itinerant nun of a
begging order collected excellent scraps from houses
where the families were larger or more at home, and
brought her offerings daily at the back door. It must
be said in fairness to her that she never asked for an
egg in return, or even hinted at such reward, but all
the more did the Harveys feel obliged to pay her a
kind of peppercorn rent of two or three eggs every
week, though standing as they did between Mrs.
Smith's unwelcome benefactions and Hilda's habit of
ostracising them whenever an egg was given away,
their position was far from enviable.

It had gradually become almost a habit with Oliver
Marling to be at the Red House. Various causes led to
this. As the days grew shorter and colder he used his
car for going to Barchester up to the limit of his petrol
allowance and gave up any journeys further afield. By
changes in the time-table at the Regional Commissioner's Office he and his secretary were often on duty
while Mr. Harvey was off, so the brother and sister
were increasingly apt to go to or from Barchester separately. It was therefore an obvious economy that Oliver should pick Miss Harvey up on his way in at least
twice a week and bring her back after work, while Mr.
Harvey went by train. And what more natural than
that she should ask Oliver in for a cup of tea or a
drink, according to their hours.

The whole question of drink was becoming acute,
but the Harveys always had gin and good gin, and
never were their guests offered with it products of
sunny England warranted to be the equivalent of the
products of France or Italy. How they managed their
friends enviously wondered and at first did not like to
enquire, but as the tooth of thirst gnawed more sharply the veils of politeness fell.

"Where do you and Geoffrey get your stuff?" said
Oliver, to whom Miss Harvey had just given an inspir-
ing mixture of gin and French vermouth. "We are
lucky if we get one bottle a month from my father's
man, and heaven knows we have dealt with him as a

family for about seventy-five years when his grandfather started the business in Barchester and solicited the honour of my grand-papa's esteemed custom. There is no gratitude nowadays."

Miss Harvey, whose not too youthful fairness stood up extremely well to the hard work and hours at the Office, stood by the fire holding her glass. The light of the flames illumined her face becomingly from below. Oliver thought how lucky he was to have such a secretary. When he looked at the highly education-conscious female B.A.s with whom most of his colleagues were afflicted, he could not be thankful enough for an intelligent good-looking, well-dressed woman of the world. Geoffrey was still not exactly his cup of tea, but harmless enough, and even if he were one's brother-in-law, of which there was no particular prospect, one wouldn't need to live with him. One of the things he admired in Miss Harvey was her firm, nay almost overbearing attitude towards her brother. He liked her spirit and did not stop to reflect that her power of bullying might be equally applied to a husband. Her sympathetic interest in Bohun's poems had been very attractive and on thinking it over he had decided that her apparent shrinking from an open discussion on *Worme Castes* was but a proof of the sensitive and diffident soul under an assured exterior.

Miss Harvey did not answer directly. The room was warm, the November afternoon securely shut out, one lamp was on the table of drinks and the rest of the room fitfully lighted by the fire. She knew that she looked well standing. She knew too that the relaxation from work, the warmth and the drink were having their effect on Oliver.

"Eyes again?" she asked, with just the right note of sympathy as Oliver shaded his face with his hand.

"You notice things too much," he said, and was rather pleased with the neat repartee.

"One can't help it—sometimes," said Miss Harvey. "I'll get you another drink. Don't move."

She took her glass, refilled it and came back to her

old place, conscious that she moved gracefully and stood imposingly.

"Where *do* you get it, Frances?" said Oliver, going back to his question.

"Black market, of course," she said lightly.

Oliver laughed, for it was obviously meant as a joke, yet the suggestion did not quite please him. He knew that his parents would look on such a thing as a serious matter, and though he assumed no right to judge other people's consciences he knew that his own conscience would make him do without luxuries that he could not get by fair means. Then he blamed himself for priggishness and put the question out of his mind.

"It was so good of you, Oliver, to lend me your precious Bohun," said Miss Harvey, "though not Bane, thank God. I have been reading him in bed and I am so delighted by his poem on the souls that know each other in this world by a secret sign and live on 'this incorporeal banquet' as he calls it, with no wish for nearer union. It seems to me so true."

And that, she thought, with the artist's pride, ought to lead to an interesting discussion, and this time I won't be such a fool as to shy at it.

"You mean that one that begins 'Not in our Flesh shall Love be consummate,'" said Oliver very bravely. "Yes, it is a thought one has often had, but Bohun has put in a way, disconcerting I admit but with extraordinary simplicity and strange magic, that is quite beyond one's power to analyse. I did a bit of research in the Cathedral Library last week and I find that there was a certain amount of talk about him and a Mistress Pomphelia Tadstock, widow of another canon. She was about his own age and highly educated and had been thrice, I mean three times, married. This poem seems to have been addressed to her and evidently describes his own feelings about the relationship. That very fine line about 'Dogs to their vomit, we to'r whores return,' probably expresses the

attraction and repulsion which he felt simultaneously
for her."

"Yes, a good line," said Miss Harvey judicially,
while with the rest of her mind she studied how to di-
vert the talk into more useful channels; for Oliver's
quotation, though a fine example of Bohun at his best,
was not so lover-like as suited her intentions. "But the
couplet that sems to me to sum up the whole poem is,

> 'To sport with *Bodies* is but *Common Use;*
> Thy *Soule* with Mine wantons in*Heavenly Stews.*'

Of course it is not perhaps exactly how one would put
it to-day," said Miss Harvey with great broadminded-
ness, "but it put what one might roughly call the idea
of Platonic love in a charming conceit."

Oliver, much to his annoyance, was again overcome
with shyness of this interesting subject and could not
at once think of a suitable answer.

"I mean," said Miss Harvey, in thrilling tones which
did her great credit, "that there are friends for whom
one feels a very deep affection which is almost a thing
of the spirit. It is almost too fine a thing to discuss, but
you are a very easy person to talk to."

Oliver, half attracted, half nervous, said yes, there
were friends, very dear friends whom one would really
not mind if one never saw again. Not that he meant
exactly that, he added, but he was sure she would understand what he meant; a generous remark as he was
far from sure what he understood himself.

"I know so well what you mean," said Miss Harvey,
thoughtfully draining her glass. "In a way I would be
quite happy if we never met again, for there would be
so much to remember. The senses" (at which word
Oliver blenched slightly) "count for so little as against
the spiritual understanding. With that safe one does
not need to see, to touch."

In proof of this very beautiful statement she looked
deeply at Oliver, though as his face was in shadow the
effect on him was annoyingly inscrutable, and going

over to the table of drinks let her finger tips rest on his
shoulders as she passed.

It was but the brush of a bird's wing (or so Miss
Harvey put it to herself when going over the scene in
her mind later), but it had its effect on Oliver. He
liked Miss Harvey very much, he admired her more
and more, he had vaguely considered what a life
shared with her might be, but it was suddenly borne
in upon him that he did not want people to go touching him, not like that at any rate, so he got up, put his
glass on the narrow marbled mantelpiece and said he
really ought to be going.

"A stirrup-cup then," she said gaily, returning with
two full glasses. "To the memory of Thomas Bun."

"Bohun," said Oliver firmly.

Miss Harvey realised that she had made a false step
and that the magic was less potent.

"I only said Bun to provoke you," she said laughingly, and moved nearer to Oliver who felt paralysis
creeping upon him. "The firelight is so lovely," she
continued, "and that faery sound of the lapping
flames."

If there was one word Oliver hated it was faery,
especially if people pronounced it in that affected
way; and yet her proximity was very pleasant. She
stood very still, very silent, very close to him. An un-
seen power seemed to him to be compelling him to put
his arm round her, thus imperilling the whole idea of
Platonic love, when the mantelpiece, suddenly remembering that it was deliberately made so narrow that
one could not safely put anything on it, cold-shoul-
dered the glass which fell with a tinkling crash on to
the hearth. The front door bell rang. Almost simultaneously Hilda opened the door, and saying, "I suppose
you're in, Miss Frances," turned up all the lights. Oliver felt rather relieved and rather annoyed. To be perfectly truthful he would have liked the moment of
temptation to last for ever with a special clause to
safeguard him against committing himself, but as this
was impossible the next best thing was to be out of

temptation. Hilda let Captain Barclay and Lucy into
the room and shut the door on them.

"Oh, hullo," said Lucy. "I've got a little grain for
your hens and Tom came to dinner a bit early so I said
we'd bring it you in his car. Hilda's got it. We're going
to fetch Lettice on the way back. I'll tell you what,
Frances, someone's broken a glass in the fireplace."

Miss Harvey said it didn't matter a bit and offered
the newcomers drinks, but both refused, Lucy because
she had a gentlemanly preference for dry sherry or
nothing, Captain Barclay because, as he quite matter-
of-factly said, he never drank cocktails just before
driving on a cold night and it was going to freeze before morning. Everyone showed a tendency to linger,
yet had nothing to say and Miss Harvey's handsome
face took on a rather bored and sulky look when Hilda
came in and said was she to put the dinner back or
not. Without waiting for an answer she shut the door
hard and retired to her kitchen. The guests took the
hint and prepared to go.

"Are you sure you are all right alone?" said Oliver to
Miss Harvey, not that he was really at all anxious but
he felt he owed her some sentimental amends for the
scene so rudely disturbed.

"Of course," said Miss Harvey almost snappishly.
"I'm always alone while Geoffrey is on duty, and Hilda
is here and Colonel Propert next door." Then thinking
she had gone too far she relented and said to Oliver,
her fine eyes downcast, "Some day one will really be
able to talk, one hopes."

Oliver said yes one did hope so and pressed her deliberately unresponsive hand. No wish to encircle her
waist revived in him, but he thought with pleasure
that they would meet again tomorrow at the office.

"Don't come out," he said, "it is too cold for you."

Miss Harvey, who was not intending to come out,
threw a touching look of gratitude towards him and
shut the door on her party.

"Oh my goodness *gracious*," said Miss Harvey aloud
to herself in a voice of exasperation. "And for the du-

ration probably. And that ghastly Bun! One might as
well be dead. Oh, *Lord*, what a set!"

It was certainly very cold outside. Oliver's little car, a
ramshackle relic which did more miles to the gallon
than most, and had a window that permanently
wouldn't wind up, cut but a poor appearance beside
Captain Barclay's just pre-war car. To be truthful, it
cut no appearance at all at the moment, owing to the
black-out, but Captain Barclay knew its face well and
had once experienced its draught.

"How would it be," he said, "if you take Lucy
straight back, Oliver? She'll want to change. And I'll
go round by the stables and pick Lettice up. It's getting a bit late."

Though Lucy was much attached to Captain Barclay she saw the cogency of this reasoning, so she got
into Oliver's car, slammed the door three times, which
was the only way to make it shut, slanted her legs well
away from the gear handle which trespassed over the
passenger's seat, and they drove off, Captain Barclay
following. He turned into the stable yard, dismounted,
went up the steep stair and walked in. There was a
good deal of noise in the sitting-room which turned
out to be Diana and Claire in blue dressing-gowns
having a treat of their supper by the fire at a small
table.

"Bikky," said Clare, holding up her biscuit.

"By Jove, yes," said Captain Barclay.

"Clare can't say biskwit," said Diana scornfully.
"Tell us about Sultan."

This was an epic, told in instalments whenever Captain Barclay met the young ladies, about a pony he
had when he was little. Having exhausted the catalogue of the real things it had done, such as scraping
him off against a wall and running away with him into
the middle of the fastest twenty-minutes the Hunt
had ever had and getting cursed by the Master with
more than human ferocity, he had rashly carried his
tale into foreign parts and Sultan was at present in

Germany, eating a German soldier every night and hiding in barns and forests by day. The etiquette of the story demanded copious illustrations which were supplied by the listeners, especially by Diana who had a very fluent pencil and always knew what her own drawings meant. Nurse came graciously in and said was it for Mrs. Watson because she was expecting Mr. Oliver and not to make all that noise. Captain Barclay said he was instead of Mr. Oliver and not to hurry Mrs. Watson, so nurse got pencils and paper for the little girls and Captain Barclay went on with his story. Just as Sultan had eaten a very fat German general Lettice came in.

"I am sorry I am not Oliver," said Captain Barclay, "for I gather it would have given more satisfaction to nurse, but he has taken Lucy back to change and I said I'd fetch you."

Lettice nearly said, That is almost as good as dropping your gloves behind the radiator, but felt the doubtful taste of such a remark in time and only smiled. The same romantic coincidence had occurred to Captain Barclay who likewise had thought it better unsaid. Straws showing the prevailing wind.

"What a nice party this is," said Captain Barclay. "I rather wish we hadn't to go to the Hall."

Lettice said she was afraid there would be nothing to eat if they stayed, but managed to imply by her voice that except for the conventions she would starve very happily.

"Well, good-bye," said Captain Barclay.

Diana said good-bye-and-thank-you-for-the-lovely-story all in one breath. Clare, a true woman, pointed a fat finger at herself and said, "New Dressingham."

"What on earth does she mean?" said Captain Barclay.

"It's her new dressing-gown," said Lettice, surprised at his denseness. "Do you like them?"

"Rather," said Captain Barclay, looking at the two blue figures. "But there's a something wanting. When we were little we all had red flannel dressing-gowns."

"So did we," said Lettice, "and the children did begin with red, but nurse said Sally Pomfret's children were having blue and so I had to get the new ones to please her. But they look very nice."

She hugged her offspring. Captain Barclay wiped their milky mouths with their feeders and kissed them. Nurse materialised and said she would have a fine time getting them to bed after all the excitement, but the remark was purely conventional to keep employers in their places.

"I had a letter from my mother this morning," said Captain Barclay as they drove up. "She enjoyed your visit awfully and so did the girls."

Lettice was gratified. She too had enjoyed the visit. There had been a kind welcome, a warm house, good food and Mrs. Barclay had taken her to several working-parties at handsome houses where she usually found some ramification of relationship that made a link. Two of the Misses Barclay had been home on leave and, apart from their extreme competence, which rather frightened her, had been very pleasant, though obviously hardly knowing who she was.

"Mother has the house for her life," said Captain Barclay suddenly, "but she always said she'd turn out if I got married."

Lettice said, Oh, and then they stopped at the side door. In the drawing-room they found Mrs. Marling, Lucy, Oliver and Miss Bunting. Mrs. Marling said they wouldn't wait for Mr. Marling as he had come in late, so they went down again to the dining-room. Soup had just been put on the table when the host entered. Looking round with distaste at his family and guest he sat down heavily and said, Why the dickens couldn't someone shut the door. Oliver got up and shut it.

"I didn't say slam it," said Mr. Marling. "What's this? Soup, eh? Oh, all right. Might as well eat it I suppose. Daresay we shan't have soup much longer."

"I heard from my mother this morning, sir," said Captain Barclay.

"Didn't know you had one," said Mr. Marling, pushing his plate away. "What's all this pepper doin' in the soup, Amabel?"

"I don't know, dear," said Mrs. Marling. "Tom didn't say brother, he said mother."

"Mother, eh? then why couldn't he say so?" said Mr. Marling. "What's this, pigeon?"

"It's the ones I shot," said Lucy.

"Won't be any to shoot before long and nothing to shoot 'em with," said Mr. Marling. "They'll be takin' our guns away and sendin' them to Russia. Time I was dead. And you know, Amabel, I can't eat pigeons. Why isn't there some beef?"

"The servants had it for their Sunday dinner, papa," said Lettice. "They seemed to expect it. And these are very nice pigeons. You know you ate three last time we had them done like this."

"Well, what's all this about your mother?" said Mr. Marling, switching the conversation to less controversial ground.

"Nothing, sir," said Captain Barclay. "She's very well and enjoyed Lettice's visit very much and sends all sorts of remembrances to you."

"Handsome girl she was," said Mr. Marling, softening. "Here, can't anyone give me another pigeon? All want the old man to starve I suppose. Very handsome she was. We had the galop together at the end of the Hunt Ball the year she married, and I wouldn't mind havin' another with her."

"I'm sure she'd love it, sir," said Captain Barclay.

"Well, there won't be any more galops, or Hunt Balls, or Hunts I daresay," said Mr. Marling relapsing. "We'll all have to turn out of our places and see them made into County Asylums. Government's cuttin' its own throat with these taxes. Enough to make a feller cut his own throat. Well, I'll soon be dead, that's one comfort. Bill won't be able to keep the place up. No one'll be able to keep their places up. Your mother won't be able to keep her place up," he said, turning suddenly upon Captain Barclay.

"Well, so long as we kill Hitler it doesn't matter," said Lucy loudly.

"Can't hear a word you say," said Mr. Marling. "What's this? You know I can't abide slops, Amabel."

"It isn't slops, papa dear, it's a cheese soufflé," said Oliver, very clearly.

"All the same thing," said Mr. Marling, helping himself very unfairly to most of the brown top of the soufflé and scraping out the crisp bits that stick to the side. "What was Lucy sayin'?"

"I said it doesn't matter what happens so long as we kill Hitler," said Lucy at the top of her voice.

"All right, all right, no need to shout as if I was deaf," said Mr. Marling. "Kill Hitler, eh? Well, we've got to get him first. Why the devil don't the Government send an expeditionary force to the Continent? Make another front. Plenty of old fellers like me that were abroad all the last war. We could tell 'em what to do. But it's all these young fellers, and the jacks-in-office at Whitehall. Enough to break a man's heart. Why aren't you havin' port, Barclay? It's not poisoned here like the stuff you get everywhere now."

"No thanks, sir," said Captain Barclay.

"I'll have some more then," said Mr. Marling. "Are we goin' to sit here all night, Amabel?"

Oliver and Lettice exchanged glances of amused despair. Papa had given a fine exhibition of Olde Englishe Squire and was now surpassing himself as Crimean General, a mood which had been known to last for three days, with a final outburst as Mutiny Veteran before he recovered. Mrs. Marling said they would all go to the drawing-room. Mr. Marling said they soon wouldn't have a drawin'-room to sit in at all and he was going to write letters.

It was with some relief that the rest of the party arranged themselves in the drawing-room. Miss Bunting, who had rather frightened Captain Barclay at dinner by sitting beside him in complete silence, took up her usual position just outside the circle. Mrs. Marling said she was extremely sorry, but they were out of cigarettes for the moment. Oliver and Captain Barclay, by an unfortunate coincidence, had empty cases. Miss Bunting got up, went out, and came back with three small packets of cigarettes.

"Abdulla? Players? Three Castles?" she said, offering them in a lordly way.

"Good Lord, Bunny," said Oliver, "I didn't know you were a hoarder."

"Nor am I one," said Miss Bunting. "I ask Mr. Hobson at the shop for a few whenever I go in and he always lets me have some. I like to have something to offer to the Tommies when I come across them."

This unexpected side of Miss Bunting filled her hearers with respectful surprise. They somehow did not associate her with the rank and file.

"Lord Lundy's youngest boy ran away in the last war and enlisted in the Guards when he was under age," said Miss Bunting, looking before her as if she saw a picture. "His father was very angry. He said he would not use his parental powers to get him out of the army, but he would not see him. Patrick came by the servants' entrance the night before he embarked and all the family were away, so I received him and made him some tea in my room. He had no cigarettes, poor boy, and I stole some of his lordship's and two of his best cigars. When Patrick was killed I felt the only thing I could do was to remember what cigarettes mean to Our Boys. It is just the same in this war and Mr. Hobson is very obliging."

"Well, it is very kind of you to include us among your boys, Miss Bunting," said Captain Barclay. "And if you'll allow me to contribute some cigarettes to your store I shall be very grateful."

"I wish I had said that," said Oliver, frankly envious.

"You couldn't, Oliver. You are not, through no fault of your own, in uniform," said Miss Bunting. "But you may contribute."

"Serves me right for being noble," said Oliver, and everyone laughed and the slight tension was relieved.

"I'm afraid, Tom, it wasn't a very amusing dinnner," said Mrs. Marling. "William isn't quite himself to-day."

"I know what it is!" said Oliver. "Papa isn't being not quite himself to-day; he is being excessively himself. Is it the supertax?"

Mrs. Marling said it was and not a very nice one.

"It has never been nice as long as I can remember," said Lucy. "Papa always makes a most frightful fuss and says we will all be in the workhouse, but we aren't."

"When I was in charge of the schoolroom at Lord Bolton's—I mean, naturally, the Marquess of Bolton," said Miss Bunting with reverence in her voice, "not Earl Bolton—" she added with a faint accent of disgust.

"He wore a pair of leather boots and cambric underclothing," said Oliver reminiscently.

"—the Income Tax was only one and sixpence in the pound, but we all suffered very much. It was at Bolton Grange that I acquired the habit of never speaking at dinner on the night after the Budget. The Marchioness and all the family did the same. It annoyed the Marquess, but if we spoke at all his language became so violent that it was not fit for young people to hear. That," she added graciously to Captain Barclay, "is why I did not speak to you during dinner. But I should very much like to hear about Mrs. Barclay. I remember seeing her once at Bolton Grange as a young married woman when I brought Lady Iris and Lady Phyllis down to the drawing-room after dinner. I think she only had one child then."

Captain Barclay said that would probably be his eldest sister as she was the first.

The evening passed very pleasantly and dully. Lucy gave a spirited and unwanted account of how she was organising a Salvage collection, all the ladies knitted, and Oliver played Patience. As he played, the Queen of Spades, a hard-faced woman at the best with her face on one side, somehow reminded him of Miss Har-

vey's expression when Lucy and Captain Barclay had
come in, and he wished it hadn't. Much as he was attracted by Miss Harvey, he was also a little frightened
of her. He had distinctly felt her luring him in the drawing-room by firelight and had not disliked the feeling, but he was not quite sure how far he wanted it to
go. To see her daily was an agreeable stimulant and
the repeated dose had not palled, but the thunder on
her brow had surprised him uncomfortably. He hoped
it would not happen again, yet he hoped it would, for
it was so unbelievable that he would like to be convinced of what his eyes had seen. It must have been a
mistake, a trick of the firelight, or she was tired. His
eyes began to ache, so he shuffled all his cards together and got up.

"Going to bed?" said his mother.

Oliver said he was, kissed her, said a general good-
night and slipped away, reflecting how blessed he was
in a mother who didn't ask questions and let one bear
things in one's own way. Lettice, who was spending
the night at the Hall, embarked on a discussion with
her mother and Miss Bunting which led to their all
going to the Red Cross storeroom to check some lists.
Lucy, who believed in rough and ready comfort for
men, brought the whisky and soda out, splashed a
drink for Captain Barclay over his trousers and the
carpet and sat down with her knees apart and her feet
turned in.

"Are you any good about knowing if people are in
love?" she said.

Captain Barclay said not frightfully good because
his sisters could never bother to get engaged on account of hunting and shooting and salmon fishing in
peace and being in uniform in the war, but he had a
few general ideas.

"I've been thinking a good deal lately," said Lucy,
so unusual a confession that Captain Barclay prepared
to listen attentively, "and I think Oliver and Frances
might get married. I daresay it's all right, though it'll

be beastly if Oliver goes away, but it seems a bit queer, and I thought you might know."

Captain Barclay said he certainly hadn't considered the subject, and would do so. Why, he asked, did Lucy think so.

"Well, she's his secretary and people always marry their secretaries," said Lucy. "Besides, they looked a bit queer this evening, as if they'd been having a row with the broken glass in the fireplace."

"It hardly seems to me a valid proof of love," said Captain Barclay thoughtfully, "but they always say women see farther into these things than men."

"Good heavens, I'm not a woman, Tom, at least not in that kind of way, but one can't help noticing things," said Lucy, indignant at being included with her sex. "But I'll tell you what, Geoffrey isn't in love with Lettice. That would be too ghastly."

"Yes, indeed," said Captain Barclay, suddenly feeling great resentment towards the innocent Mr. Harvey.

"All he says is poetry and things," said Lucy scornfully. "But I'll tell you what, I shouldn't wonder if David was."

"Good God, girl," said Captain Barclay, choking into his whisky and soda, "what a coarse mind you have."

"Not coarse," said Lucy proudly, "you mean purrient or however one pronounces it, because I've never said it aloud before, at least that's what you sound as if you meant. David comes here a lot and then he goes away and doesn't write or ring up, so I think he is struggling against fate."

"And what on earth makes you think that?" asked Captain Barclay, very glad that no one more percipient than Lucy was in the room if his face looked as red as it felt.

"No one could help seeing that he did come here a lot," said Lucy patiently, "and he hasn't been for ages, and I know he doesn't write, because all the letters get delivered here so I'd see it. And nurse said when I was helping her with her ironing last week that it was rather lonely for Lettice since she came back from Mrs. Barclay's and she wondered why David didn't ring up and take her out somewhere. So you see."

Captain Barclay felt such a surge of dislike for David Leslie that he would willingly have practised neck-wringing on him if Lucy would oblige with a few hints, but he knew that his Lucy, though often obtuse, would notice if he didn't answer, so he said he expected David was on a course.

"He was last month," said Lucy, "because he sent Bunny a picture postcard of the Berlin Opera House and said he mustn't tell her where he was; but he was at Holdings before that when we all went to tea and he's back again now, because Merry told Bunny when they had coffee at Pilchard's the day they did a bit of the Messiah in the cathedral, I mean the choir did it. Geoffrey said the organ was all wrong because it wasn't like Handel's organ, but the organist who comes to my Anti-Gas class said it was absolutely what Handel would have used, not counting its being played by electricity now, so Geoffrey felt rather a fool, except that he never does."

During this rapid survey of domestic and musical life Captain Barclay was able to recover his wits and persuade himself that Lucy was making a great deal of fuss about nothing.

"You ought to be in Intelligence, Lucy," he said. "I never knew anyone who had so many channels of information. If your family aren't coming back I'll go downstairs and say good-bye. I'm off to town on a secret mission for a few days."

Lucy said all right and she was going to bed, so Captain Barclay groped his way down the dimly lighted stairs to the drawing-room where the Red Cross stores were kept. Here he found Lettice alone, ticking off parcels on a list.

"Oh, are you going?" said Lettice, which he felt in his hypersensitive condition to be a feelingless question. "Mother is in Bunny's room doing something about Christmas presents for the maids and the estate people. She'll be down again soon."

"I won't stop," said Captain Barclay. "Say good-bye for me. I'm going to London for a week or so on some special stuff."

Lettice, instead of going pale and tottering to a seat, as he had vaguely hoped, said how nice and she hoped he would have a nice time.

Captain Barclay said it would be very nice to see London again. The devil then inspired him to ask if she knew where David was, not that he wished to know, but he hoped to have the great pleasure of making himself uncomfortable. She suddenly drooped a little.

"I think he is at Holdings," she said, "but I expect he is too busy to ring up just now."

The right answer to this would have been, "Why don't you do the ringing up yourself," but it did not occur to Captain Barclay. All he saw was that a Deceiver was Playing Fast and Loose with Lettice, who was being pathetically brave.

"I daresay I'll run across him in town," he said. "I'll let you know if I do."

"Not if he's at Holdings," said Lettice with a matter-of-factness which seemed to him childishly beautiful though annoying.

"Well, good-night. If I can do anything in town for you, let me know," said Captain Barclay, "or anywhere else."

"That's very sweet of you, Tom," said Lettice, "but I don't think there's anything."

"Well, if there is you can count on me, day or night," said Captain Barclay heroically.

"I don't see what you could do at night, but it's very nice of you, all the same," said Lettice. "Oh, Tom, I wish you weren't going. All these goings-away make one think of the day when people are really gone for good."

"I wish I could stay," said Captain Barclay. "But I swear I won't leave England without seeing you again

—that is if you'd like it." He made this noble offer the more determinedly that he was on a job of special work which would be very unlikely to take him out of England for at least six months.

"I would," said Lettice, who was enjoying being sorry for herself. "It's not so lonely when you are here."

"You'll have David," said Captain Barclay, again under the direct influence of the devil.

"Perhaps," said Lettice. "But when it's you one feels safe. You don't forget."

The slight accent that she laid on the word "you" flew to Captain Barclay's head.

"Bless you," he said, and held her hand in both of his very reverently. He was already wondering how one stopped being reverent without appearing brusque when Lucy came in.

"Hullo, I thought you'd gone," she said. "I say, Lettice, mother wants to know if you remember where we put those rolls of blue woollen stuff last year. She's just remembered about them and can't think where they are."

Captain Barclay made his adieux and went away. On the drive back to his quarters he thought a great deal about Lettice and David. He finally came to the conclusion that if to marry David was going to make her happy he would insist on being best man, partly to make himself as miserable as possible, partly to be in a position to see that David turned up at the altar and went through with it. Having settled this he spent the rest of the drive in remembering how sad and alone Lettice had looked, how she had said she wished he would stay, how he had felt her hand cling to his. So beautiful and uplifting were his thoughts and so rapt was he above mortal regions, that his Colonel who was there when he got back said if he was in for a spot of flu he had better go to bed and not infect everybody.

The whereabouts of the rolls of blue cloth were established and the Marling family went to bed. Lettice was putting cream on her face when her sister Lucy walked in, wearing bright blue pyjamas and a camel's hair dressing-gown.

"I say, Lettice," she said, "Tom and I were having a talk after you'd gone to do the Red Cross things. I think he thought you liked David a bit."

"Lucy!" said Lettice.

"David's all right," said Lucy tolerantly. "But Tom's a much decenter sort of person really. I mean if he held anyone's hand it wouldn't be just for fun."

Only a thick layer of cold cream prevented Lucy from seeing her sister's crimson face.

"I'll tell you what," said Lucy, planting herself in front of the fire in a gentlemanly way, "if you like Tom, that's all right. I mean not to bother about me. You'd better have this bathroom. I'll have the blue one."

She went out again, leaving the door ajar. Lettice got up and shut it and walked slowly back to the dressing-table. Her own face shining with grease was not a comforting sight and she badly needed comfort. It seemed to her that she had for the first time in her life been unkind to Lucy and that it was all Captain Barclay's fault. She liked him very much, she was very fond of him, yes fond, anyone might hear her say it, but that she cared for him more than as a very pleasant, easy friend was a ridiculous idea of Lucy's. He was Lucy's property and everyone realised it. Suddenly her conscience smote her. She had certainly done what was uncommonly like leading him on over the episode of the gloves, but it was only because she liked him, not because she cared for him like that. And now Lucy had seen him holding her hand and like the kind creature she was had at once offered to give up her property to her sister. She was angry with Captain Barclay for putting her in a false position with Lucy. She was also angry with David for having given Captain Barclay the impression, or so Lucy said, that she had fallen under the Leslie charm. She hated them both and in fact everybody, but most of all herself for having got

into so wretched a position. If only Captain Barclay
were here now she could explain everything and he
would tell Lucy and it would be all right. It did not
occur to her to wish that David were here now, perhaps because she knew, though she didn't acknowl-
edge it, that it would be no good explaining things to
him because he wouldn't want to hear. There was no
one to remind her that only a very few months ago she
had been used to wish that Roger was there to make
things all right. She went to bed in a state of great depression.

Lucy meanwhile went to the blue bathroom. In the
middle of her bath she remembered that the bath
water running off annoyed her mother, and such was
the reaction from her noble deed that she said aloud,
"Well, I don't care if it does." But her kinder self came
to the rescue and made her choke the flow with her
sponge which stopped the gurgling. While patiently
waiting for the water to run out quietly, she thought
of Lettice and Captain Barclay. Most young women
would have considered that an elder sister, having had
a husband, had had all she ought to have, and thought
of their own chances. Lucy, whose heart was very
large, thought it such rotten luck for Lettice that
Roger had been killed that she ought to have any consolation that took her fancy, even if that consolation
took the shape of Captain Barclay. Facing the situation with her usual honesty she saw that she did not
care for Captain Barclay in a falling-in-love sort of
way, a sentiment which in any case she despised, so it
would be pure dog-in-the-mangerishness to try to keep
him. All the same she was very fond of him and it was
she who had found him and brought him to Marling,
her very own private property; and two large tears
mingled with the final muffled gurglings of the bath
water.

CHAPTER ELEVEN

THE READER MAY HAVE FORGOTTEN THAT MISS LUCY
Marling had a large disobedient dog called Turk, but
we have not. During the entire course of this narrative
Turk had been pushing doors open with his nose and
making for the patch of sun on the floor or, as the seasons advanced, for the hearth, leaving a roaring
draught in his wake. If the door was properly shut he
had scratched its lower panels in an appealing and de-
structive manner. He had sniffed and whined continu-
ously while Lucy was out and greeted her with hys-
terical barks every time she came in. He had refused
the good bits of cake, the biscuits, the occasional cut-
let bone that Lucy gave him in defiance of all war
economy from her own plate, and eaten every kind of
unpleasant refuse in the garden or the lanes. When
Lucy was away for a night at the Cottage Hospital he
had howled until Oliver unwillingly took him to his
own room. Here he lovingly insisted on sleeping like a
Crusader's tomb on Oliver's feet, not to speak of waking up in the small hours of the morning with a nerv-

ous twitch that almost upset the bed, and howling till
Oliver, cursing, took him downstairs and opened the
back door. Turk turned his back on the door and conducted an exhaustive search for Lucy in the dining-
room, pantry, kitchen and boot-room, after which he
returned to Oliver and with liquid eyes and uplifted
paw begged him to take him back to his soft couch
and not keep him shivering in the dark house. Oliver
remarked with suppressed vindictiveness that he
would thrash him to death if it weren't for disturbing
the family, and went back to bed, chill and irate, to
toss uneasily till Turk woke him again at seven with a
loving lick of his face. Luckily a housemaid was coming down the back stairs near Oliver's room, so he
pushed Turk out to her and went back to bed for half
an hour with aching eyes and throbbing head.

These and other beautiful traits of canine fidelity
too numerous to mention, for nothing is so boring as
other people's dogs, we merely note in passing to show
that the dogs of Barsetshire, if Pomeranians, Alsatians,
Newfoundlands, Chows, Dalmatians (one of whom
lived with the Dowager Lady Norton), Samoyedes,
Great Danes and Pekinese may be included as Empire
Dogs, were pulling together against Fascism, Commu-
nism and all forms of government which tend to sup-
press the liberty of the individual; also to prevent (in
the classical and religious sense of the word) the com-
ments of any reader who may still remember Chapter
I and wonder why Turk was mentioned if he was
never to be seen again. All of which leads to the
dreadful day when Lettice and Captain Barclay
walked down to the Red House with some grain from
the farm for the Harveys' hens and Turk would come
too. And should any reader be so ill-advised as to
wonder why Captain Barclay always seemed to have
leisure to visit Marling Hall, we are quite unable to
say, except that determination does a great deal, even
in the Army.

It was a cold December day and the blight of

Christmas was already settling on England. It would
certainly be a much nastier Christmas than the previous one, with trains, presents, coupons, rations and
tempers all a little short, and many people said, Ah,
but next Christmas will be much worse, and tried in
their eleventh shop to get a wrist watch or a cigarette
lighter for friends and relations in H.M. Forces. Bill
Marling, his wife and children, were loyally supporting the Government's nervous request that people
would refrain from Unnecessary Journeys at Christmas, by arranging to travel in company with four or
five million other people ten days before Christmas instead of in Christmas week itself, bringing their nurse
and two dogs, two turkeys, a goose and a case of
mixed drinks which Bill was mysteriously able to pro-
cure.

Lettice was ready for the walk when Lucy shouted
from the stable yard that she was just off to the Cottage Hospital and Turk was somewhere about and
would Lettice shut him up in a loose box till she came
back as he had chased a cow that morning. Not waiting for answer or expostulation she drove away. Lettice came down and called Turk, who presently appeared in company with Captain Barclay, fawning on
his boots. At the sight of Lettice, whom he knew very
well, he affected extreme terror and backed into a
corner, so that Lettice thought she could easily catch
him, but Christmas was in his blood and he doubled
and fled down the drive with the air of one who has
suddenly seen a dangerous rabbit and must save his
owners' lives and property.

"Oh dear," said Lettice. "And Lucy wanted him shut
up."

"He's off hunting," said Captain Barclay with the
easy optimism of one who is not a dog-owner. "He'll
be back for his dinner. Jolly news from Pearl Harbour
to-day, isn't it. Well, well,

> The Japs
> Are filthy little chaps.

Ready, Lettice?"

Lettice said she was, gave him the small sack of
grain, and they set off in silence, for after that morning's news there was nothing to say and even saying it
wouldn't help anyone.

"I'm glad I didn't send Diana and Clare to America," said Lettice as they went through the lodge gates
on to the road.

"By Jove, yes," said Captain Barclay, at which moment Turk rose from a lair on the far side of the road
and abased himself at their feet.

"Go home, Turk," said Lettice, but so little faith was
in her voice that Turk, putting on an idiot's face, pretended he didn't know where he was and set off towards the village just too fast for them to overtake him
without loss of dignity.

"That's that," said Captain Barclay, "and really one
can't say much else about anything just at present."

United by dislike of Turk they walked on to the Red
House and went to the back door. Hilda was pegging
out the clorths (her expression, not ours) and greeted
them.

"We've brought some grain for the fowls, Hilda,"
said Lettice. "How are they doing?"

Hilda said, with the ill-concealed pleasure of her
class in bad news, that there was one of them had laid
a double-yolked egg twice in a week and it was well
known it strained them and they wouldn't find *her* laying eggs much longer and the best layer's comb wasn't
as red as it should be and one of them seemed lame
this morning.

"You know Mr. Geoffrey and Miss Frances aren't
in," she said. "I'd ask you in the drawing-room, but me
and Millie's giving it a proper turn-out to-day."

"Yes, I know," said Lettice. "We'll put the grain in
the shed and have a look at the fowls. Can I have the
keys?"

Accordingly she and Captain Barclay put the sack
into a lock-up shed with a concrete floor, supposed to
be immune to mice, and continued their walk to the

hen-run. Lettice undid the padlock and went in with a handful of grain which she threw down. The best layer certainly had a very pale comb and it was evident that she was going off laying for the present.

"I'll tell Frances she ought to give her some Chicko Tonic," said Lettice. "Oh, Tom, hold Turk!"

But too late did she speak. Turk, overcome by a sudden access of love for Lettice, burst into the run and leapt upon her with loving, dirty paws, barking loudly.

"Don't be a fool, Turk. Get down!" said Lettice angrily.

The hens rushed together into a group to defend their lives and honour, then despairing of either rushed wildly shrieking through the wire door into the garden where with innate strategy they scattered and fled in all directions. Turk, pleased at this new game, bounded after them, waking the echoes. Round and round went chickens and dog while Captain Barclay laughed so much that he couldn't help. At last five or six made a bolt into Colonel Propert's garden and a few were got home and began to eat the grain, with the well-founded hope of finishing it before their friends arrived. Turk bounded faster than ever, there was a scuffle, and a hen lay upon the ground. Turk sat down on the grass with his tongue hanging out and panted.

"Good Lord!" said Captain Barclay.

Lettice, who had the presence of mind to shut the homing hens in, joined him.

"You'd better get some string from Hilda and put it through Turk's collar," she said.

Captain Barclay did as he was told and returned with the string and Hilda.

"I'm afraid she's dead," said Lettice, pale with the reaction.

"She's dead all right," said Hilda cheerfully. "Fright: that's what done it. My sister lost a dozen pullets like that one year when Sir George Burchell's spaniel chased them, but he paid up like a gentleman."

"Of course, I must pay Miss Harvey," said Lettice. "How much do you think she's worth?"

"Oh dear, oh dear," said an annoyingly familiar voice behind them. "Poor chookie, let me look at her. I was just coming out of my gate with my basket to go to the shop for my week's rations when I saw you and Captain Barclay, Mrs. Watson, going into my house. Pardon me, but the habit of calling the Red House my house is so strong, even though I cannot afford to live in it. So I thought, Well, I wonder now. And having time to spare I just popped over to see."

"It was that dreadful Turk," said Lettice. "He's killed her."

Mrs. Smith bent over the victim, looked attentively at her expressionless face and picked her up.

"She's not dead," said Mrs. Smith. "It is shock. If there was a little brandy, Mrs. Watson—"

She led the way to the back door and went in. The kitchen was empty.

"Of course," said Mrs. Smith. "Millie did happen to pass the remark to her aunt this morning that they were going to turn out the drawing-room."

Followed by Hilda, Lettice and Captain Barclay, who now had the unrepentant Turk on a stout bit of string, she went up the passage.

"Pardon me," said Mrs. Smith, opening the door of the drawing-room where Millie was making a surprising amount of dust, "but I have an invalid here."

"It's that Turk," said Hilda. "I knew he'd kill one of them. Didn't I say so, Millie?"

"Yes, Hilda, you did," said Millie, who thought it safer to be untruthful than to contradict her tyrant.

"She isn't killed," said Mrs. Smith. "It's only shock. Is there any brandy?"

Hilda, sensible of the importance of the occasion, took them all into the dining-room, which was bitterly cold as a fire had not yet been lighted, got out the brandy and provided a spoon.

"And a small glass, please Hilda," said Mrs. Smith.

"Please pour it out, nearly full, that's right, and now take the poor chookie."

Hilda took the fair burden and pinched her throat. She opened one eye and her beak and uttered a dying squawk, upon which Mrs. Smith, with prompt skill, put a teaspoonful of brandy down her gullet. The hen appeared to be vastly surprised, but not ungrateful.

"Just another teaspoon and she'll do," said Mrs. Smith. "The glass is a wee bit too full, so I'll just drink a little."

Accordingly, before the fascinated gaze of her audience, she drank off the rest of the glass except for a driblet at the bottom which she poured into the teaspoon and gave to the hen. Hilda with great promptitude gave the hen to Millie and locked up the brandy.

"She'll do now," said Mrs. Smith, "but she needs care. I will take her across to Mrs. Cox's, Hilda. There is an old coop in the garden in a nice warm corner near the kitchen and I'll just keep her there for a day and bring her in at night as it is so cold. She'll be quite herself by to-morrow. You carry her over, Millie, and I'll come and see about the coop. Poor dumb animal," she added pensively. "Good morning, Mrs. Watson, and Captain Barclay too. He was a naughty Turk, wasn't he. Good morning, Hilda."

With a graceful inclination she left the room followed by Millie.

"Nervel" said Hilda.

Lettice apologised deeply for Turk's behaviour, said she would ring up Miss Harvey that evening, and got away as fast as she could, for she was really afraid that Hilda might scold her. But most luckily the voice of Colonel Propert was heard bellowing over the hedge and Hilda rushed out to do battle with him and reclaim the six escaped hens who, so he said, had eaten every green leaf in his garden.

"You know, Tom, what will happen," said Lettice as they walked back, "is that Joyce will keep that hen. In fact I shouldn't wonder if she means to get them all, one at a time. What will Frances say?"

Captain Barclay, showing a sad want of heart, began to laugh and Lettice, after vainly trying to be shocked, had to laugh with him.

"Oh, dear," she said, "it *is* nice to laugh, Tom. I haven't laughed so much for ages."

"Good," said Captain Barclay. "And I may add that to hear you laugh is one of the greatest pleasures this war has afforded."

"Tom!" said Lettice, laughing and expostulating. Then, looking at his face, she said more faintly, "Oh—Tom."

"I assure you I can't help it," said Captain Barclay. "It has been getting the upper hand of me for some time."

"Tom!" said Lettice again, but with such a change in her voice that Captain Barclay was alarmed.

"What is it?" he said anxiously, and carefully refraining from taking her hand.

"I don't know how to explain," said Lettice.

"If you could try to tell me," said Captain Barclay, walking on, just apart from her. "I won't interrupt."

"Please," said Lettice, a remark which when uttered in a pleading voice is somehow highly infuriating to the male sex.

"I'll do anything in the world for you," said Captain Barclay stopping dead half way up the drive and turning to Lettice, "only don't say 'please' as if I were a murderer."

"I didn't," said Lettice. "Don't be angry, Tom."

This remark is perhaps even more exasperating than the word "please" and Captain Barclay only by a great effort of will-power and affection suppressed a blasphemous exclamation.

"I'm not angry," he said, "I couldn't be. But what have I done?"

Lettice remained perfectly silent. Contending moods and words were so working in her bosom, not to speak of her head and mouth, that she found articulation very difficult.

"Tom," she gasped at last. "We can't. You know we can't."

"Why the dickens can't we?" said Captain Barclay, adding illogically, "and anyway I don't know what you mean."

"It was all last night," said Lettice, clutching his coat sleeve to make her reasoning clearer. "Lucy was a perfect angel, as she always is, but I feel I couldn't ever do anything to make her unhappy. You do understand, don't you?"

"I am sorry," said Captain Barclay, making most praiseworthy efforts to command his temper, "but I don't. I am very fond of Lucy and I certainly don't want her to be unhappy, but I don't see where she comes in."

"But you were *her* friend, Tom," said Lettice. "She brought you here. It wouldn't be fair. Oh, you do see, don't you?"

"Do you mean," said Captain Barclay, "that—"

"Yes," said Lettice in a dying voice. "At least, I suppose I mean what you think I mean."

"As far as I can make out," said Captain Barclay with an almost brutal desperation, "you mean that Lucy likes me enough to feel unhappy if I liked you better. And that's a nice fatuous thing to say," he added bitterly.

"You do see now, don't you," said Lettice.

If Captain Barclay had followed his own inclination he would have said, in a very loving voice, "You great fool," and taken Lettice in his arms right in the middle of the drive with the grocer's van passing, instead of which he pretended to be looking at the beauties of nature till the van had gone round the corner and then said, "Perhaps I had better not come back to tea at the Hall."

"Oh, I didn't mean that," said Lettice, so exhausted by her effort of nobility that she hardly knew what she was saying.

"You can't have it both ways," said Captain Barclay. "I love you quite abominably. If you don't want me to,

I can't stop, but I can keep away. I don't want to hurt Lucy any more than you do, but I don't love her and that's flat."

"You can't suddenly not come to tea," Lettice objected.

"Oh, can't I," said Captain Barclay ferociously. "As a matter of fact," he added in a milder tone, "I am coming to tea whatever happens. But to please you—and for no other reason—I won't talk about this again; not until you ask me to. And I may say that there isn't anyone else in the world I'd do that for. Come on, Turk."

He gave a tug at the string and walked on, Lettice beside him in a turmoil of emotions of which the uppermost at the moment was pure delight in the words, "I love you quite abominably," the most romantic words she had ever heard. But none the less was she faithful to her plan for Lucy's happiness and determined that such words should never be said to her by Captain Barclay again. Lucy must be fairly treated and Lettice was prepared to bear a great deal of unhappiness to this end.

The walk would have been quite unbearable if Turk had not seen Lucy in the distance and broken his string, thereby nearly cutting two of Captain Barclay's fingers off, which enabled that officer to relieve his feelings by swearing. Lucy had been organising salvage dumps all afternoon, and in breeches, a dirty mackintosh, her hands blue and her nose red with cold, looked singularly unattractive. Nor was she much more attractive at tea, during which meal she ate, talked, interrupted and told people what in a very overbearing way. Lettice, though not critical by nature, heartily wished that her younger sister for whom she had just made so great a sacrifice would behave in a manner more worthy of the offering, while Captain Barclay, though always fond of Lucy, felt that to be tied to her for life would be a thing he could not abide. Resentment swelled in him against Lettice for unnecessary, useless, female quixotism. He almost began to dislike Lucy as with increasing symptoms of a streaming cold

in the head she bored everyone dreadfully about
paper, tins, bottles, bones and all the subdivisions of
Salvage. He found himself in an odious dilemma. He
felt certain that Lucy's feelings towards him were as
untender as his for her, but he could hardly ask her
outright what they were. He knew his own feelings for
Lettice and allowed himself to guess what hers were
for him, or what they would be if allowed to run their
free course, but how could he tell her again what she
had so firmly refused to hear? It would have given him
great pleasure at the moment to throttle Lucy and
carry Lettice off on his steed, but neither course being
possible he had to resign himself and let things take
their course. Mrs. Marling and Miss Bunting talked
Red Cross shop steadily, and if Miss Bunting looked
once or twice at Lettice she kept her thoughts to herself.

It was just like things that David Leslie, back at his
sister's for a few weeks while he went to a course near
Barchester, should have come in unannounced and
confident of a friendly reception. Lettice, who was really behaving very foolishly though never remarkable
for intelligence, looked madly at Captain Barclay for
help. If he had not just asked for a second cup of tea
and taken a very large slice of dull but wholesome
cake he would have got up, kicked his chair over and
left the party to their fate.

"And how are Diana and Clare?" said David, seat-
ing himself by Lettice after the tumult of greetings
had subsided.

This again was unfortunate. David, as we know,
though he liked the little girls, neither remembered
nor cared what their names were, an oversight which
outrages any mother, but to-day as fate would have it
he had been talking with his sister who had mentioned
four times that Diana was just a little older than Robert and Clare just a little older than Edith, so their
names were indelibly and temporarily marked on the
tablets of his memory. The bait, though quite unconsciously dangled, was more than Lettice could resist

and she at once fell into David's circling charm and talked with such animation that no one would have guessed her heart was broken. Captain Barclay discussed the forthcoming marriage of Lady Griselda Palliser with Miss Bunting. Mrs. Marling told Lucy she had far better go to bed if she was feeling like that, and Lucy, her 'm's and 'n's rapidly blurring to 'b's, said she hadn't got a cold if that was what her mother meant and anyway she had promised to go down to the stables and see Clare being a fish in her bath.

"But Lucy darling," said Lettice, her mother's ear attuned to sounds of illness, "if you are going to have a cold I really think you had better not come. Clare hasn't had a cold all this autumn and nurse would be so much annoyed if she got one."

"It isn't a cold," said Lucy with a loud sneeze, "it's only because I was standing about outside Dr. March's house because he said he'd be out in a moment and he wasn't."

Again Lettice glanced madly round for help, but Captain Barclay was still deep in conversation with Miss Bunting and it was David's eye that met hers.

"By precious wud," he said earnestly to Lucy, "you are wud bass of idfectious gerbs, and I absolutely forbid you to go to the stables and so does Miss Bunting. I myself will see Clare being a fish in her bath and I may add that such is the natural depravity of female nature from the earliest age that she will find Uncle David's company far more stimulating than Aunt Lucy's. And what is more, as blood is nipt and always be foul, not to speak of the blackout, I propose that I should take Lettice back in my little car at once. Cousin Amabel, you will forgive my haste, but if I am late at Holdings Agnes will have to coo to me at least seven times how very naughty I am to keep the servants waiting, and though she means nothing by it, bless her, it might pall. Come and dine, Barclay. My mother and sister would love to see you."

Captain Barclay said he was going to town on a job

and would be away for some time, otherwise he would
have been delighted. Lettice tried to express a thousand things in one look and signally failed, so she went
out with David, feeling that all was shallow mockery.
As she left the room Miss Bunting remarked that Lucy
had better go to bed at once, and she would come up
in a few minutes with some small camphor pills which
the Marchioness always had in the house for the treat-
ment of colds.

"Oh well, I suppose I'd better," said Lucy, secretly
rather relieved at the thought of bed, "and Tom can
come up and sit on my bed and talk to me."

"That I will not," said Captain Barclay, glad for
once to be able to speak his mind. "I don't want to
catch your cold just when I'm going off on an important bit of work. Take great care of yourself."

"Ad led be dougħ wed you cub back," said Lucy
with another ferocious sneeze.

Captain Barclay promised and said good-bye. Rather to his surprise Miss Bunting accompanied him to
the door.

"We shall look forward to seeing you on your return, Captain Barclay," she said regally. "You are always welcome at Marling."

"That's awfully nice of you," said Captain Barclay,
touched. "I'd like to think it was true—I mean of everybody."

"It is," said Miss Bunting. "Lettice of course does
not always know her own mind, but she feels as we do
at heart. Good night."

Slightly cheered by her sibylline words Captain
Barclay sped away into the night. In normal times he
would have been able to depress himself by seeing the
light streaming from the stable flat and imagining Lettice listening to David's honeyed words over Clare's
bath, but the blackout made it impossible to see anything except the piece of the drive immediately before
him and he had soon passed the lodge gates. Had he
been able to look into Lettice's flat he might have been
slightly cheered by what he saw. Far from pressing his

suit on Lettice, David was entering wholeheartedly into the game of Clare being a fish in her bath, finally, to nurse's scandalised admiration, taking her bath towel by the ends and scooping Clare out of the bath as if he were landing a fish in a net. Nurse exclaimed that Uncle David had made the towel all wet and hurriedly got another from the hot cupboard, while David, his enthusiasm suddenly dropping from him, blew Clare a good-night kiss and went back to the drawing-room where Lettice was reading aloud to Diana from Grimm.

"Lovely, lovely book," he said. "My dear mamma read it aloud to us when we were small, again and again. Could we have the story about Mrs. Fox and her suitors, do you think?"

Lettice found it, and just as Mrs. Fox had decided to throw the old fox out of the window the bell rang. Nurse was heard going to answer it and Oliver came in with Miss Harvey.

"Oliver was so kindly driving me home," said Miss Harvey, "and we thought we would call on you on the way."

Lettice enquired after the hen.

"She is quite well again," said Miss Harvey. "That is, Mrs. Smith says she is, but she has still got her, and the dreadful part is that she has got the eggs too. Hilda is furious and I really hardly know what to do. Oliver is quite heroic and is going to call on Mrs. Smith and speak to her about it as soon as we get back."

She cast an admiring glance on Oliver, who did not look as if he were particularly grateful. He had what Lettice called his "eye face" and was obviously in pain. Lettice felt a slight discomfort at Miss Harvey's free use of the word "we" and told herself not to be silly.

"Is that my Miss Perry?" said David. "What a predatory woman she is. Miss Harvey! the way is long, the night is cold, Oliver is if not exactly infirm and old not the right person to drive you back when he is pur-

blind, or is it parblind like parboiled, and if one why
not the other. Let me abide at thy left side and drive
thee home with me; I mean to your home, not to mine,
for though my sister Agnes would adore to see you it
might not suit Geoffrey."

Miss Harvey gave an educated simper and turned
her handsome eyes from one cavalier to the other ap-
pealingly.

"Thanks awfully, David," said Oliver, "but I can really manage all right, and we ought to be going,
Frances."

"Ah, but not if your eyes are bad," said Miss Harvey. "Poor eyes! How selfish of me not to realise."

Oliver looked and felt highly uncomfortable.

"Not selfish," said David, enjoying himself
thoroughly. "Only beautifully abstracted from these
mundane affairs. Together we will beard the Perry-
Smith in her den. La ci darem la mano, if you don't
mind getting your bonnet and shawl on."

When David turned on his facile charm most people
fell. Miss Harvey, though she had taken a first in Eco-
nomics (for what that is worth), was not immune. Oliver made a faint protest, saying quite truly that he
would have to go out again to go home and might just
as well run her back, but she laughingly declined and
made her farewells.

"Poor eyes!" she said again, laying her hand on Oliver's forehead for an instant.

Lettice hoped that her face looked as if it had neither noticed nor resented the action, but was not very
sure, so she went on reading Grimm to Diana. When
she had finished the story she told Diana to say good
night to Uncle Oliver and go to bed.

"Sorry, Lettice," said Oliver when his niece had
kissed him and gone. "My eyes are rotten and I'm not
fit for company. I can't imagine what Frances thought
of me."

It was on the tip of Lettice's tongue to say that she
was thinking of David, but she checked herself.

"I must seem a hopeless sort of person to her," said

Oliver in a mood of self-depreciation very unlike him, for he usually kept his troubles close. "She can do a gruelling day's work and be perfectly fresh at the end, and here am I a sheer hulk. Oh, I do wish Pilman hadn't gone to the wars. This other man doesn't understand my eyes a bit."

"Poor old thing," said Lettice, and came and sat on the arm of his chair with her hand on his shoulder. There was no thrill in her presence, but Oliver felt a comfort from it that Miss Harvey's touch had not given.

"Good old Lettice," he said as he got up. "I wish I could think Frances really liked me, but I'm really not fit for anyone to like. I wish to God I had David's bounding health."

Lettice said with complete sincerity that anyone who had any sense would like him *much* better than David, and though the statement coming from a sister was partial in the highest degree it appeared to comfort Oliver, who then went home. Lettice sat musing for a while. If Oliver really liked Frances, it was obvious that he must marry her, for he must not be disappointed. The prospect did not fill her with enthusiasm. She liked both the Harveys well enough, but they were not quite her sort and she felt that once married to Miss Harvey Oliver might drift away towards Bloomsbury, leaving her high and dry at Marling. Suddenly she felt very much alone. Even David had deserted her for Miss Harvey, and though she did not love him she would have enjoyed more of his company. The road to old age stretched before her very bleak and long, and nowhere on her road could she see the figure of Captain Barclay.

David drew up at Mrs. Cox's house and accompanied by Miss Harvey went up the little path. The door was opened by Millie Poulter, who on seeing her daily employer was stricken imbecile and after gaping a good deal fled into the kitchen. From this fastness Mrs. Cox emerged and with a dazzling though wavering show

of teeth asked if she could do anything. On hearing
that they wanted to see Mrs. Smith she ushered them
into the front parlour.

"Mrs. Smith is upstairs, but I'll run up and tell her,"
she said, genteelly covering her mouth with her hand
while she manoeuvered her uppers which were rather
too easy a fit into position again.

Miss Harvey and David sat down. The room had a
dreamlike resemblance to the Red House. On a foun-
dation of Mrs. Cox's uncompromising red wallpaper
and green plush-seated chairs Mrs. Smith with patient
industry had built up a simulacrum of her home. Conspicuous on the olive plush tablecloth was the green
art velvet blotter, the coal tongs from the Red House
dining-room were in the grate, an off-white quilted
satin cushion adorned the leatherette armchair, promi-
nent on the mantelpiece with its period ball fringe was
a green glass animal with bubbles in it which Miss
Harvey had missed though not mourned from the hall;
in the window showing up handsomely against Mrs.
Cox's red rep curtains was the second largest green
witch ball from the dining-room, whose absence Miss
Harvey had vaguely noticed and mentally added to Hilda's list of breakages. In fact, wherever she turned her
eyes some familiar object, disliked long since and lost
awhile, greeted her. All this she saw in a moment and
then Mrs. Smith tripped down the stairs and glided
into the room, giving, as David said afterwards when
describing the scene to his mother, an extraordinarily
good impersonation of Mrs. Heep, her pleasure at having Miss Harvey and Mr. Leslie as visitors to her humble abode being of a quite overpowering nature.
Under her blandishments Miss Harvey felt less and
less equal to saying she had come to fetch the hen,
while even David felt his guns on the whole spiked.

"You are looking round at my little mementos," said
Mrs. Smith. "Just little things that remind me of the
happy home days before Mr. Smith was taken. Many's
the time he used that cushion, Mr. Leslie, when he
took his forty winks on the couch, and often of an eve-

ning he'd have his glass of something on the occasional table," she added, pointing to a small table with a painted giallo antico top and wrought-iron legs which Miss Harvey distinctly remembered being used for much the same purpose by her brother on the previous evening. "It was only this afternoon I popped over to my dear wee house to see if it was still there and Hilda happening to be down the garden giving the chookies their tea I just slipped into the drawing-room like a mouse and I said, Well, there's the occasional table not being used except for the books, so I thought Mr. Harvey couldn't possibly mind if I took it and I put the books on the stool in the corner and just brought the table over and really it gave the room quite a home-like air. I always say furniture knows when it is loved."

"There weren't any books on it," said Miss Harvey, speaking to David. "There were a lot of *New Yorkers*."

"That's it. American books," said Mrs. Smith, who in common with several million of her fellow countrywomen nearly always meant a magazine when she said a book. "And may I enquire after Lady Emily, Mr. Leslie."

David, not so much at ease as usual, said his mother was pretty well, adding with great presence of mind that she would have sent her kind regards if she had known he was going to see Mrs. Smith. He then fell silent. Miss Harvey looked at him, confident in his powers of extracting hens from landladies, but such was Mrs. Smith's paralysing effect on him that he did not quite know where to begin.

"I know what you have come for," said Mrs. Smith archly, "our poor invalid chookie. She's tucked up all so cosy in her coop in that warm corner just against the kitchen chimney. It seems quite a shame to disturb poor chookie to-night, doesn't it, when it's so cold, and how you would get her into the run without a torch I don't know and the A.R.P. wardens come down on you quite sharp if you so much as show a light."

Miss Harvey hastily said she quite agreed and confounded herself in excuses for having even thought of reclaiming her own hen.

"It has been quite a pleasure to assist the poor dumb beast," said Mrs. Smith, "and I must say I shall quite miss my little egg."

Miss Harvey nervously said that of course Mrs. Smith must have some eggs from the hen after being so kind. Mrs. Smith said she would bring the hen round next day, or if it were still very cold in a day or two and how truly kind of Miss Harvey to suggest her having an egg a day as it would just make all the difference. Her visitors then thought that being outwitted at all points they had better leave. David took Miss Harvey to her front door.

"Come in and have a drink," she said.

"It certainly is far more than my due," said David, "but I will not say no."

In the drawing-room Mr. Harvey was having a cocktail by himself.

"I thought you were dead," he said to his sister, waving his disengaged hand towards David. "Help yourself, David. I heard from the Tape and Sealing Wax this afternoon, Frances. Peter rang me up. It seems they are in no end of a hole about Clause 14 and Sir Edward says if I will come back he'll get me released from the Regional. I said what about you and he said he would speak to Establishments. My God, Frances, we may be out of this damned hole by the New Year."

"With eighteen months' lease of this house still to run," said his sister.

"Oh well, don't be gloomy," said Mr. Harvey. "I came home early on purpose to tell you and the house was empty and now you quibble about the rent."

"Considering I pay half of it I well may," said Miss Harvey. "And where are we to live in London? You know the house isn't inhabitable."

"Peter says come and share his flat," said Mr. Harvey.

"With how many other people?" said Miss Harvey, whose annoyance at being worsted over the hen and having to control it before David was bursting its banks. "All his rotten little friends in and out, night and day. And just as I—well, never mind that, but you are frightfully selfish, Geoffrey."

"This being one of the conversations that are so much more embarrassing to the hearer than to the speakers, and having had the last of your sherry, I think I had better go," said David, annoyed to have been let in for such a boring family scene. "Bless you both. You must come and dine at Holdings. Agnes would adore it. I must fly."

The Harveys, hardly stopping to say good-bye, continued their argument. Geoffrey said he couldn't see why on earth his sister should want to stop in such a ghastly hole when London was gaping for them.

"I hate it just as much as you do," said his sister, "and probably more. But if I did marry Oliver Marling, I mightn't want to share a flat with you and Peter."

"I thought it was David you were keen on," said her brother.

"Well, he isn't keen on me," said Miss Harvey testily. "But I can get Oliver whenever I want him."

"Please yourself," said Mr. Harvey. "Women have such peculiar tastes. Where's that little table gone that I put my *New Yorkers* on? I can't see it anywhere."

"Mrs. Smith took it," said his sister coldly.

Mr. Harvey groaned and under cover of his groan was out of the room and into the bathroom with both taps on before his sister could collect herself. If Oliver had seen her face, far from being anxious for her to like him, he would have been glad to escape even as David had done.

But David, well on the way to Holdings, was telling himself that he had been a fool to try to get entertainment from a second-hand highbrow, and that in Lettice lay the secret of content and of the peace that he had never found and almost despaired of finding.

CHAPTER TWELVE

MOST OF THE PRINCIPAL CHARACTERS IN THIS BOOK BEING by now thoroughly uncomfortable in their various ways, Christmas did its best to bring on the culminating point of horror. Bill Marling with Mrs. Bill, whom we must call by that name as no one ever called her anything else, his four children, two nurses, perambulator, quantities of luggage, several very cumbersome dead birds of immense size and a packing case of drink, arrived in full glory at Marling Hall. Bedrooms were unsheeted, extra help was laid in with a good deal of difficulty, and Lettice with her little girls came to stay with her parents for Christmas week so that the children could be with their cousins in spite of the blackout, and nurse and the maid could help in the house.

The programme, as arranged by Mrs. Marling and Miss Bunting, was to include a dinner party on Christmas Eve to which the Harveys, David Leslie and Captain Barclay were invited. This officer was to spend the night, having got leave of absence to that end in order that he might satisfactorily torture himself by seeing Lettice prefer David, and stand by to fell David to the earth if he presumed to trifle with Lettice. How Mrs. Marling did it we cannot say, but she and Miss Bunting were past masters at organising, and there was still enough feudal feeling on the estate for some of the older women to feel it was like a real Christmas to go and work at the Hall for a week. The kitchen and back yard were like Bolton Abbey in the Olden Time. More than once Mr. Marling was obliged to force his way through three tradesmen, the estate carpenter, the two gardeners aged sixty-seven and seventeen, the cowman's children, the kitchen-maid's niece, the housemaid's sister, the mothers of the evacuee children down at the cottages, Ed's mother, who was a great one for breaking whatever she washed up, and several other hangers-on, in order to get into his own back door and take his boots off in the butler's pantry, his regular habit. Tea flowed at all hours in spite of rationing, and somehow the whole kitchen had bacon for breakfast, though we need hardly say that the dining-room mostly did without.

Everyone at Marling, nay in Barsetshire, nay the whole Empire, had sworn that this Christmas there should be no over-eating while millions starved, no buying of presents when the money was wanted for War Savings Certificates. The first of these base proposals was countered by the Food Controller who released some dried fruits and sanctioned the increased ration of fats and sugar, as also by the domestic servants of England who were as a body determined that whoever suffered they shouldn't. The second was killed at birth by the malign Spirit of Christmas who forced people to go to Barchester and to town where they scoured the shops, sadly empty, or if stocked, with only the drabbest, dullest objects, and bought horrid things, or came empty-bagged and basketed home and hunted out other nasty things left over from previous Christmases. Nor were there wanting economists who said that to give Savings Certificates was anti-patriotic because it only meant that the Government would be paying you interest, and that the only true patriotism would be to take out of the bank as much money as you proposed to spend at Christmas and burn it. But as no one listened to them, or believed them, a great many people bought Savings Stamps, which they attached to a Government Christmas Card bearing a picture of a galleon in full sail, relic apparently of a *Boys' Own Paper* special coloured illustration in the late 'nineties, thereby making the recipients, who rightly expected something better, very ungrateful. Those who had enough time bought a quarter of a pound of sweets whenever occasion offered in every sweet shop in Barchester, and very poor sweets, too. A great many turkeys did not arrive till Christmas Eve and had to be parcooked at once to arrest decay, while a haggis, which was sent to Mrs. Marling every year by a Scotch cousin, never reached her at all. For this the Scotch cousin blamed the English post-office, but Mrs. Marling replied on a postcard that it must have been stolen north of the Border as no Southron would know what it was; or if he did would regard it with insular suspicion.

By an extraordinary piece of luck the Bill Marlings' nurse was called nana, which prevented any confusion with Lettice's nurse. These ladies lived in a pleasant state of fully-armed friendship, uniting in coming down heavily upon Mrs. Bill's second nurse who was called Everleen and came from an orphanage. The nursery cortège presented indeed an imposing appearance as it took its morning walk in the grounds, the two youngest Marling children packed into the perambulator pushed by Everleen, or for a great treat by the elder Marlings or Diana Watson, with nana's eye on them, the other children, when not pushing the perambulator, hanging onto its side, running on in front and being called back by nurse, or loitering behind and being sharply bidden to hurry up by nana. In this cavalcade they visited the farm, the sawing-shed, Govern's cottage, Ed's mother's cottage, the stables under

Aunt Lucy's charge, the milking shed and all the pleasant remains of a vanishing civilisation, and Mr. and Mrs. Marling felt extremely proud. Diana and Clare liked their cousins and as they were all well brought up by proper nannies, without which there is no civilisation possible, everything was very pleasant. Lettice and Mrs. Bill continually praised each other's children while the nannies continually praised their own, but they all meant the same thing, and we may say here that the Marling children though very nice were rather dull, so we shall not go into details about them.

For the better entertainment of the Bill Marlings and the Christmas Eve guests the large drawing-room had been opened. The Red Cross stores were packed away by Lettice and Miss Bunting behind two great Chinese screens, huge wood fires were kept burning in the two handsome Adam fireplaces under the charge of Ed, who sawed logs with fervour all day and brought in piles of wood with the reverence of an acolyte, for the drawing-room was to him a temple of beauty and romance. It was during this week that he had his one and only difference of opinion with his mother, under whose thumb his whole existence had been spent. Mrs. Pollett, who was for ever against law and order, spoke angrily to her son, accusing him of making a doormat of himself for people who gave themselves airs and hinting darkly that he might find the cottage door closed to him if he went on like that. Ed smiled his half-witted angel's smile and remarked slowly, "Then I'd marry Millie Poulter. She's got a tidy bit in the bank."

"And get some more fools like yourself I suppose," said his loving mother, to which Ed, whose legally fatherless condition had often been discussed sympathetically in his presence by his many friends and relations and had to some extent soaked into his muddled brain, replied reasonably, "Well, mother, who got I?" which sent his mother into such violent hysterics that she was quite kind to him for the whole Christmas week.

Although Lettice and Oliver were to some degree gnawed by their private troubles, it did not prevent each noticing the shadow on the other. Nothing was said. Lettice could not in honesty tell her brother that she wanted Miss Harvey for a sister-in-law; Oliver, suspecting nothing of Captain Barclay's declaration, thought that his dear Lettice might be pining for David, but felt the ground too delicate for questioning.

Christmas Eve had been most exhausting. The two younger Marling children had sneezed twice. The elder boy, who was passing through that very tiresome age of rudely de-bunking defenceless conjurors at parties and had refused to clap his hands when taken to *Peter Pan*, had devastated the nursery by saying that Santa Claus wasn't a real person. The elder of his two sisters and Diana had flung themselves upon him like furies, the female sneezer and Clare had burst into tears, and only the male sneezer who was of too tender years to understand remained unmoved. Nurse, nana and Everleen had been hard put to it to restore order and get the children clean to go down to the drawing-room. Here an unfortunate epidemic of sulks took place. In vain did Lettice and her mother try game after game; even Miss Bunting could not do very much. Diana was found to be wearing a ruby ring out of a cracker, property of one of her cousins, the elder Marling boy indulged in prep school wit and had to be checked, and Clare and the younger Miss Marling having discovered the awful word Beastly felt obliged to use it repeatedly against their elders' express orders. When nurse, nana and Everleen appeared to remove the nursery party the grown-ups were too near defeat to be able to exult. Mrs. Marling went to the nursery and Miss Bunting withdrew to a writing table at the far end of the room to do the place cards for dinner. Lettice looked at the clock. It was only half past six, plenty of time to be quiet before dinner, so she sat and looked at the fire till Oliver came back from the office.

"Well, darling," said Lettice, when her brother's tall form appeared between herself and the fire.

"Christmas," said Oliver with measured hatred, "comes but once a year,

Its advent we do hate and fear,

But even that is as absolutely nothing to the infernal nuisance it is when it is really here.

Have any of the children been sick yet?"

"Not on Christmas Eve," said Lettice, shocked. "That isn't till Christmas Day. When do Frances and Geoffrey come up?"

Oliver said not till dinner time, as they had both been kept late at the office and was he keeping the fire off his sister? So they sat in affectionate, anxious silence till Bill and Mrs. Bill, who had been decorating the church, came in, for Mrs. Bill was a Bishop's daughter and knew exactly what she ought to do, wherever she was. Lettice idly asked who else was decorating.

"Oh, the usuals," said Bill Marling. "Mrs. March and Mrs. Propert and Govern and Mrs. Smith. What's happened to our Joyce? She had a positively leering light in her eye and said the New Year might bring many a change."

"From what Frances says," said Oliver, "not content with spying on them night and day, she has been making advances to Geoffrey. I gather that he is frightened out of his wits."

"Bet you ten to one she gets him," said Bill, who was famed for backing losers at the regimental point to point.

"I'll take your dare," said Oliver, "so long as it's in sixpences, for more I cannot afford."

Bill wrote it all down in his pocket diary and Mrs. Bill said she could never quite approve of widows marrying again, which might have led to uncomfortableness, but everyone knew their Mrs. Bill, and Lettice said she rather agreed. Mrs. Bill, who had a very kind heart and made the best of wives and mothers, was luckily so stupid in some ways that she felt no embarrassment at all. The children were then discussed in great detail and the party drifted off to dress. Miss Bunting had by now finished arranging the dinner table, a work of some difficulty owing to the number of the Marling family present, and turning out her light allowed herself the rare treat of sitting quietly and thinking of her own affairs. For forty years or so she had eaten other people's Christmas turkey and pudding, but she could not truthfully say that the dish had ever been bitter to her, or moistened by her tears. Her heart said a small hymn of gratitude for kindness and even honour in so many houses, for affectionate thoughts at Christmas, for her place among so many pleasant family circles, for the remembrance that so many old pupils had of her each year. Already a large heap of Christmas cards was lying in her room and though nothing would induce her to open them before Christmas Day, she knew the writings and exulted. This year, as last year, far too many of the greetings would be naval, military, or Air Force cards; and this year, even more than last year, there would be gaps in the list and she would miss the friendly remembrance of the little boys who had grown up and gone from her, some to the earth, some to the cold sea, some, whether happier or not she could not tell, to prison camps with hope very far away. She felt as if somehow she had failed in her duty, as if the Bunny whom so many little boys had loved, teased, confided in and remembered ought to have stood between them and evil, as indeed she would cheerfully have done if her small body and indomitable spirit could have been the sacrifice. So deeply was she lost in her thoughts that she was not aware of newcomers till Lucy's voice was heard at the other end of the drawing-room telling Captain Barclay what in no uncertain terms.

"Rot," said Lucy, throwing her coat on to a sofa, hurling a log on to the fire and banging herself into a chair. "It's no good saying you've got to go to London to-night, it'll spoil the dinner. Everyone knows the

War Office doesn't want you on Christmas Day. If you go up to-morrow afternoon that'll be heaps of time. Besides, why didn't you say sooner?"

Captain Barclay said he couldn't, because he hadn't had the letter owing to the posts being so queer.

"Well, if you don't go the War Office will just think you haven't got the letter," said Lucy. "If they really wanted you they'd send a telegram. I'll tell you what, why don't you ring them up?"

Captain Barclay, slightly confused by Lucy's direct methods, was heard to say that he could hardly do that and anyway no one would miss him.

"I shall," said Lucy stoutly. "And Lettice will."

"I don't think so," said Captain Barclay; and we may say that at and from this moment Miss Bunting did a thing she had never in her upright life done before, and deliberately eavesdropped. Seated as she was behind the large writing table at the far end of the room, without a light, it was not likely that they would notice her. If they did, she had the dinner list in front of her which must be excuse enough.

"Don't be an ass, Tom," said Lucy good-humouredly. "Lettice is a bit silly sometimes, but I've noticed that people who get married are often much sillier than people who don't. I suppose it's all the worry of husbands and children. Look at Sally Pomfret. When she was running the beagles she was much more sensible. Now she's got Gillie and the children to look after she seems much less interesting. Well, look at me. I know I'm not pretty like Lettice, and I loathe all this business of dressing-up and going to parties, but I was thinking the other night that if Lettice is so silly about David, really I'm much more grown-up and sensible than she is."

Captain Barclay would have given his soul to ask how Lettice and David were being silly and so would Miss Bunting, but neither dared expose their position.

"*I* wouldn't be silly about David," said Lucy, who was much enjoying the sound of her own voice and the grown-up feeling of discussing her elder sister with her Captain Barclay. "David's all right. I mean he's all *right*, but you're much decenter."

Captain Barclay, such is the effect of evil communications, unconsciously copied his friend Lucy and said, "Rot."

"Rot yourself," said Lucy. "And that's what I told Lettice."

"Told her what?" asked Captain Barclay, who would have liked to shake Lucy if that would have clarified her peculiar roundabout way of telling a story.

"I told you," said Lucy patiently. "It was that night you were holding Lettice's hand in the Red Cross bundles. It looked pretty soppy, I daresay you can't help it. So I went into her room before I had my bath and told her you were much the nicest, because I thought she might think you were my special friend or some rot. I think she thought you thought she liked David. That's what I mean about Lettice; she isn't frightfully sensible really, but I'm frightfully fond of her. Lord! it's half-past seven! Besides I promised to ring-up Captain Grant at the A.F.S. I want him to let me go out with the Fire Engines. He's awfully decent except when he's cross because he isn't in the war because he's got a queer foot because a horse trod on it."

Pleased with her discourse on the folly of elder sisters, she got up with a violence that sent her chair skating across the floor into a small bookcase, knocked a sofa cushion on to the floor as she picked up her coat, and strode out of the room.

Captain Barclay, who had been too stunned to get up when Lucy went, remained by the fire in a kind of paralysis. For some months now two thoughts had given him no rest. The first was that Lettice cared for David; the second, implanted in his bosom by Lettice herself, was that Lucy had a prior claim to his affections. With this theory he disagreed and as we know had told Lettice frankly that he did not and never would love Lucy except as an excellent sort of fellow. Now Lucy herself, with no sign at all of a broken heart,

or indeed of any sentiment whatsoever, had as good as
told him that he ought to pay his suit to Lettice and
was prepared to approve any efforts he made in
that direction. He drew a deep breath, like a
diver returning from sunless depths to the light of day.
The burden dropped from his shoulders and hope
sprang again. He had been too gentle, too weak with
Lettice. When her sisterly love and apprehension had
made her put a barrier between them he had admired
her unselfishness and with her set out upon the very
uncomfortable road of renunciation. This road,
through Lucy's words, had suddenly come to an end,
or more properly given itself a shake like the path in
the Looking-Glass and brought him back to where he
was when he started; loving Lettice with no reason
against loving her. For quite two minutes he remained
spell-bound by this blissful thought. Then, as he went
over in his mind his recent conversation with Lucy, a
chill doubt crept in. True, Lucy approved his interest
in Lettice, but the words she had spoken about David
suddenly assumed a new and terrifying aspect. If
Lucy, so splendidly dense to the fine shades, had noticed any inclination towards David in her elder sister,
it must be there. Lucy could not possibly invent such a
thing. And with this thought his spirits dropped again
to zero. As far as birth and worldly position went he
and David were not unequal, but David's was a charm
that even other men had to recognise and if David
chose to use it upon Lettice how could she but re-
spond. In considerable agony he got up and paced angrily down the long room. At the further end he came
upon Miss Bunting, her light turned on, industriously
writing. As he approached she looked up.

"Good evening, Captain Barclay," she said. "Dear,
dear, I had no idea how late it was. I have been doing
the cards for dinner. Have you just come?"

Captain Barclay said he had come in with Lucy,
who had gone to dress.

"So must I," said Miss Bunting, turning out her light
and getting up. "Our dear Lucy," she continued as she

went towards the door accompanied by Captain Barclay, "is sometimes a little more brusque in her manner than I quite like, but she has an excellent heart and a great deal of common sense. If I were in doubt upon any practical question, I can think of no young person whose advice I would be more apt to consider than Lucy's," which was of course a downright lie, for Miss Bunting throughout her long independent life had never asked nor taken advice from anyone. But Captain Barclay, being in a state of bemusement in which he was ready to catch at any straw, caught gratefully at this deliberate falsehood and said he was sure Miss Bunting was right.

"I always am," said Miss Bunting. "When I am not sure I do not speak. Follow Lucy's advice and you will not be sorry."

With alarming majesty she passed through the door which Captain Barclay was holding open for her and disappeared across the dimly-lit landing. Captain Barclay shut the door behind her and went back to the fire-side where he spent a very agitating ten minutes alternately feeling sure that no woman could resist David, the one particular woman on whom his heart was set least of all, and that he must put his fate to the touch that night, that moment if it were possible, or die in the attempt. Before he could go quite mad the party began to assemble and he had to pretend to be Captain Barclay instead of a love-lorn lunatic.

Bill Marling, David Leslie and Captain Barclay being in uniform could not do the party justice. Oliver had exhumed his tails, unworn since the summer of 1939, but Mr. Marling took pride of place in his black trousers with very wide braid down the legs and a dark blue velvet smoking jacket, relic of an Oxford club of his youth. It was his pride and his family's disgrace that the revers or lapels of this coat had never been refaced, owing to which nostalgic renouncement they presented rather the appearance of Miss Havisham's bridal finery, hanging in shreds and tatters, the canvas interlining showing through, but giving intense satisfaction to the wearer. Mr. Harvey in a dinner jacket was neither here nor there.

Miss Bunting, who always wore black at night, had added a small black velvet bow to her rather skimpy coiffure, thus increasing her air of majesty. Mrs. Marling wore a dark purple woollen gown with some gold embroidery and looked very much the chatelaine. Mrs. Bill, as was inevitable, had on a flowered voile dipping a little at one side, relic of her papa's last episcopal garden party before the war, and sandals with her great toe sticking through. Lettice wore a dusty pink which suited her dark hair, and Lucy had shaken herself into a very gentlemanly dark-green house-coat which she had bought because it unzipped all the way down, though it had no particular shape. The star of the evening was undoubtedly Miss Harvey, whose fair handsomeness was enhanced by black lace and chiffon through which her neck and arms gleamed just like a heroine's. As she stood talking to Oliver, Lettice had to admit, looking on their tall elegant figures, the dark by the fair, that they made a very striking couple. Captain Barclay, observing Lettice as she spoke to David, had to admit that a better matched couple for looks and breeding could not easily be found. Mrs. Marling noted with resigned sorrow that her daughter Lucy, though she had put on bedroom slippers instead of walking shoes, a handsome concession from her to the day, had a ladder up the front of one stocking and something perilously like a woollen vest where she had not bothered to zip her dress up to the top.

Mr. Marling said in a loud voice that here we were at Christmas Eve again, which was so unanswerable that all conversation died and the announcement of dinner was a great relief.

Captain Barclay found himself very comfortably placed between Miss Bunting and Lucy, both of whom were staunch friends if a little alarming. He also had the great pleasure of seeing Lettice across the table in animated conversation with David and feeling that his house was indeed built on sand.

"Isn't it sickening," said Lucy, hardly troubling to lower her powerful voice, "Bunny's put me next to Oliver and of course he'll talk to Frances all the time about poetry and things and I wanted to ask him if I could use his car to-morrow because I don't want to waste my petrol taking people to church, so I'll have to talk to you."

"Yes, yes," said Captain Barclay, returning with a jump from his own meditations, "do let's talk."

"What's wrong with you?" said Lucy. "You must have been thinking."

The amount of scorn she put into this simple statement roused Captain Barclay's sense of politeness.

"I beg your pardon, Lucy," he said. "I was thinking, and I'll tell you what—I mean I'll tell you what I was thinking about. I thought how nice it would be if one could suddenly make one's arms very long and stretch them out under the table and catch someone's feet that one don't like and pull him off his chair right under the table and kick him."

As he said this his usually pleasant face assumed a perfectly ferocious air. So conscious was he of the glance of dislike which he had thrown towards David that he wished he had not spoken, but Lucy took it as a very good joke and laughed so much that she choked and begged Captain Barclay between her chokes to hit her on the back, which he obligingly did. Lucy then told him what, in various senses of that phrase, she would like to do to people she didn't like, and so enthralling was the subject that Captain Barclay quite forgot his troubles for the moment, and Lettice, casting a slanting look across the table, thought that if Lucy and he were made to be happy together she might as well have a little happiness herself and threw herself conversationally into David's arms more than ever.

Miss Bunting, having seen that Captain Barclay and Lucy were happily settled, was able to devote her whole attention to Bill Marling who to her represented the norm; that is he had been properly brought up by a nannie, had been to the right prep. school, the right public school, was in the right regiment, was the husband of a very suitable wife and the father of very suitable children, to whose dullness she was disposed to turn a lenient eye, and would come in for the right kind of property which he would run, if Fate allowed it, in the right way. The conversation was almost entirely about the children, and Mrs. Marling from her son's other side was drawn into it, so that Mr. Harvey with his neighbour Lettice monopolised by David found himself deserted. This he did not mind, for he was in the throes of poetry and having learnt as a Civil Servant to do his literary work in office hours found but little difficulty in continuing it in society. One or two phrases in Jehan le Capet's *Belphégor* were still worrying him and as he ate his turkey he was able to consider several variants, each of which seemed to him more satisfactory than the last. He had been looking forward to the dinner party for some time, not from any particular love for the Marlings, though he liked Oliver well enough and admired Lettice as a woman, though as an intelligence one had to admit that she simply did not exist, but because his sister had been so very testy and uppish of late that any change from her society was welcome. In vain did he remind himself that he was a Government official of proved capacity, due for recognition in the Honours List before long, a poet recognised by the people who read his poetry, that Tape and Sealing Wax and Regional Commissioners were engaged in a titanic struggle for his services; the fact remained that Frances not only looked upon him as a younger brother, which indeed he was, but would treat him as such. And considering that he was a Principal while she was simply a temporary clerk for the duration, and a woman at that, he could sometimes hardly bear it. There was the Board of Tape and Sealing Wax in London (for with its dignified conservative tradition it had been last in the race for Blackpool, Harrogate, Malvern and other health resorts and had been obliged to stay in town as noth-

ing short of a mammoth hotel would hold it) clamouring for his special knowledge; there was Peter clamouring for them to come and share his flat; and just
because Frances thought of marrying Oliver Marling
he had to put the Board and Peter off day by day with
excuses. If this went on much longer both would lose
interest and he and Frances would be landed in Barsetshire for the rest of the war. And there was the
ever-present and ever-growing irritation of Mrs.
Smith, who far from bringing the hen back had managed to get another of the Red House hens to keep it
company till its convalescence was complete, which
would be—or so Hilda said—when she had got the
whole lot. Hilda too was getting tired of Geoffrey and
was too apt to remember that she had been his under-
nurse, though very unfairly she did not so often remember that she had also been under-nurse to
Frances. Flown by turkey and some very good bur-
gundy he invented a scene in which he told Frances
and Hilda exactly what he thought of them, defied
Mrs. Smith and went up to London alone to live in
Peter's flat and reknit the threads of Bloomsbury life.
If Frances wanted to marry Oliver, let her, though it
seemed hard on Oliver.

From these pleasant musings he was roused by the
sound of voices raised in argument, one of the voices,
inevitably, being Lucy's. The theme under discussion
was Who are our Allies with divagations into the question of Who is at War with Whom, and as no one had
any accurate knowledge on the subject there was a
wide field for surmise. Mr. Marling took the view that
if that feller in India with spectacles and all his ribs
stickin' out had been shot out of hand we'd be able to
get somewhere. Natives were England's curse, he said.
Look at the world now with natives loose all over the
place makin' a mess of everything. On being pressed
for his definition of natives he said, Well, foreigners
then, which raised a storm of protest from his younger
hearers.

"But Pater," said Mrs. Bill, Pater being a name to

which Mr. Marling took peculiar exception though he had never quite liked to tell his daughter-in-law so to her face, and if he had she would only have thought it was one of Pater's funny old ways and gone on using it, "Hitler's a foreigner, but you can't exactly call him a native. He's not a nigger."

Lucy said stoutly that he was and Mrs. Bill laughed, because Lucy was always so amusing.

"Now, what about the Chinese," said David, leaping into the fray. "They are undoubtedly natives, but one would hardly call them foreigners. I think to be a foreigner one has to be a European."

Mr. Marling said things had come to a pretty pass if we had to have natives for allies.

Several members of the party endeavoured to explain to him what he really meant, but were all bellowed down by Lucy.

"I'll tell you what," said Lucy looking round with the air of a distinguished but autocratic lecturer till every one was hypnotised by her gaze and by the noise she made, "when we went to tea at the Deanery, Mrs. Morland said a very good thing and I've thought about it several times. She said the Russians weren't exactly our allies, except that us both being attacked by Hitler made us have to pull together, because they certainly wouldn't have done anything for us if Hitler had left them alone. And I think the Chinese are the same. I mean they can't exactly call us allies, because we didn't do anything for them till the Japs started fighting us, so we are the kind of allies to them that the Russians are to us."

She looked proudly round and ate some more turkey.

"A very well-reasoned and cogent argument," said David.

"Rot," said Lucy.

"—which leads us," David went on, "to a consideration of the following thesis: if the Russians are to us as we are to the Chinese, what are the Chinese to the Russians?"

"They aren't anything," said Lucy, who was much enjoying this intellectual conversation, "because neither of them have done anything for each other."

"According to the arguments we have just heard," said Oliver, "there are no such things as allies."

Miss Harvey said with the easy condescension of a university woman that David's thesis was reducible to a very simple arithmetical formula: as x is to y, so y is to z. This would give the value of z as y^2 divided by x. She then paused.

"Then," said David, looking with earnest interest at Miss Harvey, "the English squared divided by the Russians equal the Chinese."

"I didn't mean that," said Miss Harvey, flushing and looking, for a lady at a dinner party, almost cross. "I merely wished to demonstrate the absurdity of trying to reduce human relationships, or rather international relationships from which the human element can never be absent, to any definite terms."

"And so you did," said Mr. Harvey in a very unbrotherly way.

If the Harveys had been at home Miss Harvey would have said, "Don't be a fool, Geoffrey," but being among friends she contented herself with a swift look of dislike at her brother which she quickly converted into a look of exquisite tolerance for Oliver, whose eyes were hurting so much that he did not fully appreciate it.

Mrs. Bill said it seemed so dreadful about the Americans.

"Well, well, blood is thicker than water," said Mr. Marling. "Lots of fellers married American girls when I was a young man."

Everyone then told everyone else about the girls, or men, they had known who married American men, or girls.

"What I mean is," said Mrs. Bill, who had great powers of sticking to her point however pointless, "that the Americans being English originally makes one feel particularly sorry for them, especially at Christmas, because the Japanese are simply idolaters."

Captain Barclay said he felt much sorrier for us.

"But after all," said Mrs. Bill, cheering up, "we are all like one big nation now."

"President Roosevelt and ministers of state defend us!" said David. "Not now, not ever, Mrs. Bill. But truly Allies, I think, because we have done something for each other and I hope we'll do some more. If Miss Harvey could give us the formula—?"

He looked at Miss Harvey who had quite recovered her temper and shook her head laughing.

"'Oh! W, X, Y, Z,
It has just come into my head,'"

said Oliver thoughtfully, "that much as I may dislike my cousin David at times—"

David blew him a kiss.

"—if anyone tried to annoy him I should be glad to give that person a whack in the eye."

Several voices, headed by Lucy's, gave their opinions on Anglo-American relations.

As soon as a lull occurred Miss Bunting, who with Mrs. Marling and Bill had remained a silent audience of the debate, cleared her throat.

"I think," she said, her voice and expression assuming the stern tenderness which was her attitude to her old pupils, "that although the English and the Americans have been parted for a great many years, for so long that they have forgotten on both sides what the quarrel was really about, we cannot quite forget that they were our children once. Children for whom one has cared deeply—I cannot of course speak of children of my own, but of the many who have been under my care—may do many things that wound or offend one and there are times when one may feel hurt and angry. But if any of those children get into trouble we forget all that is past in our wish to stand by them, and the more so if the trouble comes to them unprovoked, through treachery and brutality."

There was a moment's silence and a slight embarrassment among the company.

"Good old Bunny," said David, raising his glass and bowing to her. "And never shall I forget how you stood up for me when John came back for the holidays and said the pony that Uncle Giles—most meanly I must say—had given to us both was only mine on Tuesdays and Fridays, which were the days I went to the Vicarage for my Latin coaching. And just after I had thrown the schoolroom kettle-holder down the back stairs too. When I am married," he added, turning to Lettice, "Bunny will be an honoured pensioner at my board and tell my children what an angel their papa was. I do hope my wife will take it in good part."

Lettice said she was sure she would.

The dessert, consisting chiefly of some ginger and some crystallised fruits mysteriously obtained by David and presented to his Cousin Amabel on the condition that she should ask no questions, having been rather greedily eaten, Mrs. Marling, who knew that her husband would propose the King's health if not checked, collected the ladies and went away. Not that she entertained any but the most loyal feelings for His Majesty, but America had been embarrassment enough for one evening.

As Miss Harvey left Oliver's side she managed to lay her hand for a moment on his coat sleeve and Oliver was annoyed to feel a slight thrill, although at the same time he wished to goodness that she wouldn't touch him so much. Captain Barclay, standing aside to let Mrs. Marling and Miss Bunting pass, saw David pick up Lettice's bag from the floor and give it to her with what seemed to him quite exaggerated courtesy. Nor did he see any reason why David should remain standing for an instant and look down into his cousin's eyes. But this was no reason why he should not talk shop to David over the port, and as always he felt the indefinable charm which consisted chiefly in being Davidish, and thought very generously that no one who competed with David would have very much chance.

"Here, you, Carver," said Mr. Marling, suddenly interrupting himself in the middle of a discussion that he and Bill were having about the re-letting of a farm on the property, "you're not having any port."

"Harvey, papa dear, not Carver," said Oliver.

"Same thing," said Mr. Marling testily.

"The bottle stands with you, Harvey," said David, suddenly becoming Peacockian in appreciation of his cousin William's peculiarities. "Buzz it and let us have a catch. Come, I'll strike up first."

"You'll never get a glass of port like this again," said Mr. Marling. "Last in the cellar."

Mr. Harvey thanked his host very much and said he never took more than one glass of port because it didn't suit him.

As Mr. Marling showed imminent signs of bursting with rage at the pseudo-Carver's milksop spirit, Bill hastily intervened and said he had been round the cellar on Tuesday and there were a dozen in the bin next to the old cider cask.

"A dozen, eh?" said Mr. Marling, determined to make the worst of it. "Well, they'll see me out."

"Come, come, sir, we all hope to see you live to a green old age and drink confusion to Boney at your great-grandson's christening," said David, to the intense delight of Bill and Oliver who relished their father's oddities.

Mr. Marling, also softened by the Davidishness of David, smiled grimly and in an access of hospitality insisted on re-filling Mr. Harvey's glass himself.

"It's a pity I don't know a catch," said David reflectively. "Something about a monk so grey and a damsel fair, And a trolling bowl to drown Old Care. Does that sound right?"

"Quite authentic," said Mr. Harvey, who could enter into a literary jest with any man in Illyria. He then drank all his port at a gulp, eyed narrowly and suspiciously by his host who could not abide to see a good

wine so treated. Mr. Marling, despairing of the rising
generation, took them all to the large drawing-room.
Here, in accordance with a long established custom at
Christmas, he did violence to his feelings by staying
with his family instead of going to write letters,
though as he went to sleep almost at once he felt the
violence the less.

Lettice would have liked to talk to Captain Barclay,
or if this were impossible, and indeed she hardly knew
what she wanted to say to him except that whatever it
was it could not be said before a roomful of people,
then to David. He had been the most delightful dinner
companion and when he had, as they got up after dinner, looked steadily into her eyes, she had taken up
the challenge and looked back, and with the cruel, secret triumph that the nicest of women can feel, had
been certain that her gaze left him troubled. But it
was Mr. Harvey who approached her first and flinging
his lock of hair off his forehead sat down near her.
Lettice made the best of a bad job by enquiring after
his translation of *Belphégor* and so by a natural transi-
tion, after Mr. Harvey had talked about himself for
nearly half an hour, to Mademoiselle Duchaux, asking
how she was.

Mr. Harvey said she had had a row with a Countess
who was head of the thés-dansants scheme and in revenge, though how exactly it was revenge he couldn't
make out, had joined the Corps Féminin and was now
a Corporal.

"I can't quite see her in uniform," said Lettice.

"No more you would if you did," said Mr. Harvey
darkly. She had, he said, forced him to give her lunch
in town, when she had sketched for him very unfavourable biographies of most of her fellow-workers
and boasted a great deal of her complete and successful defiance of discipline.

"But the really awful thing is," said Mr. Harvey,
"that she has told her nephew to come and see us, and
he rang up last night to say he was on leave with some
friends, and they had got a car and would bring him

to see us to-morrow. He didn't know what time he would get to us and it's very awkward, being Christmas Day and Hilda having most of the day off, and Frances and I were going over to Norton Park for tea."

Lettice was so intoxicated by her passage of eyes with David that kindness overflowed and she suggested that she might help the Harveys by giving tea to the nephew and his friends.

"That is very kind of you," said Mr. Harvey, obviously much relieved. "Are you sure your people wouldn't mind?"

Lettice considered this and said they certainly might mind, especially Papa, because he always wanted Christmas Day to be sacred to the family, who would mostly far rather go somewhere else.

"But I'll tell you what," she said, and even as she said it knew that Mr. Harvey would miss the use of Lucy's catchword and thought how David would have taken it up at once, "I've got to go down to the stables to-morrow to write some letters. The central heating is on because Ed sees to it, and I could give them tea there and perhaps get Oliver and Lucy to help, or Bunny, and then my people can't mind. What is the nephew's name? Is he an officer?"

Mr. Harvey said Jules Duval, but as for being an officer he could not say, because French ideas about military ranks were so peculiar and they used the word officer all wrong. All he knew was that Jules, when he saw him for a moment in London, looked like a general.

"Then he's probably a corporal, or perhaps a sergeant," said Lettice. "They dress all wrong. But anyway I can say monsieur all the time. You don't know who the friends are, do you?"

Mr. Harvey didn't, and as the port he had so unwilling drunk began to make him feel cross and low, his spirits and his conversation drooped. Lettice, rather bored, looked round for more entertainment. David was playing six-pack bézique with Lucy, Oliver and Miss Harvey were looking at a book together, Miss

Bunting, Mrs. Marling and Bill were talking family,
Mr. Marling was asleep. She looked for help towards
Captain Barclay, but he, kind by nature, was doing his
best to entertain Mrs. Bill, whom the family, although
they were all fond of her, often found left out of their
conversations. So again she had to make the best of it,
and Mr. Harvey, valiantly fighting the depression that
was overcoming him, told her at great length about his
chances of getting back to London and sharing a flat
with Peter, till she felt her face going stiff with dullness and she thought the evening would never end.

Her brother Oliver, though no one would have sus-
pected it, had exactly the same feeling. Though Miss
Harvey attracted him more than she had ever done,
though she said all the right things about the volume
of Dr. Bohun's sermons which he had found at the
back of a shelf in a secondhand bookshop in Barchester, though her hands had lain lightly on his in turning
the pages, his eyes and head made him quite stupid.
The dinner, the lights, the chatter, all conspired to
send twinges of pain through his head and make talking an effort. So when the game of bézique came to a
noisy end with half the cards on the floor and Lucy
loudly boasting that she had won eighteenpence from
David, and Mr. Marling woke up and saying it was
high time to be in bed went off almost staggering with
sleep, Oliver seized the opportunity and shut the book.

"I can't tell you how much I have enjoyed this evening," said Miss Harvey getting up. "To be here, with
your family, is one of my real joys in exile. And I am
so delighted to have met your brother and his wife."

"Bill is a first rate fellow," said Oliver, pleased by
this praise, "and he'll do Papa so much good. They
have a lot in common and Papa likes to talk to him
about the place. When the war is over we hope Bill
and Mrs. Bill will be here more. The children ought to
know it, as this will be their home some day."

"Oh," said Miss Harvey. There was a barely percep-
tible pause before she said, "You mean your brother
will come into the estate some day."

"I hope so," said Oliver. "It doesn't do to think of the chance that he mightn't."

"How young he looks," said Miss Harvey.

"People often take me for the elder brother," said Oliver, "but it's only because I'm a stupid crock and Bill doesn't know what being ill means."

Miss Harvey made no answer, but looked at him with a very beautiful expression of tender sympathy. Her eyes, like lovely pale uncut emeralds in colour, fascinated Oliver. "I wish," said Miss Harvey after a pause, "that this evening were not over."

"So do I," said Oliver. "It is the only chance of getting the creases out of my tails that I'm likely to have till next Christmas."

"But we shall meet again," said Miss Harvey, which indeed seemed probable. "Why not look in to-morrow after church and have a drink? Geoffrey," she said as her brother came towards her, "ask Oliver and Lettice to come in after church to-morrow and finish the sherry."

Mr. Harvey added his entreaties.

"Oh, I say, Oliver," said Lucy, "can I use your car to-morrow, because I don't want to use my petrol taking people to church."

Oliver, who was used to this Dominical form of blackmail from his young sister, nodded and wished he hadn't, for the motion made his head hurt more than ever. The Harveys bade slightly exaggerated farewells and went off.

"I get a little tired of those young people," said Mrs. Marling. "Oliver, what about bed?" and for once Oliver was grateful for his mother's interference and took her advice. David too said he must go.

"One minute, David," said Mrs. Marling. "I promised Cousin Emily that book of Mrs. Morland's that she lent me. Lettice, will you find it? It is in the sitting-room upstairs."

"Can I help you?" said Captain Barclay, at last seeing his chance, but Lucy loudly claimed him to help her to put the presents in the children's stockings and by their beds, and as he had promised he had to go. So Lettice went upstairs to find the book.

She had only looked in two of the places where her mother was quite certain she had put it when David came in.

"Enter villain," said David.

Lettice smiled at him and went on looking.

"Cousin Amabel has just remembered that it isn't here at all," said David. "It is in the hall, so I said I'd come and tell you."

Lettice thanked him.

"Don't go yet," said David. "I have an inordinate amount to tell you. To begin with, Robert is in the Honours List. He gets a K.C.B. and Agnes will be Lady Graham. She is very pleased because she says it will be so nice to see 'presented by their mother, Lady Graham,' in the *Times* when the girls go to court about 1950 or so. On the other hand she likes being Mrs. Robert Graham because Robert is such a beautiful name. I think she rather hoped that Robert might be created a Duke's younger son so that she could be Lady Robert, but evidently the War Office thought otherwise."

"That is very nice," said Lettice. "Every one seems to be a Lord or a Sir now. One can hardly keep pace. It will just be plain Mrs. Watson when I present Diana and Clare."

"Not so plain neither," said David, "if that was what you meant to say."

Lettice smiled again.

"Hang it all, why can I not be simple and sincere?" said David suddenly. "Answer: if I were it would only be affectation in me. Lettice, do you think you could consider being plain Mrs. David Leslie? I can't be more simple and sincere than that."

Lettice only said, "Oh, David."

"Listen, love," said David. "I am going to talk about myself and tell you what, like anything. If it is of the faintest interest to you I've never proposed to anyone before. A good many people have had little moonlight madnesses and thought I did, but we will forget that. I love you and like you. I don't think I'd be Mr. Murdstone to the children. My mother and Agnes would be enchanted, so would my father. I cannot think of any other reasons. If they are not enough please signify dissent in the usual manner."

Lettice did not move, but she looked from side to side as if searching for help.

"There does not seem to be that enthusiasm one might expect," said David. "Listen, my precious Lettice. Have I a rival?"

"Yes," said Lettice.

"Animal, vegetable—no, that is in bad taste," said David. "Is it Tom Barclay?"

"Yes," said Lettice again.

"Then bless you," said David. "Mamma and papa and Agnes do not know, and they won't know, so you must go on coming to Holdings, for it gives great, great pleasure. So good-bye."

Lettice looked frightened.

"It is not suicide," said David, "but I have a job waiting for me and can go ahead. I have no intention of getting killed. So bless you again and when I come back I hope to find you all happily settled and shall not do any Enoch Arden-ing at the window, but come in at the front door with a belated wedding present."

"Thank you very much, David," said Lettice in a small voice.

"Well, I have offered you free from stain courage and faith, and I am reluctantly compelled to admit vain faith and courage vain," said David. "But I still like you very much."

"So do I," said Lettice. "But I do truly think I would be too dull for you."

"Bless your heart, my pretty, you may be right, but that would have been my affair," said David. "Goodbye." He kissed her affectionately and she clung to him for a moment with a pleasantly mixed feeling of a little heartbreak for his disappointment and a good deal of satisfaction in a thoroughly romantic situation carried through with great propriety on both sides. David ran downstairs and Lettice went to her room, where her spirits fell a good deal and she wished more than ever that Captain Barclay were there to comfort her, for she somehow did not feel she would be dull to him.

In the large drawing-room David found Miss Bunting by herself, who told him that the other ladies had gone to bed and Bill was in the study.

"Grouse in the gun-room," said David thoughtfully. "I've got mamma's book. Good night, Bunny. I'm going abroad very soon, but I shan't be killed and I'll send you picture postcards if the Censor allows me. Oh, Merry sent you her love and she hoped all was going well, whatever that may mean."

"What is it now, David?" said Miss Bunting with a piercing look.

"Nothing, Miss Bunting," said David.

"You may have had dirty hands, but you usen't to be untruthful," said Miss Bunting severely.

"Well, to you only, Bunny," said David, perhaps glad to speak to a friend who knew the best and worst of him, "I asked Lettice to marry me, and she doesn't feel equal to it."

"My poor little David," said Miss Bunting, looking up with unexpected tenderness at her tall ex-pupil. "But it would never have done."

"Perhaps not," said David. "You were usually right, Bunny. But it is a mortification. However, this is unmanly weakness and I must go home. Don't let Cousin Amabel or anyone know. And one other secret for you. Robert will be knighted in the New Year Honours."

"That," said Miss Bunting, "is highly suitable. Bless you, David. You were always one of my favourite pupils."

"Good old Bunny," said David, and giving his old governess a parting hug he went to the back hall to put his coat on. Here he met his cousin Lucy carrying a number of parcels which were obviously going to overbalance.

"I'll tell you what, David," said Lucy. "You can help me with these. Tom is upstairs in the nursery listening to nana about how awful Everleen is. She caught him while we were doing Diana's stocking. I think nana has a crush on him."

"I'll tell you whatter," said David, removing a few of the parcels from Lucy's arms and putting them on an oak chest. "Talking of crushes, you know Tom Barclay pretty well, don't you?"

"We haven't got a crush if that's what you mean," said Lucy scornfully.

"Of course not, my girl," said David. "But will you give him a message from me? Tell him I'm so sorry I couldn't say good-bye and I'm going abroad almost at once and my best wishes and he is to go ahead. Can you remember? That's right. Good-bye, my love, and let who will be clever."

He embraced her and the rest of the parcels heartily and disappeared into the night.

Lucy looked after him thoughtfully, re-collected her parcels and went upstairs.

CHAPTER THIRTEEN

WHEN MILLIE POULTER ARRIVED AT THE RED HOUSE ON Christmas Day she found a far from Christmas spirit in the kitchen. They, said Hilda, by which sinister pronoun she meant her ex-charges and present employers, had both got up on the wrong sides of their beds this morning and were having a fine old argument last night when they got back from the Hall. Talking about going back to London they were and Miss Frances saying she dessaid she'd like living in the country and Mr. Geoffrey saying please yourself, it won't hurt me, and something about a young man not coming into the place, but I couldn't be bothered to listen any more so I shut the kitchen door and turned the wireless on. You can have a cup of tea, Millie, and finish that bacon if you like and then you can do the bedrooms.

"Mrs. Smith had a letter from her mother in Torquay yesterday, Hilda," said Millie, her mouth full of bacon and tea. "Mrs. Cox told me about it when she was stuffing the turkey. Mrs. Smith read it to her when

Mrs. Cox took her lunch in. The lady help as lived with her mother has had a quarrel with her and the old lady wants to come and live with Mrs. Smith because they had a bomb at Torquay. Mrs. Cox said she wouldn't be surprised if Mrs. Smith wanted to have the Red House back."

"Nor no one else wouldn't be surprised," said Hilda. "What she's taken out of this house since we come here you wouldn't believe it, Millie, not if I was to tell you. Mr. Govern said only last week when he come in for a cup of tea that it was a fair shame. Well, Mr. Govern, I said, it's not my business and I never was one to interfere, but two of my dusters and the egg-whisk in a week with hardly so much as by your leave and as for seeing them again I'd as soon expect to see old Hitler driving a bus."

"I like Mr. Govern," said Millie.

"That's all right, my girl," said Hilda, "but don't you go imagining things."

Millie giggled.

"That Ed asked me last night," she said.

"Well!" said Hilda.

"So I said No sauce from you, Ed Pollet," said Millie, continuing her artless tale, "and so we fixed to get married next year when Mrs. Pollet gets her old-age pension. Seems I ought to register next year, but if I marry Ed I don't get called up, see?"

"It's a regular nuisance all this calling-up," said Hilda. "Seems Mr. Govern's niece that does for him, the one that's post-woman, is going into munitions, so I said I wouldn't mind taking on the job, quite joking-like. It'll save you coming down here every day for your cup of tea, Mr. Govern, I said, so I shouldn't wonder if I was to be married first. I saw it all in the tea-cup, first night we was here."

"Did you see me and Ed in the tea-cup, Hilda?" said Millie.

But Hilda, feeling that she had allowed Millie to go too far, said Talk, talk, talk and the beds not done, and

drove her upstairs. She then went to the dining-room
to clear away the breakfast things.

It was here very plain to her that her employers
were still having what she called a fine old turn-up. To
keep up the fiction of an Olympian existence, free
from the storms that rage in more humble bosoms, Mr.
and Miss Harvey feigned to be speaking of Mlle Duchaux's nephew, Peter's flat, the Board of Tape and
Sealing Wax and such matters. Hilda, disappointed in
her hopes of hearing them argue, delayed the clearing
away in a diabolical manner as much as possible, but
finally the last crumb had been removed and she had
no excuse to linger. Unwillingly she picked up the tray
and went towards the door which she had left ajar, the
better to be able to hook it open with her foot.

"All right, Hilda, I'll shut it," said Mr. Harvey and to
her great annoyance shut it firmly behind her.

"No need to slam the door, Geoffrey," said Miss
Harvey.

Mr. Harvey said he hadn't slammed it and she must
know by now that the catch didn't work properly unless one did, and if she wanted Hilda to be able to
hear everything that was being said in the dining-
room, he didn't.

Miss Harvey said, "Really, Geoffrey," in a sisterly
way.

"Really, yourself," said Mr. Harvey rudely and without much point, so his sister got up and left the room,
shutting the door with ostentatious gentleness. It at
once swung ajar, so Mr. Harvey was able to comfort
himself a little by slamming it again with great violence. Hilda in the kitchen remarked to Mr. Govern,
who had called in to pass the compliments of the season and have a cup of tea on his way to chapel, that
they were having a fine old Christmas dust-up in the
dining-room and she wouldn't be surprised if they all
went back to London as Mr. Geoffrey and Miss
Frances didn't seem settled like.

"You won't be going, Miss Plane, I hope," said Mr.
Govern.

"Depends who asks me to stay," said Hilda.

"I'll tell you who will," said Mr. Govern, and drawing a small sprig of mistletoe from his pocket, he waved it above his head and saluted Hilda with great gallantry. Millie, coming down from the bedrooms with a dustpan, was so overcome by this sight that she dropped the dustpan and the dirt went all over the floor. Mr. Govern in a Scroogian Christmas spirit saluted Millie too, and putting the mistletoe in his buttonhole went off to chapel, leaving the two ladies to get on with the turkey and the vegetables.

Mr. Harvey, left alone in the dining-room, wished he were one of the people in history who broke china to relieve their feelings. Willingly would he have smashed a whole gallery of Sèvres, and even more willingly, because closer to hand, the green glass animals with twisted legs that inhabited Mrs. Smith's diningroom mantelpiece. The thought of dilapidations made him refrain, so he lit his pipe with a hand shaking with rage, dropped it quite by accident, broke the stem, swore, lit a cigarette and angrily paced the room.

It was high-time, he felt, that someone took Frances down a bit. There was that most delightful offer of returning to the Board of Tape and Sealing Wax, that other enchanting offer of sharing Peter's flat. The Red House could, he was sure, be sub-let with the greatest ease and they could all go back to London where people appreciated one. But just because Frances felt she was Somebody at the Regional Commissioner's Office and because she fancied Oliver Marling, she was being, not to put too fine a point upon it, devilishly obstinate. She might think she could marry Oliver and perhaps she was right, but Mr. Harvey had his doubts. Also he did not fancy the connection. Taken singly the Marlings were pleasant enough, though Mrs. Marling and Lucy did bully him dreadfully and Mr. Marling would call him Carver, but their ways were not his. Lettice, whom he had at first found rather disturbing, turned out to be rather a dull woman with no allure. And not one of them, unless it were Oliver, would fit into his

scheme of London life. Better far to leave these barbarians to their own society and return to the shades
of Whitehall, if only Frances would see reason. Last
night when they got home she had been extremely disagreeable, so that what with her temper and the unwanted glasses of port, he had spent a wretched and
wakeful night, thinking of crushing repartees. Some of
these he had tried at breakfast, but somehow by the
light of day they had lost their brilliance and cogency
and he and Frances had had a very unpleasant quarrel, Frances chilling his blood by saying that she distinctly remembered a clause in the lease by which
they could not sub-let without Mrs. Smith's approval
and adding that he could ask her about it himself, because she wouldn't. In the middle of the quarrel
young Lady Norton had rung up to wish them Happy
Christmas and suggest that they should come back to
Norton Park as she could not get really nice P.G.'s who
liked roughing it. Frances had said if he wanted to go
to Eleanor and George he could do so, but she
wouldn't, and at this moment Hilda had come to clear
breakfast away.

If by wishing Mr. Harvey could have transported
himself to Peter's flat he would have done so, but he
realised that before he could get away from the Red
House he would be obliged to go through several
more scenes with Frances as well as giving notice at
the Regional Commissioner's. It was Christmas Day,
there was no newspaper, Mlle Duchaux's nephew,
blast him, was coming at an hour unnamed, and then
he and Frances would have to drive in sulky silence or
unamiable bickering to Norton Park. In black despair
he got out his paper and began to work upon Jehan le
Capet's sonnet.

Hardly had he got into the swing of things when
Frances, looking very neat, opened the door and said
she could see he was not coming to church, so would
he, if it was not too much trouble, look at the drawing-
room fire from time to time, though she knew it was no
use expecting him to remember. Mr. Harvey pretend-

ed to have been so busy that he had not properly heard what she said, which did not in the least take his sister in, but she repeated her words, wavered between slamming the door and leaving it ajar, decided on the latter course and slammed the front door instead. With black hatred in his heart Mr. Harvey got up, shut the dining-room door, and settled again as well as he could to this work.

An hour or so passed. Mr. Harvey by a great effort had worked himself into the requisite state of translator's frenzy and had almost finished the sonnet when a slight sound drew his attention. Looking up, he saw Mrs. Smith.

"I have just slipped over," said Mrs. Smith, "to wish you and Miss Harvey the compliments of the season. I did not go to church. Last year I had Mr. Smith. Not that he was able to attend divine service on Christmas Day, for he had one of his bad turns and was sleeping it off, but it makes such a difference to have a man in the house. I felt that if I went this year everyone would be gazing upon my widow's weeds and passing the remark that things were quite different this Christmas. But you must not let me disturb your work."

Mr. Harvey looked at her with the mad expression peculiar to those who have been deeply sunk in literary composition and are too rudely roused.

"Mr. Smith was just like that after doing the year's accounts," said Mrs. Smith, sitting down. "He used to like me to sit by him. Of course I couldn't really help, but he said my sweet presence was all in all to him. Don't take any notice of me, just go on as if I wasn't here."

Mr. Harvey wished that he had not quarrelled with Frances. Had they been on better terms he would have been safely at church, or she would have been in the dining-room to protect him. He thought of ringing for Hilda, but feared her scorn.

"I'm afraid you find me rather distrait," he said. "I have to work even on Christmas Day."

"So did Mr. Smith," said his relict. "I shall just sit

here and think it is Mr. Smith writing to his uncle Joe.
He always wrote to him at Christmas. You know, Mr.
Harvey, you have quite a look of Mr. Smith as they
say."

Mr. Harvey was so frightened that he nearly got
under the table. His sister's gloomy prophecy came to
his mind, and he thought that if he found himself
forced to offer his hand to Mrs. Smith Frances would
say, I told you so. Had it not been for this strengthen-
ing thought he might have done it. As it was he went
into a kind of swoon or syncope. Through it he heard
Mrs. Smith continue,

"But of course not with Mr. Smith's eyes. You do not
know, Mr. Harvey, what it is to Love Once. That
Chapter in my Life is closed."

On hearing this good news Mr. Harvey revived,
which was just as well, for Mrs. Smith's next words
were worth attention.

"It seems," said Mrs. Smith, "quite a shame to trouble a gentleman like you, but I have no one to speak
for me since Mr. Smith passed on. The fact is, Mr.
Harvey, that my mother wishes to leave Torquay and
settle here. With our two little incomes we could make
quite a home for ourselves here. So I thought I would
have a little talk to you about it and seeing Miss Harvey on her way to church I said to myself, I will just
slip over and speak to Mr. Harvey."

Mr. Harvey thought, very quickly. Here was a
heaven-sent excuse for leaving the Red House. If he
could sufficiently implicate himself with Mrs. Smith he
might have the whole thing arranged, except for the
legal part, before Frances came back. True, she would
be even more disagreeable than she had yet been, but
with the prospect of freedom in sight he could stand
it. The whole thing would be difficult, but worth
doing. In a few weeks he might be in Peter's flat, with
intelligent or literary friends coming in and out and all
the gossip of the coulisses of Whitehall.

"What exactly do you propose, Mrs. Smith?" he said
in his best Civil Service manner.

"I will just," said Mrs. Smith, grabbling about among her necklaces and fishing out a long piece of black cord, "put my poncksnay *on* and read you my little suggestions."

She put on her pince-nez and after further grabbling in her bag produced a half sheet of paper.

"Perhaps, Mr. Harvey, it would be simplest if we let matters remain as they are," said Mrs. Smith, on hearing which words of ill-cheer Mr. Harvey thought of going down on his knees. But he was glad he hadn't when she continued, "If you sub-let the house to me, you could go on paying me your present rent and I would pay you the same that Mrs. Cox asks for her rooms without board or service, thirty shillings a week. Of course if Mr. Smith were alive he would look after my interests, but I am quite alone."

"As far as I can see, Mrs. Smith," said Mr. Harvey, "I would then be losing three pounds fifteen a week on the transaction. We must consider this."

"After all it is my own wee house," said Mrs. Smith, turning her mournful eyes on him.

Anxious as Mr. Harvey was to escape, he could not do it on such terms. After a good deal of talking, during which he was in mortal terror that Mrs. Smith might take offence and cry off altogether, it was decided that their lawyers should go into the matter. Mrs. Smith obviously wanted her house and he thought there would be no real difficulty. Luckily the lease was in his name and Frances could not, or at least would not, he hoped, kill him.

"Just one more little thing, Mr. Harvey," said Mrs. Smith, "The chookies. Of course they have done a great deal of damage in my little garden with putting up the shed and all, but suppose I just take them over and we say no more about it. Of course they will cost me a great deal to feed and I have but my widow's mite, but sooner than any unpleasantness that is what I will do."

The whole unfairness of this suggestion rose up at

Mr. Harvey, but Life was unfair, Frances was unfair
and one might as well give in.

"Very well, Mrs. Smith," he said, basely betraying
his absent sister, "I daresay that will be all right. Perhaps you will speak to my sister about it."

"Pardon me, Mr. Harvey," said Mrs. Smith, "but Mr.
Smith made it a rule never to do business with ladies.
Of course he would never have let me do my own business like this, but he is not here, though I often feel
he has an eye on me and knows how hard life has been
for me since he passed over. And I hear your maid is
going to be married?"

"Hilda?" said Mr. Harvey. "You must be mistaken."

"Trust we women to know these little things," said
Mrs. Smith almost archly. "I got it from Mrs. Cox's
Millie and she says it's a settled thing, with the estate
carpenter. And here, lo and behold! Miss Harvey coming back from church. Wonders will never cease. I
shall be one too many."

There was nothing for it but to say of course she
wouldn't and get out the sherry. Miss Harvey came in
with an air of gracious forgiveness highly exasperating
to her brother. Either the service or some other agency
had evidently much improved her temper.

"A Happy Christmas, Mrs. Smith," she said graciously. "Geoffrey, I met Oliver and Lettice after
church and they are coming in to wish you a Happy
Christmas. They just stopped at Dr. March's on the
way."

"I have just been having a little business talk with
your brother, Miss Harvey," said Mrs. Smith. "We can
break the lease at the six months, you know, and as
your maid is getting married I daresay it will be quite
agreeable to you."

Miss Harvey stared as if she were bereft of her
senses.

"It seems," said Mr. Harvey nervously, "that Hilda
is going to marry the Marlings' estate carpenter, and
as we were thinking of London, it seems quite a good
moment to make a break."

"And I shall look after the chookies as if they were my own," said Mrs. Smith, "and many a time shall I think of you when I collect a dear wee egg. Well, I must be wending my way so I will say au revaw and slip off."

With an inclination of her head she glided from the room and out of the house. At the gate she met Oliver and Lettice.

"A very Happy Christmas," she said. "You know my tenants are leaving and I am going back to my little nest. As Hilda is going to be married it seems quite an appropriate moment."

Nothing could exceed her hearer's surprise. They enquired who the lucky man was and on hearing thought it quite a suitable arrangement. But though they were pining to hear more about the Harveys' sudden change of plan they did not wish to discuss it with Mrs. Smith, so they only lingered for a moment and went on to the Red House.

But in this moment Miss Harvey had been able to say quite a good deal of what she felt to her treacherous brother. Not since the day when he was six and she was seven and a half, and he had knocked down and danced on her sand castle at Littlehampton had he seen such a display of temper. Mr. Harvey was frightened nearly out of his wits, but reflecting that the lease was in his name and that Frances had not a gun or a sword, he valiantly stood his ground.

"Great weak fool!" said his sister. "Do as you like. I hate this house, I always have. You can go to London if you want to and I shall go to Eleanor's. I can go to the office just as well from there and I wish you joy of Peter and all his dear little friends."

Mr. Harvey very wisely said nothing, which so annoyed his sister that she nearly screamed with rage and was telling him what she thought of him in unrestrained language when Oliver and Lettice came in. Naturally she stopped at once, but her voice, her face white with rage, could not be concealed. Happy Christmases were exchanged and sherry drunk.

"You know," said Mr. Harvey, greatly daring, "that we are breaking the lease in January. I have been asked to go back to my own work at the Board of Tape and Sealing Wax and shall share a flat with a friend. Frances is going to Eleanor Norton for a bit, so she will be able to go on with her work at the office."

Miss Harvey said nothing, but looked at her brother with a dislike that was very obvious. She saw in Oliver's face, though he was behaving very well in an embarrassing situation, that if he had ever thought of her with affection, that thought had melted under her eyes. Lettice and Oliver expressed quite sincere regrets that their neighbours were going and said, quite truly, that they would miss them. It was all rather embarrassing and the guests were glad to say they must go back for lunch and take their leave. To put off the evil moment of facing his sister again, Mr. Harvey accompanied them to the gate. He then walked rather aimlessly about the garden, but it was cold, he knew his sister would despise him if she saw him keeping away, so he settled his tie and went indoors. His sister was standing with a cigarette before the fire.

"I daresay you are right, Geoffrey," she said. "I rang up Eleanor while you were seeing them off and arranged for us to go to Norton Park till you go to London. Eleanor wants me to take on her A.R.P. work and I think I would find more scope in it than in the office, so I shall take some things over with me when we go this afternoon. Of course if you like to stay on with Hilda, you can."

This was all the revenge Miss Harvey took on her brother, who was so frightened by the choice offered him between Norton Park and solitude with Hilda that it was a pity his sister could not quite savour her triumph. But their misfortunes were not over, for Miss Bunting and Lucy now appeared.

"Hullo, we've come to say Happy Christmas," said Lucy. "I say, there's a car outside and some French people or something. I expect it's your governess's nephew."

Rather glad of a break in the home atmosphere the Harveys and their guests went out to the gate. A tall, well set-up young man in irreproachable uniform was standing by a car and introduced himself in excellent English as Jules Duval, the nephew of Mlle Duchaux.

"My friends here," he said, beckoning the occupants of the car to get out, "are going to visit some compatriots at the Barchester Hospital and will fetch me when I shall have enjoyed my lunch with you, and your excellent English tea. Venez, vous autres."

A yellow-faced soldier and two black-faced sailors got out and smiled at the company.

The Harveys said a general How do you do and looked enquiringly at M. Duval (for his rank they never dared to ask) for an introduction.

"I'll tell you what," said Lucy, tempering her voice in consideration of the newcomers' feelings, "they're not real French, they're a Cochin-China or whatever it is and niggers."

"Hush, Lucy dear," said Miss Bunting.

"I wish we could give them lunch," said Miss Harvey, untruly.

"Useless, mademoiselle; they go on to Barchester at once," said M. Duval.

The yellow-faced soldier stepped forward a pace, remarking, "Môa, Pléyère." His coloured friends, not to be outdone in courtesy, also stepped forward, saying "Môa Trécastel," "Môa Abdulla," respectively.

"Would M. Abdulla and the rest like some sherry?" said Mr. Harvey, feeling that the morning's nightmare would never come to an end, especially as, to his great confusion, the three strangers laughed very heartily, the nigger sailors with flashing white teeth, the yellow-faced soldier with rather unpleasant yellow fangs.

"Excuse me," said Miss Bunting, "but I think you misunderstand. Voilà, messieurs," she added, and taking from her bag three small packets of cigarettes handed some Players to the yellow-faced soldier, and to the negro sailors a packet of Three Castles and a packet of Abdullas. The cigarettes were accepted with broad smiles.

"Aha, mademoiselle parle français," said M. Duval. "On reconnaît bien à votre accent, mademoiselle, que vous êtes anglaise, mais c'est très bien."

Miss Bunting took no notice at all.

"They return to fetch me at five o'clock," said M. Duval.

"Oh, I forgot to tell you how sorry we are," said Miss Harvey, "that we shall be out this afternoon. But Mrs. Watson—this is her sister, Miss Marling, and this is Miss Bunting—has asked you to tea and we will drop you there on our way to Norton Park. I am afraid our maid will be out, so could your friends call for you at Marling Hall? Anyone will tell them the way."

"Perfectly," said M. Duval. He gave a few instructions to his friends who got into the car, the yellow-faced soldier at the wheel, and drove off.

The Harveys and M. Duval went into the house.

"I say Bunny," said Lucy admiringly, "how on earth did you know about the cigarettes?"

"Tommies are Tommies all the world over," said Miss Bunting. "I must see if Mr. Hobson can let me have a few more after Boxing Day, for one never knows when they will be useful. Now come along, Lucy. Your father and mother will be waiting to drive us up."

Christmas was passing off very well on the whole at Marling Hall. The children had all been good. The elder ones had behaved very well at church and were to come down to lunch, which was a goose, as they had had the turkey last night.

When Oliver and Lettice got back there was a large pile of letters that had come while they were out. Lettice opened hers without much interest. They were nearly all Christmas cards of various degrees of inapplicability, including a half-sheet of paper from a militant-pacifist acquaintance on which was printed in imitation copperplate, "With good wishes for as happy a

Christmas as the world will allow and that next year
may be less wretched than the last." And a few letters
from friends. But she did not much care. Last night
had not been a great success. David's proposal, though
it had not touched her heart, had not unnaturally disturbed her. It had been impossible to get any talk with
Captain Barclay. This morning he had gone off early
on business and she did not know when she would see
him again. Not that she had anything special to say,
but more and more she felt that if he were about there
was safety, and some kind of peace. However one
couldn't go running about the country after officers
and if one did they wouldn't be pleased to see one.

Her depressed reflections were suddenly disturbed
by an exclamation from Oliver.

"Lovely, lovely Christmas!" he said, with what for
him was violent excitement. "Lettice! my darling Pilman is out of the Army and practising in Wimpole
Street again. Now I can go and have my eyes mended." Lettice at once put her private trouble away,
overjoyed that her dear Oliver should have his kind
friend and oculist back again. His face looked happier
than she had seen it for a long while. She pressed his
arm affectionately and took her letters up to her room.

At lunch the chief topic of conversation was naturally the Harveys and Mrs. Smith. Mrs. Marling expressed a conventional sorrow on hearing that they
were leaving so soon, but this deceived no one. Lettice
had had a moment's anxiety that the loss of Miss Harvey might be a disappointment for Oliver, but as he
showed no signs of a broken heart and was rejoicing in
the prospect of a couple of days in London with his
dear Mr. Pilman, she decided that it was all right. So
pleased was she to see him content that she forgot for
the moment the long, arid road of life that lay before
her and quite enjoyed herself.

A good deal of lunch time was taken up in explaining to Mr. Marling exactly what had happened, and he
had the great pleasure of telling all his kind inform-
ants who were bellowing themselves black in the face

that they needn't shout and he always knew that feller Carver wouldn't stay the course, so his family left it at that.

Everyone will be glad to hear that there was a very large plum pudding for which hoarding on an extensive scale had been going on for some months. It was accompanied by rum butter which, as everyone should know, is infinitely superior to brandy butter, as is flaming rum to flaming brandy. Diana and the elder Marling girl each had a sixpence. Unfortunately, the other sacred objects such as imitation silver buttons, rings and hearts were not to be obtained, but a bone button had been provided which fell to Oliver's share.

"That, I am on the whole relieved to say, is my lot," he said to Lettice beside him as he put it on the side of his plate, and Lettice knew that she need have no anxiety about his happiness.

The elder Master Marling, who had been allowed some rum butter for a great treat, now became extremely boring and boasted how he had drunk half a glass of beer at school when Mr. Sawbridge had been called out of the room for a few moments during lunch, assuming on the strength of this the air of a jaded roué or libertine. The little girls showed symptoms of intense admiration.

"That is quite enough, dear," said Miss Bunting. "We do not wish to hear about bad manners. And the beer nowadays is little more than water."

The little girls' admiration subsided, as did Master Marling, who bore no grudge against Miss Bunting, recognising in her the voice of Authority, which his generation needs and unconsciously misses.

"I had such a pretty Christmas card from the Duchess," said Miss Bunting, changing the subject. "A photograph of Gatherum Castle with the Palliser arms emblazoned beneath it and a kind message from her and the Duke."

As no one else had had a ducal Christmas card there was an appreciable pause of respect, broken by Lucy who said,

"I'll tell you what, I had a marvellous card from Jerry."

"Who is Jerry?" said Oliver.

"Oh, you know, Jerry Grant," said Lucy. "It's a photo of the Barchester Fire Station and A Merry Xmas written with fire hoses on the top and a fire bucket below and it says Wishing you Buckets of the Best."

"Very appropriate, dear," said Miss Bunting kindly, yet letting Lucy feel that the subject was now closed.

Presently the children were sent upstairs, and there was some pleasant desultory talk over the débris of lunch and the coffee. Lettice then said she must go down to the stables and write her letters and prepare to receive M. Duval. It was not very amusing to turn out on a dull, cold afternoon, but she had promised, and there it was.

By half past three the day was so depressing that Lettice decided to black out and pretend it was tea time, so when M. Duval was set down at the stables by the Harveys he came into a room full of warmth and soft light.

"But you are altogether well housed," he said to Lettice in French. "Allow that I congratulate you on your apartment. All is in the best taste. One might almost figure to oneself that one was in an apartment in Paris. You will remark that I say almost, for there is something in the French taste which one does not find elsewhere. As for the English taste, it may be well enough in affairs of sport, but in the interior——"

M. Duval made that very unpleasant sound, dear to so many sons of Gallia and the Low Countries, a sound of contempt for which the nearest and very vulgar English equivalent is the raspberry.

Lettice said, also in her best French, that she was glad he liked her flat and she hoped he was enjoying himself in England.

"Quant à cela," said M. Duval, "je vais d'abord vous parler un peu de moi, pour vous expliquer ma person-

alité. Je dois vous dire, en premier lieu, que j'ai très
mauvais caractère."

He wagged a forefinger at Lettice, pregnant with
meaning, though what the meaning was she did not
exactly know, so she offered him a cigarette.

M. Duval said he did not smoke. It was not, he
added, that he despised the good things of this world,
far from it; but he was by nature an ascetic and was
able at any moment to deny himself anything without
in the least feeling the deprivation. "Tenez, je vais
vous raconter," he said, and embarked upon a very
long, dull story of renunciation. He had, he said, in his
youth, a sufficiently gay youth, par exemple, but madame knew what young men were and he would say
no more, been a great smoker. Thirty, forty cigarettes
a day had been as nothing to him. One day it had occurred to him to test his character. "Par suite de cer-
tains évènements, dont je désire que vous ne me de-
mandiez pas une explication, le sujet m'étant assez
pénible en ce qu'il s'agit de ma mère," he sad to Lettice, who did not in the least wish to ask any questions, he had decided that on a certain day he would
cease smoking altogether for six weeks. He paused or-
atorically.

"And did you?" said Lettice.

M. Duval asked her to pardon him, but that was not
the question. The question, he said, was, whether his
character, le Moi, would benefit or not by such an act.
A character like his own, he said, and went on saying
it for nearly ten minutes.

"That is very interesting," said Lettice. "And now I
will get you some tea. You must be quite ready for it."

M. Duval thanked her, but said he never drank tea,
except, he added, under certain conditions which he
would limit himself to precising in the fewest words
possible. As the words seemed to take an unconsciona-
ble time, Lettice plugged in the electric kettle, made
the tea and offered him a cup.

"Pour vous faire du plaisir, je ne dirai pas non," said
M. Duval, although he added, it was entirely against

his habits. Habits, he said, were a sign of the inner self. A man of his character, for example, would form habits quite other than those which a man, he would not say of inferior character, but of a different type of character would form. He paused for a moment in his analysis.

Lettice said she hoped he was having a happy Christmas.

M. Duval most regrettably repeated the raspberry noise. Christmas, he said, was well enough for the devoted. For himself, philosopher and sincere unbeliever, for unbelief, he added, had its saints and martyrs as well as belief, the rite of Christmas was of a nullity complete. It said nothing to him in the end. As for priests, he continued, and sketching again the raspberry noise, one knew what to think of those there.

Lettice said that the Vicar at Marling Melicent was very nice.

"The good vicar of madame's parish," said M. Duval, twisting his mouth, but to Lettice's great relief not repeating the noise, was doubtless a brave homme, but undoubtedly an adorer of fétiches. For a man with a character like his own, said M. Duval, all religion was fetishism, whatever the creed. He had, he said, studied profoundly during a youth, d'ailleurs orageuse, the question of religion and had decided that for a man of his temperament it was but mummery. "Quant aux femmes, je ne dis pas," said M. Duval with wide tolerance, "c'est convenable. Un point c'est tout." But, he continued, it was impossible for him, given the character that he possessed, to be impressed by it. He would explain to her, he went on—but Lettice told Oliver afterwards that at this point she thought she became insensible.

The afternoon at Marling Hall passed like any other Christmas afternoon. Everyone felt full and sleepy. Mr. Marling retired to his study where he could doze at his ease, while the rest of the party sat in the large drawing-room and thought they ought to go for a

walk. Lucy, after yawning violently, said she must go
and ring Jerry up. Presently the noise of the side door
being banged and a car being started was heard, and
secure from being told what, the family relapsed into
coma once more. Finally Mrs. Bill, who felt a certain
proprietary right in Christmas procedure, dragged her
husband out of his torpor and told him to go for a
walk. Bill said he would go if Oliver came too.

"We might go and look at Govern's cottage," said
Oliver. "There seems to be some talk of his marrying
again and, if so, that wall behind the copper must be
repaired. It really ought to have been done before the
winter."

Bill, who took the deepest interest in estate matters
on his too infrequent visits, agreed, and asked who the
lucky woman was. Oliver said the Harveys' maid.

"And talking of this and that, Bill," he said. "You
owe me five shillings."

"I never refused to pay a just debt," said Bill, "but
why?"

"Wasn't there a bet about Geoffrey and Mrs.
Smith?" said Oliver. "I know it is unchivalrous to introduce any allusion to the fair sex, but I do want my
money."

"If it weren't Christmas Day and the pubs opening
the Lord knows when," said Bill, "we'd go and cele-
brate on the five shillings."

"On my five shillings, you mean," said Oliver. "Hand
it over."

The brothers went out of the room hitting each other
amicably.

Mrs. Bill then said didn't the Mater think they
ought to be starting, as the Christmas tea for the
school children was at four. Mrs. Marling who disliked
the name Mater as much as her husband disliked
Pater, agreed that they ought to be starting and the
two ladies went upstairs to get ready. Presently the
noise of the side door being shut was heard again and
Miss Bunting gave herself up to the pleasures of a
comfortable chair, a good fire and her own company.

All so far had gone as she and Miss Merriman had foreseen. Lettice and David: it would never have done: and it was not to be. She had not communicated with Miss Merriman, she did not intend to communicate with her. She knew, and accepted the knowledge without attempting to account for it, that Miss Merriman would, by her peculiar gifts as a guardian of her employers, understand perfectly that any danger of a marriage between David and Lettice was over. She did not think David would have told Miss Merriman, she did not think he would even have told his mother; and she knew with absolute certitude that though Lady Emily might not suspect and would just think David had lost interest as he so often did, Miss Merriman would know exactly what had happened. Neither she nor Miss Merriman would rejoice. In these august matters there is no rejoicing as there is no regret. Fate, immutable, star-decreed, had taken its appointed course and the two priestesses knew that they were justified in their faith.

Rapt in these high musings she must have dozed a little, for when she returned to earth she found Captain Barclay in front of her.

"I do hope I didn't disturb you," said Captain Barclay, "but I found I could get back after all, and I couldn't find anyone except Mr. Marling and he is asleep."

Miss Bunting said they had all gone out and Lettice was at the stables, but would be back after tea.

"Stop and have a cup with me," she said. "I will ring for it now."

Captain Barclay, seeing no way of refusing without discourtesy, thanked her and sat down. Miss Bunting, who had never been afraid of servants, pressed the bell and ordered China tea for herself and Captain Barclay. The maid set a small table in front of her and went away. Miss Bunting meanwhile conducted a rather one-sided conversation with her guest. That he did not answer, or if he did, in an absent way unlike his usual good manners, did not at all discompose her.

She could not know that Captain Barclay was thinking, and had been thinking ever since the previous
evening, about the enigmatic message from David
faithfully delivered to him by Lucy when they had put
the presents into Diana's stocking, but her special
sense of what the right people were about told her
that all was going well. The maid came back, and just
as she had set the tray down the front door bell rang.

"It can't be a friend," said Miss Bunting as the maid
left the room. "They all know that we use the side
door. Milk and no sugar for you, I think, Captain Barclay."

Captain Barclay said how kind of her to remember,
to which Miss Bunting replied that in her young days
a hostess always took pains to remember her guests'
tastes and that the Marchioness knew exactly how the
wife of each of the Marquess's principal tenants liked
her tea. The maid returned.

"Please miss," she said, "it's some French gentlemen.
At least that's what they said they were, but two of
them's black, and they said they wanted Mrs. Watson."

"Those," said Miss Bunting to Captain Barclay,
"must be the Free French who called at the Harveys'
this morning. They brought Mlle Duchaux's nephew
with them and Lettice is very kindly having him to tea
as the Harveys had to go to Norton Park."

Captain Barclay got up.

"—so perhaps, Captain Barclay, you would be good
enough to show them the way down," said Miss Bunting.

In so ordinary a voice did she say it that Captain
Barclay merely thought she wished him to explain to
the visitors the route to the stables and went out to the
front door. In the hall he hesitated for a moment, then
put on his overcoat, picked up his cap, gloves and
stick and shut the front door behind him. The noise
reached Miss Bunting, who poured herself a cup of
tea, and sat sipping it with great relish. The maid said,
Should she put the scones down near the fire to keep

hot, so Miss Bunting let her do it, but she knew that never would those scones be eaten by Captain Barclay.

Captain Barclay, greeting the visitors in passable French, offered to show them the way to Mrs. Watson's. Just as he was going to get into the car, another car came up and seeing the unaccustomed sight of people at the front door stopped to investigate. Lucy and an officer got out.

"Hullo, Tom," she said. "Jerry, this is Tom Barclay, he's a great friend of mine. This is Jerry Grant, I mean he's a captain and he's going to let me go on the fire engine when they do night practice."

Captain Grant, a not quite young man with an intelligent face and a slight limp, said he would certainly not let Miss Marling ride on the fire engine and would probably be put in the Tower if he did.

"Oh, rot," said Lucy in high good humour. "What are *they* doing, Tom?"

She looked towards the other car.

"Only Mlle Duchaux's nephew's friends come to fetch him," said Captain Barclay. "I'm going to show them the way to the stables. Lettice is giving him tea there."

"Oh, all right," said Lucy. "Come on, Jerry, and we'll see if tea is ready. And after tea, I'll tell you what——"

Her voice died away as she and Captain Grant went in and shut the door.

Captain Barclay apologised to the visitors and got into the car. As soon as they reached the stables he asked them to wait and he would send their friend out to them. Up the steep stair he went, put his things down in the hall and walked into Lettice's sitting-room.

About ten minutes earlier Lettice, emerging from the trance induced by M. Duval's analysis of his anti-religious experiences, had come to with a start and said how very interesting that was. M. Duval, gratified but

not surprised, said that one of the many advantages
that French education had over an English education
was that the mind was trained to make a logical examination of its own processes of thought. His friends, he
said, might arrive to fetch him now at any moment.
"Mais, puisque j'ai encore quelques instants à vous sa-
crifier," he continued, he would explain to her in what
consisted the essential superiority of the French education over the English education which was entirely
on a wrong system. It was a question, he said, on
which he had deeply reflected and upon which he
would now constate his ideas in a manner clear and
precise. And this he was still doing when Captain Barclay walked in.

Captain Barclay took one glance at the situation,
and that glance was enough. Lettice looked white with
fatigue and her eyes met his with the appeal of a very
patient dog who has a thorn in his foot and hopes his
master will be able to take it out.

Captain Barclay, who had fought in France before
the Belgian retreat, at once recognized Lettice's visitor
as no general, but a corporal. He acted at once. Before
Corporal Duval knew where he was he had said good-
bye to his hostess, got his coat and cap and was out of
the front door, and so hypnotised was he by Captain
Barclay's air of command that he automatically did violence to his own feelings by saluting him. Captain
Barclay waited at the door till the visitor had reached
the bottom of the stairs, heard the engine being started and the party going off to wherever they had come
from. Then he shut the door and came back to the sitting-room.

"Put your feet up on the sofa," he said to Lettice.

She obeyed.

Captain Barclay pulled a chair up beside her and
took her hand. As she did not seem to mind he held
her hand in both of his.

"Do you *have* to be so silly?" he said.

Lettice, enchanted to be called silly, said what did
he mean.

"Letting that fellow kill you," said Captain Barclay.
"You haven't the first idea how to look after yourself.
What you need is a keeper."

Lettice made no answer, but her free hand found its
way to its fellow, an action of which she appeared to
be quite unconscious.

"Well?" said Captain Barclay.

"Oh, Tom," said Lettice.

"Mind," said Captain Barclay, "I am not breaking
my word. I said I wouldn't speak about it again unless
you asked me and I'm jolly well not going to."

Lettice said she wasn't quite sure if she understood
what he meant.

"Yes you do," said Captain Barclay. "Perfectly well.
But as you apparently have to be silly I will break my
oath and tell you again that I love you like anything.
I'm likely to be in England for another six months at
least, so you know what the chances are and can make
up your mind. And what is more you *must* make up
your mind, now."

He released her hands and got up.

"Oh, Tom, I cannot bear not to have you with me,"
said Lettice, sitting up. "It has been quite dreadful
being afraid that you wouldn't talk about it again and
I thought I would die."

"This is your last chance," said Captain Barclay. "If
you find you really don't want to marry me, tell me
now. If not I shall marry you and that's that."

"I can't quite explain," said Lettice. "I do love you,
Tom, so much that I feel I oughtn't to marry you. I
mean after all I am a widow with two little girls and
you aren't. I mean you have never been married before and it seems so unfair for you to have a widow
and two children in the house. It isn't that I don't love
you quite hurtingly. But you see, I did love Roger very
much too and——"

As Captain Barclay's face became troubled, her
voice trailed away.

"Very well, my precious, precious Lettice," he said.
"I daresay you are right. Forgive me if I have made

things difficult for you again. I love you too much to
try to interfere. If Roger is in your thoughts I have no
right there. Bless you."

He looked once at Lettice, walked slowly towards
the door and opened it.

"Oh, Tom," said Lettice.

He turned.

"Don't say any more," he said. "Bless you. Good-
bye."

"But, Tom, I can't explain if you don't listen," said
Lettice. "I only wanted to say something. About
Roger. Of course I did love him very, very much and I
always shall, though I mostly never think about him
now. But there was always one thing——"

She paused. Captain Barclay stood in the doorway,
wondering how long his patience would last.

"You see," she said, "Marling is rather a nice name
and though I really did love Roger with all my heart, I
have never quite liked the name Watson. Mrs. Watson
is not a very interesting name. I can't be Marling again,
but—if you didn't much mind——"

Just then nurse came along the passage, evidently
bound on some errand to Lettice.

"Just a moment, nurse, Mrs. Watson is engaged,"
said Captain Barclay, and he went into the sitting-
room and shut the door.